WHERE YOU CAN FIND ME

This Large Print Book carries the
Seal of Approval of N.A.V.H.

WHERE YOU CAN FIND ME

SHERI JOSEPH

THORNDIKE PRESS

A part of Gale, Cengage Learning

GALE
CENGAGE Learning®

Detroit • New York • San Francisco • New Haven, Conn • Waterville, Maine • London

GALE
CENGAGE Learning·

LIBRARY OF CONGRESS CATALOGING-IN-PUBLICATION DATA

Joseph, Sheri.
    Where you can find me / by Sheri Joseph. — Large Print edition.
        pages cm. — (Thorndike Press Large Print Peer Picks)
        ISBN 978-1-4104-6106-3 (hardcover) — ISBN 1-4104-6106-8 (hardcover) 1.
    Missing children—Fiction. 2. Crime victims' families—Fiction. 3. Recovered
    memory—Fiction. 4. Life change events—Fiction. 5. Large type books. I.
    Title.
    PS3610.O67W44 2013
    813'.6—dc23   2013014070

Published in 2013 by arrangement with St. Martin's Press, LLC.

Printed in the United States of America
1 2 3 4 5 6 7 17 16 15 14 13

WHERE YOU CAN FIND ME

CHAPTER ONE

October 23, 2006

The Vincent house had been new when they bought it, when Caleb was four and Lark an infant. On TV, it looked like nothing much: two-story, tri-gabled, putty-colored brick in the style of every other house in the development. Set mid-block on Waverly Way, one of the longer streets, it was hard to find without checking the address. Their half acre of bermuda turned lion-colored in fall, like the others, and though in recent years the Vincent plot could be counted on in any season to look worse than its neighbors, it had been freshly raked for Caleb's arrival. A foundation volunteer had bagged the lawn's leaves at the curb but overlooked the bushes crowded against the house behind a barricade of cockeyed railroad ties, where oak leaves remained caught between the twigs. Above the front door was a fanlight window of milky stained glass, the

Vincents' one outward quirk, depicting, if you looked closely, a rooster. All the other windows — from the columns of glass that flanked the entry to the slitted row in the automatic garage door — were backed by pale curtains or blinds, always, so that the house resembled a closed eye.

Each day required at least one visitor from outside, usually a foundation volunteer bringing in groceries, packages, the forwarded mail, in several trips up the walkway. These people, officially careful of the Vincent privacy, were on hand to assist in the house with any number of tasks but took their leave as soon as possible, generally within the hour. The last had departed that morning, leaving Marlene and Jeff Vincent alone with Caleb. This was their message to the world: *time alone with our son.* But the FBI had said *Give him space,* so inside the house they were still looking for the balance.

Lark — stashed for a few days with her aunt while Jeff and Marlene flew across the country, returned with Caleb, and got him settled — would be home soon. In the meantime, the three in the house drifted separately from room to room. Jeff and Marlene battled to keep phone calls and e-mails brief, so they would be available if their son wandered near. *Their son,* this strange tall boy of fourteen. With each other as well, they spoke only the necessary words before they floated apart to farther corners where he might find them.

Marlene was rinsing dishes, pretending the kitchen was as sunny as it would be if she dared open the curtains, when a sound rattled her. At first she couldn't place it: a bang of padded hammer to string, a burble of notes, but in a pattern. It had been years since the children had taken piano lessons, and no one in her house had ever played more than "Jingle Bells." But this was organized noise, an entire verse of something. The TV, maybe? She shut off the water. Definitely the piano.

A skillet in one hand, she rounded the breakfast bar half ready to fight. All she could conceive of was that some ravening reporter had broken down the door and invaded the living room in order to play — what? A Chopin prelude? "Ode to Joy"?

Caleb sat at the piano bench, his back to her. After their few days of monitored visits in Spokane, then the roughly twenty-six hours he'd been at home, she had only just become certain in recognizing his shape at this distance, the narrow beauty of his adolescence. The hollow at the back of his

9

neck; the gleam of scalp through hair shorn close but carelessly, a half inch to nothing, marked by the clippers. Caleb — only sitting there, it seemed, until she caught the flutter of his hands at either side and the melody proceeding in its sure tempo. She remembered him at age eight or so, struggling through scales or "Streets of Laredo" one clang-bang note at a time, whining all the while to be released from this hell. Six weeks of lessons and she'd given in, let him run hollering victory into a summer evening in suburbia, this place she and Jeff had once sneered at from their hip Atlanta youth. OTP, it was called: Outside the Perimeter. But eventually there had been no room to argue against cheap housing, good schools, streets where kids could ride their bikes and play until dark.

On soundless steps, she drew close enough to see the silvery jag of the scar behind his right ear — one of many, one of only a few he would show her — and he was still playing, no sheet music before him. From behind the metal-framed glasses he'd chosen without her, or that had been chosen for him, his eyes looked not at his hands but somewhere into the body of the piano. His face wore no expression — none, at least, that she could read — before he stopped, fingers settled into the dropped keys, and withdrew his hands.

"It's out of tune," he said. Not even a glance to see if she was impressed. He slipped up from the bench, went to the front window, and leaned an eye to the edge of the blinds.

"Still out there?" she asked. Of all the questions she was afraid to ask him, how could *What was that you were playing?* be one of them?

He nodded his answer. Then, because she liked to hear his voice, he said, "Those same three, and a new one down the street, some kind of giant black truck. And that Channel Three lady with the camera going."

At the table that had been purchased the same year as the house, they sat for dinner, unable to remember who sat where. Did they have seats? Caleb took the chair that backed to the bay window, which put Lark across from him and Jeff and Marlene at the ends. It wasn't right, but Marlene couldn't remember the order. Had the entire table been moved?

"Do you like lasagna?" Lark asked Caleb, alert for the answer. No wonder if they all prodded him with every mundanity as they would a space alien. Lark had arrived home wearing lip gloss and a skirt borrowed from her cousin, carting in the family's first meal, which she'd spent the day making herself with her aunt Bethanne's assistance.

Caleb said, "Sure. Lasagna."

Lark shrugged. "I usually make simpler stuff, like chicken with rice, or spaghetti with jar sauce, or something, when I cook for Dad." She gave Jeff an uncertain glance. "We take turns cooking. Or, I mean, I cook for Mom, too. I'm not very good."

"You're excellent, honey," Jeff said, while Marlene scooped the first cube, spilling steam and sauce, webby with cheese, onto Caleb's plate. They had not yet decided on when or what to tell him about who lived where and the rest of it, and as the days accrued, it was seeming less traumatic to let him glean it all this way, with one ear, or to wait until he asked.

"It looks great," he said. When they were dished up with salad and bread, Lark said a blessing for them, one of a few tolerable side effects of the private school they'd moved her to, the one with the highest walls. Marlene folded her hands, looking at Caleb. Caleb, with a check of everyone's hands, folded his also, then looked back at Marlene.

To her memorized table prayer, Lark

12

added, "And thank you, Lord, for bringing Caleb home." Amen. They ate, complimenting the food, and Lark watched Caleb openly. They had spent an hour together, and already there seemed to be a joke between them — though Lark was plainly self-conscious and Caleb was . . . well, what was he? Quiet, they might have said. But did other fourteen-year-old boys speak more than this?

Lark pursed her mouth, raised an eyebrow, a more sedate version of the teasing expression she'd been using with favorite older relatives since she was five. Loosely translated: *Are you some kind of crazy person?* "Who cut your hair, anyway?"

Caleb chewed around what might have been a smile. "I did. You don't like it?"

"Well, you don't look like the poster too much," she said, as if he'd flubbed an assignment for school. "And it's kind of uneven."

"Hair grows," Marlene said.

"Maybe he likes it that way," Jeff said.

Lark brightened. "Did they show you the poster yet? I'll show you mine that I drew on. I drew glasses on one, like you actually have! Also I drew a Mohawk one, and one with, like, black lipstick and some pierces, because I know a boy who does that. Mom

13

thought it was cool. She said you could look like anything, so it was good to think about all the ways."

Lark was eleven. There were moments — this the first of many to come over the next few months — when they all looked at her, her round face still androgynous with child-hood, her solemn gray eyes and hair bobbed at the chin, and thought how she was the exact age now that Caleb had been when he was taken.

As soon as Lark and Caleb had entered her bedroom, she shut the door to show him the back of it: an eleven-by-fourteen poster commanding, in red letters, "Find Caleb Vincent!" Below were two images: Caleb on his eleventh birthday and Caleb age-progressed by a computer to fourteen. The age-progressed boy mirrored the smile and pose of the younger one and looked, despite the light in his eyes, dead somehow. The hair, a lush, lustrous brown, appeared painted on. At the bottom was written, "$50,000 reward for information leading to safe return." The door was recessed from the rest of the room, so Lark had to step back and let Caleb look alone.

"*And* there's a T-shirt." She fished it from the closet and held it up on a wire hanger that dented the shoulders: white, XL, same graphics as the poster printed front and back.

"That looks too big for you," Caleb said.

"Yeah, but I can't even wear it outside. *We* can't, really, like me and Mom and Dad. Because of the attention. It's already kind of hard to like go to a movie or something."

"So no one ever saw it?" he asked.

"Oh, god, there's like a *million*. Miss Fay made them and she gives them out all over town. And the posters and buttons too. On the button it's just the age-progressed one. I wonder what they'll do with all those posters and stuff now. We could seriously wallpaper the whole entire house."

The rest of the room did not feature him, and while he took it in, she said, a bit sheepishly, "Grandma Vincent sends me all this stuff. I'm kind of into the cloud forest, in Costa Rica? You remember how Grandma went to live there?"

Her canopy bed crawled with jungle life. Stuffed monkeys and sloths wrapped their arms around the posts; toucans and coatis and iguanas lounged on the pillows. On top of her bookshelf perched an iridescent green bird — a quetzal, she told him — with a tail hanging halfway to the floor. Posters of leatherback sea turtles swam the walls beside trees caught in clouds, golden toads, butterflies of unearthly blue. At ceiling level along one entire wall was a tempera banner painted for a fund-raiser she'd organized at school. "Save the Cloud Forest!" it said, its outer edges decorated with her own renderings of a toucan, a poison-arrow frog, elephant-ear leaves.

"So I started this whole thing at school," she said. "I got kids to raise money for the cloud forest, and some other schools were doing it, too, in a bunch of other countries, so now there's a whole part of the cloud forest in Costa Rica, like a bijillion acres, that we bought just ourselves."

"Seriously? That's impressive."

As he turned his head, lifted his chin to examine the banner, she saw how much he looked like their mother. The poster didn't show it. Marlene had always been petite with a distinct jawbone and ropey little muscles — she needed her long, twisty hair, she used to say, so she didn't look like a teenaged boy — and Caleb was like a flash of what she might look like with her head shaved. Same height, same body almost, even some echoed ways of moving. He had her flattish, disklike face and her pointed chin. But not her hollow eyes. Behind the glasses, which no one in the family wore, his eyes were regular eyes, a densely lashed hazel, murky and meditative like pond water in sunlight.

"I really wanted to go there bad," she told him as he studied her Costa Rica map. "Like to go to school there and just . . . live there."

"Not anymore?"

She shrugged. "Not so much now."

Once or twice a day, someone sanctioned pulled past the news vans and into the driveway. Often it was Fay Tomlinson, the Find Caleb Foundation director, or it was another foundation representative, bringing the day's deliveries and ignoring reporters with a smile. Or it might be Bethanne McCall, Marlene's sister, who was likely to roll her eyes and yell something mock-cheerful or sarcastic in the general news-van direction. Until Thursday, the fifth day of the media siege, Lark stayed home from school, closed up in the family shell. Then twice each weekday, for a little excitement, the garage door rose and emitted Jeff Vincent's Honda CR-V, in which he ferried his daughter to her brick-walled private school, and twice more it rose to take him or the two of them back in, though it was soon clear that

17

both occupants would be unreachable for the trip, hard to distinguish behind smoky window glass. From time to time, the police rolled in and ticketed vehicles or rousted the reporters for loitering, and then the neighborhood might have a few hours to breathe in peace and not feel as if the whole world was watching.

The Vincents were no strangers to attention and for years had welcomed, in a way, almost any violation. When rumors of Marlene's drug use spawned tabloid-vulture excrement (the most insane, street-person-looking picture of her they could find under headlines like "Did This Soccer Mom Sell Her Son for Drugs?"), she was happy enough when it got her a spot on *Larry King Live,* which she agreed to do no-holds-barred, admitting to every stray ounce and bump she'd ever done, if they would put up Caleb's picture and rehearse the details. Three years later, after Jeff had moved out ("temporarily") with Lark, giving up on Marlene as he had on Caleb, she'd still been dreaming up ways to interest at least the local media enough to say his name again, post his picture. So it was no surprise if all those people induced over the years to look now wanted to hear the end of the story.

Lark, by the week's end, was the Vincents'

sole ambassador to the world, or at least she was ambassador to the girls of Agape Academy. With hardly a precedent for a "new girl" in their midst, let alone an unchurched refugee from a public school, the Agape girls had taken her in three years before and developed their own protocols, as with a celebrity, for protecting her from their own harassment. Once, when Lark was nine, a woman reporter had shoved a microphone in her face and said, "Do you think your brother is still alive?" Most of them had seen this image of Lark, a small, slightly pudgy girl shrinking smaller except for her round gray eyes, saying on their TV screens, "I don't know," and then, "I hope so." It stopped similar questions in their own mouths — no matter how badly they wanted to ask — and made them all the more eager for a chance to fend off one of the reporters parked at the school gates with a prim *I'm not talking to you,* as they had been instructed to even if the question seemed nice, like "Are you a friend of Lark Vincent's?" or "How is she holding up?"

They were all thrilled, of course, that Caleb had been returned, and, despite the power of prayer, they were quite as shocked about it as the rest of the world. Some time ago, their prayers had changed from *Please bring Caleb home* to *Please bring the Vincents Peace,* which meant a sad thing. But now they praised the Lord and shouldered in afresh to embrace Lark, reinforcing their status as friend to this girl who, if you overlooked the semifamousness, was really rather strange. Few of them were allowed near the latest TV news about her brother, and those who happened to catch some — it was hard to miss — were constitutionally resistant to the hints of secular filth. *What happened to Caleb Vincent?,* the question blaring from every channel, could be answered quite simply with no more information than was found at the surface: he had been taken by evil people, preserved for more than three years by the grace of God like Daniel in the lion's den, and brought home.

All the joyous, bubbling attention at school was just enough to keep Lark willing to go. Caleb was at home — waiting for her, because what else did he have to do? — and he was nothing like what she'd expected a returned brother to be. She'd assumed she would know him, first of all, that he would bear some resemblance to the brother she'd had when she was eight, though during the intervening years, missing him as a playmate, she'd already erased his bad qualities (his lack of patience, his refusal to include her if his own friends were around or to take any real interest in her or in things she liked, ever) until she had so transformed him that, despite the ubiquitous "Missing" posters, he had come to resemble in her mind something akin to the dashing cartoon fox from *Robin Hood.* Hadn't he even spoken with a faint British accent? She loved that fox brother, wrung her heart in her hands when he fell from the high tower and dropped like a stone into the moat. And would he surface? Only if she wished for it hard enough. Only if she stood poised at the crenellated turret above, ready with her own breath to make him alive.

Now she faced a stranger, half a grownup, a fascinating relation. It was as if some creature more endangered and exotic than the cloud forest itself had been brought into their house and placed partly in her care. She wanted to sit all day studying his secrets. She wanted to find a way to tell him that her own hard wishing, like prayer, had breathed for him and brought him back.

Before the kids were up in the morning, Jeff folded and stowed the blankets from the front-room sofa where he had slept. It wasn't to keep a secret. Marlene had told their son he could sleep in her bed anytime he liked, and she said *my* bed, not *ours,* a maternal zone made free of men in case he might need it that way. But it seemed important that the house look as normal as possible, not just to the necessary attendants but to the Vincents themselves.

Caleb did not take his mother up on the offer, though he'd been that sort of child: a cuddly child, a child of many fears. He was the boy who could not make it through a single night of summer camp, phoned crying for his parents to fetch him, and as old as eight he would still wheedle his way into the bed between them. Now he slept in his own bed, if poorly. He was the last awake each morning, and Jeff often heard his footsteps past midnight or his low voice in the kitchen, having a late-night ice cream social with Marlene or, once, on the phone to Spokane and Julianna Brewer, his favorite FBI agent, specialist in crimes against children. It was only about ten o'clock out there, and Julianna had told him to call anytime. Though Jeff eavesdropped longer than he should have, they were talking about nothing special: the Seattle Mariners, movies they'd seen.

There was no guidebook for this. He worried Marlene was being too open with Caleb, as she'd once been with Lark, out of her own uncensorable need for something — intimacy, or venting. With Lark, she had not been able to stop herself from cataloging the possible horrors Caleb could be enduring in that moment, because children could never be too thoroughly warned. It had become, at least in a certain mood, her notion of responsible mothering.

In her late-hour kitchen chats with Caleb, Jeff overheard them trading the lists of drugs they had done, Marlene saying, "Mostly cocaine. Methamphetamine. And sleeping pills. What I really want most of all right now, though, is a drink."

Caleb's voice, harder to catch: "I don't like meth too much. Roofies are nice, or most pills — the sedative kind. And liquor." A pause, and he added, "Beer. I like beer."

"Oh, yeah," Marlene said, the smile in it unmistakable, "I could go for a beer. Mostly I was drinking what I called a lazy martini, just gin over ice. It's hard to get up the energy to mix things or stock extras when you're drinking alone. And also I was very busy, looking for you. Every minute you were gone."

Marlene, a believer in the inherent value of communication, had stumbled upon this method and urged Jeff to try it. "If you're alone with him, and very quiet, and just *speak.* But like he's a grown-up, you know? Like a friend. He'll talk." But Jeff was less sure — why not value silence? Let him alone, let him heal. He was home. If the FBI seemed satisfied with their working theory of what had happened, thin on suspects and ragged as it was, why should his parents press for more?

Most of the day Jeff worked from the basement office, because they were supposed to give Caleb space — that mantra in his head less reminder to himself than unvoiced argument to Marlene. He drove Lark to and from school. He ate meals with whoever was present, dinner generally the only time they were all four gathered around the table and unattended by relatives or foundation volunteers or agents of the FBI. Once a day Marlene accused him of "going quiet again," but he was just trying to be mindful, to take it all in, stay on top of it. More than anything, he was trying, still, to hear the news that his reasonably dead-and-buried son was in fact alive. It didn't compute. Caleb was gone; before him stood his Caleb, and so much time had passed. Jeff found himself unable to put the two together.

Marlene was supposed to be in rehab. Only because he'd had to track her down in a hurry, to let her know that there was news of Caleb, had he learned she'd enrolled herself in an outpatient program a few weeks prior. Now she claimed she didn't need it. Not that she was recovered — more like she'd never really had a problem.

"Let me tell you about addicts, okay?" she said, hissing in the relative remove of the front hall. "And I've met my share, even before I started up with that group therapy . . . whatever. Half of them are just idiots with no self-control. The others are people with *real* reasons for using that can't be fixed, who had *horrible things* happen to them that can't be undone. But me, I'm a special case. I *was* one of them, but my horrible thing was undone! There's no precedent for me."

"Is that what your doctors say?"

"More or less."

Marlene had been addicted to her own anguish, to the Internet at two A.M., to the endless search. Jeff was willing to concede that the drugs had been mostly the facilitators to being awake for it or to knocking herself back down. But he knew the first mandate of rehab was "be asleep at night and awake during the day," and he wasn't sure she was accomplishing that with much more success than their son.

Caleb was not addicted anymore, if he ever had been. He'd been found living in a small town an hour outside of Spokane with a doctor, a man he called Jolly. Jolly, he said, had taken him away from the man who kidnapped him. Jolly had gotten him off the drugs.

The piano tuner said, "There must be a fire out there or something. I was like, jeez, what's going on? Had to park down the street."

It was a busy day in the Vincent house. The therapist, a pleasantly toadish woman with yellow and gray hair, commissioned by the FBI, was down in the basement with Caleb, who really could not be taken out to meet her at her office. Mitch Abernathy, the agent in charge of Caleb's case, was having coffee in the kitchen with Marlene. He said, "Maybe I could sneak him out to the field office. We could play racquetball or something."

Marlene smiled — it was hard not to get a little giddy, borderline amorous, every time she looked at Mitch. For three years, four months, and fourteen days, he more than Jeff had been the man in her life, loved, hated, endured. She, his special tormentor, called at all hours, hurled abuse as she pleased, turned shamelessly sweet to seduce from him information and pointless effort; he dog-trained her to behave and learn patience. After everyone else had given up, even the Find Caleb Foundation forced toward repurposing its resources, it had been only the two of them struggling on, Mitch using any spare time to scour databases with their thin evidence. There had never been much: Caleb's BMX bike hidden in the woods behind the elementary school, a connection to a sketchy neighbor, a sighting with a strange man, none of it fruitful. Eight months on, they found Internet photographs (blurred horrors including a boy clear enough to call Caleb, photos Marlene would not have been shown but that she raged until Mitch relented) that linked to an ongoing investigation but, as Mitch insisted, could have been taken at any time and, in any case, did not offer much hope of what they called a "live recovery." After that, nothing of note. When the FBI released the bike from the evidence locker, Mitch brought it back to the house on Waverly Way, where Marlene was living alone, and hung it on the garage wall for her beside Jeff's, Lark's, her own.

Now it was as if, after all that frustration and sorrow and suppressed wrath, she and

Mitch had just fallen into a coat closet and had some kind of glorious, planet-rocking sex. Probably they *had* wanted each other more than once through all that time, every emotion so intensified by the fact of a missing child that it bled to adjacent ones. Lingering over their coffee in postcoital paradise, they both felt the impending end. What would be left to them without the source of all that energy?

When the piano tuner was finished, Marlene wrote him a check. He said, "Oh, man, you're those people with the kidnapped kid, right? I shoulda known. I must be dumb or something. Wow, so what's it like? You must be going crazy knowing he was walking around loose like that and didn't tell no one, right?"

All but the first sentence was blocked by Mitch's intervening, dark-suited body, moving the man to the door without violence or effort, like a snowplow. "Thanks for the service, friend," he said. "We really appreciate it."

Before they had boarded the plane together for Spokane, Mitch had advised the Vincents not to concern themselves with this itchy question, the million-dollar *why*. Over pizza and champagne the night the DNA results came back, he said (though they had not asked), "It's really not all that surprising or something to dwell on too much. He was either terrified of Lundy or he felt like he owed him for getting him out of the first place. I don't have any doubt he was every bit the captive there. He was made to feel like he had no choice."

But no one had asked Caleb the question.

"What about Caleb?" Lark asked — she'd been reporting for them the goings-on at Agape over Sunday pancakes, one week to the day from his return. "Where will he go to school?"

Jeff looked at Marlene, who chewed a piece of bacon. Over her usual damp-eyed vague anxiety lay a film of bliss he felt at least partly responsible for: sex for the first time in a year, the first in three that had not put her into a temper at herself or at him. She'd always been the sexual one in the relationship, he a little in awe of a woman he had to work to keep up with, but the abduction — not just the loss but the apparent nature of it — had, without diminishing her drive, touched all sex with something rancid. Now he watched the quiet in her limbs, hoping she'd stay willing to forgo reserving the bed for Caleb, with the world peeping through the blinds. Step one toward completing the restoration of his family. He wondered, though, how long it might go on being more hers than his, she the de facto head of the household and parent of their son because she had won their all-in bet.

"Caleb won't be going to school for a while," she said.

"I won't?" Caleb asked. All of them turned to her with the same questioning eyes. It was one of those topics that had not yet come up.

"I can't let you just yet, honey. We'll have to figure something out. Maybe home-schooling."

Caleb tightened and kept quiet. Lark drew a breath on his behalf but waited also. Marlene said, "You see how it is out there. If you go out, I can't keep it from you. And I don't mean just the cameras. Every kid in your classes, every teacher, every parent . . . I don't want those people making this follow you forever."

Hard to argue with, and no one, least of all Jeff, was inclined to try. His decision to leave her the year before, to take Lark, had underscored the general assessment that her tenacity over Caleb indicated mental imbalance. If she might forgive him for it one day, she would not now, if ever again, be questioned.

"Maybe," Jeff said, "if we find the right private school, it wouldn't be so bad. Kids there have to get used to . . . differences."

Marlene shook her head, unhearing. "Even if we move," she muttered.

"I like school," Caleb said quietly, to no one. They all stopped chewing. He so rarely spoke. He almost never made a request or offered these droplets of information, each bursting on impact into a little scene. They knew — everyone knew — that for two whole months he'd been a freshman in a public high school in Providence, Washington. He'd ridden the bus, sat in class each day, had friends, and *he had liked school.* Maybe his liking school in the first place, wanting to go, was the reason he'd been enrolled in it.

Jeff swallowed, sliced another bite of stacked pancake. Was he the only one who heard defiance in that sentence? The insistent *I* of it: *I am no one you know. I lived without you. I lived while you buried me and it's too late now for you to know who I am.* God, what kind of father was he, resenting his son for taking his son away?

Marlene rose in a casual way with the butter dish and stopped behind Caleb's chair

31

to lay a hand on his head, set her lips to his forehead at the hairline. "We'll think of something. I promise." For as long as a meditative pause allowed, she stroked his bristly hair. "But for now. Until Christmas, at least."

"Fair warning," Bethanne said, unpacking groceries into Marlene's pantry. "I think Mama's going on TV."

Marlene, unsurprised, said, "You are fucking kidding me."

"I told you you should have let her come over."

Their mother, according to Bethanne's theory, was angry about being excluded from the house and having most of her calls ignored, but Marlene was certain that whatever the woman said on TV would only be worse if she had insider information to back it up.

Her mother's latest voice mail: "I want to make sure you're watching him around Lark. You know how they are after a thing like this, and you have to accept that he's going to be messed up in the head. Fourteen is plenty old to be a danger to little girls. And you know we can take Lark out here with us, any time."

This might have counted as an improvement over her previous assumption, equally damning, that Caleb would turn out to be gay — except that all of what her mother considered sexual vices could be lumped together as committable by the same person and everyone fell into one of two categories: the untouched and the guilty. Marlene would never forgive her for saying once — three years before, at the first hint of molestation — that maybe it was for the best, after all, if he was dead.

He knew the rooster over the doorway, the one he'd named Doodledoo when he was four. But the house it guarded was smaller, his room shrunken, his bed's edges closing in — more every night as if he were growing by the minute. He lay on his back in Caleb's bed impersonating Caleb, eyes closed, then open because the door was shut, so they couldn't peek in to check if he was still there, if he looked like Caleb yet. Through the bathroom they shared slept his sister. He remembered having one there, the dance of locked and unlocked doors. Amid all the house's shrinking she alone had grown, from a doll-girl into a person. Of them all, she was the most changed, though still younger than him, so he trusted her more to be herself and not a trick. His parents, in certain glimpses, could seem like very good copies of themselves planted by aliens or evil government interests.

Outside in the carpeted hall, footsteps — his mother's — crossed back and forth, a pause at each pass to listen for him. Shoulders aching, he held the horizontal shape of Caleb, a boy who would be asleep by now. It seemed as if he'd be required to endure this posture only a short time, a couple of weeks. As if being himself in this place could be no more than temporary.

When he was little he'd seen a Disney movie about a cream-colored horse with two owners. A poor boy, who called the horse Taffy, had lost it to a rich girl, who called it Bo. Whose horse was it? To decide the matter, the boy and the girl stood at opposite ends of a paddock and called the horse, one calling "Taffy!" and one calling "Bo!," and the whole town watched, expecting the horse to know which one it was.

The blinds kept out most of the light, and he woke late in the morning, glad to feel the day half gone without him. The room, a blur without his glasses, was still his room and exactly as he had left it, half of everything in it a secret code of Haylie he could no longer read. Posters for the bands she liked, a sketch she'd made of a bearded man, poems by poets only she had heard of, line drawings copied from old books of strange, nineteenth-century machinery. Haylie was his babysitter, a graduate student who spoke to him as if he were her own age and could follow half the loopy things she said. He tried, but the closest he could come to her was her music. Some of these leftover possessions — like the poster for a CD on the back of his door: a woman in a white nightgown on a yellow moor, running away, looking back over her shoulder as she disappeared into fog — made him almost remember her voice.

And the music. Though he couldn't recall a word or a note of a Metacarpals' music, he felt how their eerie, gothic melodies haunted some locked-up room in his head on an endless loop. The disappearance of Caleb Vincent could be reduced to a very short story, and maybe he alone knew it. Once upon a time a dim little boy fell in love with his babysitter and thought he could impress her by liking a band she liked, collecting the band's music, showing up at the concert where she would be.

He took a shower, dressed himself in whatever new clothes had appeared in his room the day before. Downstairs, he could count on a lingering hug from his mother just for getting up, a hand on his shoulder from his father, and he was glad for these simple things; he could lean on his parents as if a child, forget for a few seconds what they were thinking. Because they were waiting for it, he forced out some words like a line in a play. He was playing himself. What would Caleb say now? But whatever he came up with, he knew, would not stop them from thinking what they were thinking about him, the hundred-headed beast of their every thought.

His mother called it "mooning about" when he hovered from room to room, trying to think of what Caleb would say but more often forgetting that effort, just lost in his head, somewhere else. So he parked himself in the upstairs game room and noodled around on the new GameCube, a present from someone who was glad he'd been found. Funny how his mother had made all these online friends, most of them parents of missing kids, who now sent to Caleb the gifts they couldn't buy for their own children — as if taking candy from strangers hadn't gotten him gone in the first place. An iPod nano, a phone with GPS, clothing . . . boxes came daily, filled with things he once would have loved but that didn't interest him much now.

Sometimes his parents left him alone so long that he switched from video games to the TV he wasn't supposed to watch. The war in Iraq must have been on a break, because every news channel featured his eleven-year-old face, his name in a printed graphic. "WHAT HAPPENED TO CALEB VINCENT?" For a current photo, they all showed the same loop of video shot through a car window, an FBI transport that had been physically stopped, momentarily, in the road. Also there was a digital snapshot taken by a classmate in Providence, depicting the boy they'd known as Nick Lundy and Caleb himself knew as Nicky: blond, wearing glasses and half a smile, head cocked with a hint of attitude, a fourteen-year-old who looked absurdly content and unmanacled to be under headlines about sex slavery and mysterious pedophile rings. And the kidnapper had sent him to school! Caleb wondered if his parents watched secretly, if they had by now gotten an eyeful of Nicky, the boy whose head he'd shaved into oblivion but whose glasses he still wore.

Sometimes he caught a glimpse of Charles Samson Lundy — always the three names, as with serial killers — huddled under a jacket, out on bail and led away by a lawyer. It was hard to see any of his face. But in the smiling portrait from his hospital ID badge, shown as often, every feature was clear, and some bleached-blond commentator would generally be on hand to express surprise or shock that this man, aside from being "almost" attractive, appeared so friendly, intelligent, normal, which is what the neighbors and his co-workers all confirmed as the impression he made. He was thirty-eight years old. His eyes were lively behind wire-framed glasses, his nose a little large, his dark hair grown out over his ears, wisping around his neck — nothing marked him.

Caleb's mother was right. He shouldn't watch this. It only made him angry, guessing what other people saw in a picture, or what drove them to watch. The man would be no real mystery — they knew him in advance. Caleb Vincent was the one they wanted to untangle and lay bare. No one said *Hey, let's rape the kid all over again on national TV,* but that was the footage they wished for, the part of *what happened* they most hoped to reproduce. Jolly had warned him.

All this hiding in the house on Waverly Way, refusing to answer questions, granted a certain protection but only gave the newspeople more to wonder about, to fill the airtime with. Perhaps he cannot speak, the effect of the horrible trauma. He will be this way; he will be that. He must not be blamed. He will require extensive therapy. He may feel himself to be at fault, he may feel ashamed, he may identify with his molester, even love his molester, he would have been too terrified to leave, he could not possibly have wanted . . .

He lay in Caleb's skin, sleepless in Caleb's bed. *Pop* went the lock on the door, his sister done in the bathroom. He could slip into her room and tell ghost stories on the tall canopy bed, or he could go downstairs and find his mother in the kitchen. Usually he did one or the other. Once, choosing neither, he'd been caught crying by his mother, but he couldn't tell her why. She stroked his back, saying, "I'm your mother, I'm your mother," her hair making a hot tent over him in the dark. It wasn't what she thought. None of it was what anyone thought. Mainly he was ashamed to be the center of it all. He was ashamed of what they all knew even knowing so little, the parts too horrible to speak. And it was just hard, keeping up every minute with who he was supposed to be when he heard those voices calling two names in the dark.

They were not supposed to ask him much.

Even if they could, how much would they want to know? With him safely returned, it was as if he'd only been away at a particularly mysterious boarding school, sequestered in the far western mountains and later shut down for undisclosed atrocities. He was presumed to have endured something he should not have, though he'd come home changed by far more than this, by more than the hormones racing in his blood, stretching his bones long, hardening his eyes. He had come home educated.

Yet if he wanted to pretend none of it had happened, they should let him. They should let him feel their willingness to listen, even if he waited months, years.

"What do you want?" Marlene asked him, as safe a question as she could think to murmur at the breakfast bar after midnight, when they had finished all the ice cream there was. "Most of all, right now. If you could have anything."

He didn't take long to decide. "I want everyone to stop thinking about me all the time."

The high school he would have been attending had he never gone away sent him books. The algebra book was the exact one he'd been using in Providence, where a test had been given on chapter 5 the day after a pair of FBI agents had pulled him from class. It was comforting in a way to go on to chapter 6 as if he'd taken the test, even if he had to forge on alone.

He missed friends. Not the specific ones in Providence — he hadn't known them long — as much as just people to hang out with, the pack of kids and his place in their midst. His once best friend, Patrick, still lived down the block in the same house. ("Patrick mows Mom's lawn!" Lark had blurted — forgetting she was supposed to pretend the lawn had always belonged to all of them.) His mother said, "Yes, well. Patrick. Of course he remembers you," and then tried to discourage him four or five ways that danced clear of what she wouldn't say: that even if she'd consent to letting him out of the house again, ever, he would not find anyone willing to be his friend.

Eventually she'd given in, gotten on the phone with Patrick's mother and arranged for the boys to get together at the Vincent house, maybe play video games. When Patrick had backed out at the last minute, Caleb wasn't sure Marlene hadn't pre-empted it somehow. And should he be mad if she had? Was it worse to be rejected, or to be so protected that he never could be? Boys change so much between eleven and fourteen, she told him; maybe it was for the best. And yes, Patrick had new friends now, wild friends, and Caleb really could not be involved in all that.

Julianna had given him a journal before he left Spokane, leather-bound with creamy, unlined paper. "Try writing down some of that stuff you're spinning up there," she said, meaning his head. Mostly he sketched. Lots of eyes. Tattoos. Hands. Pieces of things. He wrote out some of the Latin he could remember, mixing it with made-up words, ghost words. (On many pages: *leechee bone.*) Real things, whole things, scared him. He wrote "I want to kill myself" and scratched it black before he even knew if it was true. He drew a mouth with freckles all through the lips: Julianna.

The media had finally given up on the house and cleared the street, though now and then an unmarked van drove past, slowly before the Vincent house. Plain gawkers of all types — teenagers, mostly — pulled up and pointed, their windows down, their voices loud enough to hear from inside. Solitary people parked and stared: perverts, deviants, celebrity stalkers, sad people who had lost something and needed to sit close to joy; there was no way to guess which. The police, if not parked outside, swept through every twenty minutes to move them along.

Lark tried to interest Caleb in Mario Kart as he lay on the game-room floor on his back, his legs bent over the sofa seat, arms outspread. His feet were laced into green Converse All-Stars that had arrived in the mail and had never touched the outdoor ground. Downstairs, their parents were having a semi-polite argument, Marlene saying, "I've *been* here. I'm not the one who left."

"They're not really fighting," Lark said. Caleb went to the window, lifted one slat of the blind. The rain had ended, the last half hour of daylight backing and sculpting the clouds. There were no cars out front. On the outside of the window screen, a daddy longlegs with white-striped legs felt its way along with one feeler leg, longer than all the others, tapping ahead in all directions like a blind man's cane.

Lark went on. "The only reason Dad and me left is because Mom lost her mind a little, while you were gone. But now she's fine. Now we'll all be together."

She'd given him versions of this story before, though she tried to avoid the upsetting topics. When her parents had flown out west, she and her aunt and cousins had moved all her belongings back to her old bedroom to make it look as if she'd never been gone. But they had said she didn't need to lie to him, and under that pretext Lark told him whatever she considered he ought to know, anything she'd be curious about herself in his place, though all of it was spun in this soothing, upbeat way that was natural to her. They were the stories she told herself, and she offered them to Caleb as truth.

Near the stairs below, Jeff said, "Now hold on. I thought recovering addicts weren't supposed to make any major decisions for the whole first year, or something. Isn't that right?" And Marlene said, "I am not a *recovering* anything."

What major decision? Lark wondered. Aloud, it might have qualified as an upsetting question. Caleb, listening also, turned abruptly and left the room.

She followed him down into the garage. He was behind the cars, and when she got to him, his BMX bike rested on the concrete floor before him. "Your bike," she said, staring, as if it were a ghost object he'd caused to appear from the air. She knew every little thing about that bike, mainly from listening to him — nine turning ten — describe the exact one he wanted. It might have given her some kind of déjà vu except that he was so much taller beside it.

"I'm going for a ride," he said. "Don't tell them."

"You can't!" she squeaked in whisper.

"No one's out there." He wheeled the bike past her to the side door that opened to the yard. "I won't be long."

"I'll come with you. Get my bike down."

He set a hand on her head, dipped his face toward hers. "What are you, my keeper? Wait here. You can stall them for me if they notice."

Then he was gone, leaving a panicky tightness in her chest. His hand on her hair had removed the option of ratting him out. And it wasn't like he was a child. He was fourteen. But she couldn't let him leave on that bike either, the very one they had found in the woods behind the elementary school the morning after he disappeared. The only question was whether to follow him on foot or to try to get her own bike — sparkle pink, with a white basket and pink and white streamers, untouched in three years — down from the wall.

She made a try at hefting the bike, and her hand sunk into the back tire — flat. Just as well. She didn't especially want to be seen on that little-girl bike, plus she still had on her school uniform with its khaki skirt. On her way out the door, she caught sight of the blue Razor scooter, Caleb's once. She had taken it over for a season before the pink bike. She grabbed it from its hook.

On the street, she didn't know which way he had gone, but there was a circle the family had once ridden together on evenings in nice weather, up through the lot of the elementary school, over into the park, around the duck ponds and back. He just wanted some air, some exercise, she was sure — though the man he called Jolly was out there somewhere, even if all the way on the opposite side of the country, and it seemed Caleb might be drawn straight to him on some kind of tractor beam, pedaling through the sky like one of those kids in *E.T.*

Instinct aimed her toward the school — past Patrick's house, where no one was about — too slowly on the pitiful wet-blacktop scratch of her scooter, and she was winded fast from the slight incline of the road. "Helmet," she remembered aloud, and Caleb didn't have one either, but maybe they were old enough not to need them now. It was growing dark.

A black car passed, headlights on in the

blue dusk, then turned around and pulled up beside her. "Lark," called a man's voice from the window. "Lark Vincent."

She was semi-used to strangers calling her by name, but it always terrified her. Worse than the obnoxious jokesters were the friendly ones, the ones who acted like they knew her or wanted her to think they did. Jaw set, she shoved her foot harder against the street as if she could outrun him. But then she abruptly stopped where she was. She couldn't lead some stalker creep to Caleb.

"It's Mitch," he said. She could barely see his face through the window, and he switched on the interior light. "Agent Abernathy, of the FBI. You wanna see my badge? Get in the car. How you gonna get anywhere on that thing?"

Panting for breath, she climbed into the front seat, dragging the scooter along behind her. She tried to explain about Caleb, but the agent was already turning down a side street headed away from the house, no faster than the speed limit.

"Are you watching us or something?"

"Not really," he said. "Just driving by."

She looked at him again, with a stutter of uncertainty that she had recognized him correctly. She knew the name well but hadn't been around him enough to be certain of the man attached to it. He said, "I assume this is what you're after," pointing ahead through the windshield. There was Caleb, coasting around a corner, then pumping the pedals hard into a hill.

"Go!" she cried. The car had rolled nearly to a stop at the curb.

"He's fine, don't worry. We'll give him some space." He put a cell phone on her thigh. "Call your mother, please, before we get ourselves into an Amber Alert situation out here."

She opened the phone, turned to him with a sudden curiosity. "Do you like my mother or something?"

He frowned, twitched. "I like all of y'all. It's, uh, star three."

"I can't."

He blinked at her with strange, small eyes she remembered better now, vague and distracted-looking, as if he was always a little put out, and she puffed a breath through her nose, held his gaze. "I promised I wouldn't tell. And they won't even know we're gone yet."

He shook his head, mouth folded in. "You got a bit of your mother in you, you know that?"

She didn't know that but didn't say so.

Ahead of them, a red Corolla pulled out of a side street faster than it should have, with a bleat of tires, a wave of its tail. "Seat belt, kiddo," the agent said, and she clicked it into place. The car ahead peeled off down another street of the neighborhood maze, but they didn't follow, just continued on toward the park at their leisurely pace.

At the park entrance, they pulled up and idled. The streetlights were on, glowing in the damp pavement, illuminating the empty tennis courts under the tree shadow. A woman walked an elderly golden retriever up the path toward the exit. There were a couple of cars parked back near the bathrooms, but Lark could see no other people, no bikes. "Where is he? Aren't we going to find him?"

It was hard to get too worked up, though, while seated beside a federal agent. A *G-man.* They sat for a minute, and the agent rolled down his window as if to get some air, but instantly there was Caleb on a shush of tires, headed the opposite way, toward home. The agent tipped his hand out, crooked two fingers, and Caleb stopped beside the window. Lark could hear him breathing hard. "Agent Abernathy," he said lightly, a greeting.

"Caleb. Have a nice ride?"

"Yeah. It's a little chillier out than I thought, but you get warmed up."

The agent smiled. "You headed home?" Lark, in the dark of the car, hoped Caleb wouldn't notice she was there at all.

"Yeah, on my way. I just went around the block."

"All right. You go on straight there. I'll be behind you."

Through the window, Lark could see Caleb's chest heaving in his long-sleeved T-shirt, his knee cocked up by a pedal. Maybe he was making up his mind to argue about it, but then a car coming toward them, crawling against the opposite curb — the Corolla — swung around and took aim. There was shouting, whooping, the car stopped in the road with its high beams on Caleb and at least two people in it hanging out windows with cell phones.

Caleb stood on the pedals to race away, but the agent was already out of the car, the bike caught by the handlebars. Another car had turned up behind them, less decisive than the first, but waiting. Before she saw him move, Caleb was at the passenger door, shoving Lark over — she had to quick undo her seat belt — and he slammed himself in and hunkered low, wordless and watching. The agent, with the bike's handlebars

50

gripped in one hand like a dog by the collar and his badge in the other, moved toward the Corolla, from which someone said, "Hey, man, it's just pictures. It's a free country."

The second car changed its mind and slunk away. A few people had come out onto porches and into yards. Leaning over the Corolla's window, the agent delivered a lecture and a threat and received no guff in return. Seconds later, the car creeping away backward to turn itself in a driveway, the agent opened the back door of his own car and hoisted in the bike.

With a sigh, he settled back into the driver's seat and glanced toward the two of them, still ducked and frozen together, but he didn't seem angry. "Getting near dinner-time, isn't it?" He rolled up the window, put the car in gear.

Caleb started an apology as they drove toward home, and the agent said, "No, don't you say a word. That right there is not a lesson anyone should have to learn. Just so long as you're clear on where you'd be if you'd taken off just then, because these are some goddamn yahoos who'll run you flat down in the street. They think someone's gonna give them a million fucking dollars for some crap off a cell phone, and that's all you are to them."

The phone rang — Lark had to dig it out from under her. *Marlene,* it said across its face. She handed it to the agent, who flipped it open and said, "I got 'em both. Right here next to me. We're pulling in now."

Chapter Two

For days before the big announcement, Lark overheard her parents arguing. "We could move to a different state," her father said. "Florida, for instance, wouldn't be bad from my perspective, with Harry's people in Jacksonville —"

"You're not thinking clearly."

"Marlene. If we're just patient, this is all going to blow over."

"He needs to be away, *far* away. Not just so he can go outside. I don't want it touching him anymore. Or Lark either. She's had enough. Sorry, but drastic measures are necessary."

If not always sure of the details at issue, Lark could tell who was winning. She and Caleb were seated together on the top stair, straining to catch one of many battles — this one seemingly about who liked or didn't like Grandma Vincent — when Marlene swooped to the bottom of the staircase and fixed them in her shining gaze, a hand on each rail. "Lark!" she said, breathless, almost growling with triumphant glee. "How would you like to go live in Costa Rica for a while?"

"Me?" Lark cried, startled. For years, going had been all she wanted — first to visit her grandmother for a week, later to attend school there, for six weeks, a year; her plans became more intricate as her parents continued to say *Maybe* and *Someday* and *We can't really think about that now.* They hardly told her anything about the search for Caleb or let her help, and meanwhile the cloud forest was dying! It needed her to save it!

But Caleb home had changed more than the life of her family. For Lark, the light had simply clicked off in the room of the cloud forest and clicked on in the room where he was. So remote, her old dream to study cloud forest ecology, when she might become a naturalist of Caleb, like Dian Fossey with the gorillas: sit close, absorb his secrets. No one else would know him as she did. She barely cared to go anymore to that misty, far-off place, and here was her mother horribly granting her wish, sending her away.

"Well, all of us, of course," Marlene said. "We'll go see Grandma Vincent. Caleb, what do you think? Up in the mountains! The cloud forest! Tell him, Lark."

"Like the hotel and all that? I told him."

The year before, their grandmother had invested all she had in an abandoned hotel at the Continental Divide — "semi-habitable," she called it, but she lived in it now, and so did their uncle Lowell. She intended to one day fix it up into an eco-lodge or a biological station, maybe an artists' colony. Plenty of room in it, Hilda said, for people who might help with the cause, and plenty of room for Lark back when she'd dreamed of her own bedroom with monkeys at the window. Hilda had made the purchase less for the building than for the land it sat on, part dairy pasture, part primary cloud forest. In Monteverde, much of the conservation work was about converting cleared pastureland back to the forest it had once been.

Down in the kitchen, Lark peppered her mother with questions. "It's still just an *idea,*" Marlene said, aiming this at Jeff, who peered in wary silence from behind a coffee mug, "but I think we could go very soon. Say in six weeks, right after Christmas." Caleb slumped in the door frame as if unsure these matters pertained to him. "That way you can start school there in January. *Both* of you. At that Cloud Forest School of your grandmother's you're always talking about!" Marlene sent Jeff a glance that said *see,* she'd been listening to Lark, and Lark would be on her side. "We'd stay, I don't know, as long as necessary. We could just see how we liked it."

Lark looked at her father, who rolled his eyes to the ceiling while Marlene spun out more of the plan. They'd need passports fast, since none of them had ever been out of the country. Mitch could help expedite that. Money to live on wouldn't be a problem, since Jeff had for some months been in the process of selling the family business: DoodleDoo, named for the stained-glass rooster over the front door.

Since Lark was a baby, her parents had struggled as a home-based company of two to promote the DoodleDoo software, which did something Lark never understood about inventory management. She remembered sitting at the basement table with Caleb to stuff envelopes marked with the rooster logo, for allowance money, while their parents hurried from computer to fax, speaking simultaneously into phones and often in the same sentences, like, "Our son named it when he was four!" Marlene quit the day Caleb vanished — her job became the Find Caleb Foundation — while Jeff left the business to interns for a time before returning to forge on. Meanwhile, what Marlene had always disparaged as Jeff's time-waster hobby, a blog about the daily life of the business, became unexpectedly and ridiculously popular, carrying Doodle-Doo to success along with it. In the past year he'd become somewhat of a bigwig in the "Micro ISV community," giving out advice to small-scale software entrepreneurs who wanted to run businesses out of their own basements. Besides selling the company to devote his time to the blog, he'd been contracted to write a book based on it.

"Your father can write his book in Costa Rica," Marlene said. "And work on the blog from there too. It's the perfect place."

Jeff glared at Marlene's display of unreasonable enthusiasm. "As I have said, there are a lot of other things we'd have to consider, your mother and I."

"Like what?" Marlene crossed her arms, crossed her ankles, tipped her head, as if no argument could disturb her perfect serenity. "The house will be fine. You can consult for Harry long-distance."

"I'll have speaking engagements. It's really not feasible, for *us,* to be that far away. And besides, it's a foreign country. What do you really know about this place?"

Only Lark knew much. As a distraction, her parents had encouraged her friendship with her grandmother and her obsession with the cloud forest without ever paying much attention to what she said about the country. But, Marlene argued, what more did they need to know? It was far. They had family there. Hilda's little mountain town was as safe and modernized as could be expected of any remote place south of the border, and living was cheap. There were no scary diseases; the water was even drinkable.

"Dad," Lark asked when they were alone, "are we really going?" He'd worn a look through most of this that meant *I'm not going to say it but your mother's gone crazy.*

He puffed out his cheeks, helpless. "I don't know. Your mother seems determined." That meant *not no,* shocking her with the sudden reality. They were going to Costa Rica.

Caleb could not be roused to any sort of excitement, though their relocation seemed fine by him. He'd go if they told him to, be content with it if they wanted him to be — as if all his own desires were on permanent hold, awaiting their expectations, or left back in Washington State in that boy he had been.

Nick Lundy.

Nicky. He'd corrected Lark once when she said "Nick," the name they used on the news that she wasn't supposed to watch.

If, beside him in the glow of the game-room TV, she asked a question, he'd likely ignore it. Even something simple and obvi-ous, like "Is that Jolly?" when the news showed a picture of Charles Lundy. He would stare into the screen as if he hadn't heard. It was hard to tell what the man's face made him think. Looking at it, he didn't seem scared or sad or angry or even like he was necessarily seeing it. She tried declarations instead, like "He doesn't look that scary," or "He looks kind of nice," because Caleb might speak if she was wrong. If he was silent, she'd take it for agreement, and it was like they understood each other on this level just below expres-sion.

Lundy had given a statement when ar-rested, which was printed sometimes on the screen and read by a newscaster: "I took this boy from a bad situation. I did not know he'd been kidnapped previously from his real parents. I lied only to protect him. I have been a father to him, and I love him

59

dearly as a son. He loves me. I have done everything possible to give him a good home. Ask him and he will tell you."

Well? she asked him with her eyes. There he sat, right next to her, telling her nothing.

On TV, people sometimes acted like what Lundy said was a lie, and sometimes the opposite. Lark, gathering the crumbs Caleb dropped, thought the truth was somewhere in the middle. For instance, on TV they sometimes argued that Lundy was not only part of the mysterious pedophile ring but "the worst of them": he was the doctor who treated all the kids, so no one would get caught by going to a regular doctor. And she had seen with her own eyes some of Caleb's scars — on the palm of one hand, inside his right arm, above his left knee, on his scalp — stitched, he told her, by Jolly.

"How did you get cut?" she asked him. He was sitting at the end of her canopy bed, tracing the white line in the heel of his hand. Closed off in her room, he was more likely to tell her things.

"I did it myself."

"How?"

"Different ways. This was on a window."

"Why?"

He paused to consider before answering. "I wanted to get stitches."

A pedophile ring, in Lark's mind, was a dozen or so slobbery cartoon men sitting in a circle. The boy — also a kind of cartoon stick figure, not quite Caleb — might be caught in the middle of the ring like an animal in a trap. Or he might be off in another room marked with a red cross, sitting on a table before a man in a white coat who was kind of nice.

On TV, they said Caleb Vincent was brainwashed, like a cult victim, fed on sugar and drugs, that whatever the pedophiles told him he would believe to be true. Their mother had supplied a hint of support for this, mentioning a few times that Caleb would not be testifying in court because of some problem with what he remembered. "If y'all don't even want his story," she'd said to Agent Abernathy, while Lark was eavesdropping, "where does his story go?" She was complaining, in a way, but also glad, because it meant they were free to leave the country. Caleb could have sessions with his FBI therapist by phone twice a week. Otherwise, whatever had happened would be in the past and far behind.

By the end of November, when the fever had calmed and TVs could be safely on in the house, it was easier to be caught by surprise, then snagged, flipping channels, by his sudden face — maybe the boy with ragged cropped hair on the BMX bike, stopped at a car window — or by some Dr. Somebody, speaking into the camera about Something Syndrome, and you'd realize after a few minutes that he was talking about Caleb. "It's unlikely a boy like this will ever be completely normal or able to fit in with other kids his age. Often a sociopathic tendency —"

The set clicked off — their mother with the remote, taking the third spot on the sofa beside Lark. *If you listen to those lies, you'll start believing them,* she had told them both often enough. She wasn't mad, though. She folded Lark in her arms, and Lark snuggled against her, luxuriating in her new mother's warm, abundant presence.

"I know," she said, "it's hard, to turn that stuff off." She was talking to both of them, but mainly to Caleb at the sofa's opposite end. "Even when you know it's just people making noise, making stuff up, filling up time on the TV. People who know nothing at all about you. You still want to know. What's being said, what other people might hear and be thinking about you."

Caleb blinked, listening, the smallest shift of his head close enough to a nod to count. Marlene squeezed Lark closer, kissed her ear. "But where we're going, none of that will matter. There won't be American news. You'll seem strange to them because you're an American, nothing more. And you'll be free there to be anything. Anything you want to be."

Though the implication in this that they were going away *forever* gave Lark a tremor of uncertainty, she loved this mother. As with those versions of her brother, Lark had three mothers: the one from Before, the one in the middle, and the one After. The one from Before had been only her mother, hazily remembered. The one in the middle had been often frightening, like a stranger in her mother's skin; her rigid embraces had conveyed almost nothing but fear: *Are you still here?* or *We are not safe; no one is safe.* The After mother had turned soft of arm and eye, prone to lush contentment. Still concerned only with her children, she had come to believe — and made Lark believe — in the sheer power of her will to protect them. And if the mother in the middle had really been only Caleb's, the After one belonged to them both. Having this mother, Lark felt more privileged than all the girls of Agape with their normal, stable homes; she might not need God anymore. She'd follow this mother anywhere.

"Get with it, Dad!" Lark said when Jeff came upon her drilling Spanish with Caleb in the dining room — *¿Dónde está el baño?* — and asked (innocently, he thought) why they were doing that. "It's the language?" she said. "You know, of Costa Rica?" And the next day Marlene was cherry-picking flight deals from the Internet.

It wasn't as if he hadn't been paying attention. These days he was pretty much always paying attention, ever since the night Caleb had fallen through a crack in the earth after telling his father . . . what? He was going to Patrick's? Spending the night? Something about maybe being late, Marlene having granted permission? Caught up in his basement blogosphere, Jeff could never recall the precise words his son had used to shut down concern on that summer evening, with more than an hour of daylight remaining.

Marlene might never have forgiven him that lapse except that she, after dropping Lark at a party, had "run a few errands," which included a trip to her dealer (as the news channels labeled her art-school friend Alex) and a friendly bump for the road. Jeff, the police, and the FBI soon knew where she'd been that night. The news channels were stuck with speculation that came close enough. But no matter if the reality, which she later admitted to Larry King, was far less seedy than it sounded. No matter, even, whether she'd been using enough on the sly to have compromised her attention toward the children in general (Jeff had never noticed, if so). The stop at Alex's itself had put her home an hour later than otherwise, and Caleb one full hour deeper down the rabbit hole.

Strangely enough, Marlene's mother — a small-minded woman Marlene could barely stand to be in a room with — had loudly defended her daughter, calling any hint of drug use a pack of lies, while Jeff's mother, always a little cold toward Marlene, had withdrawn even further. Hilda Vincent was not the type to speak such opinions aloud, but she'd always felt Marlene was too reckless and free-spirited for Jeff, that she would not settle down enough to be a good mother, and if Hilda would never come out and say *I told you so,* her feelings on the matter were clear enough. Even her relationship with Lark carried faint overtones of snubbing Marlene or compensating for her.

So Jeff had noticed when Marlene began

picking up his mother's calls, making her own. As early as Spokane, it had started, Marlene simply adding Hilda to her list for news relays when Jeff was tied up elsewhere — wanting, he glimpsed, to be the bearer of the olive branch. A month later, the calls had turned more social, Marlene asking about Hilda's day and about life in her country, as if Caleb's return had erased any reason for discomfort between them.

"Your mother," Marlene said, "is really not as bad as I thought. She's so much cooler than *my* mother. Can we switch?"

She was being playful to hide what he knew was a desperate earnestness. So much happy change — all of it requiring her to straighten up, take charge of the family, be the perfect mother at all times — was beginning to wear on her, and she had no reasonable mother of her own to turn to. With Caleb especially, she was out of her element. Anyone would be, and there was Marlene, trying to pretend knowing him would require little more than being his mother, this person she'd never been sure in the first place she wanted to be. An accidental pregnancy had brought them all here. She had planned to be an artist, a single woman with many fabulous loves. "I don't know if I've got the maternal gene," she would say, half joking. "You've seen what raised me."

So he understood the impulse, to flee to his mother in Eden. He could even, in moments, agree with some of the reasons. He'd been watching, spotted it coming, but somehow convinced himself that Costa Rica would pass on by before Marlene got as far as plane tickets. Who moved to a foreign country on a whim? Fine for his brother, Lowell, one of that rootless tribe of freeloaders and opportunists who'd never owned anything or taken on any adult responsibility, but normal people didn't do such things. And if the Vincents had for more than three years been anything but, they were now solvent, flush with offspring, primed for a triumphant return to the kingdom of normal.

"Are you sure you can handle us all?" Jeff asked his mother in a furtive call from the basement. "I'm not sure Marlene's thinking it through. She gets ideas in her head these days, and there's no way to talk her down. I don't know what she'll be like once she gets there."

But Hilda, it turned out, felt bad about staying so far away the last three plus years, when she might have found a way to return to the States and help. "If you all need to be here," she said, "this is where you should come."

It sounded sensible enough, but after hanging up, he wanted to dial her right back, explain again. What he couldn't quite say aloud was that Marlene should not have been right. That Caleb had been found at all was a miracle; that he was alive was an accident, a pure improbability. The universe had stumbled off balance on their behalf, and now Marlene was a monster of bad decisions.

For Jeff, their battle's nadir had come in the bad August of the second year, when he'd gone on his own to buy a casket, make the funeral arrangements. They had been advised that taking these steps was a necessary ritual, so they could begin to grieve and move on, and it was time, but Marlene didn't blame those advisers. Her outrage was all for him. "Marlene," he'd said, trying to reason her through it, "it's not a moral failing to believe he's dead."

"No, it's not. You go ahead and believe that if you need to. I'm not saying he *is* alive. But he could be, and that means we don't put him in the ground."

She didn't want to grieve, of course, thought she could decide not to, and he told her so. "You want to go on looking forever," he said, "because that's what you *do* now. The rest of us need other ways to live."

He hadn't gone through with the funeral. Making her face it wouldn't have healed anything. But in his own mind he buried his son and made his peace. The chance that what must have happened to Caleb could still, after all this time, be happening and happening . . . Better he'd been dead the same day, the same hour, he'd been on that bike.

Back from the grave, Caleb sat beside him playing video games, their daily appointment. Maybe they didn't really *talk,* maybe they only sat *next* to each other — Marlene's continual accusation. But they made jokey color commentary about the game. They had fun, playing Mario tennis or golf or the party games with cartoon candy colors, Jeff choosing this silliness over the dark narrative Caleb preferred when alone. ("Zombies," he said of the murky, photorealistic world his avatar ran through, clutching the hand of a slim girl, pausing to select from an epic arsenal. "Shoot the zombies before they eat you.")

He was healthy, polite, so clearly present in his watchful way behind those glasses, and yet. Whose child was this? Over time, some tether must have snapped. Or had Jeff only let it go? The boy in his house belonged to others, though more and more Jeff felt the subtle blame burn from Caleb's every glance. *You did this. You didn't pay attention. You didn't look hard enough. You dug the grave.*

Midnight in the kitchen. Marlene said to Caleb, "You have a say in this, you know. If you don't think we should go —"

"It's not that." He picked the skin of his thumb. "It's fine."

Day by day, as he should have been relaxing around them, he was growing more reserved. On instinct she said, "Is it your dad?" and he flinched, looked away.

Little things — she'd seen it. More than once in the past week, for instance, she'd caught Jeff ducking back from the doorway of a room where Caleb was. "What do you think the problem is there?"

Caleb shrugged. "It's okay. I mean, I get it."

"Get what?"

But he wouldn't say. She was supposed to know. His look took her measure, briefly, and he shook his head. "Never mind. Can we talk about something else?"

In their bedroom, Jeff was already in bed with the lights out, having impressed upon her the need for normal appearances. But after a few nights of sex, seeking the restoration, she pulled away from contact and maintained the central border. With Caleb home, any lingering animosity seemed pointless, and yet there it was. She had let him off easy for too many crimes besides this new one, his treatment of Caleb.

She clicked on the bedside lamp. Jeff's eyes were open, and he lifted himself to sit against the headboard. Even to herself, she'd become annoying, confronting him so often over his interactions with their son. But why would he keep taking it, except that he knew he was wrong? In all things Caleb, *wrong* seemed the position he accepted for himself in advance — *You're his mother; whatever you think* — so that now she said nothing but "You and Caleb," and waited.

"What? We're spending time together. You can see that, right?" She raised her eyebrows, let him talk. "It's like you have some kind of ideal father-son relationship in mind that's just supposed to magically happen." He sighed. "It's not all my fault. I'm sure you've noticed that he doesn't seem to like me much."

"Really?" She tipped her head sympathetically. For three years, she'd had limited space for anger at Jeff, and now she wanted

71

to grab the nearest heavy object — the lamp, too flimsy — and hit him in the head. "Wow, that's sad. I feel like crying for you." He gasped, and she cut off his objection. "You hear this. You don't even get to *think* a thing like that. I forbid it."

He blinked. "You *forbid* — what, a thought in my head? Am I hearing you right?"

"Yeah, that's about it."

Jeff glared, full of that guilty, cornered resentment, then ran both hands over his head as if removing his anger like a hat. He took a deep breath, in and out. "I'm telling you how I feel. How it feels around him. I try to talk to him, but he doesn't seem to want me around."

"You need to man up and get over it." She paced the room. "Honestly, Jeff, how you *feel*? Do you remember what Julianna said to us, when we first got to Spokane?" She waited, while Jeff looked like some high-school jock called out by the history teacher. " 'He's afraid you won't like him.' "

At the time, Marlene had practically stuck her fingers in her ears against hearing it. They had not yet seen Caleb, and the FBI was stalling with these advance directives, driving her to the verge of a shrieking demand for them to shut up and produce her son *this minute.* Julianna Brewer — this pretty, freckled young thing with hair clipped back and hands folded — all the while maintained the demeanor of a museum docent with rowdy schoolchildren, willing the Vincents with solemn voice and eyes to her level of stillness. Who were they to her? She had not spent three agonizing years with the Vincents, as Mitch Abernathy had. She had spent four days with Caleb. She said, "He wants to see you, but he's nervous. You'll need to go slowly with him. He might not want to be touched." After what seemed like hours, they were allowed to observe him through one-way glass. He was sitting at a table, reading a comic book. Then he observed them through the same glass. Just before Julianna brought him into the room, she delivered that final thought, though worded perhaps a little differently in the odd, deliberate way she chose her words: "He is very concerned . . . that you will like him."

Later they learned that the lengthy delay had not been due to the standard crawl of bureaucracy as they'd assumed but because Caleb, literally, was not ready. He'd spent the morning of their arrival throwing up from anxiety, afraid to meet his own parents. The reunion turned out better than expected, Caleb hesitating only seconds before stumbling into their arms and saying *Mom, Dad,* but instantly Marlene could feel in his very body the stillness he needed from her, and how right Julianna was. No matter how relaxed he could seem in the house these months later, she held in her mind the wary boy within. Not worried about love, that autopilot parental requirement. *Like.*

"He's a kid," Marlene said to Jeff in the bedroom. "You think after all he's been through he's even got room to worry about whether *he* likes *you*?"

"I know. You're right. I'm trying. I'm trying to like him. I *do,* I mean, he's . . ." He cringed from her laser gaze. "He's a nice kid."

"A nice kid?"

"He's a stranger. That's all. It's like I don't see Caleb there. Honestly, do you?"

"Well." She ignored the question — unthinkable, irrelevant. In the sudden lightening of the atmosphere around them, a chuckle rose into her throat. "That's a problem, isn't it?" *Stranger.* Who was the stranger here?

"Look, forget I said it." He was angry now, brooding, she knew, over her black-and-white standards, her refusal to allow for the messiness of his truth. "We should probably be in counseling, you know. You and me together. And separately. This is a lot we're dealing with."

"You're probably right," she said. She got into bed and clicked off the lamp.

Every time Caleb saw a doctor, he endured the same flurry of concern about his lungs. Crackling, lower left quadrant. It didn't bother him except for occasional random fits of coughing. "It's scar tissue," he said. "I had pneumonia. I almost died from it. It's fine." For some reason this story was treated with suspicion. Doctors were just people: all so keen to sleuth out some interesting condition in the kidnapped kid. "I lived with a doctor," Caleb said, robotic, beyond exasperation by the time he was repeating it for what must have been the tenth doctor, the one at the travel clinic. "I promise, it's fine."

They needed vaccines for typhoid and hepatitis A, tetanus boosters, flu shots. Hepatitis B they could probably do without. Caleb didn't bother to explain that he was current on hep B and the rest of it — all but the typhoid. Also, they needed Cipro for E. coli. Quinine for malaria, for lowland travel, though it wouldn't be needed in the mountains.

In the mountains, where they were going.

Caleb dreamed of driving up a steep road in an SUV with his family, but the house at the top was not his grandmother's. Somehow he knew whose house it was, though he couldn't quite see it through the fog. He began to fight, but his mother and father and sister were all gathered behind to shove him out of the car, toward the front door that swung open for him. "It's for the best," they said. They couldn't handle him after all. They were sorry, really, but they were sending him back.

On December 27, the beep of his alarm woke him at 3:30 A.M. Water hissed from the bathroom — Lark at the sink. In the dark of the floor, the open flap of his suitcase lolled like a tongue, a reminder of where, this time, he was being taken: into a misty green poster from the wall of Lark's bedroom, a safe place as far as they could get from the one he'd dreamed. But he had never known where the house was — maybe Canada, or Idaho, or nowhere on a human map — so it seemed it could be waiting anywhere he went.

Their six A.M. connecting flight to Miami was held on the tarmac for half an hour while the wings were de-iced. In the first daylight outside the plane windows, bundled men dragged hoses to the task.

"This is the bushmaster," Lark said, prim and teacherly, a guidebook open across her lap under a cone of plane light. She'd taken the middle seat in exchange for the window to Costa Rica. "It's as big around as your arm and over six feet long. It's extremely aggressive and deadly and is known to chase people." She turned the page. "The eyelash viper, like a pretty lady. It waits for its victims in the trees. The fer-de-lance, a very common species responsible for the most deaths by snakebite in Costa Rica. It is also, of course, quite aggressive."

Caleb said, "What is that, *The Big Book of Pit Vipers?*"

Marlene said, "*The Golden Book of Things That Will Kill You.*"

"Here also," Lark went on, flipping forward, "are some things that won't kill you. For instance, the charming toucan. See how pretty? It eats the helpless naked babies of other birds. Here is the howler monkey, which defends its mango trees by throwing poop." She giggled. "I do hope something will throw poop at us."

"Oh, certainly," Marlene said.

Their three-seated row could not have fit a fourth, even if Jeff had been with them. He would join them later, the story went, as

77

soon as business matters allowed. A few weeks, at most — "If," he stressed, "you all stay that long." Not even Lark had questioned the plan much. It was as if Marlene had pulled too hard, as on a snagged piece of clothing, and Jeff had ripped loose — an accident, that he fell away, and in their urgency and momentum, they could not stop to retrieve him.

Stranger. Marlene's anger would pass, yet that anger — more than the echoing word or the man who spoke it — felt like a toxin from which to remove her children in all haste. Embarking on this gamble as a single parent made her wish more than once for Jeff beside her, some better version of him. But Caleb already appeared more relaxed, more present and available to her without Jeff in the way. And perhaps without Caleb in the way, Jeff would better sort out how to be his father. Marlene could imagine this happening quite fast, Jeff wracked with remorse, turning up within the week. Until then, she'd put him out of her mind, and good riddance.

Leaving Bethanne had been hardest. "Maybe it won't be for long," they said to each other. Lark would miss her cousins, who had become like sisters, closer than any friend in those isolated after-years. But their lives had been all disruption for so long — Caleb's too, certainly — that jetting off to a strange land didn't feel much like leaving home. Marlene had come to hate the house at times, especially during the year she'd rattled around it alone, keeping it only for Caleb's sake. Lark had already moved out of it once. Now she was so excited about Costa Rica that as they'd driven away, only Caleb had glanced back, with a murmured "Bye, DoodleDoo" to the rooster over the door.

At the Atlanta airport, no one had been awake enough to recognize the Vincents or to care if they did. In Miami, they got some second glances, but more pressing concerns pulled the shifting crowds onward to other terminals. Caleb's hair had grown to a more standard length, one shade darker and richer than Lark's, and no one had snapped a clear photo of him since he'd been a blond in Providence, Washington. Though the hair made it easier to see he was a handsome boy (Marlene couldn't get enough of pondering him from all angles), he was not notably so, not marked in any obvious way. Other than, perhaps, by the glasses. They had talked about getting him contact lenses, but here they were in the airport, Caleb still looking through the very frames — a thin, rectangular pewter of ultra-current style — given to him by Charles Lundy.

Marlene had struggled the last few days with the relentless feeling that she had forgotten something crucial. In her sleep, she went over it all against her shut eyelids: clothing, passports, sunscreen, cash, credit cards, antibacterial gel, books, hats, bug spray, medications, pepper spray, flashlights, umbrellas, camera, snacks — reminding herself that they could buy things there or send for things, that Hilda would have things. Or she woke to two A.M. thoughts like "Caleb needs braces! We've forgotten his teeth!," requiring several minutes to talk herself down from. It was not important, not now. But only two days before departure, Mitch reminded her that the kids each needed a permission letter from Jeff to leave the country, so that it wouldn't look like she was kidnapping them.

The first surprise came earlier than she'd expected. Somehow she'd convinced herself that even as one parent, it wouldn't be so hard to keep two kids completely in her presence, within arms' reach, from the kiss-and-ride at Hartsfield-Jackson all the way to the sanctuary of Hilda's house. It was less than a day of travel. But in Miami, when they stopped to use the bathroom, Caleb vanished without a pause into the men's side, waking her like a slap. Until this moment, he had been effectively contained within the house, to a degree unnatural for any boy his age, and suddenly, let outdoors, there he went, utterly gone from her sight. She had no option to follow.

"Mom," said Lark. Marlene blinked at her daughter, then back at the gap in the wall that said Men.

With a breath she turned to Lark, picked out a strokable section of hair at the girl's ear to worry in her fingers. "Okay. So. I guess we go over to that side, huh?"

Lark nodded, as if participating in a decision. Someone could stand guard outside every door, always and forever, or they could let go a little bit and hope. Still, Marlene kept hold of the one she could, chose the neighboring stall, kept up a running conversation, touched her daughter's sneaker with her own under the partition, and Lark touched back.

Their seats were over the wing, which blocked much of Lark's view of what the pilot announced they were flying over: the Florida Keys, Cuba, Honduras, Nicaragua. Caleb sat in the middle, where they could guard him. Many people were sleeping, but the Vincents had yet to doze. Caleb had his iPod earbuds in, a Spanish study text open before him — Juan and Miguel go to the movies. Marlene perused one of Lark's wildlife books.

There were two kinds of people in the world, Lark decided: those who fell asleep surrounded by strangers and those who did not.

Off Cuba, the water paled to aquamarine, the shadows of little clouds above marking the water. Scattered on the surface or beneath it were dark freckles she told herself were the black backs of whales.

The flight attendant came through with immigration forms; each of them had to fill one out. Lark copied her passport number, noted her current occupation as "none," her purpose of trip as "residence." At the bottom of the form was printed the only law of sufficient magnitude to merit announcement in advance, translated into a somewhat warped English: "The penalty for sexual abuse toward minors in Costa Rica implies prison." She looked at her mother and Caleb, wondering if they saw it.

From Nicaragua the plane crossed a continent, ocean to ocean in no more time than flying over Georgia, and there below were the Pacific beaches of Costa Rica. On the pale edge of sand she could see from the window, a thousand baby leatherback turtles, each smaller than the palm of her hand, might even now be hatching to drag themselves on perfect new flippers toward the aqua blue, two thousand flippers churning over the sand. Marlene had the page open before her: the few that weren't eaten or poached from the nest, that weren't picked off the beach by gulls or coatis or ghost crabs, that did not become waylaid by debris or flip over to roast in the sun, would reach the water. They hatched knowing how to reach it, how to swim. Those that touched water might live a hundred years.

Chapter Three

"Uncle Lowell!" Lark shrieked at her first glimpse of the Land Rover — blue and white as promised, smocked in rust and dirt, the only vehicle to turn onto the airport road in half an hour. Elbows flapping, she pogoed on the curb. "Uncle Lowell, Uncle Lowell!" Marlene hadn't seen her this hyper and silly since she was eight. For three plus years she'd been like a small adult, preternaturally accepting of the often ridiculous restrictions of her life. Even Marlene's unreasonable phases of forbidding visits to friends or any activities at all outside the house had simply turned Lark, contentedly enough, toward those studious, absorbing passions she'd invented alone in her room. When was the last time this child had shouted with joy? Lowell parked beside them and emerged, sporting a scruffy beard and a floppy hat. He went straight to the screaming one, scooped her up and swung her around.

"Hi there, beautiful. Whoa, did you get big. Gonna break my back doing that. *Eleven* already. I can't believe it. And you." He turned to Caleb, set his hands on Caleb's shoulders. "Look. At. That." He shook his head, tearing up. Caleb smiled at his shoes. "Welcome home, kid." He took Caleb in a long embrace, too overcome to release it, and then pulled Lark back into the huddle.

Marlene had almost forgotten how sweet he was. Say what you liked about Lowell, he had a heart — he wasn't faking that — and a generous dose of charisma to go with it, though of the sort that brought to mind a carnival barker, maybe the ringmaster of some broken-down circus. The kids hadn't seen him since they were little, but they had both been smitten with him back then, crawled all over him, and even now they remembered him as a favorite.

He took his time before turning a wry grin on Marlene. There past the hat's shade were the eyes she remembered, their dark-browed, impish glint so uncannily like Caleb's from age eleven-on-the-dot: Caleb's photo from those stacks of Missing posters in which he carried the visible family impress less of Jeff than of Lowell. Feature for feature, the brothers looked much alike, but Lowell was taller, darker, more lively, a lot more trouble. Or was it just his manner, the promise of trouble that Jeff lacked? She was already half willing to forgive Lowell for leaving them stranded on the curb of the Liberia airport for an hour, waving off the cabs that kept circling back to flirt with them.

"Hey, lady." He held his arms out, caught her up with a slow voluptuousness, kissed her beside the mouth and put her back again, then pressed both hands over his heart as if it would burst with the sight of her.

"Hey, Lowell," she said, matching his smarmy voice and smile in weary parody.

"And those kids, my god." He held an open palm toward them as if to demonstrate, back to the heart again. "The whole gorgeous bunch of you, all together, right here in front of me."

She sighed — and there went her opening rant about where the hell had he been, didn't he know what they'd been through, didn't he think, just this once? That was the old Marlene, she told herself, forever poised on the brink of a federal-level fit, with the FBI on speed dial for any day's emergency. This was a new country, a new life, a new approach to time and existence. Lark and Caleb had already been showing it to her, entertaining themselves on the curb with a vicious hand-slap game. "Chill out, Mom," they said. Lark was happy just to have her feet on Costa Rican ground, even if it was asphalt. She and Caleb had right away peeled off sweaters and socks, found sandals in their bags, rolled up their jeans; then Marlene relinquished her fussing and did the same. Caleb was a thrill to behold, relaxed for once, set loose in the sun of a foreign land with a dry wind lifting his hair, no one around. *Freedom.* She'd hardly seen his face yet in natural daylight, might have been content to simply look at him where he sat except that she rationed her gaze by habit, worried he'd feel oppressed by it.

And she had worried so much about how he would be received — by anyone, really. Even well-prepared members of the inner circle could so easily betray a subtle discomfort, saying nothing or too much, signaling his difference in neon. Since his return, she'd ended up allowing few people to meet him at all. But Lowell had acknowledged what had happened to the right degree and stepped past it, folding Caleb in with a family equally loved. For that graceful welcome alone, she'd have forgiven a lot.

They loaded their bags into the back of the Land Rover. "Wow, brought enough stuff, Leenie?"

"Well, we don't know how long we're staying." At his quizzical look, she added, "You know the kids are registering for school, right?"

"And my little brother? He's coming?"

"Yep," she said perkily, while turned away to reach a bag. "Just a few things to wrap up with the business first."

Marlene got in front, the kids in back. Lowell turned out of the lot and toward a lavender range of mountains in the distance. "There's where we're going," he said, pointing through the dirt-smeared windshield. Lark and Caleb leaned up to look. "It'll take a couple hours."

Out on the narrow country highway, they passed a single billboard set back in a field, depicting manacled wrists: "Have Sex with a Minor and Go to Jail!" At first Marlene thought she was hallucinating — it was the only billboard for miles, like her own stray thought written on the landscape. Did other countries take these precautions, or had they just happened to land in the one that did? You'd never see such fixation in America. But then, it was probably all those American predators the message was targeting. The billboard was in English, after all, stationed near the airport, a reminder that what they were fleeing could follow.

Lowell gave her a sidelong, up-and-down appraisal. "It's good to see you," he said, sincere, unfazed when she caught him at it. "I'm really glad you're here."

She faced him for a closer assessment of her own. "So is this intentional?" She rotated a pointer finger at his week's growth of beard.

"More or less. You like it?"

She squinted, considering. "And, uh, what's going on up here?" She aimed the circling finger at the hat.

"It's not as bad as you think." He pulled off the hat and ruffled his hair: thinning, grown somewhat long, two horns of expanding forehead pushing back over his scalp. Like Jeff's, except that Jeff kept what was left trimmed close.

She nodded. "Looking good, Lowell." Under the camouflage beard, half composed of gray hairs, his face looked puffier; a belly bulged where he'd never had one before. But she wasn't lying. Same great smile, and those eyes — the template of Jeff but intensified, amped higher, darker and brighter. It was a relief, somehow, that he was not less attractive. Maybe she, too, remained herself in spite of all.

There was no air-conditioning in the Land Rover, so they rode with the windows down. Turning south, they entered a busier road, freshly blacktopped but just wide enough for one line of traffic in each direction, whizzing past at high speeds. Little towns were separated by stretches of cattle fields fenced in barbed wire. "It looks like anywhere," Lark announced over the wind noise, peering out through her binoculars in search of birds. Marlene agreed. But what had she expected? Donkey carts? The cars were the cars of America, the people more uniformly brown-skinned but wearing the same sorts of clothing as anyone in the States.

Farther on, they stopped at a roadside café with a few tour buses and vans parked out front. "We can get something to eat if y'all are hungry," Lowell said. The inside held rows of picnic tables, a sandwich counter, and a souvenir shop. Out back were several more picnic tables under an enormous spreading tree, almost bare of foliage, where Lowell led Lark and pointed. "You like birds, right? Check that out."

Lark smiled and nodded. High in the tree perched two macaws, one blue and gold and one scarlet, both clearly pets of the café though they were loose. Tourists had gathered before the tree — Americans with whiny children, some other white people speaking a couple of different languages that sounded to Lark like Swedish or German — all of them making impressed sounds and snapping pictures. *That is not the wildlife,* she itched to tell them. The blue-and-gold one wasn't even native to the country.

Her mother came at her with the hand sanitizer for the second time since landing, a dollop into her cupped palms, then handed her a lemonade. She had also purchased a spiraled pastry the size of a Frisbee for the three of them to share — they had eaten sandwiches on the plane. Caleb drank from a slim bottle of strawberry soda. Lark was alert and mesmerized whenever he made these weird choices, selecting some beverage no other kid she knew would dream of drinking, and thought *If he'd never been gone, he never would have picked that.* Or when he said something that no one said in Georgia, like *sick* to mean something was cool, or *That's hot* for some look or hairstyle he really thought was ugly or lame. Though he claimed to not "really" know how, he played the piano in their house — whole songs without the music, and if she asked what it was he'd say Schumann or Mozart or he'd name some prelude or sonata in D

91

minor, as if these were nothing special, just the normal things everyone knew.

All the time he'd been missing had coalesced in her mind to a definable thing: *the Gone*. The Gone was a great bounded mystery, the mouth of a night cavern where she waited for a light to see by and from which — if she held herself quiet enough — items might be brought forth and placed in her hand.

"Can I taste that?" she asked. He handed the bottle across their picnic table. They broke off pieces of the pastry, which glistened in a tantalizing way but was made all of dry flakes and air.

When they had finished it and each taken a turn in the restroom — more hand sanitizer — they continued to sit beneath the macaws, because Uncle Lowell was talking to a girl who worked there. Marlene, her expression sweetly tolerant, made cryptic comments that Lark found thrilling: "That's your uncle, kids. So glad nothing's changed."

"Oh, this is Elena," Lowell said, when Marlene decided they were leaving. "Elena, mi hermana-in-law, *Mar*lena. The rug rats, Clark and Laleb."

"Hola," Elena said with a coy look. She was short with a cute, round face, a blond streak in her black hair. "Hola," they all said back, while Marlene nudged Lowell to the truck.

All this seemed only a minor annoyance, if not a kind of joke between their mother and uncle. Driving with the windows down blocked most of the front-seat conversation, but they both appeared relaxed and happy, Marlene with her bare feet on the dash and her laugh pealing now and then. In her wide sunglasses, the tendrils of her hair blowing over the seat or caught up in her silver-ringed hands, her slim T-shirt baring the ivy-vine tattoo that twisted around her upper arm, their mother looked like a movie star. Lowell also had a tattoo, the broad, spiky blades of which emerged from the frayed edge of the near shirtsleeve. Their father did not have tattoos. But he liked Marlene's. "Your mother was a bartender" went the explanation ("Art student," Marlene amended), "and I rescued her." Lark was always surprised when they were at the pool and new people noticed the tattoos she usually forgot were there.

The road climbed through villages where people chatted on porches and uniformed schoolchildren ran in the street. Lark tried to place herself and Caleb among them, though none were white. *We will be the*

Americans, she thought. With Caleb she puzzled out the words on signs they passed or asked Lowell, who sometimes knew the answer but most of the time did not because he didn't really speak Spanish. This made Lark the Spanish expert in the car, she realized with a pleasant jolt of fear. Caleb was second. Somewhere within the great dark cave of the Gone were CDs for learning Spanish — he'd mentioned them, made some comparisons to the ones they used together — but only some vocabulary and common phrases had stuck with him.

An hour on, the road became curved and steeper, and the asphalt ceded to dirt, a loose, marginless ribbon over precipitous drops. "You definitely need a four-by-four up here," Lowell said as their tires churned through ruts and over rocks. "They keep the road like this to protect the cloud forest from too many tourists." Far in the distance, past miles and miles of lowland, lay the crystalline Gulf of Nicoya — they could almost squint out beyond it through a nebulous blue of clouds or horizon to the Pacific shore. Strong winds buffeted the truck (*Viento fuerte,* Lark said to Caleb, because the words came to her) and the air temperature dropped ten degrees in five minutes; they rolled up the windows. Ten minutes more and they put on sweaters and jackets rolled the legs of their jeans back down.

"Is this the cloud forest yet?" Lark kept asking as the mist and greenery thickened. Lowell said no, not yet, until they were so high that the terrain began to level out, and they rolled with less effort through a heavy, windy fog. Hills rising at some distance, dimly visible, seemed forested, though near the road was all barbed wire and pasture — the dairy farmland, Lark guessed, waiting to be replanted with trees. Another turn up a gravel drive and they were there.

Lark recognized the red, barn-like out-buildings and entrance to the hotel, all muffled under a gray density of fog. The hotel itself was down the slope, its long, cor-rugated roof a hazy suggestion roughly parallel to and level with the road. Hydran-geas and other flower bushes were in bloom, though a fierce wind laid them horizontal as flags, and all around, white wall of fog leaned close. Outside, as they scrambled to pull luggage from the back, the world was whipped away in a bleary, waterlogged wind. A carved wooden sign above the door, creaking and rattling on rusted hooks, read "Finca Aguilar." The estate was named for the farm it had once been and for Hilda's second husband, dead two years, a man no one in the family had met.

Lark was the first inside, pushing damp hair from her face as the others shuffled luggage behind her. The structure they entered at road level was only a railed landing from which stairs descended to the lodge, two stories down the side of the mountain. Below, in the middle of a wood-floored lobby, stood her grandmother, grinning up with hands on her hips. "Well, look who's here!"

The Finca Aguilar, as Hilda would tell them, had once been called La Reina de la Noche, fifteen years before. It was an overly ambitious venture, as it turned out, for its removed location. In its construction the owners had rushed more than was wise, overspent on luxury items and skimped on essentials. Open only a few years, the hotel was a honeymoon destination for wealthy foreigners, and stories were still passed around town about the lavish parties hosted there by millionaires in its first year or two. In the most persistent of local legends, a tragic room collapse had killed half a wedding party, though the authorities insisted the building's most dramatic damage had actually happened some time during the last ten years, when the hotel had stood vacant.

From its main lodge, fastened to the side of the mountain like the figurehead of a ship, two arms extended gently back, each bent at an elbow to follow the curve of the land. Each arm comprised a single row of balconied rooms, propped on stilts over the abrupt drop. Seen from the hawk's view out over the valley, or perhaps from the dense green of a neighboring mountain, the Finca Aguilar was a great glass-visored face and two arms, the left intact and the right broken just past the elbow, what had been rooms 5, 6, and 7 of the north wing shattered loose and dangling at a crazy angle or gone, fallen away down the mountain face. The pieces that had cracked through the canopy had landed and been swallowed back into jungle humus, grown over with moss and vine. The nearer rooms of the broken north wing remained intact, but no one ventured into its hallway.

The south wing was meant to house the Vincents: seven rooms ("all certified structurally sound," Hilda promised), each large enough for no more than two cozy sleepers, so the three of them would probably take three separate rooms. Marlene didn't like the sound of this. The chance of building collapse aside, she had fashioned a dream of her children sleeping in some sort of guarded alcove mere steps from her bed, if not one under each wing like chicks. But luckily the rooms were not ready yet. Workers were in the midst of tiling the floors, so their beds had been set temporarily in the dining room of the main lodge. Hilda slept in what had been the manager's suite, dropped below the main level at the south shoulder. Lowell had established himself in the mirroring room at the north end, formerly the game room. For now, they would all share Hilda's shower.

Night fell while they were saying hello and bringing in bags, thwarting Lark's plan to go immediately outside and explore. "In the morning," Marlene promised. "Maybe the weather will be better."

Hilda, her arms twined around Lark, said, "You're pretty much looking at the weather, I'm afraid. The trade winds are changing direction, which puts us right in the collision. It might clear a little now and then."

The lodge was all dark wood and cavernous space, dim and lamplit. The lobby below the entry stairs doubled as a living room with sofas and chairs upholstered in pastel patterns from twenty years before. The front desk, set along an interior wall, extended toward the dining room, where it morphed into a central, semicircular bar. Stretched across the entire valley side in front of the bar, where the ceiling dropped to standard height, was the long dining room. Their beds had been placed in a row against the wall of the kitchen and partly concealed with makeshift walls of metal utility shelves backed in bedsheets. "That will give you somewhere to unpack a little," Hilda said. Between the bar and the kitchen was a brief hallway with doors to restrooms marked Damas and Caballeros.

"Sick," Caleb whispered to Lark as they poked around. "We live in a restaurant!"

"Un restaurante," Lark said. "En un hotel." Then, eyes bugged out, she added, "¡Enfermo!," which made Caleb laugh.

Wind howled and battered at the fogged glass of the dining room's long wall of windows. Squinting out, Lark couldn't tell if the solid gray view, darkening with night, was condensation on the glass or the cloud that engulfed them. It was maddening not to see what was right in front of her.

Hilda brought in juice and tea on a tray. "This is that tamarind juice I was telling you about," she said to Lark with a wink. No surprise if Lark got most of her attention, her touches and extra hugs and private comments. For a long time, apart from her cousins, her grandmother had been her best friend — maybe her only friend. They knew things about each other no one else in the room knew. A year earlier, or five years earlier, Lark might have reveled in the favored treatment, her mother and Caleb welcomed warmly and sincerely but not equally, as if Lark were the beloved relative and these some friends she had invited along. But already she felt the subliminal stress of divided allegiances, wanted to take her grandmother aside and explain that things were different now.

Her whole life, it seemed, Lark had been told she was "like Grandma Vincent," in appearance, in personality: her curiosity, her obsessiveness, her smile, her eyes. Maybe for this reason, feeling sorry for herself, forgotten by her parents or at least unnoticed and unspecial, she'd started writing to her grandmother. She still wasn't sure of their supposed resemblance but hoped it was true. Hilda was beautiful and strange, her small, round gnomelike face almost unlined, her dark gray hair lustrous and cut like a boy's. There was nothing frail about her. She had dramatic dark eyebrows that Lark did not share but the same light gray-blue eyes, which on Hilda seemed to say she'd already read your whole book but wasn't going to tell you how it ended.

When the kids were young, Hilda, a widow with puffy hair, lonely and at loose ends, had visited on holidays. They had last seen her at Christmas when Caleb was eight and Lark was five. After that, a sudden passion for travel had landed her in a new country every month or two, until she met her second husband, a tour guide in the cloud forest. In letters, she told Lark, *If you don't remember me too well, that's for the best! I barely remember myself, some sad woman who didn't know what to do with her life just because her boys were grown and her husband gone too early.* After all their exchanges and some recent pictures, Lark's "new" grandmother was much what she'd expected, with only her gestures and facial expressions to figure in.

"Isabel was here," she said to Lark, pronouncing it the Spanish way: Ee-sa-bell. Isabel was a girl of fifteen who lived nearby, and a favorite of Hilda's. Lark knew all about her. "She had to go on home to dinner. We expected you earlier. She was sorry to miss you, but she'll be back tomorrow. That girl is a stitch. You're going to love her."

Marlene trailed Lowell into the kitchen after the promise of a cocktail, the two of them like a couple of sneaking kids. Lark sat at the table, one of the many, with her tamarind juice, while Hilda turned to Caleb, as if she'd been waiting for Marlene to leave. "And you." A hand on his shoulder, she squinted up into his face, a few inches above hers. "My, you have grown since you were eight, haven't you?" She patted his arm. "I'd never know it was you."

"Good juice, Grandma," Lark said, to fill the silence. "Try it, Caleb. It's good."

Off the dining room was a set of stairs that led down to Hilda's bedroom, the shower they would share, and the bent hallway from which they could peek into their future rooms, tiny and crowded with the workmen's tarps, ladders, and buckets. Lowell led Lark and Caleb down the matching stairs to the right of the dining room, where they arrived at a vestibule with Lowell's bedroom to one side and, facing it, a doorway boarded over with plywood and crisscrossed planks. Behind the boards was the broken wing. Caleb set his hand to the plywood, feeling for what might lie beyond. When no one was looking he pushed, tugged a board, testing for give.

In Lowell's room was a pool table with scarred red felt. Two of the striped balls were missing; there was only one unbroken cue, and the floor canted a few degrees toward the blank, moaning valley. "Y'all just let me know if you feel like playing," Lowell told them.

Caleb tested the outer floor with one foot, then jumped on it. "This is going to be the next thing that falls, isn't it?"

"That might be a good bet. First the pool table, then my bed right after it."

A Ping-Pong table, pushed into one corner, was stacked with boxes and piles of clothing. "We could move that upstairs," Lowell said, "where there's some room, except it's kind of my closet at the moment. And we'd have to get some paddles and a ball."

"Laleb and Clark," Lark said. "You used to call us that, right? When we were little. But which one is which?"

"You remember that, huh?" Lowell grinned, his hat off now to reveal a disheveled mess of hair. "I don't think it's one way or the other."

Marlene came down the stairs and propped herself in the doorway, slurping Imperial from a can. "Costa Rican beer. Not too shabby."

Caleb sidled up to her. "Can I try?"

Head lolled against the door frame, Marlene reached to finger through his growing-out bangs, then handed him the can. "Don't tell your grandma."

Lowell scoffed. "It's your kid. What does she care?"

Marlene shrugged and sat on the bed. Hilda was upstairs cooking dinner. Lark plopped down beside her mother, blinking up like a baby bird. "Me, too."

Marlene laughed. "You won't like it. One sip." Lark swallowed, then made a face she tried to force into a smile.

Caleb racked what balls there were into a diamond. Marlene said, "What do we think, kids? Are we happy? Because I am about giddy. This is going to be, I think, the right decision. An excellent new life, right here. Who's with me?"

"We're with you," Lark said, meaning it literally.

Upstairs, they gathered around the chosen table in the vast dining room. Dinner, Hilda announced, was almost all the Costa Rican food she knew how to make: baked chicken with gallo pinto and fried plantains. The gallo pinto — a murky black-gray heap of beans and rice — was eaten here, she told them, at breakfast, lunch, and dinner.

"Don't let her freak you out," Lowell said. "We eat cornflakes for breakfast."

Lowell had mixed a pair of cocktails for himself and Marlene: the local moonshine, called *guaro,* with the tamarind juice and ice. Marlene spent a good part of dinner talking about Jeff and the business. It seemed strange to Lark that they had hugged her father good-bye only that morning; that he was back in their old house, probably sitting at the basement computer, his life proceeding so far away without them.

Caleb was more accustomed to this process: one life and its people obliterated, replaced with another. *Being taken,* he thought of it, a form of travel. Only the first time had been bad. The others he'd been luckier: taken by Jolly, taken by the FBI, taken to a foreign country by these new-old people, his family. Sometimes it was scary, if he could feel himself going, but also soothing because there was nothing to be done about it — the outcome would be beyond his influence. He'd been taken by paramedics once, after a sledding accident, and had expected to end up in child services or some kind of juvenile detention or group home, but Jolly woke up and took him back.

Under the table, Lark stepped on his foot — meaning *eat* — and he tucked his fork back into the gallo pinto. He found it sweet as well as useful that Lark made it her mission to intercede for him, to make him appear normal before she had any real sense of what his strangeness was.

"So, Caleb," his grandmother said, "I know how Lark feels about attending the Cloud Forest School. How about you?"

Speak, warned the reflexive voice in his head — his shrug would not suffice. He could already feel this grandmother checking off boxes on his form, only a few blank ones left before she declared him something. "I'm kind of worried about the Spanish," he said.

"Yeah, for real. Me too," Lark tossed in with quick enthusiasm.

Hilda smiled. "Well, most of your classes will be in English. That's one of the big draws for locals, especially families in the tourist industry: that their kids will come out fluent in English."

"I know, I just wish I knew more." All forks but Lowell's paused, everyone watching Caleb the way they did whenever he spoke more than three unrequired words in a row. "I mean, I don't want to —" *be a jerk,* he was about to say, then remembered that Lowell didn't know Spanish. "If I'm living in someone else's country, it would just be nice to speak the language, I guess."

His grandmother nodded, maybe even

106

erased a check mark somewhere, while the conversation, a little boisterous because Lark was hyped up and Marlene and Lowell were buzzed, was tugged free of him.

Later, in the big kitchen that had been stripped of its dishwasher, he scrubbed the dinner dishes while Lark rinsed. Hilda, transferring leftovers into plastic containers, shouted to them merrily over the water noise: "Your school is not designed for foreign kids, I'm afraid. All your classmates will speak English. They won't give you much chance to practice your Spanish unless you make them." She moved in lithe, energetic steps between counter and cabinet, lifting dishes to high shelves, squatting to low ones, emptying, wiping, replacing. "Heck, my Spanish after five-some years is still pretty bad — that's my old brain, and the fact that I can get away with English most of the time. But you have a young brain." She touched Caleb's shoulder. "It's spongy still. Whatever you immerse it in, it's going to soak right up."

Marlene would have helped with the dishes, but Hilda said, "You sit, talk."

"Kids, help your grandma," Marlene tried instead, and they popped right up together, stacked plates, and followed Hilda to the kitchen. *Look at that,* she thought. Her kids would take up her slack, save her from Hilda's judgment.

Kids — she loved the word, the balance of combining them in a syllable that even Caleb's homecoming hadn't granted. Somehow she had not yet thought to assign Caleb even the simple chores he'd done at age ten, like loading the dishwasher while Lark cleared the table. Instead, she leapt to clear his plate or tend to any possible desire before he could think of it, while Lark, her silent accomplice, took over Caleb's former tasks. Here, though, their trussed-up lives had somehow relaxed in a great exhalation. She made no effort to do things differently. She simply lazed at the table with Lowell, observing the changes with wonder and provisional gratitude, all of it seeming right and good.

"Your mom thinks I'm a lazy cow," she said, sipping her guaro drink, which was rather tasty. "And other things, I'm sure."

Lowell scratched his grizzled stubble. "Compared to Hilda, everyone is lazy. Don't worry, after living with me for a year, she'll find you a model of responsible, ambitious adulthood. And actually, you'll notice she's lightened up a bit. 'Tico time,' as the expats say. 'Pronto' down here is like, 'I'll get to it when I get to it.' "

"What are you doing here anyway? I mean, you can't legally work, right?"

"Define 'work.' I can help out around here, which I try to. Mom would like me to go back to teaching, like at the school. That I could do, since it's an English immersion school."

After a long, dissolute youth and several misfired careers, Lowell had finally gotten a teacher's certificate and settled into high-school substitute teaching in Milwaukee. He was good enough at it to get hired full-time, teaching English to urban sopho-mores, a job he had loved in the fall and left by the spring, landing in Costa Rica soon afterward. ("Got fired, I'll bet you any-thing," was Jeff's opinion.)

"I miss it," Lowell said, examining the dregs of his drink. "But I'm not ready to go back. It's too intense. It's . . . I'll tell you the story one day. Which is not that interest-ing. I'm here until Mom gets sick of me or the right thing hits, I guess. Don't laugh, but I'm kind of working on a novel."

"About your wild youth?" At least twice, years before while drunk, Lowell had re-counted the alleged book's plot and sworn her to secrecy — she was the only one he'd ever told, he'd said both times — then never remembered later that he had told her.

He ignored this. "And I might have a few other things in the works. Ventures, you could say."

"Yeah? Come on, Lowell, I'm family. We don't have secrets."

They were not, actually, the sort of family that confided much of anything that mattered. He said, "Put it this way. There is money to be made down here if you know where to look. A good bit of money."

He was always working a scheme. Marlene prepared herself to sound interested, or at least not disparaging, but he surprised her by changing the subject. "How about you, lady? What are you doing down here?"

"Seeking sanctuary. You can't imagine what our lives are like in the States." *The States* — another enjoyable thing to say, and she paused to savor it. Just the drive up the mountain, bathed in the *us* and *we* of Lowell's anecdotes about his and Hilda's daily life at the Finca, had made her feel like one of them already, comfortably expatriated.

The kids returned to gather what remained from the table, and the mere sight of them brought her a rush of gladness. She stroked Caleb's back in praise as he collected Lowell's plate and a pair of serving bowls, surprised as always by how muscled he felt despite these months spent captive in the house. He answered with a twitch of smile, glasses flashing in the light. When they had gone, back through the kitchen's swinging door to the tune of Lark's burbling chatter, she said, "I want them to have a chance to grow up in peace. God, do you remember how hard it is just being four-teen? Imagine how you would have felt, with all the *secrets* you had then, all your morti-fying little thoughts and deeds, if the whole world knew them. And that's just the same stupid shit everyone had. Now imagine what everyone knows about him. Or thinks they know — same difference. Even Lark doesn't have a real chance for a normal life under all that."

Already she'd said more than she meant to, though it was a relief to have Lowell's ear over a drink. On the phone, she'd prepared Hilda: *We don't ask Caleb about what happened,* and she might have been happy enough if somehow that translated to *Nothing happened; there is nothing to ask.* Sooner or later, she was sure, Lowell and Hilda would confront her for her account of it all, her theory. And maybe there were things they should know. *He cries some-times; he walks around at night; he has learned to play the piano; he is not always truthful.* She wasn't sure about the last one, but she often sensed him reading answers off his questioner. Like Clever Hans, the horse that solved math problems by tapping out the solution with a hoof, he watched for some subliminal cue of what he was meant to say.

But when — if — anyone cornered her for the full account, she intended to say that she didn't want to talk about it. If it were possible, she would choose not to bring it here, not to allow it into the country. Was it so quixotic a hope that she might keep this place clean for him? That here, maybe nothing *had* happened?

Lowell chuckled. "Okay, I get it. You're übermom. But what about for *you*? What do you want here?" The guaro had eased his eyelids, stretched his smile — she hoped his brain wasn't already spinning the notion that it was *him* she'd come for. That speculation would be so like Lowell as to qualify as inevitable if she didn't do something to squelch it.

She shrugged. "I don't know. I'll do some sightseeing, I expect. See what this place is like." She had not, in truth, thought an inch farther ahead. "Maybe I'll go back to painting. You and I can be the first residents of

Hilda's artists' colony. Or maybe I'll find some *venture* to get involved in. Something in the family. You're going to cut me in, right?"

They had always been good at the joking banter, but Lowell evaded her with a grimace and now, looking back over the day, she felt something missing, or maybe something added: a worry or sadness she had never seen in him, lying underneath his jovial charm. Maybe it was only that he had grown up, as she had. But it seemed unfair that any sort of worry, or age itself, should have followed either one of them to this place.

"New tattoo," she said, pointing at the side of his neck — a black scorpion.

"Oh, yeah. Like it? Watch out for these fuckers, by the way. Seriously, make sure the kids shake out their clothes. I wanted to get something to commemorate the whole Costa Rica thing, something cooler than 'Pura vida.' And I figure this can double as a totem to ward them off."

"Or bring them to you."

"Don't even joke. Mom still doesn't believe we're infested, but I've killed at least three. Check your bedsheets."

"Lowell." She tipped her head, shook it sadly, despite all she'd seen of Lark's guidebooks. "This is too soon to go spoiling my plan for paradise on earth. I'm going to have to side with Hilda on this. There are no scorpions."

CHAPTER FOUR

The next day, they rose early and met Isabel Rosales, the girl from down the road, who accompanied them on their first hike into the cloud forest reserves. Here, on tended trails cut through dim cathedral chambers of greenery, sneakers and jackets sufficed against the mist, and the clouds that drifted in rags and scraps over the canopy granted clear views out to the Gulf of Nicoya. But back at the continental divide, where the Finca perched, they exchanged jackets for ponchos, sneakers for boots, and entered a landscape obscured by fog, the wind-whipped view extending no farther than a gray blur of near trees. On the second morning, they awoke as if in a new place: out the dining room windows appeared a plunging, tree-covered panorama of valley, a distant finger of lake touched with cloud shadow and silver. Hilda pointed out the base of the volcano on the opposite shore

— the cloud lifted only that far, hovered at the volcano's peak. An hour later, the blanket dropped. The valley, lake, and volcano vanished and stayed gone.

Their world was a cloud, made not of fluffy cotton but of water. They were all surprised that life inside one should be such a wet thing. The pictures they had studied in advance, true to the beauty of the place, had not shown that they were going to be wet all the time in order to look at it.

Even indoors, fingertips slid over the varnished walls through a film of water. Toilet paper was damp on the roll. An open door admitted visible billows of vapor. The clothes from their suitcases emerged already clammy. Towels were stored in the dryer until shower time. A dehumidifier the size of a small filing cabinet and the constantly tumbling dryer sucked up a good portion of the power produced by Hilda's first major investment for the place, a windmill generator. So far, the constant winds provided no shortage of free electricity.

"It's like the deck of a ship at sea," Caleb said to Lark, as they stood taking spray from the balcony rail over the white valley. Lark knew enough about the Gone to know it was landlocked, with mountains, like this place they were in now. But he was right —

it *was* like the deck of a ship, all fierce wind and oceanic fog. If she didn't need the experience to know it, then neither did he. In their makeshift bedroom he played from his iPod dock sea shanties in a haunted minor key that suited the mood of the place, especially in the deep gray of an afternoon when there was nothing much to do.

If Lark wanted to go out and explore the property, Caleb refused, aloof, a tease; she was to offer things. She didn't *have* a million dollars, he pointed out, and he had no interest in any of her possessions, which she named for him one after another. "*Cay-leb!*" She would be his best friend, she would draw him a picture, she would make his bed for a week, she would do anything he said. The second day, same as the first, Caleb relented with a sigh and a benevolent smile once she had promised him all within her power to grant.

From the window, Marlene watched their orange ponchos and rubber boots trudge away down the gravel garden path and vanish in the fog. The fog would return them, and by the second day she spent less time waiting there, searching for their spots of vermilion in the white, fighting an urge to follow.

The gravel path led them through Hilda's

mixed plantings, which thrashed in the wet wind: coffee bushes, pink bananas, poinsettias, guayabana, sweet lime trees with rescued orchids bound in twine to their limbs, a garden plot where the green headdresses of pineapples were rowed beside beans and carrots. From the south wing behind them came the cracks of the workmen's hammers, a squeal of a drill, a shout in Spanish. On the hill above them, hazy, loomed the broken north wing. The gravel ended at the forest's edge, where they paused to consider the soggy trail that switchbacked down the mountain, steeper as it progressed. Unlike the reserve trails, which were semipaved with cinder block, the forest trails of the Finca Aguilar were all muck.

"Let's go a little ways and see," Lark said. Hilda said the trail existed only for the sake of a lovely waterfall an hour down; some neighbors kept it cleared in exchange for access for their horses. Lark and Caleb had yet to see a hoofprint. These neighbors, who ran trail rides for tourists, were also part of the work crew on the south wing and were related to Isabel, who had already spent enough time with the Vincents to feel like a friend. Isabel had promised to take them to see the horses, even to take them riding if the weather got better. But horses were boring to Isabel. She preferred going to town, where the Vincents had not yet ventured — too much to see, Hilda said, in the cloud forest.

Lark was dying to find a monkey, a toucan, a poison dart frog, something with which to entice her father on the phone, make him say, "Wow, I'd like to see that! I'd better come." Because of the weather, Hilda said, the animals had mostly been hiding since their arrival. With nothing to see, there was always the hope that Caleb would feel talkative, but he was mostly silent on these walks, and after a while Lark would go silent too.

Caleb took the lead. In the dim woods below the Finca Aguilar, it seemed to rain constantly, steadily, everywhere the same patter of hefty drops, though Hilda had told them it wasn't actually raining. It was only cloud vapor condensed on the canopy leaves, dripping down. To shield their eyes, they wore baseball caps of Caleb's: one said "Seattle Mariners"; one said "FBI."

Broad, veined piper leaves like the ones Lark had taught herself to draw on fundraiser posters gleamed in their sheen of water. Vines hung in loops between the trees. Ferns radiated above; palm fronds flapped wetly; moss clung to every surface. Lark stopped now and then to track with her binoculars a small bird — distant, drab, unguessable in the murky green profusion in which no birds sang and there was no sound but the tick and plunk of water.

"Had enough?" Caleb asked after a while, to Lark's relief. She hadn't wanted to say it first. Caleb stepped up to a tree at the trail's edge and did something under the front of his poncho, then stood there.

"Are you peeing?"

He regarded her over his shoulder. "Jealous?"

Her mouth hung open from shock and novelty, the same surprise she'd felt when she realized that clouds were wet — knowing a basic fact and witnessing its action upon the world were two different things. Generally, she forgot he was different down there, granted by nature these strange abilities she lacked. Back home in Georgia, some nights when he couldn't sleep, he would come into her bed and tell ghost stories — about real ghosts — and because he was so close, and nearly grown, and wearing boxers, which was hardly any fabric at all, she'd been compelled to think about what would be, must be, underneath. All she'd ever seen of a penis in her life had been his, some long-ago bath time. A girl at Agape had said they got big and hairy, so she wondered about that, and wondered, too, if what was under the boxers could be damaged or gone, taken from him in the place he'd been.

"Wanna hold it?" he asked, and she realized she was staring. There was nothing to see from her angle, but she whipped aside anyway to peer into the very interesting forest. He laughed. "Aw, that's sweet. I'm just kidding, you know."

She didn't know what he meant by *sweet*, and gave him a grumpy face when he was finished, so at least he'd know she wasn't fazed. Again he led, and they attacked the slow uphill slog, sweating in their ponchos despite the cool air. He could have made her touch it — she'd promised him anything. He could have made her squat and pee, too. Such strange or inexplicable demands would not have surprised her, but he never collected on her pledges, not even the one to make his bed. He piled up her debt and forgot it, the game over.

She might have voiced these thoughts, if only to get him to talk, but she didn't want to remind him that he could make her do things. And the hike required too much concentration. At a few places, where she struggled in the sloppy footing, he anchored himself on a tree to give her a hand up. When they had reached the windy lawn, he kept walking, up the steep pitch toward the road. Halfway, he stopped to gaze over the eerie grounds as he waited for her, and they stood catching their breath.

"Ghosts would like it here, maybe," Lark said, hoping for another of his stories. On the Finca's lawn below them, a tico boy who might have been a ghost himself — he never looked at them or smiled — pushed a wheelbarrow around the collapsed north wing, where a wedding party might have died. Lark waved, but the boy made no response.

"Are there ghosts out here now?" she asked.

"Could be."

"If all those wedding people really died, then they'd probably still hang out down there, inside the broken part. Don't you think?"

When he'd first asked her if she believed in ghosts, she hadn't known how to answer. Now that she did, he still treated her as if she was a skeptic. Their long-ago babysitter, Haylie, had introduced them to a ghost, he claimed. Lark remembered Haylie, a pale college student with white-blond ringlets and eyes like a bunny's, white-lashed, always rimmed in red as if she'd been crying. But she didn't remember the ghost, whose name was Ivy. Caleb said Haylie had an antique photograph of the real Ivy, who was her great-great-aunt or some kind of distant cousin, a beautiful girl who looked like Haylie with long hair.

"Haylie used a Ouija board," Caleb said, during one of those story hours in Lark's bedroom, "for a séance to call her. But maybe she didn't do the séances with you. You were pretty young for that."

"Did you see the ghost?"

"No, not with Haylie. But later." He gave Lark one of his measuring looks. "She was there. In the place I was."

And there were other ghosts besides Ivy in the Gone. One was called Zander, a boy who had lived before Caleb in the place he was. And more, ones he wouldn't name. But he made strange references. The night they arrived in Costa Rica he had asked her, "Do you think a ghost could go on a plane?"

"Is it Ivy?"

"No, different one."

She wondered if he meant himself. He had been on two planes — or three, actually. He had died a couple of times, or so he had told her, not inclined to explain. And there were times he had been dead in her mind, dead in the mind of their father and so many others. People said it was time to let Caleb go, let him be at peace. Did that make him closer to dead? Could a ghost be someone she could touch?

And then there was Nicky, a boy he talked about sometimes, who was himself.

On the grassy hillside, wrapped in orange vinyl, he stood staring down at the clouds that flowed downhill over the north wing. Or maybe he was looking past it, where the wheelbarrow boy had gone. "Do you think that's Ranito?" Lark asked, suddenly intrigued.

"Who?"

"That boy."

"I don't know. Guess it is."

One of Isabel's cousins, the one who did not like gringos, would not speak to them. Ask Isabel one question, and she'd tell you ten things. He was always charging around on a horse, terrorizing people. "He thinks it is like a motorcycle," Isabel said, with a wide-eyed show of derision. His real name was Rafa. He did not go to their school. He was a *comehuevo,* a kind of slur that meant he was low-class. Because he was so skinny with big, fierce eyes like a frog's and also had sticky fingers, he was called Ranito, "little frog."

Lark didn't think the wheelbarrow boy was all that skinny, and she hadn't really seen his eyes yet. "How come she said his fingers are sticky?"

"She means he steals," Caleb said. Lark raised her binoculars at the flit of a bird in the bushes up the hill: one of the collared redstarts they saw everywhere, with a yellow head and a cute cartoon expression. When she turned back, Caleb was down beside the wreckage of the north wing. She huffed a breath and followed.

From the outside they could see in through part of it, beams leaning, the floorboards mostly fallen like piano keys into the foundation. Metal from the roof slumped at a precarious angle toward the valley, sheltering a dense heap of rubble that Caleb framed with one hand before him. "So that part was the room," he said. He turned to squint through the open frame, which was like a doorway pulled askew. "This is the hall."

"We're not supposed to be here!" *Nowhere near it* was the rule.

Caleb, already picking a path through the rubble, gave her a sarcastic glower that said she'd overlooked the obvious. "They can't see us."

"Um, I don't think that's the point. Like,

you could die?"

Deep inside the ground-level scattering of rotted wood and trash, Caleb pulled off his poncho and draped it over the floor beam of the hallway, near the level of his chin. "Caleb —" she said, as he gripped the beam and swung himself up. It looked simple, stable. With a grin back at her, he sidled farther in, and she cringed, eyes scrunched shut with certainty that the whole structure would snap under his weight, collapse and slide into the valley. Even now it seemed to be happening, the rumble and roar, the ground shaking as the juggernaut carried him down.

Somewhere he'd found a floor. When she opened her eyes, he was inching deeper, melding with the shadows. "Yeah, this is not real stable," he called back, as if anyone might think otherwise. Her fear was fading into annoyance, becoming a desire to follow. She was curious, at least, to see what he saw. She wanted him to think of her as a brave and worthy sidekick, not *sweet* in that dismissive tone.

"Any ghosts in there?" she asked, dry as a stone as he hopped down, brushed off his palms, and retrieved the poncho.

"Nope. None here."

■ ■ ■ ■

"We're going off the grid," Marlene had assured Jeff. "That's got to be as good as rehab, on the *slim* chance I need it."

The Finca Aguilar did not disappoint on this count, with hardly a house in walking distance, and she had no vehicle of her own. They were all sharing the Land Rover. Since Caleb's return, she had not felt that old craving, but still, she wanted to be fine, and she was relieved that so far the only thing keeping her awake in the dark of the makeshift family bedroom was an anxious ear, listening over the wind for Caleb. If not rustling his covers with frustrated wakefulness, he often made sounds in his sleep: soft moans, grunts, a mumbling of words she strained to decipher. At times he might have been arguing. A sigh could have been a wince, an unbent vowel issued from his throat a call for help. She hovered over his bed, debating whether to wake him from wherever he was. But she held back, and after half an hour or so, he fell quiet.

On the third morning, woken by the wind just before dawn, she felt the startling calm of a new reality: they were safe. Never mind the snakes, the scorpions; no matter that

Jeff was not with them. Her children slept one on either side of her, motionless beneath blankets, their breathing quieter than the wind over the roof. Whatever or whoever visited Caleb's dreams could not touch him in the flesh. No hounds had tracked them to this place, no toxic gawkers, no cameras. They had escaped.

Even Hilda's young friend from down the road, Isabel Rosales, who read American fashion magazines and was crazy for American TV shows and movies, had no idea. "Your grandmother never talks about you!" she told Caleb in a scandalized way. "She says Lark this and Lark that, but I hardly hear Caleb anything. You are like a surprise to me. She must think I am so boy crazy she better hide you."

This had been the first morning, when Isabel, a plumpish girl with enormous eyes and an abundance of wavy hair half-tamed with barrettes, had accompanied the Vincents on their first day of hiking in the reserves. Hilda took them first to her own, called the Children's Eternal Forest. Only a small portion of it, known as Bajo del Tigre, was readily accessible to the public, even that part so vast not half its trails could be covered in a day. On a map at the ranger station, Hilda showed them a remote green thumbprint representing five hundred acres, the plot purchased by the girls of Agape Academy under Lark's direction. Lark wanted to see it, but Hilda said, "We'd be hiking for days. It's all one great preserve, so any part you look at can be yours."

Lowell abstained from Hilda's treks into the jungle. "Work," he said, and dropped them at a visitors' center, taking off for the day in the Land Rover. But Marlene counted on his festive company at happy hour, so she was surprised when on their second day he boarded a bus to the capital city of San José: more business. Couldn't it wait? He'd be gone only a day or two, but still, she wasn't eager to be abandoned with Hilda so soon and was a touch hurt that he'd forgo her own sparkling presence. Maybe it was a woman. Actual business that couldn't somehow be avoided, even of a shady nature, was hard to imagine on Lowell.

By the third day, Marlene was ready for some civilization, and the tiny triangle of shops in the nearest town, Santa Elena, held all the allure of a metropolis. Hilda was due to return to work at the reserve headquarters in town, so they parked on the street and separated. For a guide, Marlene, Caleb, and Lark had Isabel, in a short denim skirt and a T-shirt that said "Eye Candy" in gold glitter, snug to the roll of flesh around her middle. "Yeah," she said with a sly smile, "my father would kill me if he knew English better." She wore mascara and sheer pink lip gloss, a color she was grudgingly allowed to leave the house in. According to Hilda, Isabel was one of the smarter girls at the Cloud Forest School, but not the kind of girl who liked to be told so.

They climbed a cobbled street steep as a staircase, the late-morning sun close and bright so that the continuous mist, gusting from nowhere, was laced with rainbows: complete and distinct, or faded and partial, high in the sky or low to the ground. Sleek dogs trotted between storefronts; more lounged with backpackers on a hostel porch. Isabel and her charges squeezed to the road's margin as a transit bus rumbled down the hill. A motorcycle zipped upward, kicking up dust. Isabel waved to people, stopped often to introduce the Vincents: "My friends," she called them when she spoke in English, "Caleb, Lark, Marlene," as if they were all her peers. And maybe they could have passed for a pack of teenagers, Marlene in her plastic sunglasses and rag-cuffed jeans.

"Oh, that one there, I hate her," Isabel

muttered in Marlene's ear, indicating a teenager across the street. "Isn't her shirt so ugly?"

"Hideous," Marlene said.

The old Marlene might have been annoyed not to be treated as an adult. But this whim of expatriation had granted her a second adolescence, and so far it felt only pleasurable, a welcome gift. She was suffused with a mood — reckless, thrilling, powerful — that she'd hardly felt since her twenties, back in the bar where she'd first met Jeff, and before him, Lowell. And if it drew her children closer, as to some glamorous older cousin or friend, what was the harm? How better to keep them near than to be one of them? She'd been a parent once to Caleb. At eleven years old, he'd been visited with his first real desire that crossed her — to see a concert, stay out one night past curfew — and without even asking, he was gone.

They withdrew some Costa Rican money at the bank. "Everywhere almost will take dollars," Isabel told them, "but colones is cheaper." Marlene gave her kids each a pretty, pastel-tinted bill labeled 5,000 colones, the equivalent of about ten dollars, so they could practice with the cost of things as she did.

In the street just outside the bank entrance, a guard stood with a sawed-off shotgun cradled across his uniformed arms. "That's a little extreme, isn't it?" Marlene asked, once they had moved on along the covered sidewalk of the level main street toward the next store.

"Nicaraguans," Isabel said, cryptically.

They stopped into a hardware store, a bakery, a shoe store. In a souvenir shop, while the Vincents looked around, Isabel leaned at the counter to chat in Spanish with the middle-aged clerk, Rosa Cruz. Marlene hoped she'd remember at least a few of these names, half the people seemingly Isabel's aunts or cousins or simply "like my family." Lark veered Marlene's way now and then to show her a wooden carving, a necklace, the prices marked on each in dollars and colones. Off in a corner, Caleb admired a machete, the steel flashing in his glasses as he turned it. His eyes slid toward Marlene, and before she could smile he jammed the blade back into its sheath as if caught at something, set it back on the shelf. It made her wince. *Play with knives,* she wanted to tell him. *Be a boy.* But hearing things like that seemed only to make him more self-conscious.

At the counter, Isabel giggled, chided the

clerk, and both of them, Marlene noticed, snuck a pointed peek at Caleb before leaning back to each other for more round-eyed, hushed, and grinning chatter. The scene brought a cold rush of panic (*They know. How could they?*), but a few blinks simplified it. Caleb was a cute boy. Her constant fear that he'd be a freak in anyone's eyes must have distorted her vision, because the thought was mildly stunning: her grown-too-tall son, pale and serious, examining postcards from the rack by the door, was a *cute boy,* one a girl like Isabel might notice that way and be teased about.

In two weeks, when school started, Caleb would be the new kid in Isabel's ninth-grade class. He would be the thirteenth student, the fifth boy, the only gringo — aside from the teachers, who were mostly young Americans. Though Isabel affected dislike for all of her classmates, according to Hilda it was only that she was bored with them, the same eleven kids she'd been with since kindergarten.

For lunch Isabel led them to a nearly empty café with plastic tablecloths. Her favorite was the pizza joint across the street, Kako's, but Hilda had insisted on the café, a "typical" place, where she would meet them. A tico in a white apron, nearly the first local they'd encountered whom Isabel did not know by name, brought them menus. "Gracias," Marlene said, one of three things she could reliably speak on the spot, the others being "por favor" and "¡Qué bueno!" Today she had added "Mucho gusto," the response when being introduced.

Across the table, her children bent studiously over their menus. The last time she'd been in a restaurant with them, they'd been seven and ten, ordering off the kids' menu, wishing they were at McDonald's instead. Now they were half strangers to each other. They had no routine, in a restaurant, for what was allowed, what was expected.

"Get whatever you like," Marlene said. "You too, Isabel. I'm buying."

Isabel made a show of protest, then fielded their questions about what was good. They ordered batidos, fruit blended with ice and milk: Lark went with Isabel's choice, banana; Marlene chose mango, and Caleb, blackberry. When Isabel located her lunch in some obscure corner of the menu, a cheeseburger with fries, Marlene was swayed by the thought and made it two.

"Mom!" Lark said. "You can't eat American food."

"We are the cheeseburger twins!" Isabel cried. "I get enough of casados at home,

134

you know? But if you like that kind of thing, they are good here."

Lark and Caleb both smugly ordered casados, which would come heaped with the ubiquitous gallo pinto and fried plantains and were served everywhere, even in the cafeterias of the reserves where they'd eaten lunch the last two days. They liked it, they said, Lark determined to turn herself tica if food would do it; Caleb seeming, if anything, to think the choice polite. Since his return, he hadn't expressed distaste for a single item of food — this child who had once given her fits with his pickiness, who had generally needed a separate meal prepared from his approved menu (eggs on toast, grilled cheese, peanut butter and jelly) and would sooner put a dog turd in his mouth than a bean of any kind. The change was one among several in him that were both pleasing and so obscurely troubling that she avoided remarking on them.

"You didn't have to work at the family hotel today?" Marlene asked Isabel, who was often on duty there to handle English-speaking guests.

"Oh, you totally saved me. If I say Hilda needs me, they usually let me go. I always try to get Hilda to need me for something, so I can escape. Hilda is going to help me get into college in the States. Maybe in New York."

"College? That's a long way off, isn't it?"

"I wish it was tomorrow! Only two more years, because Costa Rica stops at eleventh grade, so I will have to finish high school first in the States. Hilda will help me with that, too, so maybe I can stay with a family there, like an exchange student? Or I could tutor their kids."

"Your parents would let you go so far?"

Isabel stabbed her pale batido with her straw. "I am convincing them it would be good for the hotel. Learn better English, go to hotel management school, like that. But I think when I get there" — she tucked her chin coyly, glancing up at each of them in turn — "maybe I will really study graphic design. Or fashion, like clothing design. Maybe I will never come back here. Do not tell them, though. Okay?"

Her roving gaze had landed on Caleb, who blinked, shook his head. Lark, his translator, piped up: "We won't tell."

Isabel smiled into her glass. "They would like me to be trapped here forever. I would *die.*"

"America's not all that great," Lark said.

"Oh, you must be crazy, girl!" Isabel turned in a manic fury to Caleb. "*You* don't think this also, I am sure. Though how would I know, because you never talk. You should talk!"

"I talk," he said, so deadpan that Isabel, essentially shy under all her bluster and noise, backed off.

The boy in Washington who rode the bus, had friends at school, must have talked as well. He must have countered the boldness of others with enough of his own to make a place for himself there, with no mother to guide him.

One day, she and this boy were going to have a reckoning as to just who was to blame for what. Some days this was her thought, having spent more than three years with all of it charged to her account. Others she could only wonder at his resilience. God, how did he get out of bed in the morning? On trails through the reserves when he did no more than follow the group, every step could seem an act of bravery, and yet she watched him shimmy alone with casual aplomb out to a slim ledge, gripping saplings for balance, to lean into a private view of Nicoya. Or at the feeders by the ranger station where eight species of hummingbird buzzed continually past their ears, he reached out with a horizontal finger and stroked one, belly to tail, as it hovered to feed. Twice he induced one to perch on the finger, still feeding, and if Hilda hadn't called them away to the trail he would have done it for an hour, his face blank. In town, he looked new people in the eye and said "Mucho gusto," and what fourteen-year-old boy to whom nothing had happened would manage so well and not be sullen, evasive, miming boredom? She had studied the species enough to know.

His every word and gesture was a miracle; yet she was still visited, less often now, with illogical flashes of rage, too much like the mood she'd detected in Jeff. *Who are you and what have you done with my child?*

In the reserves it was easy, anywhere he went, to frame him on the screen of her digital camera, catch him there. The camera, a new purchase, was fancier than any she'd ever had, and she pretended all her fascination was for its many settings and the scenery. She must have taken fifty shots of his face, eye to eye with a hummingbird. Or up inside the cylindrical, barred hollow of a strangler fig, higher than Lark, arms spread between the skeletal upside-down branches with light striping through all around him. Truly, no matter how loudly she had insisted to the contrary, he must have been dead in some part of her mind, the part that now fired with continual surprise: *There he is, alive.*

Hilda joined them as their food arrived, ordering herself gazpacho and sea bass. So far, she'd been easier company than Marlene had expected. *Going tico,* Lowell's phrase, seemed to have dampened her old impulse to express disdain for Marlene's every word and action. Perhaps it helped as well that she was distracted by a project, one that might soon take her to Belize for a conservation summit on what they were calling the Jaguar Corridor. "It's so exciting," she told them with childlike wonder as they dug into their lunch — that all of Central America and Mexico might join together to create this one large reserve. Jaguars required huge territories, up to a hundred kilometers each, and if the territories didn't touch, the cats would become genetically isolated and die out. The Corridor was improbably ambitious, but its true beauty was that it would save everything down the food chain, the whole cloud forest. "If the jaguars can live here," she said, "then everything can."

"But who even wants them to?" Caleb asked. "I mean, if you're a person who lives there. Don't they eat your goats and stuff?"

"Well, yes," Hilda said. "Jaguars are tricky.

At the local level, very controversial. But step back a little, and they're a symbol of national pride for these countries. They draw money and get people to act. No one wants to live in the country where jaguars are long gone. But then, no one exactly wants one hunting in their backyard either."

"Bajo del Tigre," Lark said. The name of that part of the reserve, Hilda had told them, referred to the last known local jaguar, shot as a cattle raider some forty years before. But the Children's Eternal Forest had for years been putting into practice the principles behind the Jaguar Corridor initiative: it bought up land and more land in the name of biodiversity, until it had become the largest private reserve in all of Central America.

"Even for me," Hilda said, "there's the idea of a jaguar, and then there's the real thing. You'll see what I mean when we go to Stancia's." She thanked the server who brought her fish, then forked off a generous bite with rice. "The fish here is *so* good," she said, giving Marlene's burger remains a scornful glance. "Maybe today after lunch, we'll go see Stancia, since we've got the truck."

Stancia with the wildlife center — Hilda had mentioned her a few times. "But don't you have to work?" Marlene said.

Hilda blinked as if she'd forgotten this. "Oh, not really. I finished what I needed to do." Maybe it was part of "going tico," but Marlene was beginning to wonder if Hilda had as much responsibility with the reserve as she claimed. In speaking of her "work," she often sounded more like a glorified volunteer.

Stancia's place was a half hour's drive on bad dirt roads to a lower elevation and a different climate, less windy, the dry montane forest. They passed a number of shacks, often with a skinny horse or cow tied in the yard, loose chickens, dogs that bolted out to chase the front tires ahead of the trailing dust cloud. A turn took them into scrubby forest for half a mile, and the road ended at a barbed-wire fence, where Hilda called Isabel and Caleb out to help her unstring a post and fold the fence back. They left it open behind them, a snarl of wire along the ditch.

Stancia's house, appearing at the end of a forested drive, was white stucco, hugged by a lush garden. At a distance behind the house was a long, sagging barn and what looked like caging appended to both sides, animal movement visible within. They found Stancia on the back porch, feeding a squalling basketful of grayish creatures from a syringe. "Toucanettes," Stancia introduced them with a dismissive flip of her hand. "So, Hilda, this is your family I have heard about?"

"All but my son," Hilda answered, the words echoing oddly in Marlene's head. Was it now Hilda's son who had gone missing?

"And your other son," Stancia added, with a smirk that meant something. Isabel, standing beside Caleb, nudged him and gave him a look — some gossip about Lowell passing between them, apparently.

Stancia was younger than Marlene had expected, maybe in her early thirties, a pretty tica with bangs that curled back along her cheekbones, hair longer and more tended than seemed to suit a woman who worked with animals. Showing them around, she coiled it up behind her head and jammed the wad of it through a rubber band. She had a dry wit and spoke in a flat American accent; she'd been to college in Chicago.

Outside, she gestured toward outbuildings: "Compost in that shed. That greenhouse there" — a foggy, algae-covered structure near the house — "is our hospital ward for critical-care patients, plus the reptiles and amphibians are there. In the barn is, well, different things. You'll see."

Before reaching the barn door, they could smell the zoo. They walked down a dim hallway past howler monkeys, capuchins, coatis, and a sleeping sloth, as well as animals familiar from the States: raccoons, squirrels, an armadillo. "We get a lot of electrocuted monkeys," Stancia said. "They try to travel on the power lines." Down another wing were mostly birds: a long flight cage of mixed songbirds, one of small shrill parrots, one of hummingbirds, with separate pens for a vulture, a toucan, brown jays, an owl, and others with more exotic names — Stancia gave the species and history of each. Some had been crippled. Some were recovering from injuries or, like the toucanettes in the house, had been orphaned and would one day be released. Most had been confiscated by the government from people trying to keep them or sell them as pets, and some of these, Stancia said, might also be released, if they had not been kept too long or from too young an age. Two flight pens held a pair each of brilliant, squawking scarlet Macaws — "Our little captive breeding program," Stancia said.

Lark peered eagerly into each cage, identifying animals, asking questions. Isabel, who had been here more than once, lingered a little behind with Caleb and narrated a shadow tour into his ear. Now and then he smiled at a comment, muttered something back, and to Marlene they looked like any two teenagers on a field trip, more interested in their own amusing observations than in what the guide might impart.

"Critical age is very important," Stancia was saying. "It is the time each animal learns what it is, if it is a coati or a motmot or a spectacled owl." They had stopped at the cage of the owl, which blinked at them from a near branch and clacked its beak softly. "This one, he was kept by a farmer from when he was a baby, so he thinks he's a person. He can't unlearn that. Now he must live here always."

Hilda asked knowing, officious questions about why one animal hadn't been released, or another hadn't been moved to an outdoor cage, and Stancia responded curtly, as if ready to take offense. Marlene wondered if she was annoyed to have this sudden tour on her hands, in the midst of her day.

Hilda stopped at a cage of three stout, healthy-looking rodents called agouti ("Like big guinea pigs with long legs," Lark said) that crowded and hopped over one another in the back corner of a stall. "What's wrong with these guys?"

"Nothing," Stancia said. "I'm keeping them for the jaguars."

"Ah," Hilda said.

"To eat?" Lark cried.

Hilda stroked Lark's head fondly, said to Stancia, "So I've been telling them about our Jaguar Corridor project. You want to explain how the agouti fit in?"

They continued walking past cages, then out the rear doors, where more cages were spread about the property. "These two cats we have, their mother was shot in the rain forest to the south. They were about half grown then, very wary of people. But we have had them now for almost four years. Nowhere to release them. We keep them at the back of the property."

They waved to a white girl — or boy? — with spiky yellow hair and a pierced lip who was cleaning an outdoor cage, a squirrel monkey perched on her shoulder. "See that," Stancia said, an aside to Hilda. "I get these interns now. College students. They just show up and some of them even work, like Petra there."

Where the clearing ended, they followed a tire-track trail into a sudden darkness of forest shade. "We wanted to keep the cats so they don't see people, so they stay afraid. You smell it already because we don't clean the cage that much. We fast them for a day then catch them in a box trap so we can get in. I will show you them through a blind. From here" — Stancia indicated their position on the trail — "we don't speak anymore, okay?"

The smell was not merely of dirty cage but of death, of rotting flesh. Deep under the trees, the tire tracks ended at a wall of plywood and canvas, above which chain link rose to eight feet high. Lark shushed Caleb and Isabel, who continued to whisper about something that had become very interesting. Stancia directed them to peepholes cut into the wood. Marlene leaned to look. The interior of the cage appeared vast, irregular, dipping into a ravine at one end, the whole of it roofed in chain link near the perimeter and, toward the center, in cables and sagging netting. The ground inside was mostly bare earth, the bushes ragged and dusty. Lark and Isabel held their noses shut. Louder than the wind through the canopy was the buzzing of flies, and the first creatures Marlene could see were dead ones, or pieces of them, scattered through the enclosure: ivory bone, blackened hide, patches of sticky-looking hair, one stark cloven hoof pointed skyward.

Stancia stepped back from her slot and

mouthed "They are sleeping." She pointed toward a wooden shelter. Marlene searched many minutes in the shadows before she caught a bit of motion, a spotted tail curling languidly upward and smacking down into the dust. From another shadow, the second cat emerged. It slunk a few steps toward them, nose in the air, and emitted a chuff of sound. Marlene felt it looking directly into her eyes. She'd forgotten which of the spotted cats a jaguar was and was surprised at how low and heavy and broadset the animal was. It looked unreal, proportioned for cuteness like a stuffed animal, the massive paws merely plush mitts, though there was nothing cute about the pale cold eyes or the mouth that hung a little open as if to taste them on the air.

Back up the trail where they could breathe again and speak, Stancia said, "For years, we have to feed them, and what can we do? The truck comes down here once a day and we throw in part of a cow, or a goat, sometimes chickens, whatever we can get. They have to eat. The agouti we will try so they can learn to catch live prey and see what it should look like. Agouti they should eat. But it is a problem, because almost all their lives they hear a truck, they smell people, and it means food comes to them."

When their group was back in the Land Rover, driving home, Hilda said, "So, you see, there's one possible future for us. It's not ideal. Obviously, you want to get the animal back into the wild where it belongs, and we already have a tract of open land that would be big enough for them, with no jaguars on it. But Stancia could spend months giving them nothing but live agouti for dinner, so they learn to kill, and it's no guarantee they'd know how to stalk one outside of a cage. Then they either starve to death or they go toward people. Which leaves us with not just a dangerous situation but a public relations disaster for the whole program."

"So *are* you gonna release them?" Lark asked.

"Stancia's planning on it, I'm afraid. But I really don't know. It may not be worth the risk."

Caleb and Isabel sat side by side in the backseat, both of them gone quiet in the confines of the car but forced almost close enough to touch. Whenever Marlene stole a glance, they were looking mildly, studiously, away from each other.

On the drive home from the wildlife center, Caleb saw the girl again. On the dirt road

148

they passed a tin-roofed shack with a bare yard, where a shirtless fat man hung clothes on a line. Nearby, a barefoot boy near Caleb's age chased a smaller one along a fence. A toddler sucked his thumb and stared at the car. Passing, Caleb turned and there was the girl, rounding the corner of the house, looking back over her shoulder and straight into his eyes. Her arm was bound in a sling made from a man's flannel shirt — did the other hand hold the stuffed blue dog? The way she was turned, he couldn't see the dog, but the flannel sling was unmistakable. Her face was dirty, her eyes black and fierce, her hair a mess of tangles, and she seemed to glow a little, her colors more vivid than those of the ordinary people near her. Always, when he saw her, she was gone again before he had time to shut his eyes and make up a spell: *Be gone be gone. Why follow me? I have nothing for you.*

Later, he and Lark were sitting on her bed, the one against the wall in their sheeted corner of the dining room, his iPod playing a tender ballad of murder that was like melody and lyrics for the groans of the wind outside. The first time he'd heard the song, it had been from Haylie's iPod, her thin, hot, dry hands sliding over his face to tap the earbuds into his ears. The Metacarpals:

the very band he had snuck out to see the night he'd been taken, by the man with the tickets. He'd meant never to listen to them again. But something about leaving the country had made him load all his old CDs onto the iPod, and now that he was here he knew he'd been right. This place wanted them.

"Do you believe in ghosts yet?" he asked his sister. "I mean, really."

"I said I did."

Isabel, right beside him in the backseat, hadn't noticed anything, but Lark had sensed his alarm, whipped around to look herself. And what would she have seen? Some ticos in a yard.

"Do you remember the house we passed with the kids outside, the man hanging laundry?"

"That fat man with no shirt?"

"Did you see a little girl with her arm in a sling? About seven or eight?"

Lark thought about it, shook her head. "Was it a ghost?"

He let out a breath, both gratified and distressed that a real girl had not been there. "Probably not," he said.

It made three times. He'd seen her in a doorway, and in a street near other children, but always at some distance away so he couldn't be sure. He'd never seen this one before arriving in Costa Rica. In life the girl was no one he'd known, though he remembered her, a patient Jolly had treated. Nicky had helped — that was unusual. His job had been to keep her calm while Jolly made a cast for her broken arm: just talk to her, or try to, since she knew no English.

She's dead, then, he thought, though he didn't want to believe in ghosts anymore, out here in the normal world. Until today, she hadn't looked at him. But for those few extra watts of brightness imparted to the air around her, she was the color of the people here. Maybe she was from here, and that was why he'd never seen her until now. *"¿De dónde?" Where are you from?* — he seemed to recall someone asking her the question. But she hadn't answered.

His recent studies in Spanish must have called her up — no ghost, just a memory, linked to those few phrases he and Jolly had learned on her account. Had Nicky been upset that day? Maybe, in small, unspecific ways; but nothing extreme, nothing to haunt him. She was just some random girl who broke her arm once, a kid he'd spent a few hours with, and then she went away fixed. He hadn't thought about her much, afterward.

Ivy and Zander, so long ago and locked away, made fine ghost stories for Lark, but this little girl who'd chased him to another country felt like one to keep to himself. He wanted to tell someone, though — Julianna, if not Haylie. If not Jolly, whom he kept shut out of his mind most of the time. It wasn't so hard to do. Isabel might have been an option, a local substitute, but he was far from ready to trust her. And anyway, at half a year older than him, she was far too young.

CHAPTER FIVE

The day before school started, Lark and Caleb went off with Isabel for a second canopy tour. They had done it the week before with the adults, riding a series of thirteen zip lines strung between tree-mounted platforms in one of the reserves. Because her family owned a hotel, Isabel could go for free whenever she liked, and if her cousin Francisco was working that day as a guide, she could bring along friends without an adult. "They make you have one just because the guides don't want to babysit," she assured Marlene, who might have joined them, except that after many days of letting her e-mail languish she'd become obsessed with the Internet café in town. "Francisco will be our adult. We'll take the shuttle."

In the shuttle van, they shared a bench, Lark in the middle. And why not? It wasn't her job to help Isabel accidentally sit next to Caleb. Caleb might even appreciate having Lark between them. When their mother prodded with a subtle singsong "Isssabelll," Caleb gave the smallest negative head shake or shrugged one shoulder — not a very strong denial, but Lark thought she'd better give him the credit for one just in case.

Isabel seemed ready and happy to include Lark, and not even mad that Lark sat in the middle. In her way, Isabel was as mysterious as Caleb — always enthusiastic even for what she despised, an exclamation point on everything, but somehow you were hardly ever sure what she really preferred. Maybe she didn't like Caleb that way. For all Lark could tell, maybe she went home each night and told her family how weird these Vincents were, how annoying to spend her time with.

Lark loved the zip line now, though the first trip she had almost chickened out. All the night before she had sweated through nightmares of falling. But her uncle Lowell went first, then her grandmother, and after watching Hilda grin and say "Whee" as she hopped from the platform's edge and into the sky, it was hard to be too scared, even on that first long line she faced alone. One leather-gloved hand went around the line behind your head: this was the brake, but it was hardly needed. You sat in the harness, ankles crossed; you trusted the harness to hold. Caleb had gone just ahead of her, her mother behind, and once Lark had lifted her feet, passing between them seemed not much scarier than a long, fast playground slide through a tunnel of forest, with someone to catch her at the other end.

This time, in a group of twenty-odd tourists, Lark didn't care whether she went first or last. Slipping along the line between platforms was so automatic she could begin to feel in herself the soaring flight of a bird from tree to tree. She was a harpy eagle, peering into the canopy for monkeys or, on the longest lines that flung her out into the open sky, admiring the miles of her harpy kingdom with the wind in her face, rippling in her feathers.

Landed, she could also monitor what was going on between Caleb and Isabel, but Isabel spent more time chattering in Spanish with her cousin than talking to Caleb. Francisco was a lean, handsome eighteen-year-old, though he looked younger. Like most of the other teenaged guides who ushered them into position or clipped them to trees while they waited for each turn, he spoke only a few words of English. Only the two older leaders, one at the front of the line and one at the back, were fluent in

English and made jokes to keep them all smiling.

Anyone who was nervous on the zip line could ask one of the guides to go along, so the guide did all the work while the person sort of sat on his lap for the trip. In front of them in line was an elderly German man who always asked for a guide to go with him, and always wanted Francisco. If this annoyed Francisco, his face didn't show it. On one platform, the German man changed places with someone in line and struck up a conversation with Caleb. "It is quite exhilarating," Lark heard the man say in his thick accent. He asked Caleb where he was from, and later he was talking about his childhood in Bavaria or something else boring that Lark didn't catch because she was talking to Isabel.

"It'd be more *exhilarating* if he would try it once by himself," Lark said, after the man had once again arranged Francisco behind him and zipped off from a platform. "He doesn't look *that* old."

Isabel grinned and said into Lark's ear, "Every time I come here almost, there is at least one perv." It took Lark several seconds to follow this, and then the shock on her face made Isabel laugh in a birdlike shriek. "I know, gross, right? But they are harmless. And that guy will probably give Francisco a really big tip. Sometimes it is even old ladies doing it!" Turning to Caleb with a wry face, she said, "Maybe I will go next, to be by him. You go behind Lark."

Caleb did so, said nothing.

After the zip line, Caleb watched from the gift shop as the old German got into a private car with his group of relatives. Rain began to patter in the dust of the parking lot. The man lowered himself gingerly into the backseat and did not look back. Yet the car drove off with some fragment of Caleb inside it — the ghost of Nicky, being taken.

The next shuttle wasn't for another twenty minutes. "Screw this," Isabel said, and called her cousin, one more from the apparently endless supply of them. This was the one with the car. Isabel had mentioned her once or twice before: *Louise could drive us, maybe,* she'd say, if there was no bus there and no taxi money and Lowell, as usual, was off somewhere unknown with the Land Rover.

Caleb could not have said why he expected a girl named Louise to be dumpy or plain, more so than any of the other Rosales women he'd met. So far Isabel, with her lively eyes, was the prettiest of them, apple-cheeked and broad in the hips, with a roll of tummy. Isabel herself maintained complicated rankings of female attractiveness. She said many things, kind or cutting, about girls she thought were pretty and nothing much about girls who were not, and they had heard next to nothing about Louise. But a cousin might be exempt from her system. Now she said, mysteriously, "It is about time you should meet Louise. The craziest one of all my crazy cousins."

The car was a rusted gray hatchback, ancient and loud, kicking up dust as it tore into the parking lot and slammed to a stop beside them. Mist still fell, but the car windows were down and Louise leaned into the passenger seat and looked up at them. "Hola, gringos," she said, and something dropped like a brick in Caleb's chest, made him stutter on a breath. It might have been little more than the surprise of her voice, low and sultry and acid, and that she was not at all plump. She was almost bony. The scooped neckline of her dress showed her bowed clavicles. Her black hair fell limp and wind-tossed along both cheekbones, lopped straight across a few inches past her jaw. No makeup, that he could tell, yet there were fantastic shadows around her eyes and her mouth, and her eyebrows were heavy and dark as if drawn on with Magic Marker. She looked older, harder, than seventeen, which Isabel had said was her age. Though she was pretty in no way Caleb could name — she might even have been ugly — he couldn't make himself look away.

"What are you *wearing*?" Isabel asked wearily, as if it were horrible. Louise's dress — the most obviously pretty thing about her — was canary yellow with a delicate pattern, and her shoulders were wrapped in a shawl of cream-colored lace. Caleb vaguely recalled an earlier remark Isabel had made about this cousin, also disparaging and also about a dress.

Louise's response was so rapid and accented that it took Caleb a moment to realize it was in English. "Shut up, bitch, or I'll leave you and your little friends on the side of the road and you can walk to town." Her lip curled to reveal a jag of carnivorous teeth.

Isabel opened the passenger door and flipped up the front seat so Lark and Caleb could crawl into the back. Louise, an arm stretched along the back of the passenger seat, regarded them over her lacy shoulder. "Don't mind us. We speak from love."

The beater car with its musty old seats seemed sharply at odds with its sophisticated driver, more lady than girl. When Isabel got in and introduced them, Louise said, "Charming to meet you" in her throaty voice and looked right at Caleb. "Of course I know all about you already."

Isabel rolled her eyes. "No, you don't."

"I do. News goes around fast. You may call me Valencia." She spun the car in a circle and out of the parking lot.

"What happened to Gwyneth?" Isabel asked.

Louise shrugged. "Doesn't fit me. And Dante said it should be more tica or I confuse the tourists."

Isabel turned to the backseat. "Louise — I mean *Valencia* — works at the Trogan Lodge, this dive hotel in town. Dante is the manager." To Louise she said, "What's wrong with Luisa?"

"Ew, Luisa is worse than Louise. Sounds like someone's maid."

"You *are* someone's maid. Hello, you *clean rooms.*"

Louise laughed, a long, smoky chuckle that crawled up Caleb's neck, disturbing like a memory. As the car bumped down the mountain, kicking rocks into the ditch, she glanced back at him again, as if they knew each other from somewhere, as if she had a private joke with him from long ago

160

and was waiting for him to remember. It gave him a flash of dizzy panic, and he reminded himself she was just a cousin of Isabel's, giving them a ride.

Isabel gawked at the yellow dress. "Seriously. *Where* did you get that?"

"I made it, of course. Admit you love it."

"If I do, will you give it to me?"

"Easy, sweetie, I can't add more fabric."

"Oh, you are hateful."

Again, Louise looked back, maybe only to keep them included, and at Caleb because he was sitting where she could see. "I am honest," she said. Was she flirting? He blinked hard, tried to see her for pretty or ugly, one or the other. Her hair, for instance: there was something alluring in the way it flapped along her face, a curtain at the edge of her eye when she turned. But shouldn't it be ugly if it looked as if she'd hacked it herself with scissors?

Louise said to Isabel, "That boy is staring at me!"

"Because you look like a freak." Isabel poked Louise's shoulder. "Uh, will you look at the road when you drive, maybe? Maybe he's staring because he doesn't want to get killed when you run into a tree."

Lark's eyes were wide, and Caleb flashed her a little smile, his promise that they were together and all was fine and the world was stranger than they were. Sometimes, when they lay talking on one bed or another, it wasn't hard to feel younger than this girl, even to crave her comfort. She had the simple confidence granted by living all the years he'd missed in this particular world. But the impulse to protect her as a big brother came naturally enough, no matter the fates that had divided them. And such opposite fates, hers to be so sheltered and coddled that he had cast her — in a story for his therapist — as an egg with a girl's face, wrapped in a pink satin bow, seated on mounds of pillows. Still, she had turned out well. If she hadn't been such a good kid, hard to resent in the flesh, he might have felt more urge to fumble the egg, let her crack a little. Even liking her, he often calculated that a crack or two would do her good.

Louise and Isabel had switched to rapid-fire Spanish, and Caleb pretended to watch the scenery, glad for a chance to just soak in the girl's voice. *Easy,* she kept saying, which he smiled to realize was actually Isy, a nickname for Isabel. They were just entering town when Isabel let out a screech and began shouting. Louise cut the wheel to the left in front of a Tica Bus, knocking them all sideways, the car plunging down a hill so steep she had to immediately apply the brakes.

"What, what?" Lark cried, gripping Caleb's wrist.

The car slowed, turned off at the bottom of the hill and up a rutted side road, maybe a driveway. "We are fine, no problem," Isabel said. "That was our dads back there. *Both* of them, in front of the hardware store."

"Your dads?" Lark said. "Are you in trouble or something?"

Louise muttered in Spanish as she parked under a tree. "They didn't see us, I don't think," Isabel said to her. "So what, anyway? You're my cousin." To Lark she said, "It's fine. I'm just not supposed to hang around him too much." Lark shot questions at Caleb with her eyes.

They got out of the car. Louise, an inch or two taller than Caleb in collapsed red heels that seemed too big for her, flung the snowflake lace around her neck like a scarf and softly insisted, "I'm fine," as if everyone were saying otherwise. In that instant, smoothing the hair around her face, she seemed tearful, vulnerable — pretty — the next, awkward as a horse as she clomped up the rocky margin with the toes of her bad shoes turned out. They followed, single file and quickly.

Farther up the road was a log cabin with a broad front porch and curtains in the windows, a hand-painted plywood sign that read "Trogan Lodge." A path led them alongside the building toward a sprawling compound of smaller cabins. Louise turned at the back of the lodge into the shade of a porch and stopped abruptly, her back to a door marked "Staff Only" as if the building were all that would shield her from the fathers blocks away.

"Let's go up to your room," Isabel said.

Sun slanted to light half of Louise's face. "They don't want to go to my room," she said, a clotted sneer in her voice. She turned a look of cold challenge on Caleb, and if nothing else, he knew to meet it and not look away until she did. One of the many tricks Jolly had taught him.

"You want to go to my room?"

Caleb shrugged. "Sure, why not?"

Louise sighed, her eyes dropping, and muttered in Spanish. That voice — sad, seductive, sick? — rang more wrong in his ears while he was facing her. All of her was wrong. Then one blink and the oddness that had rattled him by staying just ahead, out of his reach, in the rush down the mountain landed like a dragonfly on the lace of her still shoulder.

Luis. Isabel hadn't been saying a girl's name.

He almost laughed, a sudden easing of tension. Nothing seemed strange anymore. Luis led them inside, up a narrow set of stairs to a door that opened on a heady waft of incense into what was essentially a closet with purple walls. Purple mosquito netting draped a single bed in one corner, set under a small, high window. The rest of the room was an organized riot, crowded with tables, mirrors, baskets, drawers, shelves, knick-knacks, photos, posters, gauzy fabric, dripping candles. Against one wall was a sewing machine, and standing out in the room, a dress dummy. Isabel went straight to it and stroked its gown, a long, limp shimmer of midnight blue.

"I heard about this one," she said. "You wore it on New Year's Eve."

Luis smiled, turning the lock on the door. "The sequins were falling off that bitch all night."

Lark's mouth hung open as she peered into one shrinelike niche that housed dolls, feathers, tiny animal skulls, strung beads, painted figurines. At the foot of the bed, Caleb studied photographs taped to the wall: a soccer player with tousled hair and an electric grin, a purple shirt that said "Bimbo" — the shirt of Saprissa, the best Costa Rican team. In one snapshot the soccer player stood next to a boy who might have been Luis, in boy hair, boy clothes, a low-watt smile. On other walls were photos and posters of Latina fashion models or movie stars. Were there Costa Rican super-models?

Isabel turned from the dress dummy to Luis, her face crumpled as if she might cry. "Do you know how sad your mom and Tia Sonia and Justina and Abuelita and *my* mom were that you did not come to the party? Nobody could believe it."

Isabel had filled them in on the Rosales family New Year's party, a grand annual tradition, but hadn't mentioned any absent member. The Vincents understood it to be an unmissable event, like a wedding or a funeral, no question of attending or not: *everyone,* down to the most distant cousin, the most bedridden grandpa, would be there. And it was only family. Lark had gone around for a day saying wistfully to no one, "I wish we could go to Isabel's party," but Hilda had taken them to a New Year's potluck with mostly white people, one of their few social outings that Isabel had expressed no regret in missing.

"Isy, are you going to give me a hard time in front of your friends?" Now that Luis was a boy, the acid edge of his voice seemed almost gentle, even younger than his age. He kicked off the red shoes, turned the lace shawl into a whip to snap at Isabel. "You know I can't be in a room with my father."

"He was fine. I heard him say your name twice." Isabel shifted the bed's netting and sat, made a place for Lark beside her. Next to the dressing table, where Luis leaned, was a lime-green beanbag chair, but Caleb instead stationed himself against the sewing table. The room was so small they all might have linked hands.

"And he's probably on his way over here now," Luis said, "with a pitchfork. Or a dull razor." In the dressing table mirror, his brown upper back was bared down to where the V of the yellow dress was joined with a zipper. Delicate, that zipper seemed, the thinnest one in the shop, with a track that would feel oiled drawn down or up the curve of his spine. "Are we freaking out your friends?"

"He's not coming here," Isabel reassured Lark and Caleb. "He's not that bad."

"Oh no? Maybe not when he is sober." Luis gave the visitors an imperious look, as if they doubted him. "Last time I let him catch me, he beat me up and shaved my head. And that was before I even started . . . you know, this." He flipped an edge of his skirt, performed a scoffing curtsy. His armpits in the sleeveless dress looked hairless, his fingernails unpainted; the dress was cut to hold small breasts — funny, Caleb only now looked — but nothing filled the space. He'd come across boys who had some girl in them before, and he knew there were boys who were all girl; this one struck him as maybe half. If Luis had been born in a girl's body, Caleb thought, he would not choose that dress.

Lark, who liked to make people feel better, said, "Your hair is pretty long now." She watched Luis placidly, and Caleb wondered when she'd caught on. Maybe before he had, Lark being a junior connoisseur of all manner of strange animals.

Smiling, Luis plucked a long, curved feather from a shelf and trailed it over a burlap doll with pins for eyes. "That is because I can keep the man away. I have spells on him."

"Luis is a *brujo*," Isabel said matter-of-factly. "You know this word? It is like *witch*."

"And I have bad magic. So don't mess with me, gringos." He brandished the feather at Caleb, but the challenge was gone; it was almost playful. They saw each other now, and Caleb remembered Luis in the car saying *I know all about you.* It should have made him jumpy, but he felt calmer than he had in a long time.

Into the silence, Lark piped, "You know what? You speak really good English."

Isabel doubled over laughing. "You are too funny, girl."

"I went to that English school with Isy," Luis said. "Because I was smart like her, or so they thought. But turned out I was just wasting Papi's money to become a nothing, worse than a whore."

"Shut up," Isabel said.

"Now you don't go to school?" Lark asked.

Luis shrugged. "I was almost done with it."

"That's mean," Lark said. "You have a mean dad. Why does he have to shave your head?"

His sister, the egg. In a warmth of solidarity with Luis, Caleb answered for him, without cruelty and without gentleness. "Because that's how dads are. Some things they just can't deal with."

Not all dads, would have been her automatic retort. He could almost hear it, rising in her throat to her open mouth, but his tone had stopped her. Yes, all.

The constancy of the fog at the Finca Aguilar, after a week, began to feel intolerable to Marlene. How did people live here? How would she? No matter how lovely, it was like clinical depression in the form of scenery. The haze that softened the world made her sleepy all day, and she wondered idly how a little coke might improve the outlook. The men and boys who worked at propping foundations, banishing the water, hauling materials from here to there, could not be induced to smile or speak. Her greetings seemed to burden them like an extra chore. They lived in this cloud, too, went home to their wives in it, a different breed from people she encountered in town. Even Isabel's own extended family, in her telling, seemed sortable based on elevation: the higher, the more morose.

By the second week she found it helped to spend her days in town, where it was always sunny and the mist was laced in rainbows and there was dust — dust! — on the cobblestones. Even when the wind blew the hanging boards of store signs horizontal and she had to turn her back to a pelting of dust, she found it more pleasant than mud forever underfoot. She had established a back corner of the Internet café as her own office, machine #12, and had a little Spanglish banter down with the guys who worked the counter and who commiserated readily when some kid arrived before her and took "her" spot. They were nice boys, brought her coffee in paper cups, jammed along on guitars behind the counter to jazz they played on a boom box, and mostly left her alone. "Mucho trabajo" was one of the phrases she could speak, and they would say it back to her in a flirty kind of way. When she walked to or from the more removed outposts of town in sunglasses, ticos passing in cars, on bikes, or on foot would call out "Guapa" or "Tu eres una mujer . . . something" (an adjective, presumably complimentary) or a fast string of words she could sort into something like "Be my girlfriend," but in the café they were shy and respectful. Or maybe they could see more readily that she wasn't so young.

She spent a couple of days just working through her inbox, almost all of it Caleb-related. First up was the foundation — a registered non-profit with a board of directors and a volunteer network and one paid employee, Fay — which could not simply vanish but had to be renamed and repurposed. And would Marlene consider writing an article for *Woman's Day*? Would she consider writing a book, under the guidance of an agent? At one time, she would have simply hit the Delete button, or Fay would have on her behalf. But now a book was something to consider. She had the time, they could use the money, and though she had no desire to relive or exploit the past, she could not be entirely sure that she had nothing to say. So, she would have to think about it. Think, think, think, and her inbox began to refill with messages she marked "keep as new."

Then the personal mail, so many intimacies with virtual strangers besides her real friends — and how could she not respond to parents whose children remained missing, or had long ago been found dead, who had little in life but whatever small hope or bittersweet joy they could glean from Marlene? She owed them. She worked up a vague little narrative of life after Caleb's return, one that she could copy and paste, with more specific versions for people closer to her. She sickened herself with platitudes and half truths: *He is a profound joy to us every day* and *Despite all he has been through, he seems to be adjusting remarkably well.* All claims she thought were the truth until she had to suppress the long, rambling qualifier that wanted to follow; she expunged the gray, planted a period: *Every day he is more my son. We are putting the past behind us.*

There were e-mails from Bethanne, Jeff, Mitch, the three people she had talked to on the phone. But privacy was scarce at the Finca, and the one phone, tethered to the front desk, was often in demand. When Caleb wasn't on it for his twice-weekly hour with his therapist, besides frequent calls to Julianna Brewer in Spokane, Lowell commandeered it for business. By e-mail, Marlene felt freer to share her true concerns, though the busy café often distracted her, made it difficult to pin down her thoughts, and if she did manage to sink herself to any depth of concentration, her children were likely to materialize behind her from wherever they'd been that day, giving her a start. She had put them each on an allowance of twenty thousand colones a week — an amount that made Isabel's eyes pop or she might have gone higher — and from this stash they could pay a thousand for an hour of Internet access. Lark had strict, longstanding rules for using the Internet, approved sites she was allowed to visit and school friends she was allowed to write, no

Facebook or other social networks. Caleb didn't even have an e-mail address — the FBI had taken possession of the account he'd used in Washington — but he found plenty to look at online. In lieu of a talk, she asked, "Do we need to talk about what's okay and what's not on the Internet?" and he shook his head. The café, she reasoned, was a public place, no way to hide the screen.

But here was one of those questions she might struggle to express in all its messy complexity to Bethanne or Mitch or Jeff. Who was she to school this boy on the dangers of the Internet? What was left in him to protect? In terms of adult experience, she was quite sure he could tell her a thing or two — not that he would. And then a look over his shoulder could chastise her: if not sports, his screen was likely to show a Wikipedia page or a website for some topic they had encountered earlier in the day, something that she'd forgotten (Chorotega Indians, Juan Santamaría) but which he'd tucked away to look up later. Here was an alert, curious boy with, yes, many things left to discover.

When the kids arrived at the café after their zip-line trip, later than expected ("We stopped to visit one of Isabel's cousins,"

Lark said), there were only two free machines for the three of them, so Lark waited. She hung her arms around Marlene's neck, and Marlene had to fold one e-mail and open a more innocuous one. "Mom," she said. "Is Dad really coming?"

"Well, probably." Neither of the kids had asked yet so directly. "And look." She set her cheek to her daughter's arm. "If he ends up taking longer, that's just because he's got important stuff to do for the business. We're at his mother's house, right? So it's not like" — *we're running away from him,* she stopped herself from saying — "he's not going to get here eventually. And here we'll be."

Every few nights, by phone, she and Jeff traded information about the house and the business, the kids and Costa Rica, and she listened for him to make any kind of noise that sounded like imminent arrival. "I love you, too," she answered him, automatic, and there was truth in it, somewhere. But she'd become comfortable with this apartness. In his absence, family love perfected itself, free of any strain. That he'd join them in "a few weeks," give or take, turned out to be every day's perfect amount of time, though more and more she felt she'd come here knowing he would not.

"Do you miss him?" she asked Lark.

"Yeah." Lark sat in the free chair beside her. "Can we call him tonight?"

"Of course. Caleb needs the phone too, I think."

"Caleb's always calling people." Rare to see Lark mopey, collapsed on the desk, her frown mashed crooked against one arm. "He's always on the phone but he never even calls Dad."

"He talks to him when we all call, same as you do."

"Not much."

Marlene lifted Lark's hair where it was pasted down from her zip-line helmet. "You and your dad got to be pretty good friends while Caleb was away. But Caleb is still kind of getting to know your dad. He's just got some different friends, right?"

"Juliaaaaanna," Lark groaned. "He stayed with her for, what, five days? He's been with Dad longer than *that*."

Marlene glanced across the room at Caleb, out of earshot yet close enough that she could see photos of soccer on his screen. "We talked about this, right? You need to cut him some more slack. Give him time."

Lark nodded, seemed to cheer up a little — school started tomorrow, after all — and for insurance Marlene offered her the computer while she went across the street to order a couple of take-out pizzas for dinner. If she could head off that first explosion of premature grief — particularly in the form of a child crying demands to Jeff on the phone — maybe she could pass them all safely over worry and sorrow and into the land of after, when things just were and no one waited for them to become otherwise.

That night, Lark was moony again, pincering a hand at the phone while Marlene was on with Jeff. She lingered to keep an ear on Lark's turn, which was longer and more subdued than usual. But in the end she sighed and said, "You're coming here sometime, right?" in a tone perky enough that a "Yep" would suffice as response. "Okay," Lark said. "Here's Caleb."

Caleb didn't like anyone lurking when he was on the phone, even if it was just with Jeff, their conversation little more than a listing of recent activities or plans for the next day. Marlene took a beer out to join Lowell on his porch, a sheltered nook where they had dragged a couple of cast-iron chairs and could watch the cloud play in the nearby treetops. After his one abrupt trip to San José, Lowell had stayed put as her evening drinking companion. Often he went on dates, but by the next day he was back, and even on New Year's Eve, when he'd planned to hop a bus to the beach for some legendary street party with a girl named Joanna, a teasing from Marlene had induced him to stay.

She clinked her bottle with Lowell's as she sat. Below the porch, the world dropped away fast into thrashing boughs, hazed and glowing in the lights of the garden path. A roll of thunder could go on for a full minute, a steady rumble like machinery or the volcano they hadn't yet seen.

"I've got some weed, by the way," Lowell said. "I don't know if we dare with the kids in the house. But it's good."

For some reason, this took her by surprise — as if pot should be so hard to come by in this green place. It had never been a drug she particularly craved, only one she partook of whenever it was passed her way, which in her school and bar years had been often.

"No," she said, reluctant, "I think not. And I'd sort of rather you didn't either, here."

"No worries. That's one of those things Mom will knot her panties over. I have a secret spot out in the woods."

"Oh yeah?"

"Very nature boy. Girls allowed, if you ever

feel like visiting."

"I'll keep that in mind." Though curious about where he got the marijuana, how hard it was to find, she thought better of asking. She sipped her beer and gazed into the foggy drama of the trees.

"Imagine this was your honeymoon," Lowell said.

"We'd need a hot tub."

"Oh, you're so right."

She pictured herself a young bride, in the heyday of La Reina de la Noche, carried away to this alien landscape. What would such a honeymoon signify for the life to come? If you could get past the initial urge to kill yourself, what followed would surely be nothing ordinary.

She and Jeff had gone to Bermuda. It was the beach everyone went to.

Once you were trussed up for the zip line like a telephone lineman, it was too late for a bathroom break. So after the last platform, the whole group trudged back up to the gear room, where a guide helped you out of the harness, and then you went straight to the restroom. Caleb had stopped to tie one shoe, then the other, letting the girls go ahead, because the German man was slow. The restrooms were around opposite corners and the girls had to wait for a stall, so they wouldn't notice who went when to the men's.

The man had come up next to him at the trough, not too close. They weren't alone. Caleb smiled, looked at what the man was showing. Any restroom, any man. It was information he couldn't talk himself out of needing, no matter that he had no plans to use it. The man said nothing, only checked to see if Caleb would open his hand — no, sorry — met Caleb's gaze, and smiled back. That was all. The caress in his eyes was a comfort, soft as a hummingbird's belly.

"Are you telling your therapist about this?" Julianna asked, her voice a nocturne, so careful never to be shocked. "That's the kind of thing you should talk about with her."

"I don't want to tell her that. I want to tell you."

"You can tell me. But tell her too."

"She'll just, I don't know. She sees things one way. It's all about trauma for her, you know?" Under the front desk — where guests would check in, if the Finca Aguilar had guests — Caleb had made himself a semi-private phone cubby. He knew that almost anyone in the household (his mother, Lark, even his grandmother; not Lowell)

180

would eavesdrop if given the chance. So he kept his voice low, the phone close, whether no one was home or everyone was. The partial enclosure echoed his own murmurs back to him, his breath.

"Isn't it," Julianna asked, "about trauma?"

He worried she was getting tired of him. Half the time he just said whatever he thought she'd find interesting or smart, which meant he was always stranding himself some distance away from what he meant to say.

"There has to be something that's me, right? I mean, does everything have to be this thing that happened to me? Nicky, you know, *that* kid was fucking crazy, before Jolly fixed him, and . . . I don't know, maybe a little messed up still, afterward. But Caleb sometimes feels like this person I would have been anyway. Like maybe Caleb stayed back home and waited for me." He heard her breathe. He sounded nuts. "I mean, obviously, things happened to me."

He wanted to cry. This was what he hated about talking to his therapist, what he couldn't escape even when talking to Julianna: the code. All these people were so sure they knew him, knew Nicky, and sometimes it was soothing to let himself believe it. But they had this code already

181

written in place of his experience, and he was expected to accept it and use it too: what was wrong, what was a crime, what caused damage and required recovery. No matter how much they urged him to talk, three years of his life was reduced to this infuriating formula. Some things it labeled *bad* had helped him survive and grow, while other things with the same label, *bad,* had been so much worse than their code could make room for. He wanted to talk about both extremes, because those were the parts he didn't understand, but other people heard only the code. So he had to keep tapping it like a keypad: yes, there was trauma, bad things happened, perpetrated by criminals. What was not codified could not be heard, and what was codified was already understood. It did not even require him, really, except as X, the victim, to whom Y happened. And still they said, *Tell me. Say anything. I'm listening.*

He took a breath, backed up. "Do you think I'm gay or straight? I mean, really?" It was simpler, more pleasurable, to talk about the present.

Her voice was honey, buttermilk. "I don't know, Caleb. I think you're probably straight. But maybe there's not always one answer to that for everyone."

His voice, lazy with a grit like sleep, like talking to a lover in bed. The sounds of their voices were primary, the first meaning, the words a way of making them. "So, like, I could be a straight guy who gets married or whatever and checks out other guys' dicks in the john for the rest of my life?" This was not a topic that mattered to him. He veered toward whatever might be fresh enough to keep her attention.

"Why do you think you do that?"

"For information. If a guy's that close to me, it's like I need to know what he's working with."

"But you like it too. You like looking."

"No, not like that. Dicks aren't a turn-on for me. And being looked at, that kind of creeps me out. But I know how to sort men. I can do it really fast, you know, like whether they're good or bad or neutral." She wouldn't care for this terminology; he tried again. "I mean, if the guy secretly wants to hurt you. And this guy today was just some sweet old dude. So I guess what I liked was knowing he was into me. That felt really, weirdly, *safe,* in a way. Like I wasn't alone."

"Caleb. You're not alone. You have all kinds of people who love you."

"And you'll always say that."

Julianna breathed, careful. "Your mother,

from what you've told me, I really think you could tell her anything. Anything. And she would be on your side; she'd defend you to the death."

There was a fine line to walk with Julianna. He needed her sympathy, had to draw it out without letting any note of self-pity slip through. He aimed for wounded, damaged, but stoic. Self-pity was unattractive.

"Yeah. Maybe. But what if she didn't? It's not worth the risk."

In the past, once or twice, his anger at Julianna had gotten away from him. *You're the one who made me come home! I was fine where I was. I had a life and no one judged me and no one had to be sorry they were stuck forever with this fucked-up piece of trash for a kid. If you had just left me alone . . .*

He tried not to do that too often. He knew she wouldn't forget it was there, a barb retracted beneath his gentler words. Just doing her job, but she'd wrecked him, as a storm without intention wrecks a well-constructed ship. Now he drifted, alone, his family hardly more than a raft on which he waited for what end would come. Possibly he might float on it all the way to some adulthood. More likely was dehydration, sharks, the strapped-together logs breaking away from under him, one by one.

CHAPTER SIX

On the first day of school, Lark was handed
a machete. The classroom was a sloping,
unfenced pasture in which trees, planted a
year before, had sprouted up no higher than
her knee. On her own, she would have
mistaken them for weeds, but her teacher
explained how to tell the difference. Their
task was to locate the baby trees amid the
grasses and use the machetes to cut away
any weeds that crowded too close, choking
off the resources. Sun, water, soil, air. Lower
in the field grew ranks of saplings planted
by students in earlier years; behind those,
sturdy young trees. And beyond, as the land
rose again in green density, the real thing:
secondary and primary cloud forest. In a
former dairy field, her class was making
more of it.

A machete was a fierce, chunky thing. It
had weight. The blade surprised her, honed
sharp enough to sever tough plant fibers in

a stroke. The other kids, it seemed, didn't need to be instructed on how to hold it properly or warned that it wasn't a toy. At Agape, they hadn't been allowed to use scissors with pointed tips. Later, a friendly girl with a braid down her back, Beatriz, told Lark, "They give us machetes in kinder! I don't think anyone ever cut off a finger so far."

Their regular classroom, in the main building with the lower grades, opened only to the outside, and whenever they came inside they took off their shoes and left them by the door. For more than half of each day, the shoes went on and out they marched, sometimes to work — in the vegetable garden, the compost house, the greenhouse, the baby forest — but more often to pursue some task along the school's forest trails, like net insects to identify, or count certain kinds of epiphytes up in the trees, or rescue orchids that had blown down from the branches above. The teacher was a pretty blonde from Vermont, Miss D'Angelo. She favored scavenger hunts in pairs: find three kinds of edible leaf; find three kinds of fruit. Often, she sent them to climb trees — regular trees or ones with ladders mounted on the trunks and rope bridges strung between the high boughs — or she sat in the shade, chase games starting up around her, and Lark, confused, would have to check in. "I don't get what we're supposed to be doing now."

"Now," Miss D'Angelo said, "we're just enjoying the outdoors."

This was not recess. Recess was a separate period in which the girls sat in the grass and talked while the boys played *fút,* which was soccer. They ate lunch outside, had snacks outside, trooped back in and left their shoes at the door. Then it might be time for a lesson, to Lark's relief. Math, science, English, social studies, each connected whenever possible to their theme for the six-week unit, Conserving Natural Resources. Outside the open windows and the open door, the countryside fell away in a fairy tale of green hills and blue sky, the gulf an etched puzzle piece of blue that seemed so close they might walk there for a dip.

Whenever they pleased, but always at lunchtime, troops of coatis wandered through — even the teachers called them by the Spanish name, *pizotes* — around the outdoor picnic tables, in and out of the classrooms, right up alongside the desks, and paid no attention to the people at all. The kids ignored them right back, as Lark learned after she amused her class by shrieking at her first sight of one, a cross between a raccoon and a monkey with a long tail draped behind or held straight up in the air. She knew them from pictures, from Stancia's wildlife center, but one of them strolling into her classroom was something else. Their fingerlike noses scouted out dropped food, but they didn't grab or beg, didn't even pause where kids were eating. They simply went past, between a pair of human feet if they felt like it, and marched on, blind to all but food on the ground. Garbage, sorted for compost and recyclables, had to be carefully secured.

"No homework!" Lark announced after her first day, and then most of the days that followed until it turned into a complaint. At Agape, two rigorous hours of assigned work each day had ordered her time at home in a comforting way, guaranteeing its measure of attention and praise. Her cloud forest obsession had begun as extra studies she assigned herself, and as much as she loved being in the actual place, she found it hard to *excel* at these outdoor tasks. Pale as a termite, she was the only kid in her class burnt pink the first day, so that every morning thereafter her mother had to remind her to coat her face and arms in sunscreen ("In this cloud! Amazing!"). Though she was not, thank god, the chubbiest kid in class, she was the least agile, the least at home in fresh air. Indoors, too, there were challenges, like the Spanish class she went to separately with the few other non-native students near her grade. And no matter how simple the other lessons, there were always particular spots where a new kid had to catch up. So she couldn't complain that school wasn't hard enough. It was just an *adjustment,* which was how she liked to put it when reporting on her day.

Whenever her class filed out to the forest trails, they passed some of the solitary huts where the high-school kids had their classes, and sometimes, peering into a dark interior, she'd spot a waving hand, Isabel or Caleb. Their class changed huts and teachers for each period, so Lark never knew where they would be. Some of the huts were up on the lawn overlooking the gulf; some were deep in the woods like secret campsites. She was jealous on every level — that they were together, and had class in huts, and changed teachers, and did real, serious work at their desks instead of so much "enjoying the outdoors." It was the first time she could remember yearning to be older than she was. The kids in her class seemed babyish, besides being established in their cliques, and it was hard to make friends. She'd have rather hung out with Isabel and Caleb any day.

Caleb claimed to like the school well enough, in his shrugging way. "It's a hippie school," was his assessment. As usual, this was not a protest, only an observation, though he didn't say it in front of Hilda.

Their grandmother, it turned out, was not actually a teacher at the school as Lark had assumed but had only assisted there from time to time in the past. Lark wasn't sure if this counted as a lie, but she'd started to wonder about other things her grandmother said. Was she really going to Belize to make the continent safe for jaguars?

After Lark's first day at school, when she was helping in the kitchen before dinner, her grandmother offered new insight into the world of plants: "It's important to have a good heart around green things, especially when you're wielding a machete. A plant will know your intentions. If you intend to harm it or help it, it will know."

Lark smiled, suspecting a joke. "It will?"

"Oh, yes. It's been proven in the laboratory. A plant can be rigged with electrodes to work as a lie detector, more accurate than any machine. Even water," Hilda said, the faucet open and pouring beside her, "is sensitive to human thought and can tell good intentions from bad. Don't be skeptical!" Lark blinked — it must have shown in her face. "There are many, many mysteries in this world that science has no real answer for."

Lark had never thought it *too* strange that Hilda cooed to every plant in the yard in the belief that kind thoughts and words helped it grow. A lot of people talked to plants — it was sort of like prayer. But plants that could read your mind? *Water?*

I am never alone in the forest, Hilda liked to say, and now the idea struck Lark as creepy: trees, ferns, moss, epiphytes, the water droplets on every leaf, all leering down at Hilda to judge her intentions.

In a few weeks she'd fly to Belize for ten days, leaving them alone at the Finca. "You must talk to my plants for me," she told Lark, "while I'm gone."

"What are *you* up to in the dark?" Lowell's voice as he swung into the kitchen was loopy and thick with insinuation, probably also a few drinks. It was one in the morning, and he'd just come home. He crossed the room in long, slow tango steps, all the way to the refrigerator door and three feet from Caleb before he startled back, shook his head. "Christ, kid. Thought you were your damn mother standing there."

Caleb was amused. "Really?"

"In the dark, you're twins." Refrigerator light poured over both of them as Lowell bent inside, emerged with a beer. "Uh, running a little low in here," he said meaningfully, studying Caleb in the chilly light until Caleb brought forth the bottle tucked away on the counter behind him. Lowell must have smelled it on his breath. He'd snuck only one a night, maybe four total at this point, figuring his mother and Lowell would each attribute it to the other if they noticed at all.

"Hmm. Conundrums, eh?" Lowell shut the refrigerator, returning them to the dark. "Well, don't just stand there. Not healthy to drink alone."

Caleb took his beer and followed at a creep, out across the darkened dining room, well clear of the corner where his mother and sister slept, down the stairs edged in yellow safety lights to Lowell's room. Lowell went straight to the john at the back, flicked on the light and left the door open as he pissed a long, loud gush into the toilet. Caleb watched, holding his beer, then sat on the bed. From his angle, the doorway blocked Lowell's front half. He wore a long-sleeved T-shirt that covered most of his tattoos. His brown hair curled down the back of his neck.

The rumpled, never-made bed with its skin aroma, more Lowell than Lowell himself, was familiar seating during the day — the room had only one wooden chair otherwise. But to be there in the dark, alone, waiting for Lowell to join him, stirred Nicky awake. Lowell wouldn't have any use for him, of course. Minutes before, in the kitchen, his approach through the dark had been laden with enough convoluted sexual intent to lift the hair on the back of Caleb's neck — then, in the instant of recognition, an abrupt drop in temperature, a welcome deadening. Still, he would want *some*thing, prefer Caleb to be one way or another. It began to worry him, to ache like grief: by not being Marlene he'd been a disappointment. He'd have to makes amends.

When Lowell shut off the bathroom light, the room shifted to the gray of the enormous window, its cloud dimly lit by the outside garden lights. He plunked down mid-bed and scooted back against the wall, took a swallow of his beer. "Ahhh. But we can't make a habit of this, right? I mean, it's Friday, so I don't know why you can't have *one*. Except your mom might cream my ass, so we'll just not mention it. Cheers." He leaned to tap Caleb's bottle neck with his. "What're you doing up, anyway, bruh?"

Caleb shrugged. "Can't sleep, I guess."

"How come?"

"I don't know. Not sleepy." He slid back to the wall beside Lowell, sipped his beer. Before them, he could see the pool table with its red felt, a few loose balls gleaming like pearls in the dark. "Were you out on a date?"

"You might call it that."

"With Stancia?"

Lowell snorted. "Who told you about her?"

Caleb smiled down at the bedcovers. "I have sources. I hear many things. The complete exploits of Lowell Vincent."

"Woo-hoo, listen to you. Like a tico, down with the *chisme.*"

Caleb took a slow drink. "I have heard a certain term applied to you, by the local population."

Lowell's voice was full of suppressed laughter. "And what is that, pray tell?"

"Oh, I probably shouldn't say."

Lowell hooted, grabbed him by the arm. "Now you have to tell me, don't you?"

That grip triggered a flash of shock like

jumping into a cold pool — it made him laugh, turned fast to a buzzing, gratified warmth, because he'd wanted Lowell to touch him. "Oh, I really shouldn't, I don't know," he went on in his put-on voice, while Lowell menaced him with threats of noogies. "Okay," he said finally, and Lowell released him. "The term I heard was *man whore.*"

It wasn't as funny in his own voice as it had been in Isabel's, her eyes bugged out with spastic pleasure. *Your uncle is a man whore!* Still, Lowell about spit out his beer laughing.

"And who says that?"

"People. Sources. I hear Stancia is one of your many lady friends. And that you have women all over you from here to Montezuma. But Stancia thinks she's your girlfriend. Or she'd like to be. Is that true?"

"There's a *small* possibility that is true." Lowell let out a belch. "But I don't pretend to know about what goes on in the minds of women."

Caleb nestled to the wall, content. "You knew my mom when she was a bartender, right? Before she met my dad?"

Lowell nodded. "I am quite truly the reason you exist. You and Lark. Your folks never would have met without me."

"Were you and her together before they were?"

"Um," Lowell said, "next topic."

"What, is it a secret? I don't care if you were banging my mom."

Lowell made a sound like "Ow" and stifled a few snorting giggles, one hand pressing his face into a mask of decorum. "No secret, no story. Nothing to see here. I think we'd best go back to these present-day women I supposedly have so many of and none of which are your mother."

If she and not Caleb had been in the kitchen, then she'd be here now. And then what would happen? It would likely depend on what they'd had to drink. Caleb wished he could have been her, for an hour. To see where it would have gone, to keep Lowell lit as he'd been.

Out the window was the night cloud, the howl of wind steady as a locomotive. "I think Stancia's pretty," Caleb said.

Lowell smirked. "She's pretty something."

"And then there's that girl we met on the way up here. Elena? And my English teacher, Miss McCord." This last one Caleb was proud of, and he could see in Lowell's face that he'd guessed right. On New Year's Eve, Lowell had planned to take off for Montezuma with an American girl, Joanna,

197

and some of her friends — just tagging along for the party's sake, he claimed — but would not divulge more details, no matter how much Marlene had goaded him: *And how old is this girl?*, etc. He'd changed his mind about the trip, though, to humor Marlene or maybe (Isabel's theory) Stancia. In town were at least two American Joannas by Isabel's count, but one look at his English teacher and Caleb knew she was the girl. "They're pretty, too," he said casually. "In a different way."

"*Shiii-oot.* Nothing gets past you, boy! I gotta start watching out for you."

"Young, though," he went on, monitoring the seesaw of Lowell's reaction: so far, he was still entertained, yet Caleb was in range of being a brat, another kind of disappointment. All he could do was keep talking until Lowell grasped that he was not necessarily a child. "Those other girls. Younger than Stancia, for sure. Probably not as smart as she is. Maybe, I don't know, they'd be easier to manage?"

"All right. So, you have an opinion about which one I should pick?"

Caleb thought about it. "Well, I bet I haven't seen them all, but I'd pick Stancia. I don't think you want to pick anybody."

Lowell sipped his beer. "Why Stancia?"

Caleb shrugged. "She's cool. Different. She seems really smart." He felt self-conscious suddenly, turned to his beer. "I don't know, I just like her."

Lowell snatched up the chance to turn the spotlight around. "You like any of those girls your own age? Isabel, maybe?"

Caleb was quiet for a moment, sorting the options for a reply. "I have this kind of situation. A problem. Can I run it by you?"

"By all means, bruh."

"I like Isabel. I mean, she's cute. And we hang around a lot and, you know, we have fun. We get along. She's like a friend. And there's this girl in my class who's cute too. Like, really cute." All this was true, except the part about it being a problem. In fact he hadn't given any of it much thought. It just came to him in the moment as the kind of thing Lowell would like to hear.

"Mmm-*hmm.*" Lowell gave him a squinty, knowing nod.

"But I can't really talk to her or Isabel gets all pissed off."

Lowell stroked his chin. "I see. Yes, the doctor is in. Let us take a look at this. Isabel likes you?"

"I don't even know, is the thing. Isabel hates these other girls in our class. I think she just wants me to be *hers,* maybe just as a friend would be fine with her, but as long as I'm not *theirs.* And I sort of think this other girl, maybe she kind of flirts with me just to piss off Isabel."

"Women! It starts early, doesn't it?"

"And there's not that many guys in our class. So that's part of it. Plus, they've all been together since kinder. So I'm like the fresh meat."

"Indeedio! Well, let's see. Would you care to have one of these girls for a girlfriend?"

Caleb shrugged. "I don't know. It seems complicated. I don't really want to get attached to one person right away. I mean, I just got here."

"Right. Right. That's good thinking. Play the field. Here, try this: let them fight over you if they want to. You just be a gentleman. Be charming to everyone, even the uggos, then Isabel can't get too mad at you, plus whenever you feel like making a move, you've got your pick. Am I right?"

Caleb grinned. "Yeah, that's pretty good. That's good advice."

"Caleb, I am very glad to be of assistance." He clinked Caleb's bottle again, then upended his own over his mouth. "Damn, I'm out."

One more, Lowell decided, though he was already semi-drunk. Caleb wasn't sleepy yet. They could split it.

Then all they needed was a bedtime story, chosen by Caleb, told by Lowell. Once upon a time, half the girls in Costa Rica had wanted to get into Lowell's pants, since all American men were rich and also on the prowl for tica trophy wives, a misperception that Lowell was able to bask in for his first few months in the country. Caleb prodded the story along with fascinated questions, shifting onto his back across the bed, feet parked on the wall. Lowell assumed the same position at the foot of the bed, and when Caleb awoke, before dawn, they lay more or less in these places, awkwardly folded with more than an arm's reach of space between. He sat up and for a few minutes, before he crept back upstairs to his own bed, he observed his snoring uncle.

His mouth hung open just wide enough for a finger, maybe, to slip inside the gap and up to the knuckle without waking him. His snores were not a phlegmy rattle but soft and vocal, like a moan. Like Jolly's. Caleb had a vague memory, from an hour or two before, of falling asleep to the sound.

I am eleven years plus eight and a half months old, Lark thought on the bus home from school, watching Caleb sleep two seats ahead. Isabel, on the seat between them, read an outdated issue of *Vogue* a teacher had given her. They were the last three on the bus, each with a seat to stretch out on solo as they crossed climates from sun to the cool gloom of cloud, lumbering upward toward the very last stop on the route. How Caleb could sleep leaned to the window with his earbuds in and road ruts bouncing his head all over, Lark would never know. "Teenagers," their mother had said, when Caleb was still dead to the world near noon on a Saturday, as if age explained him.

Only a week after his eleventh birthday, he had entered the Gone. For half of her own life that she could remember, that threshold had gaped ahead of her like the jaws of a whale, and now she had fully crossed it. Being him, she told herself: I have been gone over eight months. Whatever is happening to me, by now I know what it is.

Out the window, fence posts ticked their progress. If a barbed-wire fence could be pretty, these were, the black posts made from tree limbs, each with its own crooked individuality. Half of them sprouted wind-whipped green shoots, resurrected by some cloud-forest magic into sapling trees.

Looking at them made her remember her

grandmother that morning saying *Trevor.* "Trevor won't care if I'm a little late," she'd said, if Lark and Caleb wanted to catch a ride to school after Lowell dropped her at the ranger station, where she had to meet this man, the lead naturalist on the Jaguar Corridor. In her usual khakis and rain jacket, Hilda appeared so flushed and bright, chatting in the front seat about jaguars and *Trevor,* that Lark said, "You look pretty!" Hilda thanked her, unsurprised by the compliment, as if her prettiness were obvious. At the ranger station, a tall, gray-haired man with a wispy beard stood smiling in the doorway. Ushering Hilda inside, he gave the Land Rover a wave. "Hey there," Lowell said, waving back sarcastically. "If you're wondering why she's going to Belize, there's why. Been chasing him for a while, but now I think they might be, you know . . ."

"Might be what?" Lark asked.

Lowell glanced at Caleb as if they shared a secret before he answered. "Let's say romantically involved."

"What?"

"Or maybe not. Pretend I didn't say that."

When she looked at Caleb, he only shrugged. At the school gates, they separated in the crowd, and then she'd forgotten about it until just now on the bus home. Every day, the grandmother she'd once been so sure she knew became a little less that person, a little more someone else.

She was about to ask Isabel if she knew about Hilda's boyfriend when, from nowhere, a horse appeared at her window, pacing the bus. Its high, boxy brown head and high-stepping hooves seemed too close, the road it shared with the bus too narrow. The rider glared sidelong as if the bus were in his way, but only after the horse had flattened into a gallop and shot ahead of them did Lark recognize the rider as Ranito.

She poked Isabel. "Look, your cousin. What's he doing?"

A gasp of bus gears roused Caleb, who peeled loose his earbuds. In the grass beside the fork, the bus stopped to let them off, Ranito sat on the restless horse. A few times, Lark had glimpsed him racing around on this horse or another, but always at some distance.

A week before, at the Finca, he had spoken to her, though she had quickly aggravated him by understanding so little. *Horses* was the one word she could catch, and she had answered, "Sí! Caballos!" Lacking even the word for "ride," she had mimed it for him, feeling stupid. Later she asked Isabel if

Ranito was going to take them riding, or if he had meant to invite just Lark, and Isabel had given her a comically grim look. "You don't want to go riding with Ranito. Trust me."

"Why are you here?" Isabel asked him — in Spanish, but Lark was beginning to hear these simple sentences as easily as if they were English. Isabel sometimes hiked with them up the left fork to the Finca Aguilar, but today she had to go home, down the road to the right.

Ranito, his stony gaze turned toward the trees, grunted a few words that hardly sounded like any language. A rough rope was knotted snugly behind the horse's ears and around its muzzle. Its skin twitched. It lifted its hooves one by one and set them down, shook its head, began stepping sideways until it swung back into the road and nearly on top of Lark and Caleb. They had to scramble back to avoid being trampled.

Isabel rolled her eyes, annoyed. "Whatever. See you guys tomorrow." Using a stirrup and Ranito's hooked hand, she swung up behind him with surprising ease. The horse skittered off at its high-stepping pace carrying both of them, Isabel's turquoise school bag jouncing on her back.

"That was interesting," Caleb said. He

pushed fingertips under his glasses to rub his eyes as if the horse might be part of the dream he was still emerging from.

They began the hike up their own road, the crunch of their sneakers in the wet, sandy gravel making Lark wish for hooves. "Grandma needs to get us some horses. We could tie them here and then ride home from the bus stop."

Sometimes the Land Rover came down to meet them, but Lark didn't mind when they had to walk. The road was agonizingly steep in places, and where it leveled off, they were smacked in the face with a wind that was like carrying twenty extra pounds; yet she was happy for the time with Caleb all to herself.

"Okay, hello" — she swatted his arm — "did you know Hilda had a *boyfriend*?" Caleb never said "Grandma" or "Uncle" when they weren't around, and it gave Lark a little thrill to use their first names as well. Sometimes he even said "Marlene," which Lark admired but could not yet bring herself to mimic. It seemed to turn their mother into just a person they knew.

Caleb made a sleepy negative sound.

"And she's going off to Belize with him?"

"According to Lowell."

"Why do you think she said it's about

jaguars?"

Caleb was quiet for several steps, considering or falling back into a drowse. "It can be both, can't it?"

"But." Lark didn't know how to ask her question, and before she could sort it through, the Land Rover growled out of the mist ahead, Lowell at the wheel.

"Sorry," he said through the open driver's window, stopping beside them. "I'm not here to get you. Off on errands."

"Where?" Caleb asked, suddenly awake.

"Here and there. Hither and yon. Nothing too exciting, but I suppose y'all can come along if you want. Got anything else going on?"

"That's all right," Lark said, just as Caleb said, "Nothing. I'll go." He jogged around the truck, hopped into the passenger side.

"Not you, chica?" Lowell asked.

She looked at Caleb, already slouched in the seat with a contented smile as if he'd chosen the best prize from the bag. "Okay. Why not?" She got into the backseat, unsure of the appeal except that anything Caleb did would be worth tagging along for.

After they had turned at the fork, Lark remembered. "Hold on! Mom will freak out. Isn't she home waiting for us?"

"Oh, it was her idea, actually. She said if I

ran into y'all on the road I ought to see if you wanted to come along."

"Why?" Lark hated being alone in the backseat. She had to lean up between the front seats and shout.

Lowell laughed at her appalled expression and tone. "Well, I don't know! I expect she's grown tired of you rug rats always underfoot. Maybe she's performing a secret satanic ritual in the nude."

Caleb laughed. "Chill out, chica." He propped his feet on the dash like their mother always did when she rode there.

The drive to wherever they were going — "Out a ways. Have to check on some property for someone" — was mostly annoying for Lark. Even when she leaned up to hear what they were saying in the front, it would be some inside joke or secret thing they didn't want to explain to her. She gave up asking after a while, since Caleb would just give her strings of vague words that amounted to nothing, while Lowell would take the opportunity to invent joke answers. Then Caleb would laugh and add more joke answers, and it was all so funny except that Lark still didn't know what they were talking about. All she could do was add to the joke string, which was kind of pointless, a nonanswer to her own question. After a while she sat back and gazed out the window into the trees overhead, looking for monkeys.

They were driving somewhere she'd never been, on worse and worse roads until they were crawling through mud. At every unmarked, all-but-invisible fork, Lowell paused to puzzle over a map marked with someone's hand-drawn roads and boundaries. The forest was moss-dense and vine-strung and she leaned forward to ask, "Where are we? Is this the reserve?"

"Close to there. *Bajo* del Bajo del Tigre."

They arrived at a clearing of stumps and mud where a shack of tin and scrap wood had been erected near the trees. The road seemed to end there, at a brown creek. "Wow," Lowell said. "Here we are. Miracle I found it." Two mongrel dogs ran out barking at the truck. White smoke rose from a pit, tended by a boy with a thin mustache who turned to stare at them.

"This is the property?" Lark asked. The shack didn't look like something people could live in. There were visible gaps in the roof, and the walls emerged straight from the mud, so that she imagined the floor must be the same ankle-deep, churned-up stuff that surrounded it.

"Everything is property, right?" Lowell

looked unhappily out the window. "Not *his* property."

Shouting through the window in Spanglish, Lowell induced the dull-eyed boy to approach. "¿Dónde está Manuel? Manuel, Manuel! Look, dude, can you shut up those perros? Nobody needs to be cutting any more trees, okay? ¿Los árboles? No corta. ¿Entiendo? Dios mío. ¿Dónde está Manuel? ¿And quien . . . tú? ¿Cómo te llamas?" Through all this, the young man — dressed in cargo shorts, a baseball cap, and a faded blue T-shirt that said "Banana Republic" — leaned on a hoe and mostly shook his head no or shrugged, palm to the sky. He spoke one sentence, then repeated it, and both times Lowell turned to them and asked, "Did you catch that?" They had not. Caleb pulled out his Spanish text and tried to look up a word.

"Stancia, you know Stancia?" Lowell tried. "You habla con Stancia? ¿Familia? Well, this is pointless. ¿Tengo teléfono? No? Christ. If I could get a damn phone in this country, my life would suck somewhat less, I tell you. One a y'all give me a piece of paper and a pen." Lark pulled a notebook from her bag, ripped a page loose, and Caleb handed over a pen. Muttering, "I'll bet you anything this guy's got a phone in his damn pocket," Lowell scrawled a message with a lot of exclamation points and a phone number, and handed it to the boy. "Para Manuel, sí? Give that to Manuel. Entiendo?" The boy nodded, but it didn't exactly look like understanding. It looked more like *Go away, crazy American.* "Alrighty then. Hasta la vista." Lowell muttered under his breath as he put the car in gear.

Lark caught some of her uncle's errors — *entiendo,* as a question, was "Do *I* understand?" — but decided correcting him would make her sound like a smarty-pants. "Who owns that place?" she asked instead.

"A dude in Texas who never comes here."

"Well, why doesn't he sell it to the reserve?"

"Hmm, good question. I suppose that's what he ought to do, huh?"

On the way back, because they were close, they took a detour to check on another property. "The same owner?" Lark asked, and Lowell replied, "Um, you could say that."

The Land Rover crept along a rough forest path, and Lowell stationed them at opposite windows to watch for, well, anything. Any sign of human life, any clearing in the density of jungle. Was this cloud forest? Lark wondered. The trees were old, tall, shaggy with epiphytes, but the ground below the tires seemed almost dry, and sunbeams slanted brightly through the trees, undulating as they passed like fingers on piano keys.

Farther on, they were stopped by a fallen tree across the path. Lowell and then Caleb got out of the truck, so Lark followed, stepping into a sponge of humus. She imagined they must be within that vast range of green Hilda had shown them on the reserve map, dark for what they owned, a shade lighter for what they would own soon, one lighter still for what they hoped to purchase in the future.

Lowell and Caleb shoved at the tree without budging it. "You two are the naturalists, right?" Lowell led them around to where the trunk had snapped. "Did someone cut that tree or did it fall by itself?"

"Fell," Caleb said. The trunk was splintered four or five feet off the ground, the broken ends already darkened and softening into rot.

"Okay. I don't think anyone's been here, but I need to check around a little. Y'all can sit in the truck, or you can help."

Holding out a finger, Lowell said, "Here's where we are, this ridge of land like a finger. I'll go out to the end; you two go off to each side. Just walk straight so you don't get lost.

There's only so far you can go before you come to the drop-off. Be quiet, look for a campsite, a shack, a clearing, anything like that. Take a good look around when you get to the edge — any weird clear spot, smoke, that kind of thing. Then come straight back here and wait for me."

Apprehensive, Lark looked at Caleb. "What kind of people would be here?"

"Just squatters, that's all. They're not dangerous. Even if they saw you, the worst they'd do is run away. But really, I don't think you're going to see anyone. You're not going far, I promise. Right through there."

At school, a mission might send them off the path into the uncharted jungle, so it wasn't the first time Lark had picked her way through a lush tangle of growth that appeared impenetrable at first. *Always watch where you step,* they were warned. Careless shoes might crush a baby sprout, a fallen orchid, a shoe-length parade of leaf-cutter ants, the last individual golden toad that no one believed was still in existence. Rotting wood, besides making for unsteady footing, was home to all manner of fauna. She'd never been told, in so many words, *Watch out for snakes,* and when she'd asked, her teacher told her they sometimes found little coral snakes on the school grounds, nothing else poisonous. Lark was disappointed. Where was the promised fer-de-lance, the bushmaster that would chase her? Maybe in this wilder place. As she tiptoed toward the sunset that was threading fire through the trees, lighting her way to the broadest gaps, she checked each vine before she grabbed it. She looked where she put her feet, and at each step she looked ahead and to both sides for human signs. By the time she thought to look back, the Land Rover had been swallowed in green and she was alone in the forest.

The sudden rush of blood was like voices, halting her, humming in her ears. What if Caleb vanished on his own solitary trek, never came back? Only as an afterthought did it occur to her that if he could be lost, so could she. The Gone, she was certain, might be entered this fast, this close to the familiar: Dorothy up in the tornado, Alice down the rabbit hole. A door at the back of the wardrobe — go through it, and you were somewhere else. The way back sealed itself, disappeared. Run back now and no one would blame her. But she didn't feel that much fear, continued stepping forward. If this was the Gone, she wanted to see what was in it.

Elves, talking animals, even ghosts, she

wouldn't mind in her Gone. But if she saw a man, any kind of a man, she'd scream and run.

Not far ahead, the jungle ceased in sunlight. She crept out as far as she could, gripping woody vines and balancing her sneakers on exposed tree roots, until she reached a view of sky and nubbly green mountainsides falling and rising again in the distance. She saw no scars in the green, no smoke. The sun rested on the shelf of the next mountain as if some hand had set it there.

The place felt strange for a reason she couldn't name, something other than the clarity of the air. At the same moment in which the answer came to her — the wind was gone — several things happened in quick succession. First a very loud, froglike, metallic croaking sounded from her left, followed by bright movement through the air just below. A toucan, enormous yellow beak as big as the black-feathered remainder that followed. And then, as she was peering out after its progress, she caught movement in the trees overhanging the valley to her right. Howler monkeys. Seven or eight dark bodies, soundless, scratching themselves or walking idly along a branch, not caring too much that she was there. A moment earlier, she might have turned to go back and missed both toucan and monkeys, so close to her yet unnoticed.

Returning, she dawdled. How long had she been gone? Long enough for Lowell and Caleb to start to worry? She imagined their panic, believing they'd lost her. Instead of retracing her steps she wandered astray, only because the passage was clearer — this is what she would say, she decided, if called to account — and where the ground was bare, she crouched to examine prints. No human ones that she could see, but many tiny paw prints, a few twiggy impressions of bird feet, animals that might even now be watching her. And why not a jaguar? How could anyone say for sure that one was not here, or that the broad, indistinct depression in the leaf matter, alongside a pot of mud marked with smaller prints, could not possibly have been made by the great cat's paw?

Still, no one called her name. She lingered to make sure, though as she got closer to the road, there were strange noises — riveting, familiar though not heard before. As she emerged from the woods, Lowell and Caleb didn't look too worried about her. "No!" Caleb shouted, loud enough to echo off the canopy, and laughed at the same pitch, like a regular kid, louder and looser than he ever let himself go.

Lowell had him in a headlock, was delivering a noogie. "You'd better take it back, you little —"

"No way! Bite me!" Caleb cried, and then, "Lemme go, you rapist!"

Lowell released Caleb as if someone had pulled a gun, hands up and out. Both of them stood looking surprised. Then Caleb pointed at him and cracked up, and Lowell fell into a slow, bemused grin, shook a finger at him.

"Hellooo!" Lark called.

"Ah, there she is," Lowell shouted back. He hooked an arm around Caleb's neck and faked a sledgehammer punch at the side of his head. "You get lost?"

Like you'd notice! she would have snapped if they'd been paying her any attention at all. Caleb was practically crying from laughing. "I call the front seat!" she said.

Until the start of school, Costa Rica had seemed to Marlene a stroke of brilliance on the whole, a wiser move than she could have plotted in advance. The first weeks were suffused with the daily wonder of letting Caleb go, like any kid, out into the open world, even if it was a strange one. Then came tuition, uniforms, a list of school supplies to carry to the supermercado, and she awoke to the permanence of the disruption she'd created. What had she been thinking, to register her kids at some random foreign school, to subject them to this wet and shrouded life? Caleb, especially, did not need extra strangeness to contend with. Her folly appeared before her with shocking clarity, and she felt on the verge of packing their suitcases.

The afternoon of the third day of school, Caleb sat with his math homework spread on a dining room four-top. She took a seat beside him, said, "Look. That school is Lark's dream, not yours. If you don't want to be there, or *here* . . ."

He sighed and examined her. Was it only the glasses that made him appear so defended? He'd been shy about them in Spokane when they'd first met. Minutes in, he'd apologized as he extracted them from a case. *Is it okay? I want to see you.* At the time she'd fought to hold back tears: that he needed them, that she hadn't been there to help him pick them out, that he'd met her blind so as to appear less strange. Now she sometimes wanted to rip them off his face and crush them, as if they were some parasite that had attached there.

She stroked the sleeve of the hoodie he wore over the green polo of his school uniform. "I just need you to tell me. Is it too depressing here? Too weird? We could all, I don't know, change our names and move to Florida. Maybe we didn't have to go so far."

"I don't mind it here," he said. "Really."

The question she needed to ask was unaskable, hardly in reach of language. Hopeless, she tried, "Are the kids at school nice to you?"

He shrugged. "I guess. They don't pay that much attention to me."

"Well, that's . . . that's good. Right? And there's Isabel; she's kind of like a friend. She's really great."

He just looked at her, reading her. Minutes earlier, he'd been content, working his math problems, then she'd sat down and turned him all tense and wary. *I want everyone to stop thinking about me all the time.* "Okay," she said, forcing a smile. "I love you, that's all. And I'm glad you like school." She laid a hand over his and rose to leave him alone.

And maybe he *was* happy — happier than he might have been, at least, in some other place. Now, in the second week of school, her flight instinct had ebbed along with her general discontent, so that again she could picture their lives ahead, with the rooms of the south wing almost finished. She and

Hilda strolled through them, discussing furniture. "I've got a roomful of spare pieces," Hilda said, "but I expect we'll have to scare up some more."

Marlene's room was the nearest, then Lark's, then Caleb's. The impulse, desperate once, to sleep with her children in arm's reach had faded over the month in the dining room, so that the memory seemed almost silly. She was looking forward to her own bathroom, her own shower, changing clothes when she pleased. The row of bedrooms even struck her as a little crowded for long-term living, made her wonder about the thickness of the walls.

"The kids can each have one of those four-tops for a desk if they like," Hilda said. "And we can just move the beds down from dining room." They stood in Marlene's room, which, like the others, had been floored in glossy, mottled apricot tile and smelled intensely of varnish. The workmen had moved outside to the porches. Now and then a man passed the windows with nails in his mouth. Gruff Spanish seeped through the wood and glass. "Though you'll want a bigger bed, I imagine," Hilda said, with a keen interrogative note. She waited a pause. "Even if it's just going to be you in here."

Marlene crossed her arms, toed the tile.

He'll come soon would have been simple to say, but instead, picturing the big bed Hilda would find for them, she said, "He's not ready, just yet." She tried to speak with confidence, not as if she were asking questions, still figuring this out. "You know how he is. He sets a course and he sticks. He's slow to adjust. Moving him anywhere is like, I don't know, pushing a boulder."

Hilda nodded. "Maybe we should be pushing, then. Do you need him here, now? I think that's the question."

Lately Marlene had been sensing that Hilda was actually on her side, or at least that she harbored some sympathy toward her over Jeff, and Marlene liked the feeling. She stroked her bathroom's varnished doorway. "When Caleb disappeared, I think in a weird way I took it better than Jeff did. I jumped in to find him, zero to sixty, and Jeff . . . he was just stunned through it all, didn't want to believe it. Then, you know, once he starts moving, there he goes, this giant boulder moving three feet to the left, and that's it. So he made up his mind Caleb was dead, and now it's like he's still half stuck there." She shrugged. "He'll come around. But until then, no, I don't really need him here."

Hilda tipped her head with a little smile.

"Opposites, the two of you."

"Yeah?"

Sitting in the windowsill, Hilda squinting at her. "You're one to make up your mind awful quick. And I won't say you're not right. I know how you want to heal your family. You've been through hell, and I don't guess anyone else knows it like you do. Unless it's that boy you've got back."

They walked back to the main lodge, and Hilda went out to work in the garden, while Marlene wondered, as she had before, how much her mother-in-law really understood. For instance, *did* Marlene want to heal her family? In a choice between healing family — whatever that meant — and healing Caleb, she'd choose Caleb, that quick. Though she'd yet to risk much in the way of questions, she was aware that in Hilda she hoped for some kind of maternal guru with the answers. Frightening, if Marlene herself turned out to be the holder of answers, the mother of mothers.

The kids gone with Lowell on his errand of the day, she'd have the place to herself for a while. Not allowing for too much intention, she went to the phone, dialed the number from the list taped to the desk.

"Hi," Mitch said, and she was instantly relieved at his warm simple tone. There was no business in it. "I was just thinking about you."

Already this was new, as if they had stepped into a private room where they had agreed to meet. In the past, theirs had been a rough pairing, that of ice climbers in a storm, every interaction a matter of life or death. But it had been so good when it was good, never better than just before their flight to Spokane, before they had DNA results, when in her husband's presence she had seduced from Mitch what he had sworn to the bureau he would not give: his insider certainty that the boy they had found was really Caleb. All that intensity — gone, it was too great a loss.

"Are you busy?" The phone cord was just long enough to reach the plush chair with its back to the hotel desk, and here she draped herself over the arms, gazed into the high rafters. "It's just, no one's home, and that makes me think I ought to be talking to you. About, you know, whatever."

"I'm not busy," he said. "Which makes me think I ought to be doing something for you. For Caleb, the case. I still forget sometimes, wake up and think he's out there needing to be found." Pause. "How's he doing?"

"He's great. He's, I don't know, climbing

trees and learning Spanish. In some ways it's like he's better than an average kid. Is that weird?" Her slow, rambling words were punctuated with Mitch's *hmms* and soft sounds of agreement. "Not like he's Mr. Communication, exactly, but he's not surly or mean or stupid or closed off or . . . plotting anyone's death, I don't think, like your standard teenager. And the damage — oh, the damage — I'm waiting for him to *show* it and he just doesn't."

"Yeah?"

"Okay, not only is he nice to his sister but he seems to like her! Isn't there just something wrong about that? When he was ten he was no great fan of hers, and he showed more anger over that iPod I wouldn't buy him than he's shown over anything since he's been home. It's like he turned out better somehow than if I'd never lost him. What does *that* say about my so-called mothering skills?"

Sounding insane, she thought, must be the only way she knew how to speak to this man, who answered her with his customary calm. "Nothing, Marlene. It says nothing at all about you. You're lucky. He's lucky."

She laughed bitterly. "Right. You're right. What am I complaining for?"

"It's hard now, not to have something to

worry about. You're back to the everyday, a thousand little worries instead of that one big, all-consuming one. I feel it too. I've got cases, plenty to do, but nothing that important. They're not on that scale."

"It's funny," she said. "I was so miserable and . . . crazy, while he was gone, but at least I knew what to do. I had a goal. Now I'm still seeking him, in a way, but there's no logical action I can take to get there. I just have to wait. And be there. It makes me feel very foggy and lost. Like this place. You should see it, Mitch."

"I can picture it, the way you've described it."

"You should come visit."

He was quiet, as if he might be considering it, and she thought with sudden ferocity, *Come. Say yes.* So strange, that this was the man whose presence she yearned for, a man she had never kissed. This man who had so often been her adversary, her punching bag, the one who came up short at every turn and failed her three years running, though he was all she had and she was so very grateful, too. Her greatest desire on a lonely afternoon in the cloud was to hear his voice. When was the last time she had yearned for Jeff, his body, his voice? Wanted him, been aroused by him, lamented his absence, sure, but *yearning* required an extreme state of deprivation they had never experienced. Even now, if she chose, she could be in bed with him in less than a day.

"We miss you," she added, to save Mitch having to find the answer.

"You and Jeff miss me?"

"He's not coming. We're . . . separated." Saying it to Mitch before she'd ever quite framed the words for herself was like receiving news. Was it true? Nothing in her revolted against it, unless it was the prospect of telling the kids. That she wouldn't do. Maybe what was true for her didn't need to be true for them, yet. Or ever.

She took a long breath, let her shoulders loose. "I don't know. Maybe that's how it should be. It's good this way. Hard enough —" She was going to say, *Hard enough for Caleb to adjust to just one of us,* or *Hard enough for Caleb without listening to his parents fight.* "Hard enough," she said, "for me to come to terms with Caleb again, without trying to fit Jeff back in at the same time. We have things to work out. It's too much."

"That's understandable. It's a difficult situation."

He was saying nothing, yet his voice carried a melancholy undernote that referred to larger quandaries, whole paragraphs he wasn't speaking. This was crazy. Screwed-up and wrong, and probably imaginary on top of it. She shifted to brighter news, the rooms in the south wing that were almost finished — "So, pretty soon we'll each have our own bedroom, finally" — breezy and meaningless, yet it was as if she'd said, *I'll be all alone in my room, alone in my bed. Please come.*

Forget paper. If she called herself married to anyone, bonded in spirit, wasn't it more truly to this man? Wasn't Caleb's true father the one who had never given up?

CHAPTER SEVEN

Twice after school, Caleb took the bus to town, then hiked up the hill to a spot that looked down on the community fútbol pitch where he could observe the game without being noticed. A few boys from his class played with boys from the public school, and at that distance he recognized no one for certain — just a cluster of young bodies passing and blocking in the midfield green, their voices cracking against the air in Spanish. He went no closer. The third time, he skipped the charade of stopping at the field as if he intended to join them. Instead, after starting up the hill in case Lark or Isabel was watching — no chicas allowed at the fútbol pitch, his rule — he cut down the side street that led to the Trogan Lodge.

This was how he bargained with himself: avoiding the fútbol players would not count as fear if he made a braver choice. And braver was facing Dante.

The Trogan's lobby, often crowded with shabby guests sipping Imperial brought over from the market or playing games at its hodgepodge of tables, was disconcertingly empty, even the Internet station. There was only Dante, at the front desk, writing in his ledger. Any minute people would arrive, from one door or another, but Caleb didn't wait, headed straight for the menacing gleam of the Aussie's bald dome.

Dante — big, buff, bare-armed, ears pierced in gold — looked up from the ledger and stroked his goatish tuft of blond chin hair with a smirk anyone else would have taken for friendly. "Your girl's not here. She's over getting a load of laundry."

"I'll wait."

"Suit yourself, mate."

"You should fix the dryer," Caleb said. His voice was softer than he intended but steady enough to be heard. Dante ignored him, rising with booming greetings for a foursome of American backpackers entering the front door. *Dante, the man!* they called back, and proceeded to gush about the greatness of whatever adventure he'd sent them on.

"Did I tell you?" Dante said. "You can always trust Dante. Anyone else would send you up the east side with the crowds for shit. Waste a fuckin' time, I tell you."

Caleb sat at the piano and fingered a few chords, measuring his breath. *Everyone likes Dante,* Luis had said, and this seemed true the few times Caleb had encountered the man presiding over a crowded lobby with his big grin and bigger voice, charming one and all, passing out the knowledge. The only one who didn't like him, apparently, was Caleb. Or more precisely, Nicky. Nicky did the sorting. Nicky had X-ray eyes for bullies, and if he balked, that meant Caleb could not duck around to the back entrance or breeze past the desk but had to harden his spine, face the man, and speak.

You cannot be bullied; you are not afraid — Jolly's coaching voice still in his head. Under his fingers, the progression of chords bent toward a riff on "She'll Be Coming 'Round the Mountain," slowed to something cool and loungey, and he concentrated on following the whim of the notes and not wincing when one clanged awry. He was forgetting, already — his fingers forgetting music he'd once made without much thought. Would Nicky, one day, forget as well?

After the backpackers passed through toward the bunkhouse, Dante came to breathe down on him, several inches too close. "That's not too bad," he said, his voice warm and affable, his body saying, *You have noticed, of course, that I could squash you like a bug.* It wasn't about sex, even for the worst of them. It was about who you could push around.

Dante moved back a step when he heard a rubber squeak of footsteps on the wood floor — Luis, the laundry basket under his arm. Caleb felt rescued, though Luis's comically indignant look was not aimed at Dante. "You again."

"Valencia," Dante said, each syllable separate and smeared with something unwholesome. "You got a couple more rooms to do up, I believe."

"I am aware." Bold enough for sarcasm, Luis — in a lavender maid's uniform with a starched white collar and white apron sewn in over the skirt, his hair tied back in a pretty flowered kerchief — plunked one end of the basket onto the piano bench and frowned musingly at Caleb. "This is my servant."

Luis claimed to perform love spells, mostly, though he had spells for good luck, spells to ward off evil, spells to get rid of a bad neighbor, or to keep an enemy like his father away. Certain people in town paid good money for them, seeming to find in Luis's eccentricities an extra reason for belief. He would not say who bought what, though his best customer was Miguelita, the fat proprietress of Soda La Perla, where Luis took his meals. Often he could be found in the living-room-like alcove at the back, beside Miguelita, engrossed in the TV.

After school, Isabel would sometimes buy a snack at Soda La Perla and use it as permission to join the TV watchers for an hour or two, and once she'd brought Caleb and Lark along. Miguelita and Luis seemed not to mind the company, though they barely moved their eyes from the screen and spoke only in single lines of caustic commentary, which Luis, dressed conservatively in slim cropped pants and a button-up shirt, might or might not deign to translate. When Isabel goaded him for a spell to make a rival fútbol player trip and break a leg, or make a despised TV character's hair fall out, Luis protested smugly that his powers were only for good. "I make nice things happen," he said.

Yet, Caleb reflected, many of his spells involved controlling another person. What was a love spell but making a person do something he or she otherwise would not? And here was Caleb, who could have been playing fút with regular boys, folding hospital corners in the ends of limp, mismatched sheets at the behest of Luis.

He played fút now at school, his fourth week, though for the first weeks he had only watched the fierce daily games, captains choosing up sides from the combined pool of ninth-, tenth-, and eleventh-grade boys. He found it harder to assert himself with these boys than with the ones in Washington. There, Jolly had helped him work out tricks of posture and expression, ways to appear so cool he was cold. He commanded vast, deep, cross-referenced archives of sexual information, which he could use to be funny, and while his audience hooted laughter he maintained a façade of mild boredom. Everything he said was pronounced *fucked up* and eminently worthy and so he had friends, of a sort, a posse of guys willing to be seen with him.

But this school was tiny, and Caleb was foreign, presumed gone tomorrow. At recess the boys reverted to Spanish half the time. To really learn a language, his Spanish teacher said, he must be willing to speak, to risk embarrassing himself — as if more risk, more embarrassment, would not have toppled him from the tightrope he already walked. Without Isabel, he'd have been all but invisible, and a part of him would have been relieved. He still recalled the utter seclusion of the first months in Jolly's house, looking out a window on nothing but snow, as the happiest time of his life.

But Isabel had somehow nudged the boys into noticing him, calling him up as they divided teams. He hadn't played soccer since he was ten, and their first question was if he could play goalie. So there he was, stuck in his same old lonely position that no one else wanted: long stretches of boredom, seconds of terror. But why not? He couldn't have kept up at midfield, where the boys running the ball had been doing it all their lives, and at goalie he had some skills. It was better than sitting in the grass with girls, and after a week he was no longer the last picked.

But the goalie outpost bred its own paranoia. He sensed factions, guys talking about him, a smirk turned in his direction as one muttered to another. He didn't know if it was real. When they invited him to the community pitch after school, needing a goalie, he sensed a trap. Maybe it was just his old fear kicking in: too many strangers, too much exposure. That first day, he'd headed up to the pitch intending to be brave. But the game was in progress, goalies in place, and he felt an uncrossable distance between himself and them.

Luis's fútbol hero, Alejandro Zamora, called Ale-Za, had scored the winning goal against Puntarenas the day before, blowing a two-handed kiss into the crowd. Cleaning the bathroom, Luis would not shut up about it. His eyes, his lips. The kiss sent through the camera and straight out the TV screen to Luis, who had once met Ale-Za, touched his hand. (The photograph on his wall was the two of them together, a few years before.) Caleb missed half of what he shouted from the echoing shower stall, the sound carrying out the open windows to guests walking by in the balmy courtyard.

Finished, Luis slung a last dirty towel onto the cart. In the bathroom doorway, he stretched into a full-body yawn, the lavender skirt of the uniform riding up his thighs. He had nice legs for a girl, slim and glossy in stockings, the effect spoiled only slightly by white sneakers. With a running step, he tossed himself onto the bed.

"Luis. I just made that. You're getting it all dirty."

"You think I am dirty?"

Caleb smiled, amused by his own irritation. He didn't know why he was doing this in the first place, let alone caring whether it was done right. He liked his family thinking he was at the soccer field. He was glad to be away from them. And he couldn't very well hang out with Luis while Luis was working unless he helped. "You're getting body prints all in it."

"Body prints! Oh, how will we ever fix that?" Luis propped himself on two emphatic elbows, grinding each into the spread. "You are funny. And what is with all this *Luis, Luis*? You can't handle calling me the name of a girl?"

Caleb went to the cart and stuffed the towel Luis had hurled on top into the laundry bag. "I can't even remember it. Valencia? It's not your name. And Luis is . . . well, in my head it's Lou*ise*. You know, it's a girl's name in America."

Luis made a simpering frown, and Caleb regretted having said something sincere. With Luis, better to make everything a joke.

"So, in *your head,*" Luis said, "am I a girl or a boy?"

"Kind of both, I guess. Which one are you in your head?"

He, she. On rare occasions when a pronoun was required, Caleb was usually speaking to Isabel or Lark and so used *he,* because Isabel did. To Dante, he said *she.* In Spanish, where every noun was gendered, he'd learned when referring to both genders at once to revert to the masculine. But his thoughts of Luis generally called for no language, no pronouns at all to push him out of that drifty middle where he seemed to belong.

Luis rolled his eyes, as if the question were too ridiculous to answer, though a little smile leaked through, a hint that he was somehow flattered to be known for a boy despite his choice of clothing. He lay back flat, patted the space beside him. "Don't be so uptight, white boy."

Caleb settled beside him in the same posture, gazed up into the turning blades of the ceiling fan. Luis said, "I like to lie here and pretend I am a rich gringo."

The Trogan Lodge had only eight "fancy" rooms like this one, each with a small private bath and a concrete floor. With no more furniture than a rickety rattan bed and side table, the rooms still felt cramped. Most of the lodge guests slept in bunkhouses or camped in tents in the yard. "Nobody rich would come to this dive," Caleb said.

"Oh, you would be surprised." Arms crooked behind his head, Luis regarded him with a crafty sidelong glance. "Look, there is one right now."

Caleb said nothing. It was pointless to argue with Luis. "What if Dante comes in here?"

"And finds me in bed with a child?"

Child — another word Luis liked to poke him with that Caleb refused to react to. "And finds you lying down on the job, in a customer's bed I just made?"

"Dante does not scare me. And he won't come."

He said it softly, like a mantra. It made Caleb want to storm out front and punch the man in the face, though Luis had never said anything bad about him. *Everyone likes Dante.* He said, *He lets me live here; he lets me wear a dress. No one else would do that. I'd be on the street.*

"Besides, I know who is checking into this room." Luis rolled onto his side, head propped on a hand. "I will tell him you were in his bed, too. He will think that is hot."

"Yeah? He likes young white boys?"

Luis blinked, as if the question might be another idiotic one, but his initial stance toward Caleb — imperious, ready to jeer or be offended — was giving way more and more to simple bafflement. "What do you think?"

Caleb chuckled. "Well, I don't know. I assume he likes *you,* and you're not exactly either one, are you? So maybe he's only into ticas with dicks."

This silenced Luis. He actually opened his mouth and shut it again, and Caleb grinned in delight. "Is he one of them who likes you in that maid's uniform?"

Luis laughed in spite of himself, still trying to be stern. "Why are you always asking about my personal life?"

"You brought it up. So go on, tell me what you're going to do with him. You know you want to."

"I think maybe you want a job here."

At first, Luis had tried to run him off by pelting him with information: that his father had raped him to teach him a lesson about being a girl; that he had started turning tricks on the sly at the Trogan when he was sixteen, too young for the legal brothel in San José, where he intended to start working on his next birthday. When Caleb only asked more questions, Luis called him a pervert and a queer. Now Luis had turned curious enough to probe in these gentle ways, and Caleb looked for a gap, a sign. As Nicky, he'd been in places where there were other boys like him, but they had not been his friends, and in Washington the boys he'd called his friends had known nothing of his past, his life. He had Jolly, but never a friend

239

so close to his own age who might be able to really know him and understand.

To speak seemed a requirement. But he wasn't sure *what* — what words, which part, how much — and was not yet confident Luis could be trusted any more than Isabel could. He auditioned responses in his head — *I have some experience* or *I've never been paid to do it* — no more than two before he chickened out and settled for a weak, jokey third. "Looks like I already have a job here. Not a paycheck, though. You know, like slavery?"

"Strange American boy. No one makes you come here. You like to clean rooms so much?"

I have something to tell you. Caleb shrugged. "Maybe you put one of those spells on me."

They straightened the bed, parked the cart, went up to Luis's room. Luis lit candles and incense, "to purify the air of evil influences," he said. The sun was going down. Soon Caleb would have to meet the Land Rover at the Internet café, but he didn't want to go. He and Luis sat facing each other on Luis's bed, under the lavender mist of the mosquito net. Luis said, "You know, even if you were my type, which you are not, you are too young for me. So you can quit looking at me like that."

Staring, a bad old habit, but he'd conditioned himself never to flinch or even correct himself when caught. "If you knew me at all," he said carefully, "you would think I was too old for you."

For a second, Luis looked impressed, then he covered it with a comic gasp. "What, are you a vampire?"

He smiled at the thought. "Maybe. But not the kind that bites. And I'm not looking at you 'like that.' I mean, you're pretty, but I'm not really that interested in kissing you."

"Okay. Then what are you here for?"

Like picking his way across a stream on stones. "I like you. You're funny and . . . weird. I think we could be friends."

Luis howled. "Boy, you are crazy. And you are a big fat liar, too."

You want the truth? No, wrong, and he looked again, picked a different stone. "Do you believe in vampires?"

"Real ones?" Nose wrinkled, Luis shook his head.

"What about ghosts?"

Luis drew the kerchief out of his hair, finger-combed strands of it speculatively around his jaw. "Well. Ghosts. That is a different kind of thing. I believe in the spirit world. It is a complicated place."

"Can you control it? With spells or what-ever."

Luis's dark eyes narrowed in their fantastic natural shadows. "Control? Querido, I don't control anything. Certainly not spirits. But I have dealings with them. Why, you have a ghost?"

Querido. Better than *niño.* But there was more stream to cross, and he knew he couldn't rush. "It's a long story. Maybe tomorrow I'll tell you. If I can come here again."

"Already we know I do not have to invite you."

In his lunch box: ham and cheese on soft wheat bread, gazpacho in a thermos, an oat-meal bar, a whole avocado sliced lengthwise, which he would twist open and squeeze with lime and eat with a spoon. Compiled by his mother since Hilda had left for Belize, lunch was usually this combination of standard American sandwich, something left over from dinner, and something from the farm-ers' market or picked from the yard. Jolly might have almost approved. At home, Jolly had prepared strictly gourmet, high-end, farm-fresh, free-range, exotically named fare, the ingredients if not local then im-ported from some hinterland because that was the only place you could get the *good* ones. For school, though, Jolly was careful to pack healthy but normal lunches no one could make fun of — or better, something in the range of normal but calculated to inspire a little jealousy, like a carved-meat sandwich or stew. When Nicky had friends over, Jolly enjoyed the extra challenge of snack food: what to serve that was highly desired by teenaged boys yet was neither junk nor so fancy it could be thought *gay*. The idea being that the allure of the perfect foods would attach to Nicky himself, heighten his prestige.

He appreciated good food — had been schooled enough, for instance, to value the custardy ripeness of the avocado over the bland deli meat — and had learned to eat slowly and taste. But he would never again be a picky eater. Before Jolly, half a box of candied cereal might feed him for a week. Mealtime could bring the prize of an entire bucket of fried chicken, or a stale donut, or nothing. He'd lived a dog's existence, eager to perform any trick for food, and even now, he remained perpetually aware of where food was. In morning classes, a part of his brain stretched out amoeba-like to wrap around the blue lunch box waiting in his backpack, relaying soft, constant reminders that it wasn't going anywhere, that it would be there when lunchtime came, that he would eat and have enough and there might even be something left over to dump in the compost.

At noon, after math class, the teacher dismissed them outdoors to eat wherever they pleased. As they shouldered their backpacks and shuffled out into the sunlight, a girl named Ana leaned up to his ear, a hand cupped over her mouth. "Don't tell, I've got Jelly Bellies."

He gave her a scandalized grin. "Oh yeah?" The school enforced a strict "no junk food" policy, but the girls in Ana's club made a game of sneaking different kinds of candy into their lunches and sharing with the approved few. The day before, she'd asked Caleb if he liked Jelly Bellies and he'd said he *loved* them.

"Come find me later," she said, with a sly, thick-lashed look that hinted more than Isabel's ever did. She was very pretty, and probably as virginal as Isabel despite those glances and slow gestures to the contrary: stroking her long, sleek hair or playing with a strand of it near her mouth.

Caleb said nothing but smiled a little, watching her walk down the hill to join her friends at their sunny picnic table. Isabel rolled her eyes, whispered, "Gross." She and Caleb walked up to the shaded bench at the forest edge where they ate every day — a seemingly unbreakable habit — from which they could survey the rest of the class ranged on the lawn below and, below that, the green and blue watercolor wash of the western half of the country.

"What did *you* bring me?" he teased as they opened their lunches.

"Ha-ha. Let's see. Mmm, pejibayes?" She waggled a pair of the palm fruits, green and red and yellow like little heirloom tomatoes, something that on a different day he might have brought from his own yard, boiled and salted, in place of the avocado. He did like them — they tasted like acorn squash. She sighed in disappointment. "Tortillas, gallo pinto, queso. But no candy at all. I try to tell my mother, if she won't give me Gummi bears, how will I ever be a proper *slut*?" She pretended to shout the last word down the hill at Ana.

"Jelly Bellies," Caleb corrected.

Isabel stuck her tongue out at him, turned to her lunch. "Your grandmother is gone now?"

"For ten days. With her lover." He put a lascivious twist on the word.

Isabel choked on a laugh. She had not, at

first, credited the boyfriend notion, believing like Lark that she knew what there was to know about Hilda. "So she is in Belize getting it on with a professor. I hope she packed some Jelly Bellies."

"God, I can totally picture it."

"Oh, gross, stop!" Isabel shrieked, smacking his arm. "Old-people sex!" This was all partly a show for Ana, who was far enough away that some dramatic hilarity was required to reach her, but Caleb didn't mind. He found Isabel entertaining. Only he wished she were less of a virgin about everything, less the fortified prude at heart. Ana, not nearly as bold with the sex talk, had that flimsy quality about her defenses that made Caleb think of her as corruptible, a potential kindred spirit.

"You are very mysterious," Isabel said. He was used to her flirty gambits, but they'd always been a kind of performance, not this subdued inspection she was giving him now, one knee pulled up onto the bench. "You seem like you are so quiet and normal, like a good boy, but you have secrets. I think many secrets."

"Why do you think that?" He gazed out at the blue horizon, chewing his sandwich.

"It's my feeling I have about you. Don't worry; it makes you interesting. I have to figure you out." She ate for a while. "Are you playing soccer after school?"

Sensing he was still being investigated, he gave his standard response — "I don't know" — but let it tip toward the negative, left off the *maybe.*

Her look was smug, knowing. As if there were anyone nearby to hear, she leaned closer, lowered her voice. "Let me come with you."

He hadn't been thinking far ahead, but it was no surprise if his lie had come apart. Isabel had probably known from the first day, the first minute, the news telegraphed to her out of the air both that he'd failed to show up at the pitch and that he'd gone to the Trogan Lodge.

"Why?" he asked, as neutrally as he could.

"Because it is boring without you." She grimaced, embarrassed by the admission. "And Luis is my cousin anyway."

He looked away, trying to keep the anger from his face. He could resent her means, but he could not let her guess that he resented the intrusion itself, which smelled of a priggish desire to protect him from a bad influence or an impropriety beyond his grasp. Like the rest of Luis's family, Isabel had come under suspicion as possibly belonging to the vast ranks of the *them* against which the Luis-and-Caleb alliance, not yet formed, might possibly be allied.

As if to cheer him up, she nudged his arm, eyes wide. "Did I tell you I'm dating Estéban?"

This was a quiet boy in their class, the kindest of the fútbol players. Caleb said, "Bullshit."

"Oh, it is not too serious yet. But he wants me to come to the pitch to watch him play fút. That's what I will tell Lark, when I go with you, and you can back me up."

All day, he considered not going. He'd just stay in town, say he wasn't needed that day for the game. But he didn't want Isabel, who may have truly been only bored or jealous, embroidering her notion of what he might have to hide. By the time they were hiking up the hill, he had worked up a genial attitude about her presense. If no one in Luis's family was on his side, Isabel at least came closest. And maybe Caleb was exactly the person to give her the nudge she needed to get there.

He gave only cryptic answers to her questions, cultivating a mystery and a demeanor to go with it — casual, in charge — but the effect was spoiled in the Trogan's front yard by one of his coughing fits. These came upon him dramatically, for no reason, without a tickle or a snag, only a cessation of air as if his lungs had clicked shut, followed by a reflex to heave. Sometimes he woke up that way, in a great bodily gathering against the block that roused him to wide-eyed alert. Clearing it sounded and felt like rifle fire, or five or eight shovels being jammed into a pile of rocks. Seconds later, he was normal.

Some backpackers lounging on the Trogan's front porch looked at him with concern. Isabel asked, "Are you sick?"

"It's nothing. I had pneumonia a while ago. It messed up my lungs a little."

"I had a cousin who died of that."

"I almost did. But it's fine now. The coughing is supposed to go away, sooner or later."

On the near side of the porch, a solitary white man — heavy, balding, gray-haired — read a book. The coughing had not drawn his notice, but he looked up as Caleb mounted the steps and passed in through the front door. Luis's special guest, perhaps? But he didn't linger to investigate. Though the man looked in no way familiar, the eye contact imparted a fearful jolt to the animal brain — a seizure in the amygdala, Jolly would say — the irrational certainty that the man had heard him say *pneumonia* and knew instantly who he was. Other than Jolly and a few others — his family, the FBI — the only people who knew about his pneumonia were the ones Jolly had stolen him from.

Were they still looking for him? Would they ever stop? There was the man who had kept him, whose name was unspeakable, and there was the vast network of that man's friends and associates. All of them were out hunting, Jolly had said, would kill Jolly if they found him and take Nicky back to where he belonged.

At one time, Nicky had been capable of speaking the name. He didn't use it to the man's face, but if a party was large, and Nicky had been set loose to wander high in a house full of rooms, he might come upon a newcomer who would ask *Who do you belong to?* and he would answer with the name: *Chet.* Only later, with Jolly, was he safe enough for the sound to accumulate significance, to eventually induce its own bone-deep terror, as if it were a magic summons that could make the man appear. Even in his mind, the sound had become no more than the *ch* of a struck match, the roar of flame. For the FBI, with Julianna beside him, the best he could do was to write its four letters onto the edge of the sketch depicting him, the only picture they had.

Of course, it was probably not his name.

The other men, too, had taken on a supernatural quality in Nicky's imagination, as if they could see through walls, read thoughts. They could smell him like hounds. No matter how well he and Jolly hid, the men would sniff him out, appear one day and seize him. After a year, as he and Jolly went outdoors more, took more risks, the feeling faded until it was almost forgotten. But it was imprinted so deeply that a moment's eye contact with a stranger in a tiny mountain town in Costa Rica could bring it back full force. It made him reach out, unthinking, and take Isabel's hand.

Dante was on the phone, shouting, "Tuesday, yeah. We can arrange that, mate, no worries. This ain't the States." He slid a hostile glance in their direction, and Caleb continued past the desk as if he belonged, through the empty communal kitchen to the back hall. The cleaning cart was parked in its closet. Only on the narrow steps to Luis's door did he notice that Isabel was still with him.

A tinny radio clicked off at their knock. Luis opened the door shirtless, in the red heels and a gold lamé miniskirt. He wore more makeup than Caleb had ever seen on him, including some ultra-shiny red wetness on his lips, and his hair was in pigtails above his ears. The effect was of a human form divided into three vertical panels, only the middle panel male.

"Wow, that's hot," Caleb murmured, walking in as Luis stood aside for them.

"You like it?" He pasted one demure hand over each flat tit, a tall parody of a prepubescent girl. "I am trying on for San José."

As they found an edge of the bed to sit on, Caleb exchanged a look with Isabel — yes, he'd held her hand, but only to take her forward into some new mystery under his charge. He was still buzzing with the aftermath of terror, which, utterly removed, left behind a torpor not unlike sexual release, so that he hardly had to try to act cool.

Luis strapped on a blue satin bra, prestuffed with something, then knotted a sheer red blouse with white polka dots into a cradle under the new breasts. "How is this?"

"Nice," Caleb said, with barely a glance as the three panels clicked into agreement. "But better before."

"Liar!" Luis examined himself doubtfully

in the full-length mirror.

"More interesting. But suit yourself, mate." Yawning, Caleb paged through a book in Spanish that lay open on the bed.

"You look like a hooker," Isabel said flatly, as if relinquishing a last hope that he intended anything else. It came out almost like a congratulation.

In the full-length mirror, Luis examined his ass gravely, plumped the breasts, squashed his Adam's apple with his fingertips. Protruding from his elegant waterbird's neck, which would have been striking on a girl, the Adam's apple appeared oversized and obscene. But maybe it was easy to miss such a detail if you weren't looking for it, if there was enough flash elsewhere to distract the eye.

Caleb slid down onto the fuzzy turquoise rug. "You ever think maybe you wear a dress because it's easier than just saying you're gay?" He slumped against the bed as both Luis and Isabel turned to gape at him. "I mean, I'm not trying to be funny or disrespectful. I'm just saying, it's not really a permissive culture. The gender roles are kind of strict. So you put on a dress and it's a signal, for people like, well, *her.*" He cocked a thumb at Isabel. "Or whoever. So then they skip the whole thing where they run around saying *We need to find that Luis a nice girl.* And the beauty is, you never had to say it!"

"Whoa!" said Isabel. "Did you just . . . What did you just say?"

Luis's hands went to his hips, his face a comic display. "He did not just say that."

"Or not." Caleb shielded his head with one arm, grinning, as Luis aimed an open-handed smack, cursing him in Spanish. "What do I know, right?"

There seemed a dim possibility that Isabel, who was shrieking with horrified laughter, was so shut off from reality that Caleb had just outed her cousin to her. If so, he'd done them both a favor. Luis, considering another smack, squinted at him with undeniable fondness. "I'm just saying," Caleb added. "Hooker or not, gay guys usually like guys. And I bet you'd look good in some boy clothes."

"Yeah, so would *you,* schoolboy." Luis dug into a bureau drawer and beaned Caleb in the chest with a wad of cloth. "Put that on."

It was a heather-gray tank top with XOX printed across it in black letters. Caleb leapt to his feet and stripped off his school uniform polo while facing Luis, eyeing the relative sizes of their torsos. They weren't too far apart, and the tank was only a little baggy on him, loose under the arms. It looked good. *Spider monkey,* Jolly had called him, a few times, all arms as he'd grown, the effect always somehow more extreme in a tank top than in nothing. A spider monkey, it occurred to him, was an animal of Costa Rica he had not yet seen. He fingered through his hair in the mirror.

"Hmm." Luis adjusted the shirt over his ribs, goosing him. "Still a little four-eyes dork." Caleb only smirked into the mirror as if taking a compliment. He was immune to teasing, having no doubts or illusions about his appearance. He'd heard all there was to know, from the experts. On the spot, without trying very hard, he could improvise an ode to the beauty of the zit on his forehead.

"Isy, you could use some girl clothes," Luis sneered.

Caleb knocked Luis's shoulder with his own. "God, yeah. Get her a dress."

Out came puffy pink taffeta with brown-ish stains down one side of the skirt, a rescue from a discard bin — Luis was plan-ning to take the whole thing apart and rework it. Isabel, enjoying the game, put it on over her school clothes and declared herself a pink marshmallow. While she was distracted before the mirror, Luis turned to

Caleb with a meaningful look, close enough to kiss. "When am I to hear this story of yours?" he murmured.

Suddenly, a connection — thrilling, unexpected. Luis had actually wanted him to come, and alone. With a little smile, Caleb shrugged.

Luis made them both turn around as he traded the gold mini — a precious item he meant to save for San José — for white cropped pants. Caleb merely covered his eyes, peeking enough to glimpse a tight pair of shimmery panties, in which Luis seemed to be squashed flat enough to serve for ambiguity. He yanked his pigtails out and rubbed a towel over his face, reducing the makeup to a wan, ethereal smear. Caleb was surprised he took off the makeup, put on pants. Was Luis actually listening to him? Could he be that unsure of himself?

He sat before Caleb on the turquoise rug and extended his arm. "Give me your hand." Caleb took hold as if to shake and Luis, with crisp impatience, peeled the hand loose and turned it palm up. Leaning close, he ran a finger over its surface in tingling trails. Isabel knelt behind Luis to work a brush through the ratty mess left behind by the pigtails, but after a minute he shook her off.

"You have a strong life force. You are a lover, a seeker of love, but you have some trouble already. This here, is like a heart-break" — he checked Caleb's face — "or something like that. Not quite that. You have in the past maybe a health problem, but I think you have overcome it. Here is . . . travel to a distant land."

Isabel, legs folded to one side under a spray of pink taffeta, leaned in to gawk. "Ooh, *travel;* you must be a psychic!"

Luis gestured in her direction as if waxing the air. "Over here is some negative energy." He drew a breath, refocused on Caleb's palm. "You have many broken lines, disruptions. This means great change or something that is lost." Across the heel of Caleb's hand was a scar almost two inches long, a hard white line where Luis's fingers paused. *Stop,* Caleb thought, meaning read it, meaning don't read it. No mark left by the stitches, only by the wound itself, opened by window glass. That was the first time. He had wanted air, escape, wanted to send his whole body through the window, though it could not have occurred to him to try. It just happened: both palms pressed to the glass, then a crash, a rush of air and a roar of sound, blood slipping to his elbow. The men thought they had pushed him; each ac-

257

cused the other. "An accident," they said, and called for the doctor. After that, he knew how to acquire this one thing for himself, a few hours' salvation with Jolly, lidocaine, a slow needle.

Luis's fingers moved away from the scar and returned to the creases Caleb had been born with. "Here is very interesting, like a split of two destinies. Maybe it means a decision or it means a double nature that is in you."

"Like a split personality?" Isabel murmured. Luis searched his face, and Caleb returned the gaze, blankly expectant as if ready to believe. Exposing the hand drew all his emotions to its surface. He yearned to be read, and yet he doubted Luis could do it. He sensed Luis making this up as he went, fishing around the sexuality question. If in ways he was more right than he could know, that was just an accident.

"I see here . . . crime. Some violence, possibly a betrayal of trust. Maybe you feel guilty for something." At each apparent discovery, he checked Caleb's face for a sign and, receiving none, frowned again into the palm's text. "It is likely you also have special sensitivity to the spirit world. Have you by chance had visits from a ghost?"

Caleb nodded, despite Isabel. He wanted

to see where Luis would go with it.

"Can you tell me is this a person you know?"

"Well, yes and no. I mean, there's more than one." They both stared at him, Luis still holding his hand but not consulting it. "I guess I know who they are — like, they have identities. But there's only one I knew when she was alive."

"She?" Luis asked.

Like an accusation, the word made his face flush hot. "A little girl. The other ones I haven't seen for a long time." Isabel's mouth hung open. He hadn't thought to test the story, or to find a suitable lie to entertain them. But here, he saw, was a plum of an explanation for his secret visits to Luis, interesting enough to shut out any other suspicion. He turned avidly to Luis. "Do you think ghosts belong to a place? Because two of them I'd see all the time, but only ever in this one place, where I used to live. And the little girl, she's only here." As Luis opened his mouth to speak, Caleb added, "*But* the place where I see them is not the place where they died. Except one — this boy named Zander. He was stuck where he died. But not the other two. And they're both *girls*."

He could hear how nuts the story

sounded, which made him as comfortable speaking it as if it were all a lie — voice speeding, eyes flashing wide with each new turn, though he didn't himself know what to make of any of it. A part of him sat back listening in consternation, ready to call bullshit or at least explain that ghosts didn't exist, and if a pair of them named Ivy and Zander had been Nicky's tea-party companions when he was locked in a basement, well, Nicky was psycho — alone for weeks at a time, spacey and tripping from starvation if not drugs. What proved insanity better than seeing people who weren't there?

But if Caleb saw a little girl ghost in Costa Rica, that made Caleb crazy too. Or ghosts were real.

"Crazy, right?" he said, a grin waiting in one corner of his mouth like a string he could tug in an emergency, to turn it all into a joke. But he knew that Luis, and even Isabel, did not think it was crazy. "Here's something else," he added shyly. "I don't even know for sure any of them are dead. I just figured they must be, if they're ghosts."

Isabel could barely contain her questions: Did someone kill them? Did they blame Caleb for their deaths? Did they want justice? Revenge? Caleb was glad that Luis cut off most of them before he could answer. But

Luis surely had the same questions — why else had he read guilt from Caleb's palm? And perhaps guilt *was* there. Ivy and Zander could not have blamed him for their deaths, but the little girl might.

Melia, they had called her. But it wasn't her real name.

"I barely even knew her," he told them, pressing a defensive whine from his voice. "I helped her once. That's all. She broke her arm, and she was getting a cast put on it. All I did was talk to her so she wouldn't be scared. But . . . I think she needed more than that. She blames me, right? That's why I see her."

Unconcerned, Luis tipped his head and slowly stroked through little sections of his hair with both hands like an animal grooming itself. "It may be not so simple. Maybe it is something else she wants from you."

"Like revenge," Isabel whispered.

"Spirits can want many things," Luis said. "Maybe to send a message, or to show what is true. If she is murdered, she may want help to get justice. Do you think she is murdered?"

Yes, he didn't say. "I don't know." That was the truth. He had no way to know what had happened to her. She was probably alive, he reminded himself.

Luis went on marshalling strands of his hair the way someone else might doodle on paper. "Some spirits are called to people because of . . . what would you say? A sympathy. You give off an energy; to the spirit it is like a smell. If your energy is like their energy, the same, then you are like family. Familiar. So they come to you."

"What if I want her to go away?"

Luis smiled gently. "What matters is what she wants. You maybe know what it is. Here, close your eyes." Caleb did, without pausing to question, and in the darkness he felt Luis's fingertips holding him lightly by the temples. "A child is dead who lost more than her life. Think about her loss, her need, of what you have to offer to her."

He peered into the dark, where nothing was. Because the dead had no needs. Because ghosts didn't exist. What business did Caleb have dragging up into his life these pitiful toys of Nicky's? He should know better.

"Try to hear her voice," Luis said.

Caleb tried not to, with Luis's hands on his face. But later, alone on the balcony of his new room at the Finca Aguilar, he felt guilty. *Go on,* he told her, *speak if you're going to.* The wind died often now that the season was shifting, rendering suddenly

262

audible the sounds of birds or, at night, the crickets and frogs, and also a new voice from far across the valley, the faint percussion of the volcano.

Maybe it was only the volcano that spoke. *You have left someone behind.*

The words arrived with no clear meaning but sounded much like her voice, if she'd known such words in English. He answered in a whisper the simple phrase he had learned for her sake, and that for the rest of his life, in times of stress, would come unbidden to his lips to be shaped there in Nicky's cracked voice, over and over, until he noticed and stopped himself: *Está bien. Está bien.*

Winter, Somewhere,
Never-You-Mind Day

No one told him he was already twelve. If a stranger at a party asked his age, he answered eleven, because the man he belonged to said eleven was the best and Nicky was the best there was, even better than Zander.

When Nicky asked who Zander was, the man said, "Never you mind."

But Nicky knew. Zander wasn't eleven anymore. In the TV room upstairs, where Nicky got to watch DVDs if he behaved — the good ones like *Spider-Man* and *Star Wars* — a long shelf of videos had boys' names written in marker down the spines, and one was "Zander." Back when Nicky used to cry, the man might pick out a tape from the shelf to prove how much meaner other men were and what other boys could take without crying. But he never showed the Zander one because it was special.

Zander lived in Nicky's room in the basement. Used to. The man didn't say it, but Nicky detected the other boy's shape in the mattress, smelled his breath in the close air. The man didn't tell him Zander was still in the basement, behind the wall, but Nicky could feel the exact spot of the bones like heat. When he was cold he tried to sit by them, but they only burned a little and he still shivered.

The basement room was five steps by seven steps, except to go around the sink and toilet on one side and the bed on the other made extra steps. Set back in the cinder-block wall too high to see was a window the size of two blocks end to end, made of some material that turned whatever daylight there was to dusk. The floor was concrete, the walls painted a thick, unscratchable white. No TV in the room, no toys, no books. If not for the ghosts, he might have died from dark and quiet and boredom.

Zander was a ghost, Nicky was sure, because an imaginary friend would have been more fun. Zander told him secrets of the basement, like the leechee bone, but he was stubborn and tricksy and thought it was funny to shriek nonsense words in Nicky's ear when he was just about asleep. Worse, he was a baby, a wussy little wimp. He could hardly even play Raft because he was scared of the sharks, and only Nicky was brave enough to sneak across to the sink island for water. If the man was near or Nicky said a single word about him, Zander screamed and cried or just vanished, *pop,* into nothing. Sometimes Nicky felt sorry and would soothe the boy and tell stories about how the man was nicer now, not as bad as he thought.

"Better make that last," the man said when he went away, locking Nicky in with the rest of the box of cereal. He could have one plain cereal piece every half hour because he didn't know how long — a day or five days or a thousand — and always he had to save the marshmallow bits separate. That was a leechee bone. Zander told him when it was a half hour for one cereal piece, though sometimes Nicky pinched extras, and then after longer when it was enough time for a leechee bone. Pink was to stay warm, yellow to teleport, orange for a new friend, blue to fill his belly with a feast, and green, the best, to send out a rescue beam with his mind. A leechee bone was anything with powers that had to be saved for special, like cutting himself to make Jolly come was a leechee bone, too, but only at parties.

Ivy was there less often. She was more grown up than Zander and gave practical advice like *Walk the room's edge counter-clockwise fifty times* or *Get a grip!* She was a slut like Nicky only more and had lots to say about men and what they liked. When she started up, Zander crammed his fingers in his ears and hollered or popped away.

But he was useless for warnings. The man came back, stood looming over the raft knee-deep in the shark-filled sea before Nicky could grab up the rest of the magic candy and swallow. "Guess you weren't too hungry," the man said. He made Nicky put the cereal back in the box, then took him upstairs. But this time not to the hot tub to get warm and be loved, because there was a party and they had to save up.

The man cooked onions and hamburger in a pan while Nicky washed the kitchen linoleum with a rag. The floor wasn't dirty because the man liked him to be down there cleaning it a lot. The onions hissed. The man said, "I hear you been sneaking off with the doc."

Nicky looked up through strands of pale hair, which the man always said he would cut short or dye black; but he never did because Nicky got compliments. "I wasn't sneaking."

"Nothing gets by me. I know all, see all, hear all. All comes back to me. What'd he tell you? How I don't take care of you right, I suppose, and how he could do it so much better? And probably half another load about how boys ought to be given free speech and the right to bear arms and schooled in Greek so they can read Homer and Socrates in the original."

The man seemed more amused than angry, so Nicky mumbled, "He said boys should have a choice."

The man smirked down at him. "Well, sure. Don't I always give you a choice? And you're a good boy who knows how to make the right one. Go on, what else? Lemme hear it."

Something distantly familiar like anger scraped in Nicky's gut. He had a secret with Jolly, which was a yellow shot called B-12 that Jolly had poked into his thigh twice now, and he could feel it make his brain whir higher, so he could put two thoughts together and have emotions, too. "He said how you should feed me and not give me so many drugs."

"You're fed, or you wouldn't be walking and talking. And you love drugs. Drugs are your choice. Don't you fucking ask for them?"

268

The sharpening voice shut Nicky up, so the man had to go on arguing with himself, banging the pan with the spoon. "Some boys take a little help to get 'em over; it's from how they're raised. You sedate 'em, and they're fine. It's a kindness. Makes the training go nice and smooth. Ask your doctor about that; he knows. He's pissed at me, is all, the way any of 'em is pissed at me at one time or another, because they're *jealous*. All that crap philosophy they come up with is just how they do what every red-blooded man with half a working dick does, and that's justify getting what he wants. There. You're educated."

Only leftover onions in the dog bowl for Nicky, and also the rest of the cereal, which was two handfuls, so he wouldn't be fat and dull for the party. For dessert, happy juice. A party had bad parts but was still the best because (a) happy juice, (b) be probably a table somewhere with food to sneak, and (c) Jolly might be there. Like Santa, Nicky had thought, but Jolly said it was really Cholly, a nickname for Charles. The kids all said Jolly.

"What day is it?" he asked, while the man mixed his juice. Jolly had said to him once, *You don't even ask, do you?*

The man snorted. "That's cute. Like day

of the week? The date on the calendar? You got a plane to catch?"

CHAPTER EIGHT

What told you to come? the facilitator liked to ask, a starter question for group therapy at outpatient rehab. Marlene had resisted the real reasons, so ugly and mundane at once: her husband and daughter had moved out; she stayed up all night combing the Internet; she ate so little and got so little sleep that she did crazy and dangerous things.

For instance: she saw her missing son standing on the side of the interstate, back near the trees, and slapped her brakes, veered across three lanes to the shoulder as tires screeched behind her and horns blared. Was that even what he'd look like, at fourteen, if there had been a boy there at all?

For instance: she invited her son's friend Patrick into the kitchen after he'd mowed her lawn. Shirtless, tan, damp, saturated in hormones — here was fourteen — a nascent swagger and an easy blush, a rawhide cord strung with pearlescent cowries knotted around his neck, shorts that drooped below the band of his underwear. She stocked Mountain Dew by the case, baked his favorites, wore scanty dresses, deployed every trick in her arsenal short of actual molestation to keep him with her just a little longer.

Instead of those stories, she told one about a bird. A ringing thud at her picture window woke her from a blackout three-in-the-afternoon sofa sleep. Her daughter loved birds, having been drawn to them partly by the music of her own name (though in fact she'd been named, in a sweet inside joke, not for a bird but for the whim that brought her into being: "An heir and a spare," as their hip-young-parent friends liked to say; "Why not, for a lark, let's have another"). Lark especially loved the bright cardinals that came to the feeder (no feeder, probably no birds, at the depressing cookie-cutter "apartment-home" on the interstate where Jeff had taken her), and of course this one was a cardinal, dropped in the grass like a spot of blood. But breathing. Frowsy and muddle-headed, Marlene stood in the yard, watching it breathe. Then she picked it up in cupped hands, tucked it limp and soft into a pouch made from her turned-up

T-shirt, and went in to the phone.

There was a nature center nearby, where she and the kids had once taken a baby mockingbird they had found in the yard. Caleb had been seven, Lark four. Marlene dialed the number, the bird a warm weight against her belly. While she waited to be connected to the wildlife specialist she thought: *This bird has to live. If the bird lives, then Caleb lives, and he'll come home soon.*

The right person came on the line, and Marlene explained the thud, the bird's condition: not clearly harmed, eyes open, not moving except in little stutters of its head. "It's a cardinal," she said, peeking. "A male, but . . . strange-looking."

"Strange how?"

"He doesn't have that crest on his head. It's just smooth. And his wings are black. That's not right, is it?"

"Oh! That's not a cardinal. You have a scarlet tanager! Very rare." The woman was thrilled.

"Great, now I've really got to save it," Marlene grumbled. "Can I bring it in?" She had to ask. When she and the kids had brought in the mockingbird, they'd been sent away with instructions to put it back where they'd found it, on the ground, for all the world to devour. Baby birds hop out of the nest before they can fly, they were told. They have to live on the ground for a while. Every bird in the sky has survived it. Yes, the parents will come back and feed him. No, they won't care that you've touched him. True, he might be eaten by a cat, but that's life.

"Well, you can . . . ," the woman said — and maybe it was the same woman after these six or seven years. The non-interventionist. "But let me give you a trick to try. The bird is probably just stunned. He's migrating through on his way to Central America, so it would be better not to interfere with his course." The woman told Marlene to put the bird in a paper bag and fold the top closed. Put the bag in a cool, dark place, and listen. Within an hour, she'd hear the paper rustling, which would be her signal to take the bag outside and open it. The bird would fly away.

"What if the bag doesn't rustle?"

"Leave the bird in the bag completely alone for an hour. It can't be hurt any worse in there. If there's no change after an hour, then bring it in to us."

What a beautiful trick! And it worked, just as promised. The bag rustled, the bird burst back into the sky it had dropped from, and she watched it shoot south over the trees.

Caleb, she thought. *Caleb is coming home, and he will need his mother.* And so she went to rehab to prepare the way.

Actually, this was a lie. The bird had really hit her window, rustled the bag, and flown, but she hadn't had the presence of mind to make it a sign. She had not leapt for the directory to look up outpatient drug rehab facilities in her area. It was just an interesting thing that had happened recently, one she didn't mind sharing with a bunch of strangers. It was one of those stories that should mean, should be made to mean. And at the time, anything meaningful had only one meaning. All arrows in the same direction.

In Costa Rica, after the fierce winds calmed over the mountain, leaving behind fog soft as a bath, she got in the habit some mornings of walking with the kids through the enchanted land to the bus stop. On one of these walks, Lark stopped and gasped at a bird, the way she always did, her elation indistinguishable from horror so you'd think she'd spotted something deadly about to leap at them. She pointed into a clouded tree at a brilliant splash of blood. "Scarlet tanager!" she cried. And so it was — that bird Marlene had cradled between her two hands, for all she knew, arrived at its destination.

The rehab story came to mind during the week and a half of Hilda's absence because Marlene had agreed to try writing an article — this time for an agent who would place it with a magazine, as well as help her see the way from there to a possible book. The article was to recount, at least partly, her three-year ordeal, but whenever she sat down with paper, she couldn't make herself summon that time. Not because it was so painful; what she had endured simply held no interest. To recapture, for instance, her first awareness that her child was missing seemed an empty, pointless exercise. It demanded too much of the mental space allocated elsewhere. How could any of that matter, set against this boy who had come home?

Caleb these days was filling pages of his own, in the leather-bound journal he'd started at the field office in Spokane. Mostly he wrote while closed in his south-wing bedroom, listening to that sad, sad music he would play for his sister but clicked off if Marlene came near, as if she needed more than two chords to recognize the Metacarpals. In the years of his absence, she had probably listened to them more than he ever had, lying on his bed, watching that night-gowned poster woman forever running away into fog as if through a portal at the back of his door, teasing the viewer to follow. The Metacarpals: murder-suicide music. Ghost music. A week before the abduction, according to Patrick's statement to the police, Caleb had tried and failed to buy tickets to the concert, which was held the night he'd disappeared. (Wouldn't she have taken him if he had asked? Money had been tight then, but it was the week of his birthday. Of course she would have.) Over those three years as now, she knew a part of him this way, through the music that was the conduit of his leaving.

"Why do you like such sad music?" she'd asked him one night at the Finca.

"It's not all sad," he said.

A part of her wanted to forbid it. Instead she asked him to come out of his room more often, and he acquiesced, carrying the journal. Often he stepped aside to some corner to jot down a few words, a paragraph, and sometimes he'd flip the page and scribble on, engrossed, as if he'd forgotten anyone else was there.

Unless Lowell came in. Then Caleb would look up and listen, grin as Lowell strolled by to cuff him on the head or rub knuckles into his hair. They'd taken to wrestling — wrestling! — at random opportunities around the Finca, and Marlene could only shake her head in astonishment and bite back cries of *Be careful!* when they thudded into furniture or the floor, laughed, and said *Ow.* Let them break bones, if it came to that. She wouldn't be the one to stop them, not when she glimpsed in Caleb more joy than she'd witnessed in four months. For a boy who had once so resisted his father's pogo sticks and skateboard ramps and jungle-gym daredevilry, afraid of any sort of hurt, *ow* had become quite the amusing word. It was yet another mysterious change in him that would not bear too much investigation, though she added it to the list of evidence that might one day be called upon should she need to prove her child had been switched with some other.

And where had Lowell gotten the idea to try this stuff? No one else would dream of it. But then, Lowell hardly taxed himself with pondering such puzzles. She doubted it had occurred to him to wonder if Caleb might be delicate or different from other boys, and that negligence, perhaps, was the key to his access.

Often she came upon them together, down in Lowell's room trying to play pool against the incline, or in the kitchen, engaged in some conversation that her entrance through the swinging door was likely to interrupt, Caleb dropping a grin like contraband. What are you two up to? she'd ask, trying to sound only cheery and curious. Nothing. What are you talking about? Shrug. Meekly, Caleb would mumble that Lowell was just helping him with a thing, Lowell was just telling him about a thing, Lowell was just, it's nothing. Translation: she wouldn't understand. And almost before he could pass off a reasonable sentence, a piece of that grin would creep back, the two of them trading a look.

Luckily, Marlene was still Lowell's primary playmate and could claim a space beside him before Caleb arrived. From there, she could induce her son to loosen up, smile for her almost as readily as he did for his uncle. Absent Lowell's company, she had to devise meandering, sidelong approaches, point her attention elsewhere, to keep him from going on guard.

On a mid-February afternoon he sat alone on the broad balcony off the dining room, writing in his journal. Recently the clouds had been breaking open to grant them more of a view from here, and today there was a fluctuating clarity above the misty, descending treetops all the way to the lake. Marlene leaned on the rail near his chair, looking out. The roaming clouds, slipping over the canopy, altered the landscape continually, concealing and revealing, parting to nose around treetops and realigning beyond. An echoey laugh, monkeylike, rose from three gauzed birds passing low on fast-beating wings. From just inside the range of hearing came a deep, intermittent boom, like explosives detonated very far away or a distant giant forever clearing its throat. "Listen," she said.

"I know."

The volcano. Even on a windless day, some trick of atmosphere was required to make it audible. Always they watched in the rare moments of transparency for a glimpse of the cone's peak, but even when all the valley was visible, the top of the volcano remained under wraps. Later in the season, they had been promised, there would be views of lava at night.

Caleb closed the journal. "Don't let me interrupt you," Marlene said, and then, because he shrugged and gazed mildly into the distance, said, "I don't suppose there's anything in there you'd let me read."

"It's just things I'm trying to figure out." He thumbed the leather cover. "Bunch of bullshit, really. My therapist wants me to write down what happened. Then it's supposed to be like a chapter of my life that's over." A faint sneer tightened his voice.

"Does it help?"

"I don't know. It's weird to remember things." Even as she shifted another chair up beside his, he didn't look at her, which was Caleb body language for permission to join him. "Maybe I'll be a therapist one day. Because I don't think they know anything."

"Why do you say that?"

"She wants me to curse more. And yell and stuff. I don't ever really feel like yelling."

"You're not a yeller, no."

"She thinks I'm angry. I'm a lot of things, but angry is kind of low on the list, you know?" She nodded encouragement, hurting for him yet elated that he was trying to tell her something. He looked out across the valley. "Do you think you can be mad at someone even if there's not really a reason? Like, you could be mad at me for getting kidnapped, even if you don't think it was my fault? Or I could be mad at you because you didn't come to get me?"

This chilled her, locked up her brain for a moment. Before she could locate an answer — a soft truth, a soothing one — he said,

"Sorry. I shouldn't say all this. I mean, it's stupid. Of course you weren't there. How could you be? I can't be mad about that."

"Tell me," she said, her voice feather light as if to mitigate what she couldn't hold back, "about where you were." She reached for him, set a hand on his arm. "When you wanted me to come. Just one thing."

He hugged the journal to his chest as his gaze slipped inward, seeking from some interior landscape the thing he'd give her. "It was cold," he said, and shivered, and there it was, that anger he didn't think he had, tightening his jaw. He flashed her a glance, wary and challenging at once. "You want more?"

"Yes," she whispered, but he shook his head and turned away.

"I wanted you to come." The tension left his face, a little more gone with each blink. "You think if you want something hard enough you can make it happen. Or, like, if you *need* it, God or someone is going to give it to you. It's what babies think. It's stupid."

Her hand remained on his arm, insistent. "I'm so sorry I wasn't there. I tried to come. Do you know how much I tried?"

He nodded. "It's okay. Jolly came." As if that weren't sting enough, he turned in the chair to face her, moving his arm from her reach. "Anyway, it was my fault, not yours. You're the one who should be mad."

She sat back, pondering — resisting, as always, as much as she could, the automatic comfort of a lie. "We should talk about that. Someday. About how it happened. I want to know everything. I think there were some circumstances I didn't know about. But I don't think there's any way we're going to say it was your fault. For chrissake, you were ten —"

"Eleven." He was impassive. "I wasn't an infant. No one grabbed me out of my crib. I knew it was wrong, what I was doing. I *saw* it, and I walked straight into it." The anger was back, his eyes wet, not meeting hers. "I wrecked everyone's lives."

"Caleb. We all do wrong things. You know where I was that night, when I should have been home with you."

He slumped, as if to concede, an elbow on the chair back, cheek to his knuckles. Any mention of her drug use calmed him visibly, like a reminder that they could be friends, transgressors together, on this thin ledge of commonality. It made her weirdly grateful to have been such a terrible mother. "Wouldn't have mattered," he said.

"Nobody blames you. No matter what you

think you did."

They still didn't know everything, though it had started before the night of the concert and involved Todd Jeter, the neighborhood slacker pothead, who lived over his parents' garage and allowed some of the local kids — Caleb in particular — to hang out there and play Nintendo. Few of the parents had known their kids were dropping in at Jeter's place, though from the beginning of the investigation the stories were unwavering: nothing bad went on there, only Nintendo. No drinking, no drugs, certainly nothing sexual. But Caleb had wanted money — for an iPod, which he'd bought on the sly and hidden in his room; they found it later — and Jeter had engineered some kind of moneymaking scheme for the two of them involving a pedophile. "Not for anything that extreme," Mitch had assured them, once the FBI had Caleb's story. According to Mitch, Jeter was not a monster, "just a little pissant stupid shithead who didn't know what he was getting Caleb into. And Caleb really didn't know."

If, when Caleb had been missing, Mitch had ever given them information this vague, Marlene would have shrieked like a banshee until she saw every photo, heard every last theory. But once it was over, she found herself freakishly calm as Mitch explained that, first, it was not their right as parents to know everything that came up in the investigation and second, they truly did not need or want to know most of these things. They had to trust that the FBI would tell them as much as was necessary for Caleb's well-being. Anything beyond that was Caleb's to speak of or not, on his own terms.

In Spokane, he'd told the FBI enough to confirm that Jeter was the connection, the one who had known the kidnapper, and that Jeter's description of the "strange man" he'd "seen" with Caleb had not been an invention to throw them off, as had been assumed. The sketch had been an accurate likeness of the man they would probably never find. Todd Jeter had always been their best, their only, suspect, and finding out that he hadn't been involved in the actual abduction had yet to cause Marlene an ounce of regret for the torment he'd endured as a presumed pedophile or his pathetic, unmourned death — his car run into a tree, a suicide probably — less than a month after the abduction.

Beyond the basics required by the investigation, Caleb held his cards close. Julianna had relayed to them that the whole time he was gone, he believed what the kidnapper had told him: that his family knew exactly what he'd done, that everyone blamed him, that no parent could love such a bad boy, that no one ever wanted to see him again. When he discovered in Spokane that his family had been searching all along, he could explain it away with the fact that they had not actually known about the terrible things he'd done. His central mythology still stood. Marlene could sense it even now in his huffed-out breath, which looked like plain teenage sarcasm and boyish pride and meant something like it, too. That he knew better than she did. But it disguised an urgency that was life or death. All she could do was take hold of him through his slightly stiffened resistance and kiss his face, repeat her love, though she had come to understand she was speaking to a wall he could hardly hear through. He needed his myth. If he lost it, the necessity of those months, years, of torture — *cold,* the very least of it — crumbled as well.

She was so close, she could almost see his mind turning — or was she only imagining that she could, that he was a creature she could make sense of on her own terms?

"The keys, por favor." Marlene held out her hand.

Lowell sat at a four-top eating cornflakes, still sleep-mussed and slippered an hour after the kids had left for school. "Darlin', I got things to do. People and such."

She rattled the cereal box. "Hear that? That's the sound of breakfast tomorrow and the kids' lunches too."

"Isn't there a whole garden out there?" With the elaborate patience of a benefactor, he recited, "I'm picking up the propane today. Just tell me what you need at the store and I'll get it."

"Better if I do it. Unless you want to pack lunches and do the cooking."

"Cooking? Please, mujer. We're eating out."

Since Hilda's departure, they had eaten out every night, and so far Marlene had felt no qualms about the expense. With Jeff so "busy with work," it seemed fair to assume he was filling the bank account on their behalf. And the town had plenty of restaurants to choose from, with high-quality, healthy, cheap dishes better than anything she could have cooked herself.

Truly, their usual routine worked well enough, Lowell dropping her in town to work at the Internet café and shop, though it almost always left her stranded, lugging too many bags, awaiting his return. "Lowell," she growled. "Okay, I need to go look at some furniture. And . . . *things*. I'm a grown-up woman with no car!"

He offered a frown of mock sympathy. "Maybe you should take a taxi. You know, it's not so easy to drive on these roads."

"Thanks, Dad. And where exactly do you have to go that's so important?"

She knew the answer he'd give: business, this shady operation of his that involved property management and therefore driving all over creation. Sending the kids to spy had helped support the picture somewhat, but she was sure there was more to it. "How about I just come with you? Show me some more of this country I live in."

"Well, I also need to stop by and see a lady friend. So, no."

"I'll sit in the truck while you . . . whatever it is you need to do. I have some work I can bring along. What?" she demanded at his sarcastic look. "Sue me if I like hanging out with my *brother-in-law.*"

And what if she were to dig up a chunk of history, bring it forward to set alongside such a moment as this? How strange their easy banter might seem. That it required no effort of repression, that it rarely occurred to her to even recall their particular past, gave her hope for her son. All of history lay pressed in layers beneath every new minute, every breath. But it didn't have to matter so much.

That essential dorky boyishness he shared with Jeff had not been evident in the Lowell she'd first known, minor icon of the Atlanta music scene. Or perhaps she had allowed an image of him to obscure the reality. He'd been trying to front a band back then, though his only real talent lay in charming club owners into donating stage time, and most were willing to grant him return engagements because he had a lot of friends, a lot of pretty girls who went where he did, and the good sense to pick bandmates who could haul in their share of the same. Lowell at twenty-four was lanky and tight, with more hair, a flash in his eye, an effortless confidence. His singing, a tortured grunge scream requiring more lung capacity than ability to find a note, was a whole-body performance, a display of raw sexuality that worked well with ripped jeans and sweaty hair in his eyes and the ragged T-shirts that would be yanked off eventually. He looked good without a shirt.

The night they met, in the spring of 1990, they were both rolling on ecstasy at the twenty-four-hour club all the dancers and bartenders went to after their shifts were over. She had noticed him around, and what she had never yet admitted to anyone — not Lowell, not Bethanne, certainly not Jeff — was that she had targeted him from across the room, intended to take him home within the hour.

But they had only danced — the languorous, tactile dance of their drug — and compared tattoos. Marlene, besides the delicate ivy vine wrapped above one bicep, had a stark, black-and-white yin-yang the size of a goose egg at the center of her back — a slim, sinewy back that tanned well — and all her shirts were backless or dipped in dramatic Vs chosen to frame the tattoo. As a bartender, she made very good tips. Lowell had both upper arms inked: a spiky Celtic band around the right, a dragon coiled about the left; an atom spun over one shoulder blade and another random Celtic design twisted down the leftward edge of his pelvis into his pants. "You'll have to wait until later for that one," he told her.

She assumed he was kidding when he said he considered sex a waste of a good roll. He preferred touching, dancing, maybe a little kissing. Melded against her back, he held her left hand before her face and murmured into her neck, "Tell me this isn't the most erotic thing you've ever felt" as his thumb kneaded slow circles at the center of her palm.

Vivid, intense, and yes, wildly erotic, then gone — a shift of the roll, both of them distracted by friends, she didn't remember. Months later, his band started playing the Point, where she tended bar, opening semi-regularly for some of the more popular local bands. Lowell called on all the friends he could to fill the place and yell, including his straightlaced, gainfully employed brother, Jeff. Most nights Jeff came alone and sat at the bar, nursing no more than three beers and bobbing his head to the music with a wistful expression. In a black T-shirt and jeans, he still looked sweetly like khakis and a button-down. She chatted him up as she did everyone and soon, even when Lowell was offstage and had filled a table with drinking buddies, Jeff was stationed at the bar.

Never could she have guessed their future. He had a job in computers, marketing; she, halfway through an MFA and fortified with lofty ideas of her own talent and higher purpose, could not have dreamt up anyone less appealing than a guy who sat all day in front of a terminal in order to sell things. She could barely feign interest in the first sentence of what he did for a living, though professionally, slinging beers, feign she did. It was with some horror that it dawned on her, once she'd given in to a date or two, that she and Jeff were yinned to each other's yang: he a carded member of the establishment with a bohemian soul, she a kind of poseur amid the counterculture rabble, caught in one overlong act of teenaged rebellion against her conservative upbringing, until she was headed toward thirty and permanently tattooed, stuck behind a bar, all but legally banned from sleep before six A.M. if there was a party to be had anywhere. Secretly she'd always been appalled at half the freedoms taken with sex and drugs around her, including a few of her own. Some buried part of her, still her mother's daughter, wanted to crawl into a corner and hide, to get out and settle down already. And here came Jeff, oppressed by the Man, a true artist of his kind, who needed Marlene — exactly Marlene — to crack him loose just enough to go completely off the rails, quit his job to develop his own software. In each other they found both salvation and a project, someone to save.

It didn't hurt that Jeff adored her unshakably, already that boulder that would not be budged, though for a long time it made her careless. She wasn't used to being treated as precious, granted so much. After an uneventful first date, she tried to warn him off. "See that guy over there?" she said, pointing out a local hot-lister who had once cut a record with a midsized label. (She might as well have pointed to Lowell, except that she didn't wish to be cruel.) "That's who I'm into. That's my type. He'll come over here and flirt, then he'll treat me like shit for a while. Hot and cold."

"He's a self-involved jerk," Jeff said, an observation without heat.

"Exactly."

Marlene had no shortage of admirers, not because she was beautiful but because she looked sad, or smart, or soulful, and she had cute tats and was the bartender. Men looked at her all night, growing drunker while she filled their glasses. As a rule, she didn't date customers, neither the ones who were horny and pining after her for a night or a week nor the long-term obsessives she called by name.

But Jeff wasn't there to drink; he wasn't, by the end of an evening's gazing, drunk. That he was actually in love, not in the barfly way but with serious intent, was confirmed for her in a rather stark and horrible fashion: Lowell came back, hard. For many months he'd been friendly with her, flirty in a half-attentive way that meant she was merely present in the room, not really on his radar. Then suddenly, every moment Jeff was not there, Lowell was. And while Jeff sat politely on the same stool across the bar from her, Lowell, on those other nights, was all up in her personal space, following her into dark corners, waiting for her shift to end.

She knew exactly what drove him and already disliked him for it, and after she gave in and slept with him — how delicious, that initial surrender, the first kiss — he resolved fully for her into the scumbag he was. Still, she let it happen a time or two more, drunk and coked up, each episode heady at first and fairly unpleasant before the end.

It was after one such night, trying to get through her shift on not enough sleep, that she'd done an extra line to perk herself up and collapsed, head spinning, heart racing. Or maybe she'd simply had a panic attack. Jeff was the one who picked her up, clocked her out, and then, because she wouldn't go to the emergency room, took her home and sat with her all night. After that, she was sick of her job, her friends, disgusted with herself for Lowell and the drugs. Though she couldn't afford to quit bartending, she could switch to the earlier shift, go to bed while it was still dark out. She could spend more time with Jeff, who turned out to be not so boring after all.

She told him about Lowell, sort of. The news, she presumed, would not be too surprising since she'd known Lowell first. "It was a mistake, of course," she added.

"When?" Jeff asked, a little stunned but seeming ready to process it.

"In the past. It doesn't matter."

Lowell, she figured, was likely to tell him eventually if he hadn't already. She needed her loyalty in place — though it wasn't as if she'd cheated on Jeff. If there was a crime, it had been Lowell's.

Jeff was a trusting person, still caught in a hero worship of his brother he'd eventually overcome. Over the next few years he'd argue Marlene out of her every negative opinion of Lowell, and truly, once she and Jeff were engaged, Lowell became a different person. When she was family, he became a brother to her. Without a word, they expunged the record of those few nights together, so thoroughly that all these years later it seemed as unreal as a fever dream. Could that really have happened? If they flirted in the present life, it felt permissible only because neither of them ever alluded to that past. Marlene, once or twice, had considered a coy reference and stopped herself, unsure if the world might really implode.

As Jeff through the years of their marriage had grown less tolerant of Lowell's failings, Marlene was the one more inclined to cut him a break, if only in her head. At Vincent family gatherings — so buttoned-up and regulated by codes that she was certain to chafe as much as Lowell did — they were a pair of some kind, the family degenerates. This and most things they held in common. If the Vincent kin all shared Hilda's faint disapproval of Marlene and anticipation of the catastrophe she would cause, it was a feeling most of them had held even more strongly about Lowell. Those who didn't assume the two were having an affair must have at least wondered why they weren't, why Marlene had picked Jeff and vice versa. Matched with Lowell, she would have been welcomed as a good influence. Jeff she could only diminish.

Of course she and Lowell would have made a terrible couple. If he had knocked her up, as Jeff had, she would have gone straight for an abortion, her third, and in that case might still be wiping down a bar in Atlanta, biking home to a studio loft with good light to paint by. Caleb had been the game-changer, the little switchman at the tracks — of the three, this baby she'd decided to keep almost by chance. Once he was born, she couldn't imagine his not existing. But she'd never had trouble entertaining those what-ifs of alternate paternities.

In the Land Rover, bumping down the mountain toward the mysterious business of the day, Marlene said, "So you and Caleb. You're hitting it off."

"Yeuup," Lowell drawled.

"You know, he wasn't like this with Jeff. And I'm positive, if Jeff were here, he wouldn't be doing anywhere near as well with him as you are, somehow. Seriously, what's your secret?"

"Aw, c'mon, Leenie. You know how it is. He's a teenager. You're not supposed to want to hang out with your parents, or *confide* in your parents. That's what your cool uncle is for."

She still couldn't decide if it was annoying or miraculous that Lowell seemed so ready to cast Caleb as exactly the boy he would have been with a normal life behind him.

"Does he talk to you about what happened?"

As if she were digging for gossip, he gave her a savvy squint. "This is important," she said. "If he tells you something I should know, about what happened . . ."

"Don't you pretty much know?"

"Not really. I mean, in general, yes. But he doesn't talk about it with me. Does he with you?"

"I guess he mentions things. Jolly, that's this guy they arrested?"

That name, its mystifying intimacy, always punched a hole in her chest. "Charles Lundy."

"That's about all I get from him, Jolly this or that, but really basic stuff. Like 'Oh, Jolly says this.' 'Jolly says fortune favors the bold,' or whatever. Once he told me something like 'Jolly is this guy I used to know.' That's all. Like he was just a guy. And he'll say 'when I was gone' — refer to it like that, or 'In Washington.' I haven't exactly asked about it. He talks more about stuff going on here, at school. Friends. You know."

Marlene simmered with frustration. She wanted to demand transcripts. At the same time, the sheer amount of all she didn't know and never could was so staggering that it seemed pointless to ask anything at all.

"So, not to be blunt," Lowell said, "but this guy who had him . . . he's guilty of all that? Or is it more a wrong place at the wrong time kind of thing? I mean, he's pretty damn casual if the guy was molesting him."

"He's guilty," she said, meditative. "The FBI seems positive."

"But you're not?"

"Well." She sighed. "There's the story. Did Caleb tell you the story?"

What was she doing? She didn't want to let any story loose in this country, wanted the whole of it to stay back in the States sealed in a box labeled "FBI business," but at his puzzled expression, she said, "Lundy claims he never knew Caleb had a real family. He says he took Caleb from this . . . abuser, the actual kidnapper, who Lundy thought was his father. So he had Caleb in hiding from this other man, not us. Was just trying to give him a good home, et cetera."

"And this is also Caleb's story? He didn't tell the guy, 'Hey, I was kidnapped'?"

"He didn't think anyone was looking for him." Her voice caught in her throat. She had to push back sudden tears. "He didn't think anyone else wanted him. He needed a safe place." She composed herself with difficulty. "Or so they say. There's a lot we don't ask him."

They rode for a minute in silence. "And what do you think? About Lundy?"

"That is a big question." Unanswerable, she meant, but he sat waiting as if it were not. "Whatever the man was, he was some kind of improvement. Caleb wasn't terrified all the time or drugged. He was warm and fed and treated . . . kindly, I guess. And Caleb says he'd be dead, if not for that man." She shrugged, a hefting and helpless dropping of all of it. "I'll tell you this, he'd almost for sure still be missing. He's home now because Lundy put him in freaking *school.* I mean, you gotta know you're gonna get caught once you let the school into your life. He must have been crazy. Maybe he convinced himself this was his son."

"Who he was molesting," Lowell prodded.

Marlene maintained a stony gaze through the windshield. "Caleb says no. Sometimes I just think, why not go with that?" Lord, how had all that gotten out? And still she had to stop herself from shrieking a tirade against this man, this Jolly person, who may not have been the worst example of humanity to touch her son but had surely touched him. "You know, I need to have a talk with that shrink of his. I don't know that it's

300

healthy if she's making him relive all this stuff. Or be *honest,* or angry. Fuck honesty. Let him make up stories if that's what he wants to do."

Lowell gave her a wry look. "I don't think she's *making* him do much."

Stunning — yet another secret he was privy to. "Listen," she said, "Lowell. Maybe I'm saying all this for a reason. Obviously, whatever happened to him, it made him very skittish around people. I know he doesn't always act like that's the case. But he went through something bad enough that he came out of it with all his trust in that man Charles Lundy. And when the FBI took him from Lundy, he more or less transferred that trust to one of the agents out there."

"Juliaaanna." Lowell nodded as if again he knew all there was to know, but she knew he didn't. Not what mattered.

"Yeah, Julianna. And when they turned him over to us, the last thing she said was that he was going to be looking for the *next* person to attach to like that. To trust. One person. And it's not me. I think it might be you."

He lifted his eyebrows at her and waited, as if she might next qualify that statement or take it back. "Wow, huh?"

"So just be careful. That's all. I don't want you to freak out. He likes you because you don't freak out. Just . . . be aware."

"Okay."

"And," she said, "talk to me, if there's something I should know."

He was quiet a while, glancing over at her and then back at the road. "So how do I know if it's something you should know?"

Good question. "If he's in any kind of danger. Just use your best judgment." She considered him. "Or, you know, whatever it is that you generally use."

"Ha. What would Jesus do?"

She laughed, though it wasn't funny. What choice did she have but to trust her son to yet another man? To admit she needed the help? No amount of contortion on her part, it seemed, was going to turn her into that person Caleb thought he needed or make him believe that was truly who she was.

"Leenie, listen," he said, "I haven't said yet that I'm really sorry, you know, for not being around when all this was happening. I should have been more involved. Helped. I think I just had things going on in my own life, but it's no excuse."

Marlene was touched, surprised — she never expected Lowell to examine himself. "Really, it's okay. We had a lot of help. We were crazy people. I don't know if we noticed one way or the other who was there."

"And, well, you know me. I can't really deal with the painful things. But still."

The painful things. She knew the shorthand, the expression on his face. At a certain point, those who'd rallied for the search had fallen quietly back and away. No one wanted to be around the mother of a dead child, especially one who couldn't admit the kid was dead. No one wanted to spend a life searching for a corpse.

"You're here now," she said. "Maybe now is when we need you."

She'd been paying no attention to the landscape, but it looked familiar, and next they were stopping at a barbed-wire fence, where Lowell jumped out to pop the gate loose of its stays and fold it back so they could drive through. "So," she said, "Stancia. She's your lady friend today?"

"Um. She is a lady and she is a friend."

When they parked, she got out. "Whoa, there," he said, pointing her back to her seat. "Sit and stay. I recall a promise."

"Well," she said, "that was before I knew where we were going. Stancia and me, we're old pals. I'll just say hi. Seriously, I need to talk to her about some stuff."

Behind the house, a pair of young girls squatted beside a wheelbarrow teeming with food-caked metal bowls, which they washed with a hose and laid out to dry on the concrete patio. Lowell knocked at the screen door and Stancia quickly appeared, greeting them warmly as if she'd been expecting Marlene as well as Lowell. She ushered them inside the roomy back porch where Marlene had first met her. The nursery, Stancia had called it. Though homey with curtains and flower-cushioned furniture, the room was given over almost entirely to animals. Tables along the walls were covered in cardboard boxes, incubators, kennel cages, jars of formulas, medications, instruments; to one side, a battered refrigerator hummed beside a sink full of more dirty bowls. Creatures, mostly unseen, squawked and whined and cheeped. At the porch's center, mismatched wicker sofas and rocking chairs were gathered around a coffee table, also covered in bowls, wadded towels, syringes, a basket full of dozing, partly feathered birds. At the back was a closed door, presumably the entrance to Stancia's home, and Marlene wondered how sharp the line was that separated animal space from human. Could Stancia keep it all on this side of the door?

"You two have met, right?" Lowell said.

"We have. So nice to see you again." Smiling, Stancia wiped her hands on a towel that hung over her shoulder. Her hair, pulled up, fell in strings around her face, and her scrub shirt was covered in three or four colors of splattered mess. She edged up to Lowell with an intimate look but no kiss, then nodded toward a far corner where the bleached-haired college girl, last seen waving from a monkey cage, stood glowering in an injured way, arms crossed. "Lowell, you remember Petra."

At her introduction, Petra twitched them a sarcastic smile. Up close she was striking, with blue-black eyes and lucent skin on which the sterling studs of five or six piercings — eyebrow, lip, nostril — appeared as beauty marks. For all the armor and severe haircut, she was childlike, fragile, flushed with some emotion that willed them to leave.

"Marlene, I have been hoping to see you," Stancia gushed, to Marlene's surprise. "I wonder how you and your family are getting along in Costa Rica. Would you care for some coffee?"

"Oh, no, I'm fine," she said. Lowell declined as well. "We're settling in nicely, I think," she said, and offered a few details, which Stancia snatched up so avidly that Marlene couldn't help responding in kind, until they were gabbing back and forth like sorority sisters, to Lowell's evident consternation. Wow, a new best friend, Marlene thought. Either that or their arrival had been a convenient intermission in some confrontation with Petra, who had turned away to busy herself with boxes on a table.

"He will tell you," Stancia was saying, with a fond jerk of her chin at Lowell, "about trying to get me out of this place. You know, have dinner, drinks, a social life? I go out for maybe two hours, but then it is time to feed the monkeys, or the parrots . . ."

"Tube feed a snake," Lowell said. "Seriously, last time I got her out into civilization, that's what she said. Had to go home and tube feed a snake! I said, and that's a euphemism for what, exactly?"

Nearby, Petra squatted at a large airline kennel, slipping what looked like pieces of raw organ meat through the metal gate to something inside that grunted like a pig.

"What *is* that?" Marlene asked, trying to see into the dim interior of the crate.

"You can let him out, Petra," Stancia said.

Petra squeezed open the gate and out hopped an enormous, black, oinking, feathered thing, with so much quick energy that

Marlene stumbled back, the expected pig now crossed with a turkey. It came only a few steps and turned toward Petra, puffing itself round and shaking its wing feathers as if doing a rain dance for her attention. A vulture, Stancia said, a baby one, though it was hard to imagine an adult would be any larger. Its head and neck, protruding from an elegant cowl of feathers, were obscenely naked, wrinkled and black. Petra made a tunnel of one hand, into which the vulture pushed its vicious-looking beak, oinking.

"He always thinks he's hungry," Petra said, looking up at Marlene as she crept closer. "His head feels really cool. You want to touch it?" The vulture went on grunting and thrusting into Petra's hand, though no food was there, and Petra closed both hands loosely around the beak and eyes, offering the back of the head to Marlene's fingertip stroke. Beneath a Mohawk of ethereal blond fluff was skin, soft and warm.

"Kind of pornographic, isn't it?" Petra said.

It was, though Marlene had just thought *sweet*. The grunting, so clearly a baby sound, put her at ease, and she rested her fingers on the creature's mobile head. Petra moved her hands away, pinching and rubbing the long, polished hook of the beak.

The eye was surprisingly large. Behind them, Stancia and Lowell were arguing symbology and whether a vulture — or, as Lowell insisted, a *buzzard* — was inherently creepy.

"He's beautiful," Marlene said. But then Petra released the beak, and the bird shuffled eagerly at Marlene, grabbing for her fingers. She stood up fast.

"Better put him away," Stancia said. "He is not mean, but he'll annoy us all to death."

"To death is right," Lowell said.

Stancia glared at him. "You are as bad as my mother. Why does an animal have to *mean* something? A vulture, a snake, it does not mean. It just is."

"Will you be able to release him eventually?" Marlene asked, recalling the owl in the barn.

"I hope so." Stancia frowned at the crate, where the vulture's eye gleamed. "It is very hard, some of these animals, to know what to do. For instance, a baby hummingbird, you would not think it was possible to raise by hand a thing so small, but I can do it. When it gets old enough, I put it in a flight cage with other hummingbirds, and it learns to fly and feed; it has many others to watch. I can turn it loose by the reserve feeders where there are dozens of them, and it has a chance. But the vulture — I don't have a flight cage that big. He can't even learn to fly, so how does he learn to find dead things from half a mile in the sky? I don't know. I would like to build him a flight cage, but I don't have the money. Just to keep these animals fed takes more than I have. If I am logical, I have to say it is all mostly point- less, all this work. I can help a few. And who knows. Maybe even those hummingbirds don't know enough. They just buzz around the forest for half a day, all confused, and then drop dead."

Stancia grinned and shrugged at this prospect, a flip of her hand at the fate of the hummingbirds. But Marlene saw the point — how could anyone know? If there existed a radio transmitter so small, how would you attach it? And what would it cost, in money and effort, to discover how a single hummingbird fared in the world?

Lowell drew Stancia away, saying, "Petra, can you entertain *that* one for a bit? I'd like a little private time with my lady here."

Stancia smiled with coy embarrassment. "Please excuse us," she said, and allowed Lowell to conduct her outside, around the house. Perhaps they went back inside at a different entrance. But their manner struck Marlene as a sham. She already suspected

Lowell had more reason to be here than sex, and it was hard to imagine them kissing and groping once out of sight.

"Don't let her fool you," Petra said. She sat on the sofa and lifted the shallow basket of fat bird babies from the coffee table onto her lap.

"About what?"

The birds awoke at the first jostle of the basket, squalling, heads bobbing on spindle necks. Three of them — parrots, to judge by the beaks — their gray skin spiked all over with feathers opened only at the tips like a hundred tiny apple-green paint-brushes. Petra drew a muddy substance into a syringe and began feeding it into one of the oversized beaks. "About this place," she said. "All that about the work being point-less? Kind of true, but she doesn't believe it. She would do anything for these animals."

Whatever the cause of Petra's earlier distress, she seemed placid now. She slipped the syringe deep down one bird's throat, which swelled into a pouch as the plunger sunk, then the bird was left wobbling and sated while Petra filled the syringe full of sludge for the next. They were ugly things, even uglier than the vulture, yet Marlene felt the same swelling tenderness and urge to touch them. Now was the time to press

Petra for insight into what was going on between Lowell and Stancia, but her curiosity had left her. She wanted to do the feeding.

"Where did they come from?"

Petra shrugged. "Someone cut down their tree, I think. We've had them since they were just hatched. White-fronted Amazons." She lifted one that had been fed. "Do you know you're a parrot, doofus?" she asked it, and set it, a hefty, warm, beating density, into Marlene's open palm. Its claws sought purchase, then it settled and dozed.

CHAPTER NINE

On the Thursday of their fifth week of school, Lark and Caleb returned home to find the Finca empty. Their mother had mentioned doing some volunteer work at Stancia's, but the Land Rover was parked in the road, and no Lowell. They hollered down Lowell's stairs, up the south wing, into the echoing recesses of the main hall. Caleb rounded on Lark with a sinister look. "I'm your babysitter."

She clapped her hands. "We can have a séance! I want to see ghosts." She hardly ever had him to herself anymore. Most days after school they took the bus to town, where he was likely to dump her at the Internet café and disappear with Isabel. *Let them have a little time on their own,* her mother told her, but whenever they went off without her, she could guess from their cryptic references that Luis was involved.

Caleb spun on a bar stool. "We could take

the Land Rover."

"And go where?" He looked so serious that she felt a twinge of alarm. "Do you even know how to drive?"

He shrugged, examined his fingernails. "It's not that hard."

"You don't. Where can Lowell be?"

"Bet I know." Caleb put his jacket back on. "You stay here."

But he couldn't make her stay. She followed him down the lawn in a direction they never went, to the edge of the forest, where he kicked through brush for a hidden trail. Lark fumed. How could he know of a trail she didn't, on their own property? And he was plainly trying to keep it from her, as if he needed more secrets. They had just started down it when Lowell appeared from the jungle. "Aha!" Caleb cried.

At least Caleb didn't know where the trail led. "You caught me," Lowell said with a groan. "Guess I might as well show you my secret lair." They followed him along not much of a trail, ducking vines in a gloom that deepened as they went, until they came upon a wooden staircase that rose two flights up. The light brightened as they climbed. At the top was a platform railed on two sides. "Be a little careful," Lowell said. "The floor of this thing is rock solid, but I don't know about those railings. Just stay in the middle and you'll be fine." Behind them spread the gnarled cap of one great epiphyte-laden tree; before them unfurled the cloud-thatched upper canopy down to the finger lake.

They had heard of this place, even looked for it: the first platform of the unfinished private zip line planned for the old hotel. "There's supposed to be at least one platform around here somewhere," Hilda had told them, while Lowell whistled into the rafters and said nothing. They were not far below the Finca, though the big tree hid it from view.

"It's like a tree house without the house," Lark said. "How long did you know this was here?"

"Let's say I found it round about today."

Lark pretended outrage. "You didn't want to show us!"

He gave her a sleepy smile. "Girly, this is my private paradise in the clouds. You're lucky I'm showing you now." He sat cross-legged on the platform, gazing out at the valley with peaceful, light-soaked eyes. Lark sat beside him. Some familiar aroma wafted from his canvas jacket, pungent and almost sweet.

"You should have shown just me," Caleb

said, sounding genuinely miffed. There was room for one more to sit along the valley side opposite Lowell, but Caleb remained standing. He gripped the rail, testing it as he took in the view.

Lark pointed. "Toucans!" The *crick crick crick* call alerted her, before one and then another sailed by over the treetops at a little distance.

Lowell was stoned, Caleb told her later, but his spiteful mood made her unsure whether to believe him. To her, Lowell had seemed merely inattentive, as he was sometimes, musing on his own thoughts, so that it was only Lark who turned and saw Caleb climb the railing. "Um," she said. And then there was nothing to say because he was standing on the top rail, feet braced apart, arms outstretched as if he were preparing to conduct the orchestra of trees or taking in the applause of an earth-wide audience.

Lowell got up quick. "Dude! Fuck."

Caleb grinned over his shoulder, his hair spiky and damp, and Lark thought of the fox brother he'd been for her sometimes while gone. Knees slightly bent, he began to step crabwise toward the trunk, the rail wobbling as he went. Lowell gripped his own head as if it might fly off, looking for a belt loop or something else he could grab.

Lark, having risen only as far as her knees, said quietly, "No, don't, don't," her voice pleading but not yet panicked. Somehow, from her angle, she felt certain that Caleb's footing was fox-steady, that the rail would hold, and that if he fell it would be from Lowell's making the wrong grab at the wrong moment.

Then Caleb jumped. He gave a yell as he did, laughing as he hooked a moss-covered branch, thick as a man's arm, inches above and away. Leaf matter rained down. For a second, turned full around to face them, he looked uncertain of his grip, kicking at the air. He kicked harder, swung, let go, and landed back on the platform before Lowell could finish saying, "You little shit. I am going to fucking kill you."

Caleb only laughed. Lowell took him in a double-armed headlock, not yet smiling though it seemed now as if nothing all that bad had happened, as if there had never been any real danger.

On Friday night, they went to dinner at a club called Luna Nueva, where they could claim a booth before the crowds arrived. For weeks, after dinner at Kako's or Restaurant Marquéz, their favorites, Marlene had led them on a stroll past the club's door so she could gaze wistfully in at the salsa dancers and the band. Lowell claimed no one would care if they took the kids inside. As promised, some other kids were there, even one unparented cluster Lark recognized as eleventh graders from school. When the band took the stage, no one told them to leave.

According to Lowell, the crowd was mostly backpackers from the hostels, with a smattering of local men known as *gringueros* — he pointed out a few — who were there to meet "smokin' hot gringettes, like someone we know," wink wink. Marlene smirked and waggled her wedding ring at him. Though she had worn a red sundress for the occasion and wedge-heeled sandals that laced up her ankles, she claimed she had no plans to embarrass herself by dancing in this crowd of young people. But as soon as Lowell was up and gone, in pursuit of a long-limbed, long-braided girl, a suave young gringuero presented himself at the table — Randáll. "Salsa is a dance for partners," he told Marlene, and she gave Lark and Caleb a sheepish half shrug, allowed herself to be led onto the floor. Lark watched her in the crowd as she tried to move to her partner's instruction, throwing back her head to laugh so loudly they could sometimes hear her over the music. At the other side of the floor, Lowell danced with his girl in a lazy, grinning way, a beer in one hand.

Lark was pleased with their privileged spot, enjoying the dancers. "You'll get us kicked out!" she hissed across the table at Caleb, who was sneaking drinks from the bottle of Imperial Marlene had left behind.

"No one's looking." He replaced the bottle without a glance, like a sleight of hand. "Age limits are totally arbitrary anyway. If they even have one here. Check this out." Their server was passing by, and Caleb pointed at the beer bottle, held up two fingers. She nodded, and Lark clapped both hands over her mouth. Caleb smiled. "For them. I'll give you ten to one neither of them even asks who ordered it."

Lark peered around the room, rocking her shoulders to the salsa rhythm. "We should have brought Isabel."

"Are you kidding? To this den of iniquity? We should have brought Luis."

"Do you have, like, a crush on Luis or something?"

She said it mainly to rile him, to get a re-action, though she sensed he liked her better every time she blurted the kind of auda-cious thing most people would flip out over.

If Caleb got irritated, it would be over something you'd never expect, like you'd say the sky is blue or flowers are pretty and he'd get all haughty and offended by your wrongness.

He grinned, lobbed a question back. "Do you have a crush on Isabel?" If he drank some more of the beer, she thought, maybe she could get him to spill about whatever was going on with Luis.

"There's some teachers over there," she said. "That booth in the corner. Don't look!" Lark had decided that as soon as she was old enough, she would come back to teach at the Cloud Forest School. The teachers were all so attractive and had so much fun together both at work and after, like camp counselors. Most of them taught for just a few years after college, a bit of foreign adventure before beginning their real lives. Miss D'Angelo had recently become engaged to Caleb's science teacher. Lark looked for them but didn't see them in the booth.

"They make a cute couple," Caleb said. He meant their mother and Randáll, who had synchronized enough on the dance floor to try some spins and dips. Lark heaved a sigh, though she'd been thinking something close, enjoying her mother's happiness whenever her gaze turned toward the dancers. Caleb was always saying things like this, as if to annoy her. He said, "She's on the phone with her boyfriend" if Marlene was talking to Agent Abernathy, or he called Marlene and Lowell "Mom and Dad" whenever they were all out to eat in town, table for four like a family. To their faces! Marlene, if she reacted at all, would sneer at him fondly and say, "Har-har."

Lark was almost past wondering if her father would come. The last time she had asked him on the phone, he'd said, "You guys might get tired of it there pretty soon, don't you think?" As if he'd been waiting them out, expecting them to turn around and run back home. "After school is out," he would say — as if summer would bring the change, as if Costa Rica had summer, and she had to remind him that there was only rainy and dry (kids at school called the dry season summer, which was what they were in now, in February), and that anyway, school was in six-week blocks all year, with breaks between, not in semesters like in the States. "We'll see how y'all are feeling about things," he said, "after school is out."

Their mother loved it when Caleb made jokes. He was allowed to say anything he wanted to, even swears, and Lark understood why. Yet he was starting to seem to her like some quietly malevolent force that could make their parents split for good, just by speaking as he did. She wondered if that was what he wanted, a kind of revenge for their being a family without him, together while he was gone. Together for a while, at least.

"Are you mad at Dad?" she asked.

He blinked. "What?"

"You always say that stuff." But just taking him off guard made her feel sorry, recall all he'd been through. She might have listed for him the evidence, just to be helpful — she'd been keeping a list — but instead she muttered, "You shaved your own head, you know. It wasn't Dad."

He smiled at her in that way that meant she was *sweet,* a child to be dismissed. On the dance floor, their mother had moved on to a new partner, a gray-haired gringuero with a stern expression and the flashiest moves on the floor. When the song ended, she returned to the table, wiping sweat from her forehead, just as their server arrived with the fresh round of beers.

"Oh, wonderful. Gracias," Marlene said, and drank from the cold bottle. "How you guys doing? Having fun?"

"A blast," Caleb said. "Can I go see my

friend Luis? Just right down the street."

Marlene considered him. "Luis — that's Isabel's cousin?"

"Yeah. I just have to tell him something. Like, fifteen minutes." His manner was exceptionally casual, as if he didn't care one way or the other.

Marlene glanced toward the open door with a grimace. She never wanted to say no to him. "I don't think so. Not at night, by yourself."

Lark almost wished he would argue. Any other teenager would. But Caleb only shifted his gaze up and away, like he was ignoring an unintended insult. It was the mildness that worried her, the *Yeah, we'll see* expression. Sometimes the Gone felt so close, a hovering presence steps away, and he knew its secrets so well that finding the door wouldn't require an effort. A blink later he was just her brother, unwilling to push for much after causing all their troubles.

"What if I go with him?" Lark said.

Marlene mouthed "No," as if this idea were twice as ridiculous. Before Lark could gather her argument, Lowell returned, snatched up his fresh beer, began teasing Marlene about her dance partners. Even with the band on break, the place was getting so crowded they had to shout to be heard. When the music started up again and another gringuero stopped at the table for Marlene, Lowell said, "Actually, amigo, I got this one." He stood and flourished a hand to Marlene, led her out onto the floor over her feigned protest.

Caleb's smile was goading. Lark grumbled, "Don't even say it."

"Say what?" He propped his chin on a hand, sliding Marlene's beer closer. "Girly, you have no idea what all I *don't* say to you. You're a very protected little egg." Unhurried, he kept his eyes on hers as he swallowed twice from the bottle. When he put it down, she took it, daringly, and he waited to be amused. But he knew she wouldn't.

Lowell had also left his beer behind for once and was putting some actual energy into spinning their mother about the floor. Alongside the real dancers, they seemed to be inventing a parody as they went, laughing and then serious. A song later, they were still at it and starting to look as if they were really dancing, their faces close, until Lark wished they'd go back to acting silly. Caleb watched as well, inching toward the booth's edge, and she saw that he was only looking for the moment they were farthest away, most distracted. "Going to the restroom," he said.

Her mouth opened in mute indignation. If he thought he was sneaking out into the night without her, he could think again. He went into the men's room, and she monitored the door with a laser sight until he emerged and moved into the shadows of one wall, closer to the dancers. But after a song or two, he came back to the table. Maybe he'd seen her tracking him.

Later, Marlene stood talking to a skinny-armed, platinum-headed person who slouched against a post, looking too cool to dance. "That's Petra," Lowell said when Lark asked — the one who worked with Stancia and the animals. Her name had come up over dinner a few times, Marlene saying, "Petra hates me," then "Petra's my new best friend" and asking questions of Lowell like, "So is she a lesbian or what?" Marlene had now spent a few days at Stancia's, helping to raise some baby animals, but Lark thought she might be doing it only to provoke Lowell. He was touchy on the topic of Stancia. Though he pretended she was sort of a girlfriend, Lark was pretty sure she was involved in his secret property business. She had overheard enough phone calls, added to her adventure in the Land Rover.

"She's kinda hot," Caleb said, meaning Petra, who smiled as Marlene spoke through a cupped hand into her ear. "They make a cute couple too." Lark tried to kick him under the table but couldn't reach.

They stayed another hour and left before midnight, later than Lark had ever been out in Costa Rica except on New Year's Eve. Past the final fork, as they drove up the private road to the Finca, a cab passed them coming down. Hilda was home.

So many secrets. Lark was beginning to feel as if everyone around her had a secret life — all adults, at least, which included Caleb. Over breakfast the next day, Hilda recounted the progress of the Jaguar Corridor, how agreement had been hamstrung by this person and that ambassador, meetings stalled by crises in one country or another.

"Meetings, that was all you did?" Lark asked.

"Oh, I did quite a lot of hiking," Hilda said. "It's a beautiful country."

Marlene lifted an eyebrow without looking up from her cornflakes. She had warned Lark and Caleb not to mention any boyfriend. "It's her life," Marlene said, "and it's not our place to pry."

She'd said a lot more than that, of course, because the topic came up at places like dinner when Lowell was present. She'd said, "Just because you're someone's mother, or grandmother, doesn't mean you stop being a person with needs. *We* are not here just to live for other people!" Then she and Lowell had started a discussion of how old they "really" were, in their minds, the age they had somehow been frozen at and would always feel themselves to be. Marlene said thirty-two. Lowell said twenty-two. Or maybe nineteen. Marlene said, Hmm, maybe twenty-six, and Lowell gave her a funny kind of smile.

Someone had cleared the dining room tables in the night and returned them to a grid of order, which had not happened before Hilda's return despite Marlene's repeated insistence that "We *really* have to clean this place up before your grandmother gets back." But then Lowell would remind her that Hilda was no longer the uptight person she'd been way back when. Costa Rica had changed her.

"How old are you really?" Lark asked her grandmother.

"Well, goodness, I suppose I'm sixty-four," she answered before Lark could clarify.

"Like, not for real but in your mind."

"Hmm. This is not the year I want to go back to, right? Because I'd say I've had very good years this past, oh, decade." Hilda smiled to herself, pondering. "But how I feel is maybe thirty-nine, forever."

Lark glanced at Caleb, who was eating mango slices from the point of a knife. He had not answered this question during their earlier discussion. It had not been put to him, nor to Lark, who would have answered "Fifteen" because she thought she could keep up with Caleb and Isabel just fine if they'd let her. Isabel was fifteen flat. But Caleb, what was he? Twenty-five? Eleven?

A few days before, when Marlene had sent him out to the garden for a pineapple, he'd left his journal lying on a dining room table. The FBI had assigned him to write something called a victim impact statement, to help with the prosecution of Charles Lundy — this, Caleb had told them, was what he was writing in there all the time. ("It's supposed to be how I've been affected. Like an essay, 'How I've Been Affected by My Summer Vacation.' ") The journal held only pieces, he claimed, many pages of what he might or might not say. Since no one was around, Lark flipped it open to the last written page. Under a whole lot of something covered in X's, he'd written, *I tried to stay eleven, but I couldn't.* More black scrawls of obliteration, before the final words on the page: *If it wasn't for Jolly, I'd be buried in a basement with Zander, haunting the next boy. That's how I've been affected.* He had underlined *affected* three times.

"There goes your boyfriend," he said to Lark, nodding out the window.

"Boyfriend?" Hilda exclaimed with relish.

Lark leapt up to catch a glimpse of horses striding nose to tail, disappearing in the fog down the waterfall path. "It's just Ranito," she said in a disgusted tone. A few times a week or more, the horses went by, if not down the lawn's edge and into the forest then along the road above the Finca that on the other side quickly turned impassable by human foot or vehicle. Ranito usually rode in the front of the line, and another boy, one of the brothers or cousins Lark could never tell apart, rode in the back. Strung on the horses between them were three to eight people, usually white, often shouting to each other in voices that carried through the dense air and the Finca's glass. Ranito and his partner seemed never to speak, their faces sullen and locked.

Once, on a sandy clop of hooves, the horse train had emerged from the fog while Lark and Caleb stood at the fork, waiting for the school bus. Ranito the show-off, with a glance in their direction, spurred his horse into a trot. Lark lifted a hand in greeting to the startled tourists, distracted as their own horses shuffled into a jog after Ranito's bay. She and Caleb were not the local fauna they were expecting in this removed place.

"Have you all been riding yet?" Hilda asked.

"We're going tomorrow," Lark said. "But —" Her eyes slid to Caleb's. "Just us. Me and Caleb. And Isabel. And Ranito, I guess."

"They just happened to have that many horses free," Caleb explained. "Otherwise we'd have to wait for, like, weeks."

Hilda said, "Lovely. How fun for you. Rafa will take good care of you," as if she saw nothing fishy in this arrangement, but Lark knew something weird was going on. From the first mention of the ride, Caleb and Isabel had been tight-lipped. Lark didn't press the matter, though, since she was being included for once, and the scheme had gotten them horses. She was excited to ride, eager to see the parts of the Finca property and beyond that could not be reached any other way.

"It will be a long ride," Caleb had warned her. All the better.

Sunday dawned almost windless. Hilda, as if to compensate for her long absence, served scrambled eggs and gallo pinto on the balcony. On exposed branches below the rail, three-wattled bell birds perched to sound off, beaks yawning wide to emit their single reverberant note like a bell in a distant tower. Howler monkeys, unseen, bullied the air, one in the distance like a deep-throated dog barking, then many, closer and closer, layered into a roar that became monstrous, oppressive, interrupted conversation. In their wake, the forest's lesser calls — a fluty trill, a laugh, a catlike cry, too various or subtle to identify — seemed more like silence than sound, the singers shrouded like the monkeys somewhere in the green and cool drift of clouds.

"Howler monkeys are the loudest animal in the whole world," Lark informed them in her guidebook voice.

"They are mighty close today," Hilda said.

But not even the howlers could wake Marlene and Lowell. Lark sort of wanted her mother to get up and see them off on their ride, to make sure she was put on a safe horse and that someone would watch out for her and that they would only walk. Ten minutes early, though, Caleb told her they should wait in the road for the horses, said to Hilda, "Tell Mom we went, okay?"

"Okay," Hilda said with a note of worry as they rushed out.

Fishy things were up, and Lark didn't have to wait long for the first incident: Luis's hatchback chugging up the road. The sight flooded her with fear. All she could think was that they weren't riding horses at all but getting into the car and going somewhere, into the Gone, never to return. But Luis parked the car in the road and joined them to wait for the horses. He was dressed in jeans and a rain jacket like a tomboy, but he had added a straw hat that looked a bit girlish. A backpack that appeared to be empty was strapped over his shoulders.

"What's in there?" Lark asked.

"Suntan lotion, darling. And my lipstick."

Caleb snorted a laugh, then muttered into Luis's ear something he could barely get through for laughing, with a shriek high and wild as a child's. Luis swatted him. "Your brother has no manners, did you know that?" he said to Lark, but he couldn't help smiling. *They make a cute couple* echoed in her head.

"I didn't know you were coming," she

said, careful that her tone wouldn't sound rude. "I thought there weren't any extra horses."

"One of them is for him," Caleb said. "They need enough experienced people to handle the horses."

One in the front of the line and one behind — but Caleb had said Isabel would cover the extra role. And why wasn't Luis down there saddling horses instead of waiting here in the road with the tourists? After the horses arrived, Lark put the question innocently to Isabel, who said, "Oh, Luis, he is always late!" Why didn't anyone trust her with the truth? Before they had finished sorting the horses and mounting, Lark had figured out that Luis wasn't supposed to be riding with them. Isabel had surely lied to her uncle, saying the extra horse was for Marlene, for the family ride she'd been promising the Vincents since their arrival.

And Ranito, as far as Lark could tell, was in on it. Though he spoke as usual, in grunts directed only to his cousins, he betrayed no surprise or outrage about Luis's presence. All seemed simpatico.

Lark was helped onto the horse she had hoped for, white with brown spots, the one Isabel assured her was also the calmest. His name was Pepper. The saddle didn't have a horn like the ones she recalled from long-ago pony rides, just a high ridge of leather in front and behind. This alarmed her somewhat, along with the surprising height of the animal, but her mother showed up at the last minute before they left, which made everything seem okay again. She checked their stirrups and had Isabel wrap Lark's a second time so they were short enough. She charged Isabel directly with keeping her kids safe, "especially Lark." "Don't worry," Isabel said. "It will be no problem."

The horse's big loose steps as they started out felt impossible to control, but everyone else — even Caleb — seemed at ease with all this motion, so Lark tried to act the same. Isabel rode beside her and coached her in how to sit, how to hold the rope that looped to both sides of the horse's head. "Don't pull, just leave it really loose. He knows what to do." Caleb, ahead of them, turned in the saddle to catch Isabel's instruction.

They shifted to single file, Luis behind Ranito, then Caleb, with Isabel at the back behind Lark, though Lark was soon unaware of much beyond the horse under her and the task of not falling. They were walking as promised, but it hardly mattered — once the Finca was out of sight, the trail became rough, then rougher. Every few steps her horse seemed to drop from under her, in a skitter down a slope or in a sideways slip. Pots of mud sucked the horses in nearly to their knees, so that they might scramble or leap to extricate themselves. She had just enough free attention to glimpse Caleb's horse ahead or hear it, bursting from the muck with a smack, and she'd know what was coming. "Isabel?" she said, unsure whether she called out before or after her horse heaved out of a deep spot and she was hanging half out of the saddle, struggling to right herself. "Whoa, stop!" She had to drag herself upright as the horse kept walking, following the others. "I almost fell!"

"Oh, you're fine," Isabel hollered. "If he jumps like that, just lean into it. On the downhills you should lean back." Caleb glanced back at her, but a horse-length ahead was far away, and she couldn't tell whether he thought she was being a baby or was simply too intent on his own battle of staying upright to pay attention to hers. It seemed unreasonable that the horses ahead kept proceeding forward through so much muck.

Just like the zip line, she told herself. Scary only because unfamiliar. If no one had died on this ride all the countless trips before her, then she'd live too. Right?

They were heading down the mountain through former dairy fields, half forested. A light rain fell. When Lark felt secure enough to look up at the landscape for a few seconds, the horses ahead dropped away. She followed helplessly, down into a claustrophobic chute where vertical walls of mud brushed both knees and rose high over her head to a strip of sky above. She could see nothing but tight mud walls and, below, the back of Caleb and his horse, which seemed to be sliding ever downward as hers was after it, through belly-deep sludge. When should she scream? Why wasn't everyone screaming?

They emerged onto solid ground, where she caught her breath. Views opened all around, misted and green. A big morpho butterfly flitted past, electric cerulean blue. At a pond, a black hawk lifted from a meal in the grass and winged away. "Caleb, look," she kept saying, though it was hard to admire the scenery for more than an instant before there was another channel with vertical walls, or more mud in which the horses were slipping or mired, staggering loose. It felt like riding a bronco. After one such spot, her horse groaned like an old man, dropping his head for a great rattling exhalation, and she thought to reach forward and pat him on the neck.

Caleb hadn't said a word. Isabel, too, was uncharacteristically quiet, and Lark remembered her saying, *Trust me, you don't want to go riding with Ranito.* Was this one of those rides? So far, Lark felt slightly more exhilarated than terrified. But if Marlene had been along, she surely would have stopped them in the first half hour — "Are you crazy?" — turned them all back, the trek too risky and no place for children. Which they all were, even Ranito. And they were two hours or more down a mountain they would somehow have to climb back up.

The air grew muggy enough that she broke a sweat. Ahead, Luis and Ranito paused on a grassy stretch to confer, and the line turned off through a boggy field, into the gloom of the forest. Vines reached for them; ferns and branches whipped into the faces of the followers, flinging water. Lark's horse stopped a few times, trapped by vegetation, and Isabel had to come to rescue her, while Luis and Ranito argued over whether or not this was the path: *sendero,* a word Lark knew well from all the marked trails at school and the reserves. "We're lost, aren't we?" Lark said, feeling drugged with exhaustion, distant from the answer. They emerged into another field and tracked along the forest edge. The valley spread below them, the volcano twice as close, the full cone visible behind a drifting collage of cloud and lit with spectacular touches of broken light, more like a painting than something real. A bird flew over that Lark was sure was a quetzal. For a while, observing the landscape in a kind of private ecstasy, she forgot that she was on a horse at all, that she was being carried into the unknown and might die.

They stopped for lunch — sandwiches and juice that Isabel had packed and carried. Lark was shaking all over from the long exertion of the ride and needed help dismounting. Luis and Ranito stayed mounted, turned their horses off into the woods. Lark noticed that Ranito carried a machete sheathed at his hip and wore a pack that seemed empty like Luis's. "They'll be back," Isabel said — they were just scouting for a better trail. Caleb seemed calm and was backing up Isabel's story that they weren't lost at all, everything was fine. *Está bien.*

As little as she wanted food or drink, it revived her enough that she began to cry. They were very far from home, so low the volcano had become lost somewhere behind the trees, and home was straight up the mountain. "Are we going back the same way? All the way up?"

"No," Isabel said. "We are circling, so it will be a different way. It will be easier."

Lark didn't believe her. This was the Gone. When Luis and Ranito returned to lead them onward, she said, "No. I'm not going." They couldn't make her. She was going to sit right there on the ground, her coat of mud hardening, until someone went and got her mother. Her mother would have to drive down here and pick her up.

Caleb was already on his horse, looking down at her with eyes shadowed by his hat. Isabel crouched beside her. "No car can come here. A helicopter even cannot come here. You have one way out, on the horse."

"What if I was hurt?" Lark whimpered. "If I fell and broke my leg. Then what?"

"Then we put you back on the horse and you ride out."

"Is something wrong with her?" Luis asked, moving his horse up beside Caleb's.

"She's fine," Caleb said, a bland statement of fact. His horse stamped, as if performing a trick he'd made it do. "Come on, Lark, toughen up." In his voice was a note almost like disgust, even hatred — it was a slap to the face, breaking the grip of fear. This was a test. *Three years,* he might have said, *in a place worse than this. You think a tantrum brings your mommy to get you?*

For him, she got up, wiped her face and said she was sorry, accepted a boost from Isabel onto the horse. She had a way out, and she wanted out. She was with people she knew, people she could trust to get her home if they didn't die trying. Caleb gave her one nod of approval, more heartening than words. Maybe, she thought, she hadn't embarrassed herself too badly. Ranito had not even come near, waiting grimly at a distance, as if Americans were always slow.

Farther on, at a clear, stony stream where the horses drank, another odd thing happened: Ranito alone left the group, was gone twenty minutes or more while they waited and Lark pointed out blue-gray and crimson-collared tanagers that flitted in the vines along the bank. It was pleasant now to be sitting on her horse but going nowhere, able to really look around. All this, she reminded herself, was unseen, unseeable, by anyone but them.

Starting out again from a rest stirred her resistance — more horrors surely lay ahead — but it was easier now to be stoic. There would be more beauties too, she reminded herself, beyond guessing, waiting to be discovered. Even if no one else cared about her birds and butterflies and startling views, she would.

She had been dreading the mud, the tight channels, the scramble of her horse struggling to climb through it. What they got instead was worse: slippery rock ledges, then grassy slopes that the horses might suddenly surge up in a kind of gallop against gravity. Lark was more than ready for the ride to be done. More than six hours had passed, though she had lost all sense of time. At some point in the grueling ascent, before they entered the forest and joined the waterfall trail, she noticed that the packs Luis and Ranito carried were bulging on their backs.

Mud doubled the size of their shoes, caked their jeans to the knees, splattered them front and back to the crowns of their hats; mud freckled their faces and Caleb's glasses. Hilda had them peel off their outer layer at the door, and they went straight to shower in their rooms. Lark's legs were bowed and wobbly. Dressed again in clean clothes, she hung close to her mother most of the evening and followed Caleb's lead, downplaying the more extreme details in the story for their mother and grandmother and uncle. There was some mud, they said, and some steep parts, but it wasn't too bad. Just long! Longer than it was supposed to be. They got a little lost. Lark freaked out once, just a little, but then she bucked up like a trouper. She let Caleb do most of the talking, noticing how the ride became tame in the telling. Home unharmed, she began to wonder if she'd been silly, childish, to be afraid. She also had leisure now think over elements of the ride she'd had no space to register when it was happening.

For instance, Ranito still didn't like them. "Did he ever say one word to you the whole time?" she asked Caleb at dinner, when this occurred to her. She now managed rudimentary conversations in Spanish, but only if the person she spoke with was very patient. Ranito would never be patient.

On the phone to her dad, she started to tell a scarier version of the day's trek than the circumspect one she'd cobbled together with Caleb, needing her father at least to feel her peril, to sense in the horse's every lurch and slip some new piece of evidence that her mother wasn't keeping her protected enough and might need help. But in the end, she chickened out, said it had been fun and not so bad — which was also true. She told him about the dancing, figuring no one else would have, and maybe took a little pleasure in describing her mother's various partners, ending with Lowell.

She and Caleb went to bed early by silent agreement, and after she changed into pajamas and brushed her teeth, she knocked on his door. She had probably seemed mopey much of the evening, though really she was just exhausted. Caleb shut the door and folded her into a long hug — which was new. Sometimes he would put an arm around her, a hand on her neck. Maybe a hug had not been called for until now. "Aw, baby," he said, in a pouty kind of baby talk, *bebee,* and took her face in his hands, stroking the hair over her ears. "I am so sorry. That ride was awful."

"It was?"

"Oh, yeah. Seriously. I should not have gotten you into that. But you were brave, I'll give you that. And a little rough stuff is good for you."

Relieved, she heaved a great sigh for all she had endured. Minimizing the ride had felt good, their words constructing a shared experience that had actually been fun, but now it felt even better to have the fear confirmed, to know she had survived something hard. She collapsed on his bed and he sat beside her, nudged her in the hip. "Roll over, bebee. I'll give you a back rub."

She flipped onto her stomach and he began to knead her neck and shoulders. "All right," she said — the vulnerable position made her turn crisp and no-nonsense. "I want to know what that was all about. No more *lies.* I'm not a baby, and I know everybody but me knows what those two were doing out there."

"It's a secret." Caleb's fingers pressed softly down her spine. "You can't tell mom or Hilda or anyone. Not because it's anything bad. Just because all of them will get in trouble for taking the horses out there. You have to promise."

"Fine," she said. "I promise. I know they were getting something. It was in their backpacks."

"It was plants."

"Plants?"

"Special plants. Luis needs them, for spells. You know how this hotel used to be called Reina de la Noche? Well, it's kind of a flower, queen of the night, also called hell's bells. There's some special variety that's extra powerful. Spell quality, I guess. It doesn't grow just anywhere."

"A spell for what?"

"Lots of things. One is ghosts." He sounded weary. "I told Luis about them, but I'm sort of wishing I hadn't. I wish we could just drop it, you know?"

She didn't know. "Is the spell to get rid of them?"

"I guess. Talk to them, get rid of them. Something. But they're my ghosts." His voice sharpened with anger. "Nobody else can tell me anything about them. I'm starting to think I know more about ghosts anyway than Luis and his spells."

He shifted to the end of the bed, straddling her feet, began working his hands up her calves. "But, hey, we got to go riding. That was an adventure, right?" At her thighs, where she was sore as a bruise, his hands softened. "And a major accomplishment for you, kid. You can always look back on today and know you're not a wimp." The massage felt good, though it also made her nervous as he shifted higher. Would he know he was supposed to stop?

After reaching the tops of her thighs, he sat on the backs of her knees and poked the dough of her left butt cheek, which was like being goosed and made her cry, "Hey!" in a comic way. "Look at your cute little butt," he said. "Bet it's pretty sore." He began tapping it with two open hands as if he were playing the bongos, and she burst into a real laugh, then scrambled loose. Sitting on the bed facing him, safe, she quickly regretted ending the massage. She loved the attention, and he seemed now as peaceful and distant as Lowell could be, half in his head and not even thinking about her.

Unready to go to bed, she prompted him to talk about the ride. They relived the scariest episodes, the times they had almost fallen, the moments when Caleb admitted he'd been freaked out as well. The rock ledges on the way back, Lark decided, were the most terrifying part, where hooves clacked and skidded and she had felt not just as if she might fall backward onto the rock any minute but that her whole horse might fall with her. "Wow," she said, popping her eyes, "you'd be in *so* much trouble if I fell off the mountain and died. How would you tell Mom?"

"I wouldn't let you die."

He said it so sweetly that instead of challenging him on exactly how he would have stopped such a thing, she said, "Really? You wouldn't?"

"No way. I've got enough ghosts."

Cheeks flushed with heat, she looked into her lap. "When you were standing on the railing on the zip line platform — for a second I thought you were going to die. Then maybe you'd be a ghost and you'd haunt me." His placid expression as he considered this made her add, "You wouldn't try to die, right?"

He shook his head, but without conviction. "People who kill themselves, I've decided, they have to really want to die." He shrugged. "And I guess I don't care that much, one way or the other. I've been there. I'm not afraid of it, that's all."

She watched him for a while, her big brother, sitting cross-legged and picking at threads on the bedspread. Going on five months home and he'd hardly told her anything, only these stray, sideways references. She said quietly, "You should tell me more things, you know. I'm your sister. I won't tell anyone."

"You're too young."

"You weren't," she shot back — too quickly, like defiance. "You were eleven, like me."

He looked away, his face clouded. "You think it was fun or something? Think you're missing out?"

"No," she said, with a little squeak of alarm.

"Well, I was too young." He was mumbling — an ear pressed to the door could not have heard him — and blushing with some emotion. "Lots of things I still don't understand. And there were kids younger than me, too. Just be glad you don't have to know."

"Okay," she said, worried, wanting to soothe him, to make him trust her. "I am. I'm glad. If that's what you want."

"It's a long story," he said. "I don't tell it because there's no part I can tell, by itself. Nobody would understand without the other parts, and there are parts I don't know." He was rambling, and she held herself very still, Dian Fossey with the gorillas, waiting him out. "Which is good. I mean, I have a pretty good idea about the parts I missed, but, well. Don't let anyone ever tell you, little girl, that drugs aren't good for something."

He seemed to have stopped, and her mind skipped to the flower, queen of the night. Squaring herself firmly, she said, "Caleb, don't let Luis drug you with that stuff."

He blinked. "What, queen of the night? It's not a drug."

"It is too!"

When they'd first arrived — maybe Caleb had not been in the room? — Hilda had told them that locals used the flower to make a kind of hallucinogen, like LSD. She'd told them, "Once I saw a pair of boys trying for half an hour to put a canoe into an outhouse. That's queen of the night."

"No, I mean the spell is not a drug."

"Well, what is it?"

He shrugged. "You'd have to ask Luis. I'm sure it's a bunch of bullshit. Now go to bed."

Before she would go, she said he had to promise to let her be there, when they did the spell. "You have to have someone you can trust there to look out for you. And that's me." He wouldn't promise, but he said he'd think about it.

And of course he wouldn't trust her, wouldn't bring her along. He said, "It's not today" the next time he and Isabel went off together, and the next, and days later when she asked again about the spell he said, "Oh, we already did it. It wasn't a big deal. No one got drugged. Nothing even happened."

"What did he do?"

"Nothing much. Silly stuff."

She asked if he still had his ghosts and he said, "I don't know."

November 30, 2005

After four days of Vicodin, Jolly tried a
needle full of lidocaine straight into Nicky's
gum and that was it; the next morning they
drove into Spokane to find a dentist. "We're
traveling through, had a little emergency,"
Jolly told the receptionist. "Any chance
you'd take a walk-in?" All through the drive
he'd been wound tight, nearly in tears, listing every potential scenario of calamity, but
at the desk he was calm, a warm ungloved
hand on Nicky's neck.

In chairs in the empty waiting room,
Nicky leaned at Jolly's shoulder to watch
him pen numbers into the form: twelve for
his age, which he looked, instead of thirteen,
and a birth date that backed it up. An address in Colorado; a made-up social security
number. For previous dentist, he wrote,
"Not sure. Can find out and call back." He
ticked no, no, no down all the medical

conditions, paused on "cancer," then "pregnant" with subtle, checking glances at Nicky.

"No," Nicky said, cracking a smile.

When the dentist called for Nicholas Lundy — the real last name in case they asked to see Jolly's ID — Jolly went too, saying, "You don't mind? My son, he gets a little nervous with strangers."

Almost three years without a checkup, two of those on little but sugar, must have shown in his mouth. The dentist made displeased noises and Jolly apologized. "His mom left us a few years back. And I been out of work, but that's no excuse not to be getting him to the dentist regular. We'll do better from now on. Right, son? How's that gas?" Nicky gave him a thumbs-up.

They were lucky: the dentist didn't normally fill a tooth the same day, but he'd had two appointments cancel because of the predicted snowstorm. Nicky got a cleaning, X-rays, and three more small cavities filled besides the deep one that had nearly split the tooth. Jolly counted out bills onto the counter, and they walked out the door, easy as pie.

As they drove back home to Providence, eighty miles south, the snow began to fall. "Wow," Jolly said, seizing his hand across the bench seat. "You're still here."

Nicky had been less worried, only because the tooth had been louder than other concerns. He examined his mouth in the visor, pressed his numbed lips, which were already tingling back to life. "I did good, huh? I was hardly even scared when he put me back in that chair."

"You did great. I saw you faking him out for more gas."

"But man, it was lame gas!"

Jolly chuckled warmly. "As soon as you can feel your mouth, we'll have a feast."

"Roast beast."

"Mmm, those porterhouses. For lunch something soft, like the pumpkin ravioli with sage butter?"

Fine snow blew over hilly farmland fringed in pine and up over the small pickup's brown hood. "Will it be a white Christmas?" Nicky asked, Christmas being lately at the top of his thoughts. He'd missed two not even knowing what day it was, and Jolly had promised an extra-big one to make up for it.

"Usually is. This will be early if it sticks like it's supposed to."

Home was an acre on Raven Ridge. Their lichen-colored gingerbread house sat at the end of a rutted driveway, a house off to each side, nothing behind but woods. In the kitchen door frame were the eight closely spaced marks of Nicky's height, one for each month he'd been there; pinned to the kitchen wall were charts and graphs recording his increasing times on the elliptical machine and the stationary bike, with the free weights, his resting heart rate after each set. Up in the long, skylit, blond-wood attic was homeschool, where they faced each other most days, Jolly at the computer for his online job if he wasn't teaching and Nicky at the table or on the sofa with schoolwork that had gradually ascended to levels somewhere above what could be called the eighth grade.

He enjoyed his lessons. Whenever he pleased, he took breaks to play the piano or blow off some steam in the home gym or play chess with Jolly, then back to the books. Only sometimes, if frustrated with difficult material, he might grumble, "Why do I have to know all this if I'm never going to see anyone?" And Jolly would say, "You will, one day," but not like a real answer.

"You know," Nicky said, copying out geometry problems, "maybe since the dentist worked, that means I could go to regular school."

From the computer, Jolly pondered him. "You think you'd even want to? With all those people?"

He shrugged. "Maybe. Not now, but . . . sometime." Actually, he wasn't so sure about this, but he knew Jolly would like hearing him say so. It would count as progress for one of their charts.

Mouth in a twist, Jolly shook his head. "Not possible for us, I'm afraid.".But Nicky could see he was thinking about it. He came to peer over Nicky's shoulder at the geometry. "Anyway, public school? Bleh. Full of morons."

"I can fake being a moron."

Jolly laughed. "I bet you could. I think you could do anything. Try this. 'Let us roll all our strength and all our sweetness . . .' "

Nicky was supposed to finish the line. " 'Into one ball, and bowl —' "

" 'And *tear* our pleasures with rough strife . . .' "

" 'Through the iron gates of life.' But it should say *bowl.* Because the ball knocks down gates, like bowling."

Jolly perched on the table, legs swinging. "Ah, but it's really about fucking, yeah?" His mouth was a snarl of pleasure.

"You mean 'making love,' " Nicky mocked, which is what Jolly said sometimes if Nicky said *fucking.* He socked Jolly in the knee.

"Ow," Jolly said, still grinning. "Now kiss it."

"Fuck off. Or help me do these."

Outside, the icy dust of snow turned heavy and soft, erased the yard and kept falling. By nightfall, the white land glowed under a waxing moon, down to the snow-laden trees. Not long asleep, Nicky roused to his whispered name, Jolly kneeling at the bed's window in bluish snow light. "Come look, quick."

Out in the pallid yard, deer stepped from the woods, perfectly visible against the snow. They moved toward the house in precise, unhurried steps — four, five, eight of them; they kept coming — to disappear along the lower side. The snow showed how they must have walked on other nights in the black dark, unseen.

"Wow, look at them."

"You like that?"

It was beautiful and strange, but he shivered with fear — of them or for them, how vulnerable they had become, believing themselves invisible. Nothing outside the house was safe. He leaned into Jolly's arm, the fingers stroking his neck, Jolly's fine attention all on him as if the deer were a gift he'd made while Nicky slept, a bit of magic

to charm him with. It was the kind of thing
Jolly would do.

CHAPTER TEN

Eyes closed, earbuds in was the only way for Caleb to get any privacy or peace from Lark, who was forever crying "Look!" at something she saw out the bus window. The Chicken Bus, Lowell called it, because it stopped for chickens, or any creature sentient enough that the driver might think it needed a ride or feel inclined to commune with it for a while. Someone waved and the driver pulled over, leaned there at the window for a good twenty-minute chat while everyone on the bus, ticos mostly, sat unfazed. They were rolling now, Marlene and Lowell in the seat ahead — deep into each other and behaving more like children than Caleb and Lark ever would — north on the Pan-American Highway to the Nicaraguan border.

The wheels on the bus go round and round . . .

Once again, he was being taken. Only for

a few days — school was out for a week between blocks, so they were headed to the beach in Nicaragua, a three-day forced vacation to renew their visas. And it was different in other ways, from those other times. Not since the first (its record mostly lost or muted to a weird drug dream) had he felt such a heart's tug backward to the previous life and state. Maybe because this time he knew he'd be going back, to the cloudy mountain behind them. Maybe because he was starting to wake up. With Jolly he'd made his own choices, or thought he had. But Jolly said no, he was only making progress and had farther to go before his brain might fully emerge from the slave state. For one, he still operated too much on the survivor's instinct to conform, appease. He depended too much on guidance. Any upset, like the sledding accident on Nursery Hill, Jolly loaded into an ambulance amid a small crowd of concerned sledders ("Are you his son? Go along with him. I'm sure he'll be fine"), and he simply turned off, went where any authority figure told him to and waited for the next life to take him in, as if he had no option to affect it. However sick with fear of what would come, he didn't fight. Even when the FBI took him and all his answers were numb, uncalculated denial — had he ever once so much as nodded to his own real name? — something in him had almost immediately surrendered to the fate. To feel that tiny kick of rebellion, the simple wish not to go that was his will flexing a fist — this was new.

Not that he had much reason to stay. Luis, who was impossible. Isabel, whom he had kissed once, all because she claimed she'd met a boy while visiting cousins in Cartago and it made her seem suddenly like a girl to be kissed. Luis had been with them when he did it, so it was almost like a dare and nothing shy. He thought he'd go ahead and show them he knew how. "How's that compare to your Paco?" he'd asked, and she, shocked, recovered enough to declare he'd fallen short. Bolder, he tried for a second opinion from Luis — "Don't be scared" — who twisted away in disgust. Caleb landed a peck below his ear.

With regal aplomb he collapsed with his head in Luis's skirted lap, and Luis, as if appalled, said, "Look at this. Isy, who is this strange boy you bring to me?"

Caleb, saturated in dreamy confidence, at peace and a little in love with both of them, said, "I'm not strange. This is what we're like in America."

This was before their horseback adventure, before the usual incense aroma of Luis's room was overpowered by the dying queens, creamy bell-like flowers laid to dry over every surface. Luis claimed just being in the room gave him wild dreams, and that if they sat in it for an hour they'd be halfway to tripping, though technically the flowers would need to be boiled, or dried and then burned, to activate the drug. Caleb was curious to try it, this drug, but Luis said, "Oh, no. This kind, you do not mess around with it. It will make you insane."

"What if you're already insane? Will it make you sane?"

Luis frowned. "Was that a joke about me?"

Often Caleb was surprised this way — he'd been thinking only of fixing himself. Maybe it was the language barrier, or the cultural one, that could so often step them back into this cautious formality, not quite getting each other even when the words were there and working.

While the flowers remained fresh, they performed the spell intended to call up the ghost girl, so that Caleb could ask what she wanted. The standard séance having failed the week before, Luis had set about piecing together what he recalled hearing from a bruja in Escazú: first, locate the blooms, rare cousin of the garden variety and roadside weed, which grew only in certain remote and inaccessible parts of the cloud forest; then place the flowers bell-down over the eyes and nose of the haunted person. Both séance and flower spell should have been performed in the location where the ghost resided, but they didn't know how to do this since Caleb had seen her in different places, all of them open and public. So they settled for Luis's room, where Caleb, deprived of his glasses, supine and smothered with hallucinogenic flowers, became instantly giggly.

"Now what?" he asked, his voice nasal. With a breath of laughter he toppled the flower cone from his nose. "Now be still," Luis said, a cool hand on Caleb's forehead as he replaced the flower, adjusted the others for closer contact. Caleb had decided against bringing Lark. No Isabel either, only Luis to administer this task, though it was clear by now that Luis didn't know what he was doing. He was only pretending to remember this spell — one that conveniently required the very flower he knew how to find, if with some extraordinary effort, and wanted anyway for other purposes, hence the abundance. Why would some bruja in Escazú, which was in the capital city, San José, and not the cloud forest, name a flower only Luis could get?

And how would Luis, Rosales family pariah, get the horse on which to get the flowers? Even with Ranito's assistance, they needed the excuse of a trail ride for the Vincents. Once, visiting the Trogan, Caleb had come upon little Ranito bent under the open hood of Luis's rattletrap car, working a wrench, Luis beside him and the two of them muttering together like conspirators.

However used he felt, Caleb was not fully ready to disbelieve, to dismiss the ceremony that brought him into Luis's keeping, and he breathed carefully from the flower, willing it to let him see.

"Shouldn't you say something?" he asked Luis after a while.

"I don't know past this," he admitted.

"Say, 'Melia, está bien. ¿Melia, cuál es tu nombre?' "

"What?" said Luis, because Caleb had not yet in all this time, even when they tried the séance, told him the girl spoke Spanish. He had wanted to see what Luis would know without his help.

"Shh," Caleb said, and began murmuring it himself: "Está bien. Está bien, Melia. ¿Cuál es tu nombre?" He could hear Luis's breath going shaky above him. He needed more words. *Come to me.* "Ven acá," the call of mothers in the market to their children, which he repeated until he could think of the next. *What do you want?* "¿Qué quieres? Dígame." *Tell me.* "Está bien, Melia." Then all his air was gone — it was as if she pressed his lungs with her small hands — and he wiped the flowers from his face, sat up coughing and coughing.

On the bus to Nicaragua, he caught himself forming the words again in silence, seeking more. Lark tapped his knee, mouthed when he cracked an eye, WHAT ARE YOU SAYING? He pointed to an earbud, shut the eye.

The thing was, he didn't believe, not in the spell and hardly in the ghost herself. She was part of Nicky, part of his experience, and "ghost" was just another one of those code words that translated it into something other people thought they understood. In his journal, while trying to write "the truth" — whatever that was — it occurred to him that all words were code and false, all words altered what was real and then began to take its place, so you were left with a warped, tamped-down approximation of the elusive object; you could hardly write or speak without doing it permanent damage. The vivid thing you meant to capture might still be waiting for your better effort, but not for long. Soon there were only the words, replacing it. But if you wrote nothing, said nothing, it was all too big, too much, too real, poised to flee or change. Certain men hunted exotic animals this way, or children — trying to touch and get hold of an essence they'd kill in the act.

He didn't want to kill Melia again. Or whatever her name was. But then she, what remained of her, was in no danger from him — she wasn't his to kill. Nicky was. Nicky could be killed with words, if they were made false enough. It was what they all wanted him to do.

"I have to tell you something," he said to Luis, when his lungs had found the air again. He had figured out how to say it, so simply, without having to — not all, but enough to start. He'd say, *Go to the Internet café and search on my name.* But could he expect Luis to keep a secret so freely available to anyone? Once it was out, there'd be no putting it back. And more and more, he distrusted Luis's honesty in certain things he said about himself.

He motioned for his glasses, and Luis handed them over, a comforting hand on his back. The room's edges returned — but he hated the glasses sometimes. He remembered when he hadn't needed this barrier between him and the world, translating it into something he could see but also distorting it, the periphery forever blurred.

He said, "My glasses. They sort of flash, sometimes." He looked around the room, seeking the effect, but every photo and flower and candle wick seemed clear enough. "I don't know, maybe that's all I'm seeing. Maybe there's no ghost."

"I think she was just here," Luis said. "I think she said something to you and you are, how you say . . . blocking it."

He felt so tired then, sickened by the smell of the flowers, and out of nowhere, embarrassingly, he began to cry. "Luis, there's so much I need to tell you, and I don't know how. I can't do it."

"You can tell me. Just tell me."

He cried on Luis's shoulder, trying to stop, wanting to stay. "Why can't you tell me?" Luis asked, and Caleb thought maybe only the truth would work, or maybe the tears, the flowers, had made him stupid enough that the truth was all he had left.

"I don't trust you," he said.

Luis sat back and regarded him, trying not to look stung — but the thing with Luis was that under all the attitude and costume, and though he was seventeen, he was as sensitive as a child and took everything

364

personally. It was frustrating, because you couldn't tell him anything about yourself without Luis thinking it was about him.

"Maybe you should leave now," Luis said. He didn't sound angry, just hurt.

At the door, Caleb paused. Luis pretended to be busy rearranging flowers in his T-shirt and ragged blue jeans, the sort of outfit he was more and more likely to wear if he knew Caleb was coming. "Look," Caleb said, "you should wear a dress if you want. Don't listen to me. It's pretty."

It was a gallant thing to say, but minutes later, walking away, his jaw locked with resentment and he thought *No, the reason I don't trust Luis is that Luis is untrustworthy.* He wouldn't expect the same of other people, but it seemed terribly unfair of Luis, to be otherwise so perfect and still somehow not the person Caleb needed him to be.

That had been Monday afternoon, the flowers still fresh from gathering. All that week, the last week of school before the break, Caleb kept himself away, hanging out with Isabel ("It wasn't a fight, exactly," he told her. "It'll be okay."), who acted like he hadn't kissed her at all and went on talking about her new boyfriend, this Paco. Often he wanted to ask her advice about Luis, to

365

ask if she'd seen him, but he didn't want to hand over that power. She was still kind of mad at him anyway for excluding her from the flower spell, even though she'd been half the reason the séance had failed, all her shrieks and blurted questions.

She said, "Can I tell you a secret? Paco is really named Scott. I met him online. He's an American, from Michigan! He plans to visit here soon."

Caleb made her show him the guy's e-mails — which were tame and friendly but full of misspelled romantic suggestion — and also the photos, two face shots, one in a baseball cap, of a teddy-bearish bearded guy in his twenties. Each document she quickly minimized, peering around the café for spies.

"Pedophile," he said.

Isabel shushed him wildly. "He is not! He thinks I am eighteen. Which I think I can totally pass for, don't you? And he is only twenty-one. That's six years apart, and my parents are ten!"

She showed him the website she had joined, ticababes.com — must be eighteen to play — which was dedicated to hooking up Costa Rican women with white foreign men. Her older cousin in Cartago had shown it to her, so Isabel had joined "sort of as a joke, to look around and stuff. My cousin says a lot of the guys are rich, and this friend she has is getting married to one who has a plane and a boat and all kinds of things."

It wasn't hard to laugh at this, and a snicker seemed wiser than showing too much concern. "So," he said, after they'd left the café to sit on the steps outside. "You're gonna run off with some supposedly rich dude from Michigan? This is your dream in life?"

"No," she said, uncertain but cowed by his scorn.

"Well, of course not." Tipped back on his elbows, he proceeded to pick her romance apart, in a tone that assumed she couldn't be stupid enough to think otherwise. "The pictures are probably fake. Your boyfriend could be, like, seventy. And obese. And covered in warts." He named more afflictions for his own amusement. "And that website, whoa. Way trashy. Those women on there kind of look like prostitutes. I bet most of them are. And half the guys are probably Russian mafia collecting sex slaves — that's what they do in third-world countries."

"All right, enough," she said. "I'm not going to *do* anything. It's just some e-mails, jeez."

He reported the episode to Julianna that night, not because he was really worried about Isabel but because he thought Julianna would appreciate his performance. "And that, my friends," he said, "is *peer pressure.* It could be like my community service, right? They should send me around to high schools undercover."

"Hmm, I don't know about that," said Julianna. "Let's not forget the chat-room incident."

"Oh, whatever." In Washington a teacher in the computer lab had caught him goofing around in a man-boy chat room for the amusement of his posse, half a dozen boys hooting at the screen — in hindsight, one of several mistakes on his part, each negligible in itself, that had eventually brought the FBI to his classroom door. "That was just for kicks. Like, to show how dumb it is? See, my point. And that was Nicky anyway."

By week's end he still hadn't seen Luis, though he'd once or twice strolled by Miguelita's soda, hoping for a chance meeting. Should he offer to pay for the spell? Would that help or hurt? Some gesture, a gift, might be better. Even if Luis could never be the friend he wanted, he felt an intense need to at least make Luis think about him, make him regret the loss and the strange boy's absence.

In one shop, while Lark went to nose around in the books, he considered flavored cigars — peach, cherry, vanilla — bracelets, carved wooden boxes and bowls. Nothing was right. Luis, he thought, would turn up his nose at this local souvenir stuff. A man, also examining the bowls, brushed against his shoulder and said, "Hi, there" with a warm smile, a purr of a British accent. He was dark-haired, pale and narrow with a hooked nose; in less casual clothes he would have looked like a lawyer or someone's father, though Caleb recognized him as one of Luis's men. In the right mood, Luis would point them out for Caleb's judgment. ("I'd suck his dick," Caleb had claimed dryly of this one, and Luis answered with a scandalized scream of a laugh, taking it for the joke it essentially was.)

The man must have known that Caleb hung out with Luis. The smile assumed an intimacy without setting off alarms — this was a good guy — so Caleb returned the smile. "You know Luis, right? Or Valencia, whatever, at the Trogan? Would he like this or hate it?"

The guy gave him a blank look. "Sorry, I don't . . . know who you're talking about."

"Oh." If the man was being discreet, Caleb thought maybe he'd better backpedal quick before he got Luis in trouble. He glanced back to where Lark sat on the floor in the book aisle, safely out of range behind a shelf. "Sorry, I was just —"

"Ohhh" — the guy's eyes narrowed fondly — "you mean the housekeeper. Little cutie in the maid's uniform. Yeah, he's a shy one. Can't say I've gotten too close." He rubbed his lips together, giving Caleb a slow look that traveled the edge of his face, down his neck, into his shirt. "I hear no one does."

"Oh." His heart was lifting toward his throat.

"You hear otherwise?" He was being chummy. When Caleb shook his head, the man said, "That's all right. He's not really my type."

"My little sister's here." This came out level and cool, now that it was clear where they stood. A sidelong glance showed Lark alerted like a good sheepdog, standing and watching them from her corner. He and the guy turned away from her, back to the table of wood carvings, shifting a little apart. Caleb ventured, "I guess you heard something about me?"

"Oh, no. Nothing . . . specific. Just . . ." He waited for Caleb to look up, meet his

gaze. "That you might be open. To something."

"You heard wrong."

The guy broke into a grin, as if this were
an adorable thing to say. "It's Harold, by
the way. My name. I'm headed to Arenal in
a few hours, but I'll be back at the Trogan
end of next week. Nice little town, this."

Caleb hadn't quite sorted through this new
information before he was on a bus to
Nicaragua. Some part of him resisted it, as
if he could pretend it hadn't happened. But
it added support to what he'd just begun to
suspect, that Luis was flat lying about turning tricks and probably wasn't all that
experienced. There were too many contra-
dictions. And the more Caleb demonstrated
he could keep up with any sex talk thrown
his way, the less of it Luis threw.

So was Luis now spreading rumors about
him? But Harold would have acknowledged
their mutual friend right off. So who was it?
And where did they get their information?
If someone had linked him with his personal
media blitz — it could happen any day —
would his family have to move again?

His mother knocked on his bedroom door
while he was packing his duffel for Nicaragua. "Hey, you okay?"

He sat on his bed. He was trying to talk to his mother more, as Julianna and his therapist were always telling him to. "I had a fight with Luis. Kind of. I meant to talk to him before we left town, but I didn't."

"We'll be back soon. Look, you and Luis, are you just friends? If not, that's okay —"

"Mom." She waited with lifted brows as if this was not an answer, so he sighed and said, "We're just friends."

"Okay. Anything else on your mind?" In a cold flash he remembered her sitting him down for nearly the same interrogation when he was days from turning eleven, when she and his dad were always fighting about money and she thought maybe it was that, the thing that was worrying him. He'd pretended she was right, since he could think of no way to tell her about the hidden roll of cash, the photos of him partially clothed that Todd Jeter had snapped and posted to a pay site on the Internet called Nicky's Room.

He breathed, shook loose the memory. "Nobody knows, right? Around here, about me? Or . . . they don't just *look* at me and think I'm gay or something." With all he knew about his own appearance in that other world, in which any boy was a sexual object, it was jarring to realize he might have no clear sense of how people saw him in this one.

"I don't see any reason they would."

But he couldn't let her know he'd been propositioned out of the blue by some middle-aged stranger — it would get him put on permanent lockdown. Worse, she'd get crazy upset over this Terrible Thing that had happened to him, which in itself hadn't been any big deal. He said, deflecting, "I mean, Isabel met some guy, this white kid in Cartago, I guess, and now she's all crushed on him. Not that I care. But, like, she didn't even think I was an option."

So now his mother thought he was pining over Isabel. After she had soothed him uselessly for a while and left him alone, he curled up on his bed, tearful with the need to call Julianna — someone, anyone, who could take just a little more of his shit than his mother could. But if he called Julianna, she'd be sure to guilt him about the victim impact statement he was supposed to be writing. *This will help you sort things out and move on,* she'd say — the same crap his therapist fed him. They were trying to make him put Jolly in prison and, more than anyone, it was Jolly he needed to talk to.

Marlene tried to remember the last time

she'd heard Lowell speak of his women. Had it been since the night they'd gone dancing, or before, that he'd stopped suggesting to her, fictitiously or otherwise, the vast reserves of pussy awaiting him outside the Finca's door? Stancia, he now admitted, was more of a business associate. All those dinners without Hilda — Lowell curiously never a minute late, never missing a one — had started Caleb calling them "Mom and Dad," and those names felt quite near to fitting in every room but the bedroom, Lowell the stand-in father to her children and the adult person she most wanted to spend time with. But to acknowledge it would be to leap a chasm. She could feel him watching her now with that quiet separate self, waiting for the seismic shift, the waking up.

They had not kissed. Nor come close — of course not. At night, alone in her room, came an unavoidable fantasy or two, but only that. Under no tortured circumstance could she begin to imagine taking up with her husband's brother as a viable choice, not to mention the very Lowellness of Lowell himself, often a handy cooling agent. Yet she was glad, borderline giddy, that he was making the visa run with them. (Or they with him, since his was due. She and the kids could have waited another month, though by then, school would be back in session.) Together they shaped a family, the four of them, safe and competent travelers, as happy in most of the daily, important ways as the original had once been.

The problem didn't crystallize for her until they got into the cab that would convey them, with their newly stamped passports, from the two-hour border crossing to the beach: she felt a pull of deprivation simply because Lowell was in the front seat and unavailable for the remainder of the trip, less than an hour's drive, to tip her shoulder against or touch in a dozen other innocent ways. But maybe she was just in a good mood, euphoric to be escaping the cloud and going to the beach. She snuggled Lark, kissed her temple, turned to Caleb and kissed his cheek an obnoxious number of times until he was forced to grimace and lean away. The cabdriver grinned, eyeing her in the rearview.

Separate rooms, of course. Not that it would matter so much if the kids were with them, maybe in one big room.

"There's a lot of trash in Nicaragua," Lark said, peering out the cab window. Marlene agreed — it was the first she'd noticed how unlittered a country Costa Rica was. They passed more poverty than she was accustomed to seeing, and she recalled Isabel sending them all off with a cheery, "Try not to be stabbed in the street!" All Nicaraguans, according to her, had violent tendencies and were to be presumed thieves and murderers, though in her broad-minded way she added, "Poor things, they can't really help it. It's how they are." Lowell assured Marlene that Isabel was full of shit. The nicas he'd run across were pretty nice folks, and San Juan del Sur, their destination, was practically a tourist town.

And in fact the town seemed tidier than most of what they'd passed to get there, pretty in a rustic way, with low buildings painted pink and turquoise and, beyond, a glimpse of silver bay dotted with boats. Lowell directed the driver to a place he'd stayed at before, an American-owned bed and breakfast called Casa La Piña — clean, cheap, and likely to have vacancies on a Sunday. And, he promised, Lark would like it. They pulled up to a green and yellow house with a hammock on its porch of roughhewn rails, a garden of spiky birds-of-paradise. "If they're full, we can walk to a bunch of other places," Lowell said, and told the driver, "Aquí es bueno. Gracias." Marlene pulled out bills she'd changed at the border.

Inside the sunny, tiled lobby, a parrot on a gnarled perch called "Hola!" "That's Hector there," said the bleached and tan woman behind the desk to Lark, who immediately began talking to it. The woman was Greta, one of the owners, whom Lowell greeted with expansive charm — always hard to tell, with Lowell, how well he actually knew someone. "You saved me a room, right, darlin'?"

"Now how would I know you were coming?" Her mischievous smile, though, suggested they were in luck.

He turned to Marlene. "What do we need, two?"

"God, I don't know." She leaned beside him at the desk, hoisting her duffel. "What are they, doubles? How many beds?"

"The Vincent rooms, yes?" Greta said. "I have them reserved for you."

Marlene glanced at Lowell, but he looked as mystified as she was. Lark got it first, following a flick of Greta's eye toward the sitting area opposite. "Dad!"

"Surprise," Jeff said, standing to enfold Lark.

It was just easier, he explained, to drop in for a visit here, a simple cab ride from the airport at Managua rather than the arduous climb to Monteverde. He'd been told where

377

they planned to stay, had even called ahead and reserved them rooms, which he knew would never occur to Marlene, much less his brother. He couldn't stay long anyway, so the three days sounded about right, and besides, this way he could really surprise them. Surprise!

And how could Marlene be other than happy to see him? "I'm just, well, surprised," she said, barely able to force a smile. Had she been less stunned, she might have smacked him in the face.

He wore Bermudas and a faded surf-shop T-shirt, a summer uniform she hadn't seen in years. It made him appear oddly like a time-traveler, popping up from nowhere in the form of his younger, more carefree self. She considered her own appearance, hair freshly colored and coiled up in a pair of knots with loose sprigs like pigtails — a girlish style Jeff had always favored, calling it "cute" — a loose skirt swinging above her knees, bracelets up her wrists.

At least he hadn't assumed they'd be rooming together. "My room is big enough if the kids want to stay with me," he said. "Or they can stay with you. Whatever you think." He stood with an arm around Caleb, squeezing and assessing the expanded bones of his shoulder, and Caleb seemed comfortable enough, maybe even pleased to see his father.

Lowell had cried, "Brother!" with a whoop of genuine-sounding enthusiasm — not that he was such a good actor. He simply possessed the ability to enter afresh each new moment, with no emotional residue from the previous mood clouding the way. It occurred to her that Lowell had long ago stopped asking when Jeff would arrive. Never pressed, she had not deployed for him the serious word *separated,* and Lowell went along with the family pretense that Jeff was coming, one day, eventually. She knew why. Yet she wondered now if it might actually require explanation, that she and Jeff were not sharing a room.

The kids followed her up to her room, entered by a balcony shared with Lowell's; Jeff had taken the garden room below them. Marlene used the bathroom, needing a minute to think. When she emerged, Lark stood solemnly beside her bag. "Am I staying here?" Caleb leaned one temple at a window, looking out.

"We'll figure it out."

Lark's eyes were round with awe and a little worry over whether it was okay to be excited. "Can you believe Dad's here?"

"No, not really." Marlene sat on the larger

bed — she and Lark could share it, and there was a twin for Caleb. She smiled at Lark. "I bet you're happy, though, aren't you? Why don't you go see his room? Or go see the parrot. I want to talk to Caleb a second." Lark clapped her hands under her chin, a parody of joy, and ran off. Marlene held out both hands, then set one palm on the bed beside her, and Caleb, wonderful thing, folded himself there into a cozy fit against her shoulder. "You're really a good boy, you know that?" she said, meaning mainly this compliance, his placing himself exactly where she meant him to. This much contact was not their routine, though she still made a point to lay hands on him, somehow, at least once a day.

Sure, he said, when she asked, releasing him to sit — he was glad his dad was here, and Marlene echoed the verdict. It would be good to see him. "Your dad surfs, you know," she said. "Kind of. You remember? Maybe he can take you out, show you how?" She folded a knee and a bare foot before her. "But if you ever don't feel like . . . spending so much time with him, you don't have to. It's your choice. You don't even need a reason. Just remember that."

"Okay," he said, almost a question, and she could feel him searching her face and words for what she was trying to say. *I won't let him hurt you* — she wanted to seize hold of him and declare it. Maybe he'd be past his discomfort with Jeff. Maybe Jeff had come ready to do better. What she knew for certain was that he had one chance. She'd give him one chance to be as good as Lowell, and if he blew it they were gone.

It was a mess, though. She mulled the final exigency as the five of them strolled amiably along the village road toward the harbor beach a few blocks away. ("There's a shuttle that goes out to the good surf beaches," Jeff said, and Caleb said, "Aren't there a bunch of jellyfish here?," and Lowell said, "Sometimes, depends," and Lark said, "Snorkeling! Can we go snorkeling? Mom?," and Marlene said, "We'll see.") If it became necessary, she'd take Caleb, cut off contact, go anywhere. But how could she keep Lark from her father? He might take Lark. She glimpsed them in their separate walled camps, her daughter no longer hers, brother and sister separated — too awful to think of. It was why, perhaps, she'd so easily convinced herself that their undeclared separation was the best and only option.

God, why did he have to be here? Why couldn't he just leave them alone?

After a walk along the curve of the shore

and out to a rocky point, the water sliding over her pedicured toes, they ended up on the broad deck of a waterside restaurant under a roof of thatched grass. The sun was beginning to set behind the dozens of fishing boats crowded at anchor in the bay. At the round table for five, Marlene took the chair beside Lark, who sat beside her father, which gave Marlene the necessary distance from which to observe him. "Sit here," Jeff said to Caleb, which put Lowell beside Marlene — just as he'd put their rooms curiously side by side. "I swear you've grown two inches. Don't get taller than me, all right?"

"It's all that good Costa Rican food," Marlene said. "Right, Caleb?"

Funny thing, though, about a pitcher of margaritas made from limes just picked, a salt breeze, and the lap of water against the hulls of little boats: they were soon enjoying themselves. It was hard to keep up her vigilant mood. They all had funny stories to tell — even Caleb ventured a few or added details to Lark's — and Marlene remembered that, underneath it all and some distance back, the five of them were people who really liked one another. Look at what they had lost! It made her tear up, after only one drink, and she had to pretend a bug had flown into her eye. All that Caleb had missed — and he was smiling, elbows on the table, while his father and uncle tag-team teased him about girls.

As night fell, lights came up to illuminate a white wall behind them where the restaurant's name was painted in script, *El Gecko,* and little lizards with suction-pad toes made moving designs of themselves, chasing insects. Ingenious: the wall's light drew the insects away from the diners, and the geckos waited there like dinner theater, a beautiful silent array of bug zappers. Lark required them all to look, then look again. *Did you see that one? Did you see?*

On so pleasant an evening, was it worth listening for trouble? Little things, maybe nothing. Jeff, on his second margarita, said, "Yes, I heard there was dancing" when Marlene mentioned their night at the salsa club — nights, now, because they'd gone again the previous weekend — and she said, "Oh, did you? Well . . ." and went on casually with innocuous details she bounced off Lowell and the kids, as if she hadn't caught a note of suspicion. It was only that he looked at her when he said it rather than at his source, probably Lark. But he didn't press it. He refilled his glass, topped off Lowell's, signaled the server for another pitcher as their food arrived. He asked Lark about school, and Lowell jumped in as well because he'd helped her find the pipe cleaners for her final ecology project.

But any glance, any shift of the conversation, could seem more meaningful than it was. Jeff may have had no motive for this trip beyond missing them, and duty. He was so damn dutiful. The space of the table between them lent support to Marlene's hope that he understood their separation exactly as she did, nothing that need trouble them for a definition or prevent a visit now and then.

They were the last of the restaurant's customers, still talking — if there were further hints of tension, tequila blurred them from notice — as the servers swept up. Petra, who had been to San Juan del Sur for her own visa runs, had told Marlene it was pretty safe there; just, as a woman, she wouldn't walk around alone after dark. (And Petra was no flower. She was a drug dealer, as Marlene had discovered after some prying — "Just for friends," as the small-timers liked to say, but a dealer all the same — and Nicaragua was one of the places she came to replenish the supplies of certain items she had trouble finding elsewhere.) But walking back to the hotel with the kids and Jeff and Lowell, even through pockets of black hard to navigate without a flashlight, Marlene felt entirely safe, the unknown foreign town like a stage set built just for them.

"¡Plátanos!" cried the parrot, narrating their breakfast. "Would you like juice? Huevos con queso . . . Youuuu . . . eat like a pig!" Its pupils swelled black, contracted to mesmeric pinpoints as it sang in an old-lady vibrato, "Happy birthday to you." Greta disparaged the choice, on such a beautiful morning, and the bird sang, "Oh, what a beautiful morning . . . ¡Con leche! ¡Café!"

The adults slightly hungover, they changed for the beach before too much of the morning was gone and caught a shuttle that left from a nearby hostel. *"Guapa,"* a passing boy growled at Marlene as she waited to board in her bikini top and sarong, inspiring Jeff and Lowell to spend the bumpy ride to the beach — perched on railed benches in the back of a truck — amusing themselves with *guapa* in different voices, pitches, and speeds, at random moments, their expressions innocently disassociated until they collapsed in laughter. Later it became her name, without inflection: "Hey, Guapa, style me up some sunscreen" — the sort of boyish joke they might add to for hours in the right mood. Caleb chuckled at this more than once, and Marlene found herself pleased that Jeff was reverting to his immature self under Lowell's influence. It was promising.

At a beachside shack, they rented three boards. Marlene shared one for a while with Lark, the two of them using it like a raft while the boys took turns on the other two, but the water was ten degrees colder than she cared for, and Lark agreed. Only Jeff, who could be obsessive about his athletic pursuits, had real stamina for repeated trips, and Caleb was game for longer than Lowell, determined to get his feet under him. She'd learned, too, that in almost any unstructured social situation, where Caleb was likely to freeze up or withdraw, he appreciated some simple prompt or signpost for his role in it. For their beach day he'd clearly taken from her, committed to heart, that his role was to be instructed in surfing by his father. It hardly seemed to matter to him what he was assigned — he didn't resist adult suggestion as other boys did, but applied himself single-mindedly and with visible relief. Seated on the shore, she held his glasses, but he was too far away for her to study his face without them. She'd gotten used to seeing him shirtless from all the times they'd shared a room, including the night before: skinny but strong, with faintly defined muscle, a body grown more capable of withstanding the nightmares she couldn't help superimposing on it (that one awful photo she'd badgered from Mitch, the tamest of the bunch for certain) if she looked too long.

She walked the broad wet margin of the sea with Lark, hunting shells, and they came upon fresh, deep, vehicular tracks — as if a four-wheeler ATV had plowed directly out of the sea or into it. A sea turtle, Lark declared, must have laid its eggs the night before, and sure enough, they could see the depression in the sand where the tracks ended, back near the grass. The boys were on a surf break when they returned, seated on the beach towels, and Marlene tried to sneak up, catch the conversation. But it was impossible to monitor Jeff every minute he was with Caleb, as part of her meant to.

From a beachside cart they bought agua de pipa — green coconuts hacked with a machete down to a paper-thin skin, through which a straw was then popped to drink the water with — and fried pockets of meat and cheese. ("Are any of these vegan?" an American surfer chick wanted to know.)

Afterward, Lark begged for someone to walk with her to the volcanic rock that capped the north end of the beach in a hunt for more shells or hatchling turtles, and Jeff and Caleb acquiesced. Marlene let them go.

"I do like that swimsuit," Lowell said, from the towel beside her — more shy now than he would have been without his brother present, however far down the beach. But he didn't pry into her preoccupation. They chatted as if they were not alone, as if it were only expected that Jeff was here. She wondered if her duty to the kids might be to reunite with their father. Begin pushing the boulder to Costa Rica. Stretched beside Lowell, mentally following that Celtic bramble down the sucked-in edge of his abdomen to where it disappeared into black swim trunks, she proposed to herself how simple it would be, at the least, to pack up her erotic impulse and knock with it later at Jeff's door — nothing to regret.

When the others returned, Caleb was in one of his pensive moods. He chose a spot a distance off from which to observe the water or them, this curious alien tribe he'd been set among, and she tried not to blame Jeff. But of course she did. Even if there had been no particular incident, Jeff's mere presence would be stressful for him, another set of expectations he had to meet. She let him be for a time before she went to ask how he was. Fine, he said, only a little tired.

Later they found they'd all turned pink in various spots, but Caleb — perhaps from too many trips into the water with Jeff — had gotten the worst of it. She didn't realize it until after they dragged home, dazed, to nap at the hotel. When Marlene woke, Lark was gone and Caleb was standing shirtless before the bathroom mirror. "Where's your sister?" she asked. He shrugged.

She turned to find her shoes, thinking at the same frantic moment that Lark was visiting the parrot, or down with her father — she knew not to leave the hotel. Marlene spoke all this aloud, talking herself down as she stepped into the bathroom beside Caleb. One side of his face, his ear, his neck and shoulder, a swath of his torso, and the tops of his feet were all bright red. "God," she said, fumbling through her toiletry bag for the aloe gel, which wasn't there, gone like her second child, and she stopped — was she even awake? — and stared at them both in the mirror. "It's awful. It's too hard. I can't stop it. I can't . . . do it." She hardly knew what she was saying, her voice climbing higher, and she shut her mouth against his unburned shoulder, but it was Caleb whose eyes in the mirror had gone as red as his skin, who started to cry. "It's okay," he said.

"Honey, do you feel sick?" Sun poisoning — maybe both of them, as addled as she felt; maybe all of them. "I'm fine," he said. "It's fine." He smiled through tears. "Está bien." Maybe he was only upset that she was upset, cracking apart before him, among the other untouchable, unnamable reasons, and she pushed both palms into her face, breathed. This was Jeff's fault, too. A second parent should have halved her burden, instead of giving her twice as much to worry about.

She sat Caleb on the toilet lid, found the aloe. "And Lark," she said, with effortful calm, smoothing gel along his neck with the lightest touch she could manage, "is down with the parrot, and this is hardly the worst burn I've ever seen, and I'm not an incompetent mother." He sobbed a laugh at that, sitting all the while very still, his fingers pushing methodically under his glasses to wipe tears. "We're just tired," she told him. "Too much sun."

A little more sleep, after locating Lark, a cool shower, and fresh clothes — amazing how much better she could feel, ready for a cocktail and company. Caleb, like the mirror to her mood, smiled as he pressed white fingerspots into his burns — "Ow" — seeming pleased to show the reddest war wounds among the men. After dinner on the harbor at a wood-fired pizza place recommended by Greta, the mood still congenial but quieter than the previous night, it was decided without anyone's saying so that she and Jeff needed to speak alone. Perhaps Jeff had arranged it with Lowell, who took the kids back to the hotel while she and Jeff lingered over the last of their drinks.

"It's great to see them," he said. "They seem happy. Caleb seems good."

"He is," she said. "He's doing well, and I think they're very happy. Considering." Already she was on the defensive, as if he meant to imply something else. But he wasn't fighting her. He gazed out at the moonlit water, elbows rested on the table, and she said, "Caleb, he tries very hard, you know, to be this idea of what we all want him to be. He's very good. A little *too*. It's going to be a lot more therapy, I think."

"I talked to Mitch," Jeff said mildly. "He says he can have the therapist as long as he needs. And did he tell you about the extradition? Not happening. They're actually wondering if they have a case at all."

She shook her head — Mitch had warned her. Their evidence against Lundy went shakier every week: nothing demonstrably illicit in the home or workplace, the smattering of photos from other sources inconclusive, the criminal associates lost in the wind, and no victims to point a finger, other than Caleb. Mitch and Julianna both had promised he would not be called to testify, but she knew that was partly because no one had believed he would do it. "I can't think about that right now," she said.

He took a long breath. "I've missed you."

"No, you haven't."

"I think you should come back home," he said, like the thought was just occurring to him; one he was still uncertain of. He scratched the back of his head, checked her reaction. "I miss Lark. And Caleb. I don't want him to grow up not knowing me, or me not knowing him."

"Nobody's growing up yet." This show of sincerity annoyed her — it sounded scripted, somehow — and she should have repeated the obvious: if he wanted to be with his children, then he should be with them. "Look," she said, "maybe it's me. Maybe I still have too much to work out. God, I'm still just trying to figure out how *not* to be looking for him. And you only made things worse, leaving when you did. You left me. When I needed you. How am I supposed to trust you?"

"I didn't leave you," he said. "You know I didn't. I took Lark, that's all. She needed to be away from you. It wasn't good for her. You know I'm right. We were always coming back . . . eventually."

"Were you."

"I think so."

"When I forgot him." The words were almost garbled with bitterness. "That's all you wanted from me. That was your choice, for him, to let him go."

He shut his eyes in a slow flinch. "Can we please not . . . open all this up again? I chose wrong. You don't think that kills me? But it was a million to one, Marlene. I was" — he laid his palms flat, addressed the table — "trying to find a normal life. For all of us."

"Okay." She was tired of how much hatred she could feel for him, for past actions no longer in play, though these days she rarely had cause to turn up that dirt. "I knew you were right about Lark. I wasn't completely able to be her mother at that time. So I didn't fight you. Now I have to say I think Caleb is doing well partly because you're not around." She held up a hand. "I'm sorry to be blunt, but that's how it is. It's not your fault, necessarily. But you make *me* tense, and he feels that. Or we fight, so he has to worry about that. And you have to know, he senses your . . . reserve around him. He knows you let him go." A harsh jab, and she could tell it hit home. But he deserved it. "Honestly, even in the middle of nowhere Costa Rica, he's at his limit of things to worry about."

He looked helpless, his gaze wandering anywhere but her face. "So, what, then? How long are you planning to go on living with my mother?"

"How would I know? As long as necessary." She tried to be gentle and firm, but his thwarted expression made her say, "What is it? Have you got a different life to get to?" Her suspicion, not even present before, began to coalesce. "Is there someone else?"

He sighed, as if she were crazy. "No, there's no one else. But I met someone."

"You what?"

"That's all. It's nothing. Nothing's happened. I met someone, and you should know."

Her mouth fell open. "Are you fucking serious? This is what you came down here to tell me? You *met* someone?" All her simmering anger boiled up into a froth more like glee than fury.

"No, it's not why — I wasn't even going to say it! Marlene, listen, you don't have to worry that —"

"Oh, I'm not worried. This is wonderful news. Fucking fantastic." They were drawing looks from other tables. She thought of marching off into the night, out to the beach or into the street, but she didn't trust Jeff, following, to keep them safe from the alleged muggers. "I think you should go and explore, with my blessing. Explore what you might have with this person you met. I don't think I really care who it is or what you do with her. Hell, it could be your chance to *get on* with life."

He closed his eyes against the onslaught, that gesture habitual since Caleb's return, an effort to restrain dissent. "The sarcasm is really not helpful."

She sighed, cleared her face. "No sarcasm. I mean what I say. This could be for the best."

Often, over those three terrible years, she'd privately conceded the wisdom in moving on. Almost everyone in their lives had sided with Jeff on this, against her. But in her heart she'd been unable to escape the conviction that a man who gave his child up for dead had some inherent defect in his capacity to love that child. Setting her anger aside at Caleb's return, for Caleb's sake, had been like forgiveness, but Jeff's failing appeared now exactly as it had been, undiminished, toxic to all of them.

"Look," he said, "that came out wrong. It's not what I came here to say. I don't want *permission*. I want us to be a family, together, at home. A normal life for our kids."

"And for you. That's the problem, Jeff. Normal isn't an option. Maybe it won't ever be. So you should look for it somewhere else."

"You've got it all figured out, don't you? And you'll always be right." Defeated, he shook the ice in his glass, seeking more drink, then gazed grimly out at the bay. "And how about you, Marlene? Have you met someone?"

CHAPTER ELEVEN

Lowell had philosophies. One was "Be open to the moment." "That's one you just *know* when you're a kid, right? It's that natural curiosity about life and *engagement* in what's happening." In the walled back garden of the hotel, he and Lark and Caleb sprawled in a hammock under the lime and mango trees, folded in like three different-sized puppies in a womb. Caleb had heard versions of this philosophy before, but none so expansive. "You don't know yet what's supposed to be important, so you can be watching, like, a ladybug on a leaf and that's *fascinating;* something's happening! But all the while you got adults coming in, parents and teachers and everyone working against that, trying to teach you all the rules, and what's good and bad, and all the blinders you're supposed to look through, right? Don't touch that, don't try that; here's the shit that matters, pay attention to that. And with rules, you start learning, like, agendas. Ambition. You're supposed to make *plans,* right, and have a job, a career — a job, that's the *worst* for killing your ability to perceive the moment. Or take something really basic, like you want to get laid" — he glanced Lark's way, slapping a hand over his mouth — "or something less crude, like you want to get . . ."

"Romantically involved?" Lark suggested. She had launched this forum by asking if he was sorry he had to be with her and Caleb, walking them home, when he might have been back at the restaurant bar with a pair of drunkish ladies who'd been flirting with him.

"There ya go," Lowell said. "You want to get this girl, or guy, and suddenly you start missing out on everything but that goal. That's why I like hanging out with kids, or hell, old people, or anyone. I like to see whatever's there, in the moment before me. Right now that's an opportunity to hang with y'all. And if getting some girl is in the moment before me, then that's a beautiful thing; I'm way down with that. But if you get all fixated on some abstract goal, like chasing tail, that's like some idea you have ahead of time about something that's not even there yet. See? That's blinders. It's how adults go blind. It's also why time goes fast when you're grown up and slow when you're a kid — because most adults don't have that much left to look at and actually *see.*"

"Because if it's not what they meant to see," Caleb said, working it out, "it's like it's not there?"

"Exactly."

Overhead, fruit ripened; stars glittered in black spaces between blacker whispering leaves. "Carpe diem." The words lifted and peeled loose from some recess of Caleb's memory. "It means 'seize the day.' That's like the moment, right?"

"Why, yes indeed." Lowell sounded impressed, offered a fist to bump. "Right there, my man. Boom."

"There's a poem. About bowling through the gates. . . . But it's kind of about sex, I guess."

"Well, sometimes that's your moment," Lowell murmured, the conversation becoming private because Lark, who'd skipped the afternoon nap, was already losing her fight against sleep, her eyes dropping shut, opening again.

"Do you know that poem? I can't remember it now. Something about how you're going to get old and die tomorrow." Jolly had pulled it from one of his musty college books when they were studying Latin, though the poem was in English. "Youth doesn't last, so use it now, do what feels good." Lowell's crotch was close, in reach of a hand with one small shift, and there was no way not to know this or envision the less abstract thing that might be seized — almost a simpler prospect to ponder with Lark so close. Because what could Lowell do? Of the few options, one would surely not be the one Caleb most dreaded: any kind of time-out confrontation, angry or otherwise, about the sort of behavior considered deviant by regular people.

"Isn't that most poems?" Lowell said, a lazy smile in his voice. "Songs, too. Come on, baby, life's short, do me now, all that shit."

It wasn't that he was lusting after his uncle, exactly. It was more that these things came to mind, made their pictures, presented him with options. He felt sure that if they could get past the awkward starting part — too big an *if* — then Lowell would like it, and want it again, and then they would belong to each other in a way blood kinship couldn't touch. But he'd never had to seduce someone before. He'd never learned how. As party boys went, he'd been famously shy if more than half conscious, called a prude, the ridicule instigated or egged on by the other boys until any mean shift of the mood could get him singled out for a round of Let's Make Nicky Do Things. He could almost picture one of those nameless bolder boys he'd never been, one who would have known how to make short work of Lowell, without a second's hesitation.

He reached to pluck a fallen leaf from the weave of the hammock, a move that allowed a wayward elbow-brush of a thigh, inches off the mark. He seized a leaf — even Jolly would laugh at him. "Car-pe di-em," Lowell said in a hick voice. Talking to himself, looking at the stars.

"Can I ask you something?" His heart was suddenly rattling at his sternum. He wasn't sure what it would be, what he would ask.

"Sure, but — let's get out of this thing."

With careful moves, they extricated themselves from the hammock without waking Lark, shifted to the nearby lawn chairs. Lowell got a beer from the honor bar and set it in the shadows between them. By then it was gone, the thing Caleb might have said, or done. Almost from resentment he said, "You've got some pot in your room, I bet."

Lowell smirked. "Do I? You think so?"

"I could smell it last night." He felt a little sorry now. "Like, through the door."

"Anyone else?"

He shook his head.

"You won't tell on me, will ya?"

Caleb leaned back and considered, lifting the beer. Lowell smiled like that was an answer. "Hey, listen, speaking of pot. You ever seen it growing?"

Caleb shrugged. "In pictures, I guess."

"Not around, like, say, the Finca?"

Caleb tried to scan the vast and varied stores of greenery he'd come across — it would never have occurred to him to look in the forest for pot. "Is there some?"

"Just a hunch I have. I think some of your little caballero friends have a patch some-where out there."

"Oh. Yeah, I guess that would make sense." Lowell eyed him, and he said, "I think Ranito might have, you know, resupplied, during that ride we went on. I wasn't sure why he was coming with us, but I knew there was a reason. Then he rode off by himself once." Caleb had assumed it was to get more flowers, though it had been odd that Luis hadn't gone with him the second time.

"Well, interesting." Lowell stroked his chin Sherlock Holmes style. "That'd be pretty sweet, if I could find myself a patch to nip a smidge from, no one the wiser. Guess you don't know how much there might be. . . ."

He shrugged. "Ranito got himself a backpack full. It was all he could carry without us knowing."

"Crikey." Lowell burped, closed his eyes.

And then he'd be stuck blowing Lowell every day or worse. That would be miserable. Why did he want these things he didn't want? It was only that he felt so anxious all the time, uncertain of these people. He needed someone to feel certain of. Making a move on Lowell, though, would either fix Lowell in place or drive him away, more likely the latter.

And he couldn't think of it here, with his father so close, poised to be disgusted by confirmation of all he already knew. Caleb's therapist wanted to get them in a room together, to show Caleb that the actual man and the one in his head, put there by Chet, were not the same. He knew this, in a way, knew that his father was a decent guy who was trying and that the fault was all in his own failure to be a recognizable son. *Are you Caleb yet?* His eyes were always asking, always hopeful and then disappointed. Walking along the beach with the man, learning to surf, he'd been happy enough but for his numbed dread of being a disappointment, his certainty that it was already happening and had happened. Every pathetic second, his own hope might resurge into some effort to change the unchangeable, as if catching a wave at the right spot, getting his feet on the board where his father wanted them, could erase all his wrongness. Jolly had told him, too, and it made so much sense: the father you're born to can love only what reflects well upon him, despising the rest, while your true father, who waits in the world, is the one who can love every part of you.

"What'd you want to ask me, bud? Or was that it?"

Caleb swallowed from the beer, which Lowell would not have acknowledged as theirs and which was almost gone. "This guy," he said, a bold stab in one direction if not the other, "back in town, don't tell Mom, but he kind of came on to me. And he was a tourist. Like, he came *looking* for me. You know what I mean?"

Lowell nodded thoughtfully, not quite the response he'd expected.

"And nothing happened, obviously. I'm just wondering. I don't know *why.*"

"Why nothing happened?" Lowell's voice was careful, quiet — if Lark had been faking sleep on the hammock she wouldn't have heard them — and Caleb searched the words and tone for some hint, an indication that he might even now be speculating along the lines Caleb had been. *Open to something.*

"Why me," he said.

Lowell scratched his chin. "Might be something to do with your friend in the dress?"

"No. He didn't even know we knew each other."

From the shadows, Lowell looked at him a long time. "I might have an idea. I was wondering whether I should say something. And I guess I should. Let me grab another beer. Don't go anywhere." Saying this, standing, Lowell reached to cuff him behind the ear, a head pat that morphed into a brief thumb stroke along his jaw, and Caleb leaned into it, so slightly that maybe Lowell wouldn't notice. Then he was gone, and Caleb was left with his own quickened breath and the night.

Back in his chair with an open bottle, Lowell said, "Okay. How do I put this?"

Caleb, arms crossed, could meet his eyes only from a ducking, wayward angle. "Just say it."

"First, you know how bad the tico gossip can be. I buy some girl a beer and before I

405

get home, Hilda's heard we're married." Lowell took a double swallow from the bottle, handed it over. "So, the thing is, you might be getting a little reputation. It's about how maybe you're getting a step too close to some guys in the john?"

"What?" In Santa Elena, there was hardly a john in the whole town that was more than a single closet, one person at a time. He flicked over the few he knew and came to rest on one, the urinal trough at Luna Nueva. That first night he'd waited to slip out of the booth until one of his mother's gringueros, the younger one, had gone in. The choice was obvious — the chance to see the very thing his mother might have been thinking about, brushing against, earlier. But the trough was small, and after hardly a peek he'd chickened out, waited by the sink. *You're gonna get beat up doing that,* Jolly used to tell him. It was both serious warning and wry approval, and after extracting promises for restraint, he wanted the report: What had Nicky seen? What was it like? Caleb had found it somewhat frustrating that he couldn't give his mother such news, except in his mind.

"That guy," Caleb said, "Randáll, the one Mom was dancing with that night. I didn't go anywhere near him. But he gave me kind of a mean look." And there had been other episodes, even less dramatic, but maybe just obvious enough to be noticed, to amount to a pattern if the right people compared notes. And of course there was Lowell, who never bothered to close his bathroom door unless the females were about, like an invitation.

"Look, don't sweat it too much. These little towns, things get blown up from nothing. I'm just telling you so you know to be a little more careful in the future. Some of these local guys can be a bit more sensitive, maybe, than in America. Maybe the distances are different. I don't know."

"I'm not some queer, you know," Caleb said. "I'm not, like, coming on to guys in the john. Is that what you thought, that I was some kind of —" He stopped while he could still control himself. His voice had stayed quiet but was going shaky and quick.

"No," Lowell said.

"I'm not," he said. "I don't like it. I just —" He had to stop again. Tears were close — he might have been defending himself over the very pass at Lowell he'd not had the guts to make. Lowell waited, with what seemed too much patience, and Caleb snapped, "Did you *tell* them I wasn't? That they're wrong?"

"Well, now, this wasn't exactly firsthand. But I sent word they ought to shut up."

"You know I like girls."

"Dude. Bruh. Come on. Dial that back a bit, all right? I'm your family. I got an investment here. I care about you. I don't know anything for sure about who you like, and neither do you, I bet. I'd be frankly shocked if you *didn't* eyeball whatever dick came your way, and the fact that you might do so says squat to me about you liking girls, boys, ticos in dresses, monkeys, cats, what have you. Let's call you a work in progress. I'm just saying be a little more careful where your eyes go, unless you want people to think what they'll think. I'd tell you more than that, but I don't think there are a lot of grown men in these parts gonna hurt a kid over that kind of thing. You feel me?"

"Yeah," he said, shaken, confused, obscurely aggrieved to be so exposed. He glimpsed how much of this must have passed between his mother and Lowell over their many drinks together; then all those men in town — it could not have been half a dozen, let alone the hundreds he imagined — discussing him, laughing at him and his proclivities. Had he really thought he could manage what other people thought of him?

408

Caleb finished the beer. "Let's have another." Lowell only looked at him steadily, and he said, "No, I appreciate the information. Thanks. It's helpful." He wasn't sure why he was so angry, and creeping up behind anger came the same desperate sorrow that had come upon him that afternoon with his mother. It should have been a relief, this open-ended acceptance, but something in him wanted to crawl into a hole or hurtle backward through time, back past Jolly and all the way to Chet, when nothing was in his control and no decision his to make. It was exhausting, having to be himself every minute, every act attaching to him and speaking for him.

They didn't get another beer, because his parents came home then. His father picked up Lark, a girl still small enough to be carried by a man, if awkwardly, limbs pendulous and heavy as the fruit overhead. His mother put an arm around him, which he didn't want, and did: he wanted her to carry him to bed or fold him up small enough to keep in her pocket and also to leave him be. No satisfying his scrambled soul, no matter what these people did.

Alone in the house on Waverly Way, Jeff had been watching all the old home movies.

He'd found it far too painful, when Caleb was missing, to go anywhere near them, though Marlene had drifted through phases of poring over them late at night, for hours, as if they held clues. At intervals among the beach trips and zoo trips, the school pageants and family reunions, were the episodes that featured Jeff performing tricks on some new athletic toy — the pneumatic pogo stick, the trapeze jungle swing, the bike ramp — acquired "for the kids" when they were still too small. The video showed a series of Jeff's flights and flips: sailing from the driveway ramp, tires twisted BMX style, while in the street Lark and Caleb rode their own bikes in contented circles, shouting a half hearted "Cool" or "Go, Dad!" when prompted to admire. Next, the ramp modified to its most minuscule child dimensions, the camera settled on Caleb, who stood, feet grimly planted, while Jeff called out encouragement from behind the camera. "I can't!" Caleb insisted, in his high child's voice, that slight southern *cain't* he'd since lost just as certainly. Astraddle his bike at the top of the drive, he frowned with heart-sick resolution at the ramp. "It's gonna hurt," he said, as if committing to the attempt as well as the injury to follow, for which he already blamed his father. But in

410

the end he didn't budge.

Jeff had forgotten how often this episode had been repeated over the years and how intensely his son's resistance, his cowardice, had nettled him — the hubris of a man with no concept of loss. He showed pieces of the video to Kimberly, a recent college grad on loan from his parent company to assist him a few days a week, generally at the house. "Oh, look how *cute* he is," she said. "And your daughter, and you. All so cute!"

"He turned out to be a great little athlete, later on," Jeff told her. "Soccer goalie. No one could get past him." Kimberly loved to hear about Caleb. She possessed a softness Jeff was unaccustomed to in women, a steadfast compassion that drew him out, and speaking to her of his son made him miss Caleb almost more than he'd ever allowed himself to. But here was his child caught in the video, blowing out candles, feeding a goat, laughing or running or making faces. Still on earth, if far away.

In the chilly Pacific swells, Jeff caught flickers of the boy he remembered drilling in the backyard with the soccer ball, that expressive concentration. No wonder if he hadn't glimpsed this particular Caleb before now. The surfing offered their first chance to be outdoors and alone together. "Bend your knees," Jeff instructed as Caleb struggled to balance on the pitch of the board. "It's like your goalie stance. Remember that?"

"Yeah." Caleb's fierce squint was trained in the direction of travel, as Jeff had directed.

"My wife doesn't want me there," he had explained to Kimberly. "Not that she'd say so. She has ideas about how things ought to be, and she makes the rules. True, I don't have to obey them, but she doesn't leave me any room to be a father." He wanted to tell Caleb the same, as they both rested beside their boards in the roll of the sea. This son struck him as capable of understanding such complicated, grown-up matters. But as always, he would not allow himself to undermine his wife to his children.

Hilarious, or not funny at all, that Marlene looked to be replacing him with his brother. How long would Lowell have stuck around tending to her crazy ass? Jeff had stayed longer than he should have when even Mitch had said go, though Jeff knew well the other motives there. A man they could not escape, in their house daily, lusting after his wife — it had honestly never bothered Jeff much. How could he object

412

when the most tangible effect was a more tenacious hunt for his son?

After he carried Lark up to bed — a struggle to get her up the stairs without appearing to strain himself, his brother and wife looking on — and Lowell had slipped off to his own room, Jeff suggested to Caleb they take a walk.

Marlene shook her head. "Not away from the hotel."

"Fine," Jeff said, without pointing out that Lowell had just escorted both kids alone through the Nicaraguan night, or that Caleb now had beer on his breath. So much for her brand of safety. But he was determined that if their son were to detect any hint of parental tension, its source would be Marlene.

Caleb followed him down through the empty lobby, out to the front porch, where Jeff stopped at the top step, looking out into the dark street. "Remember," he said, "how you and I used to sneak out for fast food? Arby's or Checkers or those little Krystal burgers. Your mom was on some health kick and didn't approve. So that was our thing for a while, just the two of us. When she wasn't looking."

"I remember." They both stood toeing the porch edge as if Marlene's stricture were a physical barrier.

" 'Men need meat.' We'd say that, remember? And fries, of course."

"We salted the ketchup," Caleb added. The image brought the memory close. He moved past Jeff to hoist himself onto the railing, where greenery crowded at his back. A shadow folded him in.

"The last time we did that," Jeff said, "you were telling me about the band you liked. That band." Jeff couldn't say the name, still. He felt his throat constrict with tears. "I should have listened better. I missed something." From the rail, Caleb peered down at him in wary silence like some night creature that had alighted there and might vanish at a whim. Jeff stepped closer. "Your mom and me, we were so careful to set aside time for you and Lark, apart from the business, but we were distracted. I was distracted. It's unforgivable."

"Dad, it's not —"

"No, listen. It was my fault, what happened to you. I lost you. You were gone, and there was nothing I could do." He stopped, bewildered, having intended to say something entirely different about why they were not together for now, as a family, and about how much he wanted that, no matter what Marlene might suggest to the contrary.

Caleb pulled one foot onto the rail between them, hugging his knee. "Dad. Let's not talk about it. Like, maybe we could just pretend it didn't happen."

"What . . . didn't?"

"Everything." He spoke with a soft, musing interest, as if testing the idea. "Pretend I wasn't gone. I was always here. And then we just decided to go live in Costa Rica for a while."

The proposal struck Jeff with its preternatural strangeness, at once adult and childlike. "But *you* can't do that. Pretend it all away. Can you?"

Caleb breathed audibly, in and out. "Sure. Why not. It's better, isn't it?"

Some part of Jeff had stumbled after contact with the boy who had been missing, but this boy on the rail — his never-gone son — seemed, if possible, even more elusive. How could this child have need of him? And how could Jeff quibble, insist on the full accounting, if Caleb himself argued otherwise?

"Look, what I wanted to tell you," Jeff said, knowing that he still didn't have it, that he'd never get near it. "What I wanted to say is, we'll all be together again. As a family." He meant this, at least. Kimberly, however appealing in her youth and new-

415

ness, was no one he could imagine a life with. "One day soon, we'll be like before. This, all of this, is only temporary. You know that, right?"

"Right," Caleb said, with a nod of approval, as if Jeff were getting the hang of it.

Breakfast in the garden, their last full day in Nicaragua, and Lowell had gotten it into his head that Jeff should return with them, extend his visit. "Man, why not? It's so simple. Just ride the bus with us. You know Mom wants to see you." There was an edge in his voice, and Caleb listened with some interest. His parents were both behaving as if nothing had happened or been decided the night before, and it was pissing Lowell off.

Patiently, Jeff said the trip wasn't possible right now — he had too much to do, a meeting with a publisher on Friday — but Lowell would not let it drop. "Move your meeting. You got a meeting that can't wait a week? If not now, when exactly *are* you planning to come?"

Marlene, slumped behind her black bubble sunglasses and affecting a headache, said, "Jesus, Lowell, will you give it a rest?"

Her wish was Lowell's command. Lark had begged to go snorkeling, and Lowell and Jeff decided they would take her. Caleb was grounded by his sunburn, and his mother refused to let him stay back at the hotel alone — only because she had work to do anyway, she claimed — but he didn't mind so much. They lingered over breakfast after the others left, Caleb sampling the milky coffee Lowell had left behind, inhaling from the skin of the lime Lark had plucked. Or was it lemon? Limón — the intensely sour kind that when sliced looked like an orange in lime's clothing. Fruit with an identity complex.

An older couple took seats at the next table, speaking in German. For them, he decided, he was the American boy, someone named Caleb, whose thumbnail grazed the lime's flesh, a languid only child on vacation from his elite boarding school, alternately amused and bored by his incognito movie-star mother. It was pleasant to be this person.

"Will Father be joining us in Costa Rica?" he asked.

"Father?"

"The patriarch. *Pater noster.* The lumber baron of upstate New York." He held the lime as if it were a little world between them. "Remember you said I could make my own identity?"

417

Their chairs were scooted close to share the one patch of shade left at the half-cleared table. She reached to stroke the hair back from the sunburned side of his face, and that was pleasant too, a public caress from his movie-star mother. "I have an idea for your new identity," she said. "What would you think about contact lenses?"

He took off his smudged glasses and looked at them. "Yeah. I guess then I could see when I'm surfing." Then maybe the ghost girl, the flash in his glasses, would go away — though he had not seen her in weeks. Maybe she was already banished.

"So that's a no," he said, rubbing the lenses with his shirt. "He's not coming. Like, ever."

He expected another question for an answer, a shrink question like *How would you feel about that?,* but she looked at him for a while and shook her head. Why should this give him a cold little thrill? The honesty of it, maybe, the wordless intimacy that treated him as an adult. Or the crack of things breaking on his behalf: exhilarating and a little sickening at the same time.

In a corner of the lobby, opposite the parrot and facing the room, was the Internet station for guest use. Caleb logged into his school e-mail and found the two messages he expected: one from Isabel, one from Julianna. Isabel was in Cartago with her stupid cousin, who was busy talking her into a meeting with Internet Scott — not soon, but maybe in the next few months. *She says we will make it a double date. I don't know. . . .* Probably this was Isabel creating a school break drama for him to attend to, but he wrote her back — easy, obvious, out of the way — before he opened the one from Julianna, knowing what it would say. She didn't e-mail him often since they talked so much on the phone, but when she did — his trip to Nicaragua provided the excuse — she could be counted on to dust off the rhetoric.

I need you to be brave for me. I know you can do it or I wouldn't ask. I could really use some help, and it's all in your hands, Caleb. You're the only one I can turn to.

Julianna, his princess in the castle tower. She really was that beautiful — and what was it about women who looked as if they were always about to attend a funeral, and another the next day? *Melancholia,* he'd written under a sketch of her in his journal. *Beleaguered* was another word that came to mind, despite her perfect composure. *Help me, Obi-Wan; you're my only hope.* Her tawny red curls a mess after too-little sleep, and he wanted to brush them for her, smooth her wrinkled clothes. Haylie — his babysitter, his first love — had those same pink-rimmed, rescue-me eyes, but hers had held more mirth and mischief, more wildness. Julianna's were only somber. Even in play (and they played checkers and gin rummy, went to the zoo, ordered six different scoops of ice cream with six different toppings for the hell of it), you'd have a hard time forgetting that her badge read "Crimes Against Children."

He wanted to help her. Or at least to please her, and it was in his power. He could give her exactly what she wanted, and she would love him for it. For a while he'd doled it out in dribbles, hoping to be loved for each drip and drop and that in this way he could extend their time together, increase his total portion. But he knew now that in holding back he only disappointed her, over and over again.

And it was hard to keep track of how much he'd actually told her. "It's okay, if you don't want to say it," she used to tell him, whenever he hesitated over some detail. "We already know." So he didn't say it, and they moved ahead as if he had. Sometimes he was sure she tricked him purposefully, acting as if he'd said things already, and it was easy to forget if he had. He imagined saying them, different things, all the time. He dreamed them, in his bed beside hers, in the secret hotel room where no one could find them.

But he would not speak in their favorite words, those choice morsels that made him cringe, like *molestation* — not about Jolly. *Never say it; never write it down.* The slavering news reports, the endless questions and speculations . . . he'd never again be allowed his own life, the simple life he'd had in Washington when no one knew. He would not have admitted it about Chet either, but they'd put photos before him — party photos, blurred and grainy, without full faces or body parts, but startling in their simple clarity beside his brain's murky, jumbled notions of how it had been — and it did not come to him until later that he might still have denied it, no matter what they said. Maybe that was some other boy in those photos. *He* didn't fully believe it was him, so how could they know?

Pedophile, another favorite word — as in "pedophile ring," by which the FBI meant parties, though he had once corrected them at length. There weren't that many pedophiles at parties, and anyway, they were nothing to fear. The pedophiles were the good ones. They gave gifts to their crushes and tried to please. It was the bullies you had to worry about. This was true anywhere in the world — his experience was hardly special — so why the insistence on a word meaning "lover of children" for men who merely wanted to fuck something weak, easy to control?

What about Jolly? Julianna asked then. *Is he a pedophile?*

No, he told her. *Jolly's not into children. He likes teenagers. That's an ephebophile.* You would think the FBI would know these things. Or was that a trap? But liking was not a crime. And what was "molestation" but a category dependent on some arbitrary age limit that changed on a whim over time? By the end of such a daisy chain of logic, he could answer no to their favorite words and he'd told them the truth.

He relinquished the Internet station to his mother, settled on the lobby sofa under the slow ceiling fan to ponder his journal. In it were many questions, more questions than statements about what he had lived through, and who could answer these? Some were picky little things: *How did Jolly know I liked the Metacarpals? Who gave Chet the drugs?* Some were troubling but irrelevant: *Who is*

Zander, and where are his bones?

Some were too big to wrap his mind around. In Spokane, they had made him see a different FBI shrink named Puckett. The next day he'd overheard some agents talking in the hall. Puckett has a theory, one said. Jolly, that's a pretty odd nickname for Charles, right? And Chet, also a nickname for Charles. So maybe the kid has split the one man into two. One's the good side and one's the bad. Like a coping thing, so he can feel safe sometimes.

Julianna and the other agents didn't believe this theory. Or at least, in his presence, they behaved as if they didn't. No one had ever suggested to his face that Chet wasn't real, that Jolly was the one who took him from Georgia. In the journal he'd written, *What if Chet and Jolly are the same person and I'm too crazy to know it?*

What if Caleb and Nicky are not *the same person?*

What if it was all a dream? A hallucination? At times, he could almost convince himself of this, so hazy were the memories. Sorting through his early recollections of Jolly, he failed to find the beginning, the proof, of his separate reality. He couldn't think of a single instance when he'd witnessed Jolly and Chet in the same room. They didn't

423

like each other. Jolly — Chet called him Doc — was always on his damn high horse about nutrition and proper treatment, snooting around in other people's business like he was better. And Nicky didn't have too many moments of clarity to sort through in the first place.

Jolly had not been in the FBI's party photos. Chet himself was barely in them, but all Caleb needed was an ear, the side of a jaw. Chet. The nod he should have refused them brought a flood of instant relief, and strength, and he kept going, named all the men he could and said which were the really bad ones. It wasn't much: a few nicknames, all he had. He was safe in the custody of armed federal agents, a vast unseen network of them surrounding his quiet room with Julianna and her partner. Within the first hours, he'd learned that his every request — a strawberry milk shake, a roast beef sandwich from Rocky's, a break — would power the network into action, and whatever he'd dreamed up would shortly be set before him. He said, "You're finding them, right? Go find them, and kill them. Kill them all."

His saying this moved Julianna, if not out to do his bidding then closer to guard him, closer in her sympathy — the others, too. It was what they wanted him to say about Jolly, Jolly more than anyone because Jolly was who they had. It took time for him to grasp this. They hardly seemed to care about finding Chet or the others, and maybe they didn't believe him. Maybe he wasn't worth believing.

"It's complicated," he'd said, when Julianna asked why he'd stayed all that time with Jolly. Who in his life, for the rest of his sorry, mangled life, would ever love him without questions? Jolly knew it all, had been present for half of it, watching from a corner, biding his time. There was nothing to explain, nothing to confess. He could not be a disappointment. Jolly said never, not even if Nicky ran away or turned him in. "I'd be sad. But if you decided that was what you really needed to do, and you took that action all on your own, I'd have to be proud of you, wouldn't I?"

This wasn't hard to believe. Jolly was never angry with him, or annoyed, or distant. His most negative mood was a kind of sorrowful disapproval that started, "Oh, *Nicky,*" if Nicky expressed desire for something beneath him: pepperoni pizza, trashy movies. "Oh, Nicky, really? Must we?" There was a limit, for sure — no refined sugar, no video games. His body and mind had endured more than enough systematic rotting for one lifetime. But when he started leaving the house, an hour at a time, to hang out with the boy next door — whose house had Nintendo and a refrigerator full of soda that went straight to his head like a drug, not to mention strangers who might influence him — Jolly swallowed all his objections. What really mattered, he said, was that Nicky have this chance to test his bravery, to put one foot into the world by his own choice. "You go show that kid who you are," Jolly said — by which he meant smarter, tougher, but also a normal, well-adjusted boy worthy of friendship.

From the haven of Washington, it had been hard to see back over the divide he'd crossed — at least one state line — in escaping the previous life, where Jolly's rare appearances had seemed the only reason to live. "Let's not think about all that," Jolly said. "It's over. And I'm done with those people. I have you to think about now."

Not that Jolly wouldn't answer when asked. Caleb still had questions even now, some of them buried deep, but most had been answered some time ago. *Did Jolly go to parties to have sex with boys?* Of course not. He went to help kids who wouldn't otherwise get basic care. *Why didn't he steal*

Nicky sooner? He tried, more than once, but there wasn't a way. *And if there had been no way, a year later, to steal Melia, why not call the police?* Because more rapacious men would only arrive to fill the void, while Jolly would lose the access that allowed him to go in as a doctor and help one child.

But if he still had that access, had he stolen Nicky at all? Maybe not exactly. This was the sort of question he kept buried. Did it matter so much, how he was acquired?

And buried deeper: *Did Jolly ever have sex with Nicky at a party?* If so, Nicky had no memory of it. And it seemed unlikely. Yet there were rules. No man could show up at a party and not participate, and a new boy was a debutant, initiated by every man present. So it was possible. Jolly claimed he'd been necessary enough to them to be exempt.

Had Jolly known all along that he was Caleb Vincent, a boy who had been kidnapped? He must have. But he also knew that Nicky would never again be that boy, that Caleb had no chance at a life, but Nicky did. It was not discussed directly — Nicky's world couldn't bear it. But in some part of himself he'd understood that his hazy, faceless parents, if provided with all the information, would have agreed with Jolly that yes, this arrangement was best for everyone. Maybe not perfect. But even now he knew he'd been happier with Jolly, on balance, all things considered.

He glanced up at his mother, who faced him but didn't see him. She peered into the computer screen with her lower lip between her teeth, rolling and clicking the mouse.

Some of his questions had festered over his time with Jolly, emerged in jags of crying and flashes of bitter mood. None of that had been fair to Jolly. Forget that Jolly had saved his life, twice — since if not for the happenstance of raging pneumonia, his death would have come next and soon by Chet's hand. (Zander had told him how: *knife to the throat; bones in the wall,* though Chet had mentioned the yard in one memorable threat.) His life, so what? It was because of Jolly that he could walk and speak, read a book, make a decision or an A in school; that he wasn't terrified of men or groups of strange people or just walking out a door. If Jolly had wanted his love, his compliant gratitude, he could have gotten it with kindness and food and stopped there. There was no way ever to repay the debt, and after half a year or so he'd given up trying. Nicky was a little shit sometimes. And Jolly only smiled, calling any brattiness or laziness or contempt a good sign: that's how teenagers are.

Was Chet really after us? Part of him shut down at the question, resisting disbelief. But he could glimpse how the claim might have been a sort of fairy tale to keep Nicky careful, keep him close. A way of not mentioning his parents, the people who were really looking for him, which might have cracked his mended self on its axis. Jolly was minutely attentive in this way to his emotional needs, anticipating each one long before it arrived.

This is the important part. Caleb had written that on many pages of the journal, so often that as an indicator it became meaningless. The words were in Jolly's voice, spoken in bed, where Nicky was buzzed on the bliss of his new life and safe despite the hand on his rib cage, Jolly's hand enormous in memory, twice its natural size. They had much work to do, slow and careful repetitions to overcome his reliance on drugs, his negative associations, to make it possible for him to enjoy everything a healthy growing boy should. It worked, too. He was fine with sex now. And once puberty arrived, to much celebration, Nicky was granted all the choice he'd been promised. Mostly Jolly had to beg, and was thrilled to be refused, adoring the boy he'd made capable of the decision to scorn him.

If some of the answers sat uneasily at times, like a meal that might later come back up, nothing in the journal troubled him as pointedly as this ghost of Melia. And why her? He'd seen any number of brutal acts committed upon children, not many of them worse than those done to Nicky himself. He'd seen things so twisted he could not be sure they'd really happened, that he hadn't confused hallucinations and nightmares with life. Yet what showed up to haunt him was this sniffling, fierce-eyed little girl with a broken arm wrapped in a man's shirt, getting an X-ray, getting a cast — a girl who was only being helped. Maybe the reason was simply that he remembered her, having been sober when he met her. More than sober: he studied Latin, piano, chess; he knew the phrases of Spanish he'd practiced with Jolly on the drive to a gated lodge back in the woods, a place neither of them had been before. A random day trip, an exception, to help out a friend of a friend.

Hey, chiquita, over here. His own voice softly sweet, his face down beside hers on the bed, Jolly standing opposite with the syringe. *Mira. Look at me.*

If he'd known how to find the place, he

430

would have told them. He could remember no towns, no roads, only that it was in Idaho, somewhere around Boise. Probably Chet's house was in Idaho, too, though while in it Nicky had convinced himself it was Canada. He remembered the angles of incline up the dirt road; he remembered the view from the back window and the light through the trees, summer and winter, down into the ravine and over to the next mountain, no other house in sight.

The point, the point. The important part. What mattered was that he couldn't help them. There were criminals in this story, crimes had been perpetrated, and the best he could do was point to a sketch, write the name *Chet,* say Canada, or Idaho, maybe. Nothing more.

In the journal, he jotted more questions, quicker than the thoughts chasing them: *Is Jolly thinking about me now? Does he know where Chet is? Does he know where Melia is? If she's dead, is that my fault?* But when the words were sitting there looking at him, he began to lay meticulous hatch marks over each letter. His journal might have been some sensitive government document, half redacted into black.

Is Julianna thinking about me?

I could really use some help, and it's all in

your hands, Caleb. . . . He wrote the words inside a bubble rising from her freckled mouth.

From behind him, his mother set a hand on his hair, and he dropped the journal to his chest. "You hungry for lunch yet?" He shook his head. "I'm done with the computer for now if you need it."

Greta was away from the desk, the parrot on her shoulder. Marlene and Caleb were alone in the lobby. "Mom?" She settled on the opposite end of his sofa, drew her bare feet up beside his hip. "Do you know what's happening with the case? With, you know, Jolly?" He could never bring himself to say Charles Lundy, though *Jolly* made her flinch every time.

"I don't, really," she said. "Julianna doesn't tell you?"

She didn't. Had he noticed it before? She never told him, never explained why she needed his help *now,* their session in the closed room long past. Mostly, she insisted that what she asked of him, however painful or difficult, was for his own good. *Be brave for me. This will help you.* And his mother was lying, too, he was sure, or she wasn't telling him something.

He returned to the computer and opened Julianna's e-mail, not really seeing it. On the sofa, his mother read a magazine. Only minutes before, watching her work, he'd been struck by the fact of the computer's position, its extreme privacy, the wall tight behind the chair. Words that would not have drifted into mind at the exposed café in Santa Elena went tapping into a search box: Charles Lundy, Caleb Vincent. Thousands of hits. He skimmed them, clicked open one item after another, though the connection was annoyingly slow. Most were rehashes of the same stuff, unworthy of his time. Mixed in he found odd bits to pause on: a photo of Jolly that looked recent, a photo of Nicky in Washington that he'd never seen, an interview with a girl named Sarah Parkhurst who had sat beside him in English and wore gobs of purple eye shadow and whom he'd been deciding maybe to like. "I sort of had a crush on him, I guess," said Sarah, her words in quotation marks on the screen. "He was really funny, sometimes."

He didn't have time for this, though, not even to look too long at the picture of Jolly — who looked puffy, tired, the way he had after his sledding concussion — because each click spun the computer into its long doubtful consideration of whether or not to grant his wish, as if it were aware that Caleb's Googling his own name was an illicit activity. Pornography, Jolly would call it, under the name of news, so that respectable people could feel smug while jerking off to it.

But he could find nothing about the trial, not even that it had been scheduled. Shouldn't it be happening by now? From his mother's phone calls he sometimes overheard things, like efforts to extradite, problems with the evidence — but online he found no mention of either. And what evidence would there have been? A locked closet full of expired medical supplies; the collection of artwork featuring boys, which Jolly had moved into the attic once their lives became more public. The FBI had set before him some of Jolly's photos of Nicky, but even the nudest of the nudes were nothing extreme — a mistake on their part, to deal them onto the table after those party shots — and he laughed without trying. "You've heard of art, right?" or "That's just us goofing around" or "He's a doctor, you know. And I'd been really sick. That's because of how much better I was."

He clicked back to the article with the recent-looking photo of Jolly, just his face and shoulders. He seemed to be in street clothes, maybe caught in motion, some kind of building behind him. The article under it said he was "awaiting trial in connection with" and then more rehash, including his initial statement to the police — and maybe that meant he'd said no more, wasn't talking now at all. *I have been a father to him, and I love him dearly as a son.* True, though less like a father than an older brother, a camp counselor, serious in those protocols of health and education, but otherwise their lives together were like one long sleepaway camp, full of pranks and silliness. Nicky's friends were jealous his dad was so cool. *He loves me. I have done everything possible to give him a good home. Ask him and he will tell you.*

Had Caleb told them? Or had he held back, afraid to say the wrong thing, implicate himself? But at night, murmuring between their hotel beds, he'd told Julianna so much more — even about the beginning, when Jolly had only been his doctor but had sometimes swept him into embraces and whispered crazy things in his ear, like *I'd get you out of here if I could.* "I was all goofy in love with him," he told her, because they were talking about love, the different kinds of possible love. "He was all I could think about. Not in any kind of sex way. I just wanted to be near him. It was like religion, or like the way you love your parents when you're really little. I *believed* in him."

He told her about his scars, how Crazy Nicky learned to bleed himself just deep enough to make the doctor appear. Jolly begged him to stop, but he had to be there to say it. A year later, Nicky could still feel dizzy over the improbable luck of it, the whole, real man beside him to talk to in the dark, any night he pleased.

"I know it hurts," Julianna said to him, when he was in one of his moods with her. "Ten times more when you're young." She knew.

Scanning through different articles, he found he was looking less for news than for Jolly's words. This was what he wanted: anything Jolly might have said to them that he hadn't heard yet. Jolly had always been good at explaining Nicky to himself, why he did things or felt things, and not just about sex or his various damages but the kind of person he was. The person he would be. Would he try to get Nicky a message? Would Nicky still matter, now that he was Caleb?

For all of Jolly's fits of paranoia, his short-lived epiphanies that school was a mistake, that they should sell the house and move to Canada, he had never really seen the end coming. He had never prepared Nicky for it. "You'll be okay without me" — had he

436

ever said that? So often, especially at night, Caleb tried to hear that in Jolly's voice. If the goddamn FBI had let him have *one minute* to say goodbye, he was sure it was what Jolly would have said. He'd lived with the man for a year and a half. What made them think one guarded minute through cell bars was going to hurt him?

He studied the new photo as if it could speak, but it looked all wrong, Jolly's eyes turned toward the camera but so dull he was not quite there, a dead man propped and posed in motion. As if he couldn't see that Caleb, Nicky, was right there looking at him — and that was it, of course. In Nicky's presence, he'd always been lit. At first it had been paradise, then almost a burden, the feeling that Jolly required skin contact or the sight of him in order to breathe. And if he'd slowly weaned himself, letting Nicky venture farther and farther from the house alone, Nicky had never once returned without that light coming on, Jolly's whole heated life force aimed his way. To see him so dimmed was a claw to the heart, like looking into a coffin, and he shut the link.

Under it sat the interview with Sarah Parkhurst, whose photo did not appear. In another week, but for the FBI's untimely arrival, she might have been his girlfriend. He'd begun to waylay her at her locker with flirty small talk, had already imagined what it would be like to kiss her in that spot, in front of everyone. Jolly would not have been thrilled, but in another way he would have loved it. As the prime cultivator of Nicky's public persona, he reveled in all the ways Nicky showed himself to be a regular kid, a popular one. He would have been concerned over whether Sarah was hot enough to enhance Nicky's standing with his posse of boys and beyond. First thing, they would have opened her Facebook page. . . .

His mother yawned, looked up at him. "Almost done?"

"Yeah," he said. "One more thing."

Why, why in hell, would Nick Lundy's Facebook page still be there, sitting where he'd left it? But it was. In seconds he was logged in. His profile photo looked extremely young to him — maybe it was the blond hair — with a kind of sleepy, smirking expression meant to be cool. There were some new postings on his wall, but oddly few, and that was because the page was accessible only by the thirty-three friends he'd collected from his school in Washington. There in the box of his friends, right on the profile page, was Sarah Parkhurst looking up at him, gloomily sexy in her purple eye shadow, and she'd posted on his wall: "I miss you Nick, or Caleb I guess. Hope your ok." (Jolly would have complained: "Oh, Nicky. Can't we find one that can spell?")

He opened the list of his thirty-three friends, thumbnail photos of familiar faces all the way down to Roy Thompson, his only friend whose hometown was not Providence, WA. Roy was a lanky kid with an overgrown sheaf of bangs pointed toward one eye — more than one girl had asked, "Who is that cute friend of yours?" and secretly they sent Roy messages, trying to draw him out. Roy did not respond to them. On his profile page, Roy listed for interests, "I like working on cars." He was a Christian; his hometown was "Trailerparkville, SD." Compared to the pages of other kids, Roy's was stark and empty. He had only one friend: Nick Lundy. There were no photos other than the profile shot, which was a polaroid of Jolly at fourteen, snapped in an actual trailer park in South Dakota by the man named Roy who'd taken him in after his so-called family fell apart. "Went to shit," was how Jolly put it — or he'd be stuck there still, probably a mechanic with his very own trailer, never having formed the notion that he might be smart enough to go to medical school.

Caleb's mother was up from the sofa and stood chatting with Greta, who was back behind the desk. Another guest who had wandered through earlier, eyeing the computer, returned, prompting his mother to say, "Cabe, almost done?" She'd taken to calling him Cabe in public, in case some stray tourist might recognize him.

"Yeah, one minute."

From the profile page, he clicked open a private message box. There was nothing in his head, no plan, only the sense that time was short. He wrote, "I'm in Nicaragua. Where are you?" and clicked Send. A few hours later, or at midnight when everyone was asleep, or the next morning as they were checking out of the hotel, hugging his father good-bye before loading into separate taxis, it would have been simple to log on again, briefly, just to check. A response, the chance of one, was beyond imagining. On the bus home from the border, crawling through switchbacks up the mountain, he could imagine no farther than his own words as they would appear, beside the photo of Nicky's sleepy, half-smiling face.

CHAPTER TWELVE

Lowell had been on the phone all morning. "Look, man, what can I tell you?" he said, as Marlene passed by from the dining room to the kitchen. "It happens. It's a foreign country. What's the saying, no free lunch? I know. It's" — he met Marlene's eyes — "bad luck, I guess."

The table near the window where she and Hilda and the kids had gathered for breakfast was too far from the phone for her to overhear Lowell, and he was on guard for anyone wandering into eavesdropping range. Still, Marlene caught a few more tidbits — something about the law, the cops, the courts, and references to some third party who could fix whatever had been broken. "This guy, I'm telling you, he's your best option. Ten, fifteen percent, it's a good deal at this point. I'll guarantee it's your best way out."

"What is all that about?" Hilda asked.

Marlene mimicked, "*Investments,* I assume. Management of property, and the like."

"Hmph." Hilda glanced at Lark and Caleb, who looked at each other. Lowell was so vague in his explanations of what exactly his business entailed that Hilda seemed to have decided it was drugs, if not something even more illicit. "That boy. I do wish he'd go back to teaching. Or if he must strike out on his own, I wish he'd take a little direction from Jeff. He's always had so many talents."

Marlene was starting to wonder about drugs herself, having glimpsed the links from Lowell to Stancia, Stancia to Petra. When Marlene began volunteering, Petra had been hostile at first over the idea that Marlene had come to learn to raise the orphans, any kind of young creature, and only that. "I can show her how to clean a cage," the girl had snapped at Stancia. "Sorry, but that's where she starts." Stancia flared back that Marlene was not "a *college intern*" and they could use the help. Marlene would work in the nursery for a few days, get some training, and then — since she lived far away, without a real vehicle — maybe she could take some birds home to foster.

Petra stewed for a while, but Marlene was not so far past her bohemian bar life that she couldn't convince a young person she was cool. Stancia was often away, and after a day of diligent chumminess Marlene had the girl in a full reversal. Now she and Petra were friends of a sort, with confidences. Once she'd gotten Petra to spill that she was dealing, Marlene had the freedom to ask almost anything. So what were Lowell and Stancia up to?

Petra shrugged. "She doesn't tell me. Something shady, right? Involving her family, I think?" Petra tried hard, Marlene could tell, to make neutral observations about Stancia, but they got away from her, veering between bitterness or worship. "I'm sure on Stancia's end it's about money for the animals. That's who she is."

And Petra seemed to Marlene in equal measure devoted to the animals. So did her narcotics enterprise also fund them? "Sure," Petra said, "it funds me, and I'm full-time help." But the answer didn't seem to align with the meaningful looks and hints of stress exchanged between Stancia and Petra. Maybe it was only that they were lovers, and secret ones if so — Marlene had not yet asked that. But Stancia made pointed references to money, and Petra gave every impression of being pressured into something she was not happy about. If it related to money, perhaps it was connected to whatever was going on between Stancia and Lowell.

"He's an interesting one," she said grimly to Hilda. Since Nicaragua, Marlene and Lowell had been somewhat less cozy. She'd disliked Jeff's implication of something between them, and Lowell had surely been hit with some of that as well, though he hadn't told her so, only asked if it was true that she and Jeff were separating. "For now," she said. He didn't ask what that would mean, only if she was okay, and she said fine, really fine, it was better this way, et cetera. Easy enough to predict that Lowell would skitter back like a frightened bug as soon as she looked available. And there was always the chance he was growing a conscience. On her side, she felt how she'd committed herself, at least for the present, to this alternate version of a family, and it flung all of Lowell's flaws into relief. Over these few days, they'd been struggling a little to find the rhythm that said nothing had changed, there had been nothing there *to* change.

When Lowell was off the phone, he got himself a cup of coffee and collapsed at their table with his face in one hand. "So," Marlene chirped, "how's business?"

"Fantastic. If a guy with a Texas accent calls, I am not here. In fact, tell him I left the country."

"Disgruntled customer?"

"Something like that."

"The guy who owns that land?" Lark piped up. Lowell slid her a quizzical look and she said, "You know, that place we went where the guy was and all the trees were chopped down."

"Where was this?" Hilda blinked to attention from a long gaze out the window, the inquiry aimed at Lark, who pressed her lips shut, looked at Lowell.

"A place," Lark said, uncertain, Lowell a little wild-eyed but failing to cover. "Where we went." Each word was laid down separately, then her next sentence picked up speed, having found a truth that sounded innocent. "Where a guy was cutting trees but Uncle Lowell told him not to."

"Just a property I sort of look after for someone," Lowell said, cautious, upright in his chair like an upright citizen. Then he relaxed, as if it all made sense. "Yeah, and so, that was the guy on the phone. From Texas. It's some squatters out there, the guys doing the cutting. I tried to stop them.

And of course to get them out of there, but . . . too late, I guess."

"You call the police," Hilda said. "The police will move them out."

"I did. But they're saying it's too late, they've been there long enough." His eyes flicked over the kids, Marlene. "Squatters gets rights in this country pretty quick. Throw up half a tin shack and it's basically theirs."

Hilda watched him narrowly. "What property is this?"

"Oh, out a ways, down lower. It's . . . far. You wouldn't know it." Lowell sipped his coffee. Hilda looked keen, as if she'd caught him at something. Depending on the crime, she might not call him on it. With Jeff the Vincent darling, Hilda had always and often seemed to Marlene at secret pains to correct the imbalance, tsking and shaking her head as she cleaned up Lowell's messes, doctored his flaws.

Caleb, spotting the opportunity to help his uncle and himself at once, said, "Hey, Lowell, can you take me and Isabel into town later? Like in an hour?"

Lowell turned to him, said "Well, *sure,* let's see," and applied himself to the details with more vigor than necessary.

Lark frowned at Marlene, disliking these

arrangements that would not include her. "Is it time to feed the birds yet?"

"Close enough, I guess."

Lark leapt up to follow. Marlene had been sent home with four of a species she'd been told she couldn't break too easily, or that the world could spare if she did, despite their exotic, important-sounding name: Montezuma Oropendola. They were hefty chunks of birdlet bristling with pin feathers and long, pointed beaks. Grown, they'd be crowlike, with cinnamon bodies and yellow tails. When hungry they squalled like hornets, and she fed them once an hour or more, sunrise to sunset, dog kibble soaked soft with water. With her fingers she poked one piece at a time down each throat until the mouths stopped opening for more. The birds varied in age, being from different nests that had blown down in a colony, but all were strong, with suction in their throats that seemed ready to swallow her fingertips. Lark wanted to feed them, but they were unnerving in their voracity, and she usually stopped after one mouthful and watched Marlene finish.

"We should name them," Lark said, leaning at her arm.

"No names, because they're not pets. They belong to themselves."

They had already talked about how the birds were not to be touched or even looked at apart from feedings. Lark, of course, knew as much as Marlene did about the species. There was a colony of them in an old dairy field near the Finca, easy to spot with its many woven nests drooping like stockings from one tree. The males kept harems of females and displayed for them all day, emitting a watery musical call as they flung themselves over the trapeze of a branch, wings thrown wide, and righted themselves again.

"So when they're grown," Lark said, "maybe they can join our colony, right?"

"That would be nice." Marlene had been considering these questions, though she wasn't sure how much influence she would have over their future. Stancia seemed to open cage doors on a whim, the instant she noticed that the orphans inside had grown enough. Clear them out, make room. Except when it concerned the more unusual or endangered species, everyone was simply too busy filling mouths and cleaning cages to think about an individual animal or ef- fective methods of release.

"They already know you're the food lady," Lark said. "How will they know they're themselves?"

"Well, that's a big thing I'm wondering about." She tapped a spongy chunk down the smallest one's throat until it gave a satisfying gobble. "Stancia says maybe they'll look at each other, imprint that way. We could also try to feed them through a blind, so they can't see us. You know, let's try that — right now, before they get too full." She had meant to do this from the start, and here it was the birds' second day in the house. Even with only four to think of, she'd been distracted with the process of feeding and keeping them clean, and then everyone wanted to look at them, including her.

Making a feeding blind, it turned out, was harder than it sounded. After much debate and trial and error, she and Lark relocated the birds to Marlene's bedroom, where they'd be less exposed to human voices, and composed a wall of towels clothespinned to random items recruited to the purpose: a bucket, a lamp, the bed table. This seemed the best way to let the birds have daylight while also keeping them contained and accessible. But Marlene had to scoot along the floor on knees and elbows to keep them from seeing her, and then could not see well enough herself through the clipped towels to tell what she was feeding or cleaning.

Food became lodged in the grooves of beak or elsewhere on the squat bodies, and she had to lift the birds out and clean them — so much for any positive effect of the separation. She was sweaty, dirty, and exhausted from one feeding, and the birds probably felt the same. No wonder Stancia, with her vast numbers and species, could not be bothered with blinds for any but the most delicate — though had Jeff been there, he might have engineered some simple marvel of functionality in five minutes.

"Well, that's a mess," she said to Lark as they closed the door to the room. "We'll have to think about this some more." What she wouldn't say to Lark was that she was already wishing the birds gone. They were a pain, and she was clearly unable to provide them anything of value beyond the meager care on which they would probably fade and die. Stancia, every morning on her back porch, made the rounds of incubators and collected a small heap of corpses that had passed in the night, most from an unknown cause. These she tossed into a bucket to be fed to something else.

In the main lodge, Isabel had arrived and was sitting on the sofa with Caleb, his hair damp from the shower. Marlene, with Lark beside her, paused to spy from the opposite

side of the bar. They might have been training binoculars on the colony of oropendolas
across the misty field. On the sofa, the
couple sat curled to face each other, holding hands. They were talking, too quietly to
be overheard.

How had it happened? A few days before,
the morning after their return from the visa
run, Isabel and Caleb had gone for a walk
in the forest, out to the old zip-line platform
that Lowell had considered his secret lair of
doobage until the kids found it. "She has to
tell me something" — Caleb's offhanded
reference to some intrigue from Isabel's
trip, all quite as usual. They were gone for
hours, returned holding hands. Or had they
left that way? Marlene had been busy elsewhere, not really paying attention, and when
she caught sight of them out in the billowy
white of the garden, wandering through the
pink bananas with their heads bowed together, their hands joined, she had to blink
and look again, ask herself if this was new
or if she had seen it before.

"What is *that*?" she said, thunderstruck.

Hilda, beside her, smiled out the window.
"Well, it's about time."

"It is?"

She recalled well enough his brooding
over Isabel and some boy in Cartago —

451

surely a factor in today's meeting if not its topic. And what male had ever needed more reason than a rival to make him perk up and notice a girl? But of course it was that predictability, as much as anything, that left her bewildered.

From the garden, they had entered the house still hand in hand, walked up to Marlene and Hilda, and spoke about ordinary things as if their joined state were nothing new. Or Caleb did; Isabel had gone shy, ducking a bit from their inquiring glances. Her departure for some requirement at home was a tragedy that took them off to a corner, well in view, for an hour of murmuring.

Marlene's first thought was of Isabel's father, a frightening man with limited English, with whom she spoke on occasion in town; Isabel's mother seemed friendlier but spoke less English. "Her parents," Marlene said to Hilda in the kitchen. "There's no way they're going to go for this."

Once, in town, as Marlene struggled through pleasantries with Señor Rosales outside the supermercado, Isabel had come up with Caleb at her side to ask some permission, and then the two of them had gone off together down the street. "Your son is a good boy," the man said sternly, like a command, watching them go. She got the distinct impression he meant to say *Your son had better be a good boy.* Or maybe, *I don't trust you people in the least, but if I declare this to be true it will be.*

Hilda said, "Oh, they like Caleb." This was news to Marlene. "Isabel has more rules than a lot of the girls in this town, and I'm sure they'll be watchful of her. But I doubt they'd stop her from dating. They might actually be happy. She could do worse."

"They won't care that he's a gringo?"

"That's half of why they like him."

Marlene blinked, shook her head. "And is this a good idea?" She forgot, sometimes, how little she spoke of Caleb's history, how little others knew of even the little she did.

"We'll find out, won't we?" Hilda pursed her lips, considered. "They're good kids. Both of them. I feel certain."

This shifted everything in Marlene's mind, all her concern having pooled at Caleb's potential heartbreak if the relationship were forbidden. Had she hoped for such a barrier? Her unease was diffuse, hard to name. She wanted his therapist on the phone, saying something reasonable about how a girlfriend, so soon, was not advisable. And what was Isabel getting herself into?

But the instant she sat Caleb down, her

objections fell apart at the look on his face. It was restrained exhilaration, the earnest, open face of a child. With Isabel fastened to his arm she had noticed a strange new quality to his demeanor, and here it was again: his guardedness was gone. He was inviting her in.

"So how did all this happen?" she asked, suddenly thrilled, even if not quite ready to trust the reality of it, the too-perfect normalcy. "I thought you two had settled on just being friends."

"I don't know. I just decided." He leaned in, pleased with himself. He might have been reporting to her on some complicated maneuver they had planned together. "I think I was nervous before, but it was really easy. Like, to switch."

"So I guess she didn't take too much convincing?"

He shook his head, suppressing a smile. "She was kind of surprised, but no, I guess not much."

"Well." She stroked his hair, which was getting long enough to flop over his forehead. "I'm happy for you. Just be careful, okay? I don't want you getting hurt. Or upsetting her parents. I think you know, too, that Isabel is a very sheltered girl. I'm sure she's never had a boyfriend; she's very . . ."

Innocent, she wanted to say, and the word caught in her throat with all its multiple implications of what he was not. Was it too soon to be talking about sex?

"I know," he said.

"Just don't . . . get too serious. And I want you to talk about all of this with your therapist. That's important."

He nodded, almost eagerly. A day later, she'd worked herself up to a more direct broaching of the sex topic, and he answered with disarming composure: "I know. We know. Nothing's gonna happen, I promise."

Even to her, it seemed an absurd thing to believe so easily, but over the next couple of days, when Isabel was often at the Finca, she had ample opportunity to back up belief with observation. Their demand for privacy was minimal. As if they'd agreed to a chaperone — and maybe they had, for Hilda had taken on the task of reporting each day to Isabel's parents — they no longer walked into the woods or went to Caleb's room as they used to, but instead cozied up in some corner of the Finca's public space, where mostly they talked. Kisses were rare and brief.

Lowell doubted it was real, and maybe he was right. He'd confided to Marlene that he and Caleb had talked about whether people

455

in town thought Caleb was gay, and that Caleb had become upset. All along, she'd been continually astounded by how well Caleb hid his scars, as if he'd suffered no damage at all, and she knew now that being the unbroken son they wanted was his first guideline for any action. (God, she thought sometimes, he must be terrified of us.) If he saw a way to appear normal, he'd take it, and how simple and effortless was it to take the hand of a girl who was right next to him? One gesture canceled half a dozen concerns.

But, Marlene contended, that didn't have to mean it wasn't also authentic.

"Let's think of something better for those birds," she said to Lark, who moped all day in Marlene's shadow. The birds were a lucky arrival, a distraction and a project for the two of them as they waited for school to start again, only a day away now.

"You should make them a mom," Lark said. "Like a mom puppet."

Marlene said, "Ha-ha. I can barely feed them with my hand."

In Washington, the posse of boys who had known him as Nick Lundy had come to him by way of the boy next door and some of Jolly's subtle, behind-the-curtain management. Starting high school together, they had no fixed place yet in the social strata but were the right mix of college-bound, athletic, Christian, and reasonably good-looking to get their small chances at experience without being likely to go off the rails. Of them, only Nick had done real drugs, though the list he provided them was abridged. He slayed in any contest of sexual knowledge. But what impressed them most and sealed his privileged place in the pack was that he was not a virgin. A few had proffered shaky claims to hand jobs and blow jobs, all of which crumbled before the knowing bespectacled gaze of Nick — the shrimpiest of them all, the odd one they'd dubbed Homeschool at first — who had actually fucked a girl.

This was true, though as with the drugs, he was obliged to modify or suppress some details. For instance, he left out that Jolly had arranged it. Also that the girl was a prostitute, and that Jolly had watched. It was a gift, a chance for Nicky to see what girls were like. "It didn't suck," he told the boys with a lazy hint of a smile, when they pressed for an assessment, and this was also true. "But, I don't know, it didn't make me see God or anything." Maybe the letdown was the fault of the girl — "some skank," he called her, no one he knew. Between the girl and Jolly, he'd have picked Jolly. Yet afterward he still felt attracted to girls. Maybe, Jolly said, because girls felt safer. Or he might be bisexual, like Jolly's "father," Roy, who'd had a common-law wife named Beetie and had moved freely between their two beds. Even after Roy died and Jolly was grown, he still considered Beetie his mother, and she was Nicky's grandmother, a hairdresser who bleached and cut his hair whenever she was in town.

"An older one," Jolly had said to the man in charge, "fifteen or so. Very calm, very experienced." The event had not been planned, and this girl, called Yolanda, was naked from the waist down and splayed on the bed before Nicky could guess why she'd come into the room. "Don't be ridiculous," Jolly said, grinning and giddy. "She's for you, of course." The surprise of it helped somehow, as did Jolly's presence. Nicky could still be timid, prudish about sex — Jolly was forever calling him "sweet" over one thing or another — and with the girl he couldn't help hesitating, asking permission for every touch, looking to Jolly, who slumped in a nearby chair, one hand over his mouth and the flux of his expression: love, arousal, fear, anguish.

"Mírame. Look at me, no him," Yolanda said with a little smile. She was placid as a cat, amused to be his first, and once Jolly got ahold of himself, the two of them began to talk him through it in a festive, companionable way that helped him relax.

He wore his first condom. The boys wanted to know about that: "Did you wear a raincoat?" And "How was your, uh, performance?" He said she seemed to like it. Yolanda and Jolly had both assured him he was a stud, so there was that, an accomplishment for his résumé. But afterward he'd felt sad that in all his blundering he'd forgotten to try kissing her. The lie would have come easily, if it had occurred to his posse to ask if he'd ever kissed a girl.

Isabel, then, had been his first. Having already planted one on her in Luis's room without much noticing the novelty, he figured doing it for real wouldn't be so hard. They climbed up to the zip-line platform, where the fog was dense and drifting. She pressed him for advice on Internet Scott. She was flushed, pretty, her plum lips parted, her hair gauzed in tiny beads of condensed cloud. "Do you think I should meet him?"

"No," he said, more nervous than he'd thought possible. When he leaned to kiss her, his heart was shaking his whole body, as if he'd never kissed anyone. Their mouths barely touched. He sat back, waited out her blinking shock, and she smiled and closed her eyes for another.

After that it was simpler. The strangest part was the feelings that came with it. By the time Lowell dropped them in town for their debut as a couple three days in, Caleb thought he might be in love. Tangled up in this feeling was that he'd told Isabel so much he'd never planned to, only because she'd long ago sensed his secrets the way girls did, because she sat before him wide-eyed and waiting to sponge up his pain. He wasn't such a mystery to her. He'd been abused, by someone long gone. His ghost was another child he'd known, also abused. She didn't mind that he remained almost this vague; in fact, she was poised to nod at his smallest hint. She wanted to be the one who understood.

It was a strange sort of accident. Violating the rule of *never say it,* he discovered that telling one person was almost the opposite of telling everyone. Had he invented it from nothing, he couldn't have devised a swifter means to win her love, her devotion.

In town, they strolled along the street and into every store, holding hands. It was perfect. Caleb brought money to buy batidos, shaved ice, sugared figs, any tidbit Isabel fancied, and she was in heaven, trying to pretend she didn't care about running into other kids she knew, making headlines, inciting jealousy.

If he were Nick Lundy in Washington, walking the North Providence mall with Sarah Parkhurst, he would have been more aloof; he would have actually been thinking more about sex, because that was Nick, the regular boy. Who was he now? Damaged, for sure. Too damaged to be anything like regular, though it was the reason Isabel could be so at ease and he could be generous, cuddling her and whispering stupid things just to seal their privacy. They walked past his British friend Harold, who surely looked twice, though Caleb didn't even glance up from nuzzling Isabel's hair.

In Soda La Perla, a boy from their class muttered in Spanish to his friends, and Isabel gazed on him with voluminous pity. No one could make her unhappy. "He is jealous," she said to Caleb. "The girls are worse. I say we let them all eat their hearts out." She said this tipped against his chest, almost nose to nose, and he fingered the bangs back from her forehead as the cluster of kids moved past them and out the door, staring. Even Caleb knew that Isabel with a boyfriend should have been radiating insecurity. Give her Nick Lundy's hand to hold, and her eyes would be darting everywhere, her voice louder, and before they'd made it down one street of town she'd be silent with imagined hurt or hiding in some bathroom, just because Nick was in one way or another being a boy. With Caleb, she was serene. They both were. Maybe the others would think it was because that American kid didn't know how to act right.

Chin on her shoulder, Caleb studied the dry-erase menu board, all in Spanish, though he pretty much knew the food words now. *Casado,* for instance, Miguelita's mainstay, had been for him a mixed lunch plate long before he learned it meant *married.* No one stood behind the counter, though Miguelita's son, a brawny beauty with hair clipped close to his head, was bussing tables. Manny. Luis had a crush on him, or claimed to, not that it was hard to believe. Manny was shy, sweet, and Caleb had seen him send a look or two in Luis's direction that could have passed for interest.

"Are you hungry? Split some plantains?"

Isabel tipped her face back. "Only if you want."

Luis appeared in the doorway of the back room. "Here is the happy couple," he said. His look was fathoms deep — those fantastic facial shadows, unaided by cosmetics. That he was wearing a dress escaped Caleb's notice at first because he looked so natural in it, a casual drape of peach and white.

"You heard?" Delighted, Isabel curled their joined hands up beneath her chin as if displaying a ring.

"How could I not? Quite a surprise." Luis, arms crossed, examined them narrowly. He took his time before granting a smile. "That is lovely for you. I should get for you something to eat. To celebrate, yes?" He went behind the counter as if he worked there, began naming items that were good. "Miguelita, she would insist, I think. She is a big fan of love." His voice carried a note of something between zest and anger. Or Caleb was only listening for the attack.

He had already faced her parents, a brief sofa sit-down at which he was fed sliced fruit and asked questions about his interests that had not mattered until now. No one had alluded to their status as a couple, but her father shook Caleb's hand as he left and also smiled once, which felt like the approval Isabel had promised. Ranito and some of her other cousins were less than pleased, she reported — no surprise. He hadn't asked what Luis might think, but knew that facing him might be tougher than facing any of the others. If anyone could puncture his balloon, it would be Luis.

"You can share, I assume." Luis placed on a table one plate loaded high with arroz con pollo and plantains and one can of guava soda, and beckoned them to sit. "Maybe you can share a fork, too. I don't know," he said, though he provided two napkin-wrapped sets. He opened the can for them. "Go on, eat! It is good today. I have eaten it already."

They thanked him and began picking bites from the plate. Caleb wasn't hungry; he ate only to be polite as Luis sat across from them looking satisfied. "So tell me, *how* did this happen? This, this —" He gestured as if indicating something they had spilled on themselves.

"It just did," Isabel said, with the emphatic gusto of someone telling a fascinating story.

Luis rolled his eyes. "I would like more details, please. Then I will be able to make sure the right story is told. You do not want falsehoods to be spread around town, do you?"

"Like what?" Caleb asked.

Isabel, poking through rice, said, "Don't be a cow. We are adorable, and you are jealous." In these few days, even in her usual banter with her cousin, her voice had altered toward her general serenity. Holding Caleb's hand seemed equivalent to holding a baby, an act that matured her five years. She laid her head on his shoulder. "We were friends, and then we realized we are meant to be more than friends. This story you can tell anyone who asks."

Luis looked to Caleb for confirmation. "Maybe we're soul mates," Caleb said, unable to resist Luis's term for his fútbol player, Ale-Za. Isabel smiled up at him, liking that.

"Oh, that is sweet," Luis said. "And you must share so much, yes? You have someone now to tell all your secrets to." This was directed to Caleb.

"Yeah, well," he said. "I guess that's what you do in a relationship."

Luis blinked, caught off guard. "I see." He looked to Isabel, disbelieving, and she answered with a little wide-eyed nod.

"I doubt it's what you think it is," she said, chewing. "He told me everything there is to know. It is just about some things that happened to him in the past."

For a queasy second, this felt like the vault

slipping open, but she was done speaking, and Caleb perceived the subtle sting in her words. They all knew this. They called it by the name of *ghost,* their one concrete clue to the mystery. Isabel was saying she knew and Luis would not.

"Is it?" Luis said pointedly to Caleb, as if he knew better. Until this moment, Caleb had almost forgotten all Luis's lies, which came back on a tide of hurt and anger, and his body tightened with an urge to throw a punch or the plate of food. Instead he returned Luis's gaze coldly and said nothing, which was all the truth he figured Luis deserved.

"Well," Luis said, looking away first. "You be careful with my cousin. Or I will have to come after you." A punch might have hurt Luis less, and Caleb's triumph was touched with remorse, a feeling that he was losing something. But it needed to be lost — kicked aside, crammed into a hole, covered with dirt and forgotten.

"Yes, be careful with me," Isabel said to Caleb, smiling as if to say, *See?* As if they had gotten away with something.

It was all so much easier than he'd expected. He felt powerful and calm, fortified by Isabel. He had a girlfriend. Here, it seemed, was *Caleb,* this essence of himself he called Caleb, stepping out of hiding and looking more impressive than he'd dared to hope. With a girl on his arm, he announced himself, and if no one could call bullshit, then why shouldn't he go on becoming this person, himself, before his own eyes? Soon even his father would look and say, *There he is. That's him.*

At four o'clock, Isabel had to meet her father and some hotel guests at the travel agency. Caleb went with her, stood holding her hand as she introduced herself to a honeymooning young couple from the States. "This is my boyfriend, Caleb," she said, hesitating over the word she had not yet tried before others. The perky young woman started to say something, then stopped. "You look so familiar!" she said. "Sweetie, who does he look like? Mary's boy?"

"Kind of," the guy said. The town was crawling with these fresh American tourists who, unlike the long-term residents, had likely been soaked in the news of him. But these, he realized with a start, were the first he'd been introduced to.

The bride, grinning, swiped the air in dismissal. "I don't know. Probably someone from TV."

They wouldn't know his face, he reminded himself. They might know Caleb the eleven-year-old, or Nicky. The one who had come home Caleb Vincent had effectively evaded the cameras.

"Let's wait outside," he said into Isabel's ear. The newlyweds smiled with understanding. Young love!

Outside, they leaned against the wall talking over the impressions they had made in town, and he played with her hair until her father's van pulled up to the curb. Caleb had been planning to ride along with them to the fork, but he told her he thought he'd stay behind instead; he had things to do in town. He'd see her at school. "At the bus stop," she corrected him. "Come early."

Besides needing to stay clear of the Americans, he wanted to walk through town without her, to see if the new Caleb remained. Also, his e-mail had gone unchecked for five days, since Nicaragua, and he felt that in his solid new selfhood he could just about stand to look. He resisted the urge to head back toward Luis, hammer his point a little harder. A second encounter was sure to get complicated and end badly.

Outside the Internet café was the pack of eleventh graders that ran loose in town at all hours, flaunting their freedom, boozing

468

in the dim corners of bars; whenever they were stationary, at least one pair of them would be on top of each other, making out. "Hey," a boy said to him, with an upward jerk of his chin, "you dating Isabel now?" Caleb said he was. The boy, Greibin, was king of this group. Isabel had an obvious crush on him, not that he'd ever consider a lowly ninth grader. He gave Caleb a light punch in the shoulder. "Good for you, man." Another of the boys gave him a nod. Caleb grinned and said, "See ya" with a wave as he went inside, hoping he didn't look too thrilled.

No one he knew was inside, though most of the machines were in use. He paid for an hour. In the only mailbox he had, the "cvincent" one he'd been given at school, Julianna's last plea sat unanswered. He was surprised to have no new message from her, since he had not called either, and she seemed to have a rule that she wouldn't contact him by phone. All he could do was log in to Facebook as Nick Lundy and see what was there.

What he'd thought of, what had been worrying him as much as anything, was that any message sent to his Facebook page would be copied into Nick Lundy's e-mail. And the FBI had that. Maybe Julianna herself received red-flagged alerts whenever someone contacted him there. Maybe they monitored the Facebook page too. They could have left it up as a trap and he'd walked into it, led Jolly in after him.

For Jolly, or someone, had answered. The reply was two lines long. The first was a fragment, the answer to his question *Where are you?*: "Home, where I wish you were." The second, dropped below, was not exactly a sentence either:

earnest judgment impedes eager hounds, don't count foxes before dawn

It was a shock, first to see a response, then to see so little in it. It felt like a rejection. After all this time, no contact since Nicky had left for school one normal-seeming morning, Jolly should have gushed for pages.

He read it again slowly. The first line was reassurance. The second was something like *Wait, be patient.* Meaning more would come later? But the most riveting element was the grammar. Why no capital letter, no end punctuation? *Pay attention,* it said, because Jolly would never omit these from laziness, or use a comma splice besides. *Earnest judgment impedes eager hounds.* . . . Like a Latin translation, or Greek — they had attempted to learn Greek for a while until Nicky rebelled at the difficulty. He tried to parse it from scratch. Hounds would be the FBI, the eager agents who might be reading this even now, so Jolly was the fox. *Don't count foxes* — like don't count chickens? Don't make assumptions? Maybe the message was that he wasn't caught, would evade them yet.

Caleb typed the phrase into Google, got nothing. With no pen or paper, he opened a Word document and typed it in. He typed it again more slowly. Ten words.

It sounded like a mnemonic. *Every good boy does fine,* the notes of the treble clef. Jolly had a dozen of these for medical things. The bones of the wrist: *Slowly lower Tommy's pants to the curly hairs.* He pulled initial letters of each word, *ejiehdcfbd,* but he couldn't guess what they'd correspond to. Maybe some other kind of puzzle. As part of his homeschooling, they had worked through half a book of word puzzles, then got distracted by something else. Anagrams, for instance. He started pulling letters out, rearranging. He pulled the final letters, *ttsrsttsen,* then letters in numerical succession, *euped,* before it fell apart. He pulled every other letter, every third letter. He arranged the words on top of each other. He wrote the words backward, then the letters of each word.

"Fuck, Jolly," he muttered at the screen.

Don't get frustrated, he heard Jolly say. They were side by side at the attic school table, working a puzzle. Nicky tended to slam books shut, throw things, if he didn't grasp a problem's mechanism right away. *It's never as hard as it looks.* He remembered this too. Jolly showed him the answer, and it was almost always so simple he'd gone right past it.

Turn the question around: What did Jolly need to say? Something private, something that had to be obscured from spies. If he'd wanted to tell Nicky he was free, the hounds had failed, he could have just said it. Likewise, he could have said *I love you, I miss you, how are you? Be brave.* And why *not* say these things? Why give him so little? He looked at the initial letters again, none farther into the alphabet than *j,* and counted up to *j* on his fingers. Tenth letter. Ten words total. He typed the numbers that corresponded to each letter. After the first three, 509, he knew. All his calls to Julianna had burned into his brain that 509 was the area code for Washington.

He borrowed a pen, wrote it out on a receipt in his pocket. He deleted the Word document, then signed out of Facebook and off the machine, leaving Jolly's message unanswered like Julianna's. Ten digits, a rope tossed from a boat into open water. Just having hold of it was calming. He wasn't sure what else to do with it. An hour later, the need to call surged upon him, then subsided as fast into nothing. Came again, retreated.

After dinner, he said he was going to call Julianna. He went to dial the number but couldn't finish. He wasn't afraid, exactly — he couldn't be afraid of Jolly — only overwhelmed in that moment, phone to his ear, with what to say. There was too much. And Caleb was a different person now. He had a family, a girlfriend, he lived in Costa Rica; he had no business crossing time and space, upsetting the universal order, to touch his old life. He put the receiver back in its cradle and sat crouched under the desk with the phone in his lap for a long time. School was starting the next day, and he pictured how it would go: whispering with Isabel on the bus, holding her hand on the hike up to their first-period hut, the various semi-public spots around the school grounds where he could steal a kiss. He was looking forward to the audience, to seeing how Ana would respond.

Some hours past midnight, after Caleb and all the Vincents had gone to sleep, it was Nicky who woke up and made his way along the dark hall and up the stairs, threading the tables of the dining room and ducking under the desk with the phone. "Nicky," Jolly said. "I would know your voice anywhere."

CHAPTER THIRTEEN

At first Lark's idea sounded ridiculous. Feeding nestling birds was tricky enough without involving a puppet in the process. But Marlene began to dream in papier mâché. Lark's best guidebook showed the Montezuma Oropendola as a bird with a face that wanted to be recreated: a narrow black head neatly tapering into a lancelike beak bright orange at the tip as if dipped in wax, a bald patch of pale blue under each eye, a demure pinkish wattle. The puppet, she decided, might not need to feed them. She could lure their attention with the mother's face and slip the food in with her own hand underneath.

Art school had not given her much practice in papier mâché, but she knew it was simple enough, and most of the supplies could be found at the Finca: flour, cardboard, masking tape, back issues of the *Tico Times*. The bird's head, all she needed to make, was the simplest of shapes, a long cone just large enough for fingers to fit inside. After she found some better photographs, it was only a matter of playing with the dimensions, building small details — beak grooves, wattle, inset eyes — experimenting with toilet paper and paper towels to mimic the texture of feathers, the bare patches of skin. She cut the beak at the natural mouth line so that fingers inside could scissor it open slightly on a hinge of masking tape. At the drugstore in town she found acrylic paints, as well as a sketchpad and charcoal pencils, and she began to sketch from the Finca's colony while looking through binoculars, or sitting in the Internet café from photos online. The sketches were not strictly needed, but she'd forgotten the pleasure of rendering life on good paper, a pastime while the layers of papier mâché dried. It took her three days to fashion a working model, a week to make one she was happy with, a slick and beautiful replica of a mother oropendola.

By this time, the birds were fledged, hopping around, ready to learn to feed themselves. They were so big and active she had to shut them in her shower with some sturdy tree limbs set on the floor as perches, feed them through the cracked-open door.

Though she left them bowls of softened kibble to pick at, they crowded the door when it opened, caterwauling for attention, and she went in first with the puppet. Birds are highly visual, Stancia had told her, and oriented to color. All those dazzling avian hues would not be there if birds were color-blind like most mammals — they use color to find their own kind, to attract and choose mates. Since their new enclosure did not allow her to hide herself very well, she wore a veil of mosquito netting, so at least they would not see a human face. The trick partly worked. She succeeded in getting the babies to beg from the puppet, and she drew their gaze with it while she poked food into their throats with her other hand, but if they saw the hand go to the food bowl they would follow and beg from it as readily. Once they were sated she sat very still on the shower floor behind the puppet, preening the babies with the puppet's orange beak tip, and they responded with drowsy trills and wing flutters as they drifted to sleep.

She didn't want to give them up while they were still taking hand-feedings, but they had to learn to fly and feed themselves. Reluctantly she returned them to Stancia, saw them put into a flight cage, where they would take their own kibble from the bowl or starve. They were not hers. "How will you know if they're eating? How will they learn to find natural food?" No one had time for these questions. No one had time to hide live insects under leaves in the floor of their cage, were such a feat even possible. All she could do was secure a promise that when they were of age, she could release them at the Finca's colony. Stancia preferred to release the songbirds directly from the center, where they could return for hand-outs from the stocked feeders, but Marlene promised to visit the colony daily with bowls of kibble, banking on the remote chance that the bewildered orphans, knowing nothing, would choose to stay near these marginally familiar creatures and might find the food she left before scavengers did.

Stancia was impressed with her papier-mâché puppet. Marlene was a little impressed herself — it was beautiful. She would have preferred better eyes, made of glass, but otherwise she'd been able to get the proportions and colors and textures to mimic life recognizably, if a few degrees richer and shinier. "Too bad we have no more oropendolas right now," Stancia said, trying it on her hand.

But there was no shortage of other species. "I would have said you could take as many of these as you want," Stancia said, indicating a box of songbirds, smaller than the oropendolas and all mixed in together: kiskadees, clay-colored robins, grackles, a few other common, hearty species that would take no special skill to nurture. "But that won't work, I see, the mixture. Maybe you need something a little fancier that wants a puppet mother, yes? Like these." Stancia slid a box forward from the back of a table. "Can you guess?"

The three pin-feathered nestlings inside were smaller and rounder than the oropendolas. They were shaped like parrots, and a few feathers on their backs were opening parrot-green tips, but the beaks were pointed. "Blue-crowned motmots," Stancia said. "We hardly ever get babies because they nest in burrows. Some bad little boys dug these up."

Marlene knew the motmot, a favorite of Lark's. One lived near the school-bus stop, where it could generally be counted on to be perched on the same tree limb in precisely the same spot, very still, its long, paddle-tipped tail hanging down. Several crippled adults were housed in the barn, so Marlene went out to examine them: chunky, big-headed, no-neck birds with crimson eyes, a black bandit mask beneath an iridescent blue halo, the rest green. She took out her sketchpad and began to draw the head to scale. "They will make a pretty model, won't they?" Stancia said. "Maybe you can work your way through all the birds. We will then have mothers for all of them."

"But does it even help?" Marlene wondered, knowing the answer wouldn't alter what she did. "Do you think it changed anything for those oropendolas?"

Stancia shrugged. "It couldn't hurt them."

"My little hobby," she told Lowell, during their postdinner cocktail hour on his porch. "I think making these birds might be more interesting than raising them."

"And this is somehow about Caleb?" Lowell had shaved, a rare occurrence that left him looking scrubbed and new.

"It was. From the outside there's a metaphor, you know? But the more I get into the details of it, the more I lose the connection."

"Why not look at those jaguars? They were with their mother until they were like half grown, then taken by strangers for however many years. Now the question is getting them back where they belong."

She nodded, grim. "Yeah, and what am I

going to *do* exactly? Make myself a full-body jaguar outfit?"

Lowell chuckled. "Then they eat you. I bet you'd be delicious."

"Birds are about my speed. Plus they imprint more predictably, so I'm told. You know, that mother jaguar was shot, but if she wasn't? If those cats could be put back in the wild with their very own mother, she wouldn't recognize them. Or they her. They'd probably kill each other. I don't know — like Stancia says, maybe an animal is just itself. It doesn't . . . have a message. It doesn't tell us anything." She shrugged, finished her drink. "Anyway, I'm learning something. And helping, a little. Maybe it's good, being involved in something unrelated to him." She shook the ice in her glass, contemplating another in the breezy damp of the night garden. "Hey," she said, thinking of it, "what was that business out in the garden with the Rosales boy today?"

"You saw that, did you?" He crooked a finger for her to follow into his room. Inside a zippered jacket pocket was a plastic bag he did not extract but opened under her nose. The herbal aroma was heady and dense. He brought it to his own face and inhaled, gave a little groan of sexual bliss. "Some extraordinary shit, can you tell? Local, organic, sustainable, just generally good for the planet and all. Wanna take a walk out to my fort?"

"That is tempting."

"Aw, c'mon, what could it hurt? Did I mention organic?"

Everyone else was upstairs, Lark paging through the bird books Marlene had borrowed from Stancia, Caleb on the phone, Hilda around somewhere. "I'll just go let them know —" she said, but then shouting broke out upstairs. Caleb.

"You don't listen! I'm done with you, I'm done! Leave me alone —"

Jogging up the steps, she caught "pervert" and "child molester" amid the shouting, then a loud cracking sound. In the dining room, Lark sat wide-eyed at a table and Caleb, back by the phone, was on his feet, smashing the receiver repeatedly against the desktop until some piece of it flew loose. When Marlene reached him he was sobbing into his hands, saying, "You fucking evil cunt." She took him by the shoulders — the height and proportion of her own — then thought to retrieve the phone in case the line was still open and hang up the broken receiver.

"I'm sorry. Fucking Julianna. Fuck her." The tears were past, but he seemed ready to collapse, blinking dazedly. "I . . . have to call her and apologize, I guess."

"Not right now."

Lowell stood at a little distance with his arm around Lark, waiting for triage; Hilda peered up from her staircase in the corner, and Marlene breathed, oddly calm. A meltdown, finally, and she somehow had the right question ready, casual and direct. "You want to talk to me or Lowell? Pick one."

"You," he said, no hesitation, as if the easy tone of her question had chosen for him. She waved the others off, took him to the sofa. All week, under Isabel's influence, he'd been relaxed and accessible. She hadn't seen him write once in the journal. He talked more, usually about Isabel and their day at school, and a few times he'd become animated in ways she'd never seen — breathless and somewhat erratic in speech, his eyes extra wide and his smiles twitchy, like a happy person on half a hit of speed. Lark said she'd seen it before. "He does that sometimes, like when he starts talking. He gets excited."

"I'm just tired of her using me." He took off his glasses and rubbed the lenses with his shirt, pressed at his eyes with the back of an arm. "She's an adult, and I'm a kid, right? And she wants me to do her job for her."

"I thought you'd want to help her. You seem to like her so much." Marlene had an assignment here, like Caleb's. Mitch had alerted her that Caleb was cooling on Julianna, shutting down, that he might need a nudge of encouragement if they were to have any hope of locking up Charles Lundy.

"I just want to get on with my life." He replaced the glasses and drew his knees up in a tight huddle, looking away. "Don't I deserve my own fucking life?"

"Of course. But, you know, maybe your life has to start with closing that door first. Telling all the truth there is, all you have."

His face was half buried in his arms, only his hooded red eyes visible, not looking at her. "So it's for my own good?"

She might have said something like that, but the edge in his voice made her careful. "You could do it for me," she suggested. "I think I have almost as much trouble as you do with the past, after these years of looking for you, just wanting you home. It's hard to go forward, knowing he's out there, unpunished. And I wish you didn't have to be involved, or that you could wait until you were older, but this is your one chance to have your say, to make a difference."

She hoped not saying the name would keep him unreactive, pondering, and it seemed to. He tensed but stayed quiet, still not looking at her. Her notion, half formed in her last talk with Mitch, was that Caleb might be guided by that ruling quality that most worried her: his tractability, his desire to please and be good. On the phone with Mitch, it had seemed fortuitous, a bonus for their side, but now stepping into this spongy territory made her queasy, and she could feel the anger he'd loosed upon Julianna expanding to include her as well. Blinking with the memory, she asked, "Did I hear you call Julianna a child molester?"

Blank-faced, he looked at her then, met her eyes for several seconds. "No." Daring her to call the lie. She'd done it somehow, said exactly the wrong thing.

"Caleb. Please talk to me."

"About what?" The steel doors had closed. Before she could answer, he stretched both arms over his head in a yawn, saying, "You know, I'd better go call her back. I'm fine now. I just get like that with her. She pushes my buttons."

"I think you broke the phone."

"Oh. Well, then I guess I'll fix it."

Never in her life had she craved pot, much

485

less wanted it as badly as she did now. Maybe because it was the drug she had, the scent of it still in her nostrils, but it sounded ideal, and she needed badly to talk. She sent Lark off to her bedroom with some reassurance about Caleb, then gave the same speech to Hilda before begging her to keep an eye on him from a distance. In the meantime Caleb had found electrical tape and was patching the earpiece together. "It works, I think," he said, cross-legged on the floor, blinking up at her. "Just this plastic part broke."

"You're going to call Julianna back?"

He nodded. "You don't have to stick around here or anything. I'll be good."

"Are you okay if Lowell and I go out for a little bit?"

"What, to town?"

"Yeah, maybe." She suppressed a cringe at that, but she sensed he would read too much from the truth. "Your grandma's here, okay? And you'll get to bed in an hour?" He nodded, his expression bleak, and she crouched beside him and kissed his forehead. "I love you." She resisted adding *no matter what you think,* since he was pretending he wasn't angry with her. "You be nice to Julianna. But don't let her push you around. You're right, this *is* your life."

They needed a flashlight to find their way, but once they were above the trees, half a moon lit the platform's edges and the canopy. It suggested the lake far below. Frogs and insects called all around, fluttery whistles and jingle bells and flat mechanical whines, a distant whooping that might have been an owl. Lowell lit a fat joint he'd already rolled and passed it to her. "So I am the worst mother in the world," she said, and drew deeply and held it.

"That's pretty unlikely." Taking his turn, he said, tight-voiced, "Uh, Julianna the child molester?"

"Thank you! And now I'm one too, it seems." She took another hit, turning over the incident. "The thing is, he knows when he's being manipulated and when he's be-ing sweet-talked. I think that's what he's feeling, all these adults ganging up on him." The thought jerked tears loose, and though she held up a hand to keep Lowell at bay, they were sitting close, and she could feel his fingers moving softly in her hair. "But isn't that my job as a mother?" she went on. "I'm here to convince my kids to do all kinds of things they don't want to. And then they thank me later."

"Or they blame you later." He held the joint to her mouth, and she took it, their fingers brushing. "Or you *don't* push them, and they blame you for that."

"I know. You can't win. But we're talking about letting his molester go free. Not even free on parole, as a registered sex offender. Free to do whatever the hell he wants. Either that, or I pressure my kid into spilling his guts. And probably he flat refuses, that's A and B is he hates me forever."

Lowell sat back. "Well, have you wondered if maybe it's not worth it? I know it sounds horrible, but this is one guy. Not even the one who took him, or did the worst stuff. And all of *them* together is hardly a drop in the bucket of evildoers out there. Maybe it's not your problem anymore. Maybe you and him both have given enough to it."

She had thought of this, though it wasn't something she could remember when on the phone to Mitch, when the assumption was that there was only one path, only one outcome best for Caleb or any of them. She exhaled smoke, the generous roll half burned. "Damn, this is good. Just what I needed. 'Soccer Mom Gets Stoned in Tree House . . . While Kidnapped Boy Cusses Out FBI.' "

"Good thing we're about as far as you can get from a news camera. Check that out." He leaned close, his beery breath on her neck as he pointed out over the valley. In the distance was the full cone of the volcano, black under the moon with fringe of fire at the peak. *Boom,* it said, the softest percussion as it coughed lava into the sky. Minutely visible filaments dripped over the edge and were snuffed, cooled to invisibility as more followed.

"Wow." She was mesmerized. "Did you know this was happening?"

"This is the first I've seen it this year." When she started up to go get the kids, he caught her by the arm. "No, no, no. Not tonight. It'll be here, I promise. They can see it later. Finish this. I've got another ready to go."

"God, I'm not *that* horrible a mother, am I? Let's let this one sit awhile. Let's look at that." She felt just enough effect for a pleasant trance of staring, the distant volcanic light shifting steadily in pops and drips, a tracery so bright it was seared everywhere she turned in the darkness and behind her closed eyes. In a little while the clouds took it back, a cup over a candle flame. Absent the distant forge, the dark seemed cooler; the insects and frogs went on calling.

"Do you think you could stay here forever?" she asked. "In this country, this place?"

"Sometimes. Though I never expected to stay this long. You?"

She considered. "You know, I haven't been able to see very far ahead. Hilda doesn't seem to mind us here. You or us. It almost feels stable." In the moonlight she could make out his mouth, his sleepy eyes fixed on her. "Except for this business you're in, which I'm guessing is not the sort of thing that offers a great retirement plan."

"It won't be forever. Hell, one day I'll go back to teaching. Why not?"

She winced, unready to let him sidestep her as usual. "Lowell. Honestly. Should I be worried about you?"

"Naw. It's sorta legit. Mom wouldn't agree, I'm afraid. But otherwise."

"So it's not drugs. Drug-related."

"No, not drugs."

"Yet you seem to be in the business of pissing people off."

He chuckled. "That I am. That is more or less what I do. But they're very stupid people very far away who would have a lot of trouble finding me." With two fingers, he found her hand resting on her crossed shins, hooked one finger lightly. "I like it that you're worried about me."

He didn't move closer. She didn't withdraw. She felt tender toward him and grateful and was thinking oddly about Mitch Abernathy, imagining his fingers curled around hers and how the two hands would compare — the hands of these two men she loved in such large part because of the care they took of Caleb, in their almost opposite capacities.

"What are we doing?" she asked.

Slow to answer, he seemed unafraid. "Whatever you say."

They sat thinking about that. In a tone of reason, she said, "I say we head back to the house."

The first call had been furtive, disorienting. "Where are you?" Jolly asked, his voice constricted, and it was as if Nicky had stayed out too late, worried him by forgetting to call and report his location.

"I'm in Costa Rica."

"Wow. Not Nicaragua?"

"We were just there for a few days. We live here, I guess."

"Who's we?"

"Me and . . . my mom and my sister." The words tripped him, making him claim these people who were Caleb's. But there was no other way to speak. "We're staying with my grandmother in Monteverde, up in the mountains. She lives in this old hotel in the middle of nowhere. The cloud forest. And my uncle's here." He went on adding bits into the silence, troubled at how each new detail seemed to increase it and separate them farther. He smiled. "Am I blowing your mind?"

"God, your voice. It's deeper, you know. Just a shade. But still so you." Now he could hear Jolly breathing as if they were in the same room, a sound as distinctive and personal and tonal as speech. "Should I call you Caleb now? Just say so, I will."

He thought about it. He was used to being Caleb. Nicky was that blond boy who lived in Washington, though the line cast through space to Jolly made him at least half Nicky. It didn't matter to him which name he was called, so he said no. But the word came out disgusted, and suddenly the decision felt like serving justice to the betrayer called Caleb who tried each day to erase him and take his place.

Minutes into the call, Jolly made him hang up and dial a different number. "I went and got these phones they sell to drug dealers," he said, chortling over his outlaw status. "Untraceable. I'll burn that first one, so if they're as smart as you are, which I doubt, they'll get nowhere with that number."

It meant that even if his family happened

to study the Finca's phone bill, nothing on it would tell them he wasn't dialing some alternate number for Julianna. In the week following their first talk, he called Jolly every night and Julianna only twice, the second ending in the explosion that broke the phone. He'd startled himself with that, had assumed he could control himself better. But he had meant what he'd said. It had spewed forth without much intention behind it, but later, thinking it over, he meant it more. Instead of calling her back, he called Jolly.

"She's dead to me."

"But you'll have to call her, I think, now and then. Your mother is going to hear about it if you stop completely. You need the excuse."

"Yeah, okay. I guess. But I won't like it."

"Just remember she was always a trick. It's probably not even her fault. She's like a robot they created just for you, designed to match your vulnerabilities. You're right, it *is* evil. And smart. But you can be smarter. You'll show them." The little curl of pleasure in his voice was pure Jolly.

They had the FBI for a common enemy, rather than his family. "Are they nice to you?" had been one of Jolly's first questions, twisted with anguish, and he had answered with the truth — yes, they were nice — though Jolly wouldn't want to believe it. They were glad to have him back, and they tried to understand him, and he didn't blame them too much if they couldn't. "I lie a little to everyone," he said. "Different lies. Or I just don't say stuff. It's necessary. It helps things go smoothly." But he'd never had a reason to lie to Jolly, and why start now? What should he withhold, except those deep-kept things that had always been too complicated to express or the questions that might be incriminating? Jolly could be certain his phone was unbugged but not that the house wasn't; the FBI had pried into every inch. And Caleb wondered if Julianna had a way to tap the Finca phone. He put no magic of technology past them.

Jolly was out on bond, his passport surrendered, fingers crossed that his lawyer was right in believing the charges might be dropped before he ever went to trial. He didn't sound worried, though the process could take months, even years, and the world counted him guilty regardless. "I think I'll have to move," he said. The house had been egged, a window broken — "But it's no big deal. Mostly people just avoid me." Luckily, he'd never loved people, nor his job at the hospital, and it was easy to go back to the online medical consulting he'd done from home before deciding a public life of his own would help with Nicky's transition to school — as would the extra income for his college education.

"But enough about me," he said. "Let's talk about you."

So quickly it seemed normal, talking most nights for an hour that might have been safely taped and played for a jury. In almost every way, the conversation was an extension of one started the previous year, when Nicky had begun to leave the house. On his return he would sit down to relive every minute for Jolly's avid analysis: what his new friends were like, and their houses and possessions, who said what, and everything they had done. Jolly was like an obsessed coach reviewing the tape, praising Nicky's best moves, breaking down the weaknesses of his opponents, suggesting alternate strategies. He'd maintained scrupulous mental portfolios on each of Nicky's friends, as well as on some of their parents, and, once school started, on his teachers. Because Jolly remained a teenager himself in most of the ways that willing it allowed, everything Nicky brushed or battled against was fascinating. Any detail might be dissected to yield revelations.

Now it was as if in the past five months, Nicky had merely ventured exceptionally far from the house and so had much more to report. In a week, Jolly was on intimate terms with most of the players and events in Caleb's life. Any new reference tossed into a story and Jolly would say, "Wait, who is that? Where is this?" and ask a dozen questions to pin down location, appearance, personality, history, before he was satisfied and said, "Okay, proceed," as if Caleb's day were some engrossing soap opera in which everything mattered. The latest events covered, Jolly was ready to probe more deeply into the mysteries Caleb often forgot to find interesting: his grandmother's love life, his parents' marital troubles, Luis's lies, his own ambivalent relationship with Lowell. Jolly formed measured opinions about all of these, drawn from the evidence, and often it would be some eye-opening bit of illumination followed by "But you knew that, I can tell. You hardly need me to tell you these things."

"I do, though," he said. "I didn't know that before. Not really."

He shouldn't have been surprised that Jolly required so little convincing to be open-minded and sympathetic toward his family. One of Jolly's worst failings, to

Nicky's view, was his reluctance to condemn anyone. He could find Hitler's good side. He contended that Chet, however misguided and emotionally disturbed, had once acted from love; he was a passionate man whose values had been warped. Though he'd once been certain that Nicky's real family would not be interested in or capable of giving him what he needed, he was willing to believe they weren't so bad. Not the ideal caretakers, of course, but he gave Marlene credit for leaving Jeff behind, among other things.

Night after night, Caleb told his stories and waited through the response for a purpose to emerge, the apocalyptic solution. But Jolly never suggested a future. Always he said, "I miss you, kid. I love you," but he never talked of seeing Nicky again. Did he really just want to hear about this boy Caleb's life? Early in the stuporous days with Chet, still confused by what was being done to him and why, Nicky had found and read through stacks of pornographic comic books named for boys, in which thought bubbles above the heads of the men cleared up much of the mystery and told him almost everything he would ever need to know about Chet and what he wanted. Jolly was a complicated person and no cartoon character, but it was still hard to trust that his love had no more powerful motive behind it.

Not that Caleb hoped for a future. By day, he'd become quite suddenly content to be Caleb, as if the phone calls relieved some itch or gave him back a limb he'd been missing, and sometimes he felt so natural in this skin that Jolly seemed a nuisance to be dealt with or a threat. But it didn't occur to him not to call. By evening, he was as eager to get out of Caleb as out of stiff clothes and hear Jolly's voice.

"Your house must not be bugged," he told Jolly. "They wouldn't let you talk to me this long, even for a trap. They have this idea you'll damage me."

"We wouldn't want that. Are you feeling damaged?"

"I'm pretty tough. Maybe you should try harder."

Though Jolly did not behave like a comic book man, he'd been known to talk like one. In the past, any lustful mood awakened some demon that compelled him to describe exactly what he wanted to do and what would happen next until Nicky — whether he intended to let it happen or not — would say, "Gross! Will you shut up about it?" Now, sitting in bed in the little lichen-colored house in Providence, Jolly might say, "I can picture you here next to me," and stop there. Tempted with Caleb's men's-room encounters or his urge to seduce his uncle, Jolly eagerly probed the particulars, but with an interest mainly intellectual. The lascivious pleasure that leaked through seemed oddly impersonal, as if they were discussing some hypothetical boy.

Maybe it meant Jolly had moved on to a new crush, like Nicky's tennis instructor. Eighteen years old — he was even legal. Nicky had passed two birthdays in Jolly's house and by fourteen had generally gone cold on sex, disdainful and withholding, until Jolly's eye started to wander, and then in a flash he'd be wracked by tantrums of jealous passion. Jolly took all the blame for these episodes but explained that Nicky was reacting from deep insecurity, the kind that went back to fear for his basic survival. "You still don't trust that sex isn't love. Say no to me all you want — it's not why I love you."

Even now, he would have felt better with the stamp of sex to confirm it. But he knew he was still loved. He could hear it in Jolly's voice, sometimes in the pained restraint of his breathing. Any worry or unhappiness in Caleb's stories might launch an urgent diatribe against the fate that had separated them: "I can't stand that you're so far away, and there's nothing I can do to help you. It's not fair, to either of us. The world is so screwed up, I swear to God, and hardly a soul in it knows right from wrong."

But mostly they both avoided strong emotion in these calls. They spoke in bedtime murmurs that grew more casual each night. "I'd better get off," Caleb said, "before I alert the spies. Call you tomorrow." Jolly said, "I'll be here."

At dinner, his mother wondered aloud if they ought to invest in a car. But a four-wheel drive was a must, and it was hard to come by an SUV in these parts that wasn't a hundred years old and overpriced. "I guess that's what we get for living in a place all the tourists of the world can't drive to."

"You know," Caleb said, "Monteverde might be the next big overseas retirement spot for Americans."

"Is that so?" Lowell said.

Caleb couldn't help himself. "They want to come because it's remote and unspoiled and uncrowded, but then as soon as they get here they'll pitch a fit to get the roads paved. Because Americans have to ruin everything."

"And who says this?" his mother asked. Caleb shrugged.

He was aware that his new pet phrase was "someone said." If he caught himself about to use it twice in a conversation, he reworded — "I heard somewhere," perhaps — or skipped the attribution and offered up some idea of Jolly's as his own. It was hard to stay quiet, especially over the psychological analysis of small family dramas that before had tended to float past him like Luis's telenovelas without seeming relevant or fully intelligible. Thinking of how he would relate some scene from his day for Jolly required more attention. Listening to Jolly gave him insight that begged to be offered up.

"Who *is* this someone who said?" Marlene had asked more than once, with a penetrating look. Some kid at school, he told her. Isabel's dad. Luis. His therapist. Sometimes he had to dance for a legitimate answer, because there were only so many likely sources his mother did not know as well as he did.

"Aren't you talkative these days," she remarked, in a tone both pleased and perplexed. He'd also become more inquisitive, because Jolly continually stumped him with things he should know. How old was his mother? Did Lowell play an instrument? How had his grandmother met her Costa Rican husband? "Oh, Nicky," he'd moaned, "you're better than this. What's happened to that sharp and curious nature? I hope it hasn't wasted away so soon." Later, softening, he said, "I suppose you just haven't committed yet to being where you are. Is that possible?"

Caleb supposed this was right. He felt somewhat more grounded at school, where the novelty of a girlfriend gave him purpose and focus, a role in which he was accepted. He was Isabel's boyfriend. And Isabel was more truly his friend — they were friends who kissed. Sometimes he made up his mind to love her. Choosing one person to love was an anchoring act. But at home, without her, he continued to feel stashed in a temporary existence, waiting for the next upheaval to take him to some unimagined place with all new people.

What's your mother like? What's your sister like? As much as he had ever considered them as individuals with lives apart from his, he'd done so with an idea of what he would tell Jolly about them one day, only because Jolly had given him the habit of thinking this way. He had not expected the day to come, and yet now that it had, the world turned calmly onward, all its structures intact. It had not collapsed at the breach, one life flooding the other. Did it mean he could have both?

What was his grandmother like? Rare sunlight passed over the garden in waves where she scissored the guayabana bushes with pruning sheers. From inside the house he could see her lips moving from time to time, or she smiled faintly as she often did when no one was around, as if she were enjoying something in her head. "She thinks plants can read people's minds," he'd reported smugly to Jolly, but then admitted he'd heard this from Lark. He wasn't sure he'd had a single conversation with her longer than a minute that was just between the two of them, with no one else around.

He went outside to where she worked, cleared his throat to get her attention. Whenever required to call her something, he said Grandma Vincent, such a long and formal name for someone he lived with, but both Grandma (as Lark said) and Hilda felt wrong. "Do you want some help?" he asked.

She peered up at him as if identifying an old friend, and he felt for a moment like a talking tree. "Only got one set of clippers." She snipped the air between them. "If you want, you can grab my bucket over there and pick up trimmings."

He did this for a while, and then he took over with the shears and followed her directions, on from the guayabana to the flowering hedge along the walkway. "They enjoy a good cutting," she told him. "You'd think it would hurt, but they're quite stoic when they know you're doing a thing in their best interest. A nice trim helps the flower and the fruit. Plus I think some plants are quite vain about their looks. Speaking of which, I'm about due for a haircut myself!"

He paused to scrutinize the iron-colored hair she pulled forward around her face. When they had arrived in Costa Rica, her hair had been almost as short as his own, and now it was just a little longer, creeping down her neck and turning in curves around her cheeks. "I like it like that," he said. "It's very hip."

"Oh, but it's trouble," she said with a laugh, "being this hot."

He asked how her husband had liked her to wear her hair, and she said, "Which one?" For there was Gregory Vincent, his grandfather, who had liked it dyed and curled in the salon, and then there was Javier Valverde de Aguilar, who liked it more or less as it was now, and then there was Dr. Trevor Youngblood, almost her husband, who liked it very short. Of course each of them had merely expressed appreciation for how she had worn it at the time, and maybe they would have liked it a different way just as well.

Caleb said, "The doctor was almost your husband?"

"Oh, we were working together, you know, on this Jaguar Corridor, and we got very drunk one night and wound up in a wedding chapel in Belize. A beautiful little place, but luckily not Las Vegas so no one was there at midnight to marry us. I came to my senses the next day, and now I'm afraid he's upset with me."

"You don't love him?"

"Oh, I do. But *Javier.* You didn't know him, of course — we had so little time together, really. He was special. I am who I am today because of him, because of what he taught me about this place, and what he discovered in me and coaxed into flower." She chuckled. "That sounds quite grand. What I mean is that I was already this person, before I met him, but I didn't know it. Maybe I wouldn't have, without him. And he was so dear, terribly flawed too, but you forget the flaws when you lose someone too soon. I have so much love for him still that sometimes it just goes out and lands on any old man, draws him right in. It's not my cute haircut, I'm sure. I get frustrated with Trevor, I do, but it's only because I want him to be someone he's not. He won't ever be Javier."

Snipping wayward fronds, Caleb turned that over in his head. "You won't ever get married again?"

"Oh, I might. You never know. I try to remember that it's easier to love the idea of someone than the actual person in front of you. So much simpler to love Javier now. Even my little Lark — of course I adore her, but it's a bit different than when she was far away. With separation comes all that yearning. You create a person in your head who cannot exist. These people in daily life, they can be so dull and demanding and, I don't know, repetitive! There they are again. And you run out of things to say."

He laughed, surprised at the bluntness. She said teasingly, "And you — how is your love life?"

"It's pretty good."

"Isabel is a sweet girl. Of course she doesn't know she is a pale second to the one you talk to on the phone." At his questioning look, she said, "But don't worry about that. A little love is plenty for her. Lord, what would she do with more of it?

We're done here, I think. Help me get some lemons."

He retrieved the long fruit hook from the shed. Walking side by side through the pink bananas toward the orchard, they were halted by a snake. A yard ahead of them, it slid down into the path — broad-nosed, flared in the jaw, a head the size of Caleb's fist — and twisted around to look at them. The body was slick and argyle patterned, brown and gray. Caleb gripped the fruit hook like a quarterstaff, thinking fer-de-lance, his heart racing though he didn't feel afraid. His grandmother's hand was on his arm — "Oh! Look at the *pretty*" — as the snake oozed fat-bodied across the path, maybe five or six feet of it, and into the green. "Little boa," she said, in a charmed and chiding tone as if the snake had done something cute.

"Not poisonous?"

"Oh, *no*. Most snakes aren't." Farther off, the snake was invisible but for the grass laid down in an unfurled ribbon where it went, all the way down to the woods.

"Big boa," he said, getting his breath back.

"Just a youngun. They get big enough to eat baby goats."

She twined her arm through his and they angled away from the snake's path down to the sweet lemon tree, where the upper fruit had yellowed, most of it in reach only of the wildlife. Their approach launched the weighty flight of half a dozen oropendolas flashing the ochre of their tails. "Who do I love on the phone?" he asked, like someone unconnected to his own life. "Julianna?"

"No, not her." Nose wrinkled, she grinned at the worry in his face, shook her head. "Don't you look at me for a lecture! And I'm not going to tell on you. You love who you love. In its way it's very romantic."

"It's . . . not like that," he said.

"Romantic," she said suddenly. "That's the word, isn't it, for the kind of love that has to cross all that space, the loved one so far away? Any kind of love. Even the way I loved your sister from afar. Maybe the way your mother loved you." She pointed out branches for him to hook down into her reach, and she filled her jacket pockets with the fruit called limón dulce, another one with an identity complex: a regular lemon to the eye and the nose but sweet as an orange to bite into.

"Maybe some mangoes, too," she said, and they walked down to the mango tree. "And this place, all the clouds." They were strolling into a thicker bank, and she waved a conjurer's hand at the atmosphere. "I think it affects us all, how we see the people around us. It distorts. Love goes awry. Your mother, for instance. Doesn't know which way to aim herself. And you, well, aim is less the question."

She spoke in wise tones, but Caleb couldn't tell whether she was making sense. *Loopy* was his mother's word for Hilda in a certain mood, when in the next breath she'd sound fully reasonable. "The love we have," she said, "for people far away or gone from this earth, it goes out like rain in these clouds; it comes back to us. Look, the monkeys have been here, no surprise. So maybe even all that misfired love, wrong love, can't be a bad thing for the world."

Hooking the fruit-laden branch she desired, he was startled when she said, "You disagree."

"No." He'd only been trying to follow, not thinking of a counterargument, but he said, "For some people love is . . . a tool." The fruit hook in his hands, bringing the mangoes she plucked, made him smile. "It's power. They use it to get what they want."

She gave him a musing frown. "I will have to think about that. That would not be a good sort of rain at all." He shrugged. "You know," she said as they walked around the tree, "I don't dream anymore about Javier appearing at my door. But if I could talk to him on the phone, wherever he is, I suppose I'd do it every day." She chuckled. "And if it was really him and not my own dream, he'd remind me pretty quick of the difference between a person and an idea."

"Or maybe he wouldn't," Caleb said. Three mangoes tucked into his jacket, he gave her his arm again, and they began walking back to the house. "Maybe the idea is all you have anyway. Lowell says something like that. About how you get stuck with an idea even when the person is right there. You don't see reality, only your idea of it." He'd been relieved when the topic shifted away from his phone calls, but now he tried to apply his thoughts to Jolly, the real Jolly and his clouded idea of him. He wished Hilda would ask a question or argue so he could hook it closer, but she grew vague, and as they passed through the upper garden she spoke only of the plants and their needs.

CHAPTER FOURTEEN

He had been dating Isabel three weeks when here came the thing he had kicked aside and buried, in a white dress with a band of white flowers in his hair. Caleb had gone to the drugstore to pick up a tube of ultramarine acrylic his mother needed and was walking back on the Soda La Perla side of the street to meet Isabel at the Internet café. If not for the stories he'd been telling Jolly, he might not have thought of Luis once since their last meeting, and it seemed strange that someone who belonged to his unsteady past should still be here in town, standing in front of the church like a bride.

"Where is your soul mate?" Luis halted beside the brick post of the church gate, arms crossed, trying to look badass despite his pale pink lipstick and sparkly eye shadow. A slender, ethereal rainbow that seemed to emanate from the crown of his head arched behind him over the upper half of town. But Santa Elena was so lousy with rainbows they mostly went unnoticed.

Caleb answered the snide question with another. "Who's the groom?"

"Manny." Luis nodded toward Soda La Perla next door, eyes alight, and Caleb, who wanted Luis not to exist and not to be standing in front of him requiring acknowledgment and who intended to walk past and keep going, stopped before him, took in this wedding picture, and cracked a laugh.

"Miguelita's little grandbaby is being christened," Luis said, examining neat, unpainted fingernails. "Is why the dress. But you have maybe heard that Manny is my lover now."

"Bullshit."

They were both smiling as if the mood were light, but an undercurrent of anger crackled faintly from both sides. Luis said, "You have an imaginary girlfriend, so I will have my imaginary boyfriend. And how is your ghost? Do you see her still?"

Caleb stepped up close enough that Luis flinched but didn't back away. "Don't talk about my life when you fucking lie to my face about everything. Okay? Yeah, I know you don't turn tricks at the Trogan, and by the way you're never going to San José and you're probably going to die a fucking virgin, because you're basically a coward. You just invent the idea of who you want to be and you try to hide behind it. It's pathetic." Some women walking by emitted a murmur of Spanish, the sound of worried hens. If Caleb had not been standing in the middle of town, where at least a dozen people were always somewhere in view, he might have seized Luis by the throat with both hands.

But the words had stunned as much as a stranglehold, left Luis blinking and flushed. He shrank behind the brick post and Caleb followed, the column not broad enough to hide them. "Your expression, I think," Luis said, "is 'It takes one to know one.' " Lank strands of hair narrowed his face, the beauty there so different from Isabel's, so different from any male Caleb could think of, with that persistent expressive melancholy that called to mind no one so much as Julianna, and he felt a pinch of remorse for calling the lie.

"Why?" Caleb growled against a sudden threat of tears. "Why me? Why lie to me, all those stupid lies, when I'm the one person —"

Luis straightened, his expression stern, waiting while Caleb tried to continue, wanting to say this but his obstinate throat closing on him. " 'The one person'?" Luis said. As if to name him, he took Caleb's face in both hands and kissed him. It was an act as aggressive as a slap, and for a moment their mouths were pressed together hard and closed in battle. Caleb could feel the faintest whisk of stubble, all his anger sliding toward despair, toward thwarted desire for nothing remotely as simple as sex, and it was a pure relief to feel their mouths open, their tongues push together. He grabbed tight around Luis's waist, where the dress was drawn into a silky bow in the back.

After only a few seconds, he registered the scuff of footsteps on the walkway. He looked up at Luis, whose lipstick was smeared, his gaze fixed outward through the iron bars of the fence. Caleb, his own view blocked by the post, didn't move, and the man strode past quickly without a word or a glance. Isabel's father. Still Caleb couldn't release the lock of his arms, and he leaned his cheek against Luis's shoulder to watch the man depart. The white dress, nubbly against his cheek, smelled of mothballs and flowers.

Sagging with sudden lethargy, Caleb loosed his hold, stepped back against the post. "Great. My life is over."

Luis took up the spot beside him, hands behind his back, gave him a sad little smile.

"Don't be dramatic. That is worse for me than for you."

"Make a spell," he whispered. He didn't want the kiss back, only to stay as close as they were, shoulder to shoulder and calm at least, nearer to friendship than he'd felt with anyone since Jolly.

"There is not a spell for everything," Luis said.

Lark heard about it from a girl named To-masina in her class. "Your brother kissed the boy who wears a dress. In front of the *church.*"

Everybody knew by lunch, but as far as Lark could glimpse from her distant sixth-grade routine, Caleb moved through the school day as usual, holding Isabel's hand. On the bus home, he sat with Isabel. Lark, who began the ride in a seat far from them, heard some boys snickering behind her about the kiss, but no one seemed to taunt Caleb or Isabel directly. No one threw things. She wondered if Costa Rican kids were nicer than American ones or if they were only disarmed by Caleb's casual man-ner, which made him seem older and more worldly than the other boys in his grade.

"Do you know what people are saying?" she asked Caleb from the seat ahead, once the three of them were alone on the bus.

He smirked. "Just ignore them. It's not a big deal. Luis kissed *me,* and it wasn't, like, for real. He was just being crazy, or making a point or something. You know how he is."

Lark couldn't help looking at Isabel for a second opinion — the last few times she'd seen Caleb and Luis together, Luis had been rather prim, Caleb the crazy one. Isabel matched Caleb's above-it-all expression with a roll of her eyes. "It is not going to bother me." She looked up into Caleb's face with a velvet solemn expression, and he brushed the hair back from her forehead. But since they'd been a couple, Isabel was always looking at Caleb this way, as if he were very beautiful and had a terminal illness.

Everything wasn't fine, though, because Ranito was at the bus stop on his horse, wordlessly collecting Isabel, and the next day Isabel was no longer free after school but needed at home. Caleb said her father only wanted Isabel clear of the gossip until it cooled off and that he seemed to blame Luis more than Caleb. As far as the gossip went, Lark gathered that a boy kissing a boy was a serious misdemeanor, and doing it in the middle of town in broad daylight was worse, but neither compared to the gravity of committing the act in the shadow of the cross, as if deliberately spitting on the church. Caleb pretended not to care, but he stayed away from town; he was quieter at meals and the rest of the time was either closed up in his room or on the phone. He said he was calling Isabel — they could still talk on the phone — but when Lark wandered nearer than she should have, she heard him saying *she* and *her dad* and *her family,* talking about Isabel to someone else.

Since the start of the second session of school, Lark had made a friend of Tomasina, the only girl in her class who rode the bus to town every day. Tomasina's family owned a souvenir shop that also served coffee and pastries and had a bank of washing machines in the back where tourists could do their laundry. While their clothes tumbled, tourists hung about the shop drinking coffee, and because the owners spoke no English, any questions were directed to Tomasina or her little brothers, Pablo and Antony, who all attended "la escuela inglés." "When is the mail picked up?" "Do you sell stamps?" "When does the bus come?" "Does this shirt come in other colors?" People gathered around fascinated as seven-year-old Antony spun long-winded, improbable answers to anything ("If you call on the phone to the man who makes the shirts, he will maybe have other colors. Maybe he will have green, and blue, and yellow, and some other colors you will like. If you ask him maybe he will make the other colors for you"), then they asked more questions as if pulling the cord on a talking doll and bought more coffee and knick-knacks. Tomasina, less adorable at eleven and so less in demand, was generally free to go here and there in town with Lark and sometimes another girl or two from class who had come with them.

The shaved-ice man parked his cart at the bus station most days, and this was usually their first stop. Tomasina's favorite treat was a grape copo, shaved by hand from an enormous block of ice with a wicked steel blade, "con leche," which meant that after squirting in the purple syrup, the ice man — who was thickset and hairy under a straw fedora — would glop over it a pale brownish mound of sweetened condensed milk. Lark started ordering her copo "con leche" as well, with strawberry syrup, though the concoction was almost unbearably sweet and she could rarely finish the cup. They considered themselves particular favorites of the ice man, who grinned half toothlessly at their approach, called them "mis chiquitas," and recited their expected orders.

People sat on benches and milled about in front of the station, waiting for the bus. On this day another girl, Sofia, had come along with them, and she ordered last, taking her time to ponder flavors before she chose a cola ice, no leche. Mashing the gooey milk into red ice with her spoon, Lark kept glancing toward a teenaged boy with a duffel on his shoulder who stood apart in the shaded overhang of the station. Three times, at least, she looked, and he seemed to be looking right at her. Then he said her name, almost too quietly to hear.

Enough people were close by that she went over to him. "Where's your brother?" the boy said, and it was only from the voice that she recognized Luis. He wore jeans, a dark nylon jacket, a blue baseball cap that bizarrely said "Braves."

"He's at home," she said. "What happened to you?" He stood in the shadows, turned shyly aside from her squint, but she saw that one eye was swollen half-shut, and there was a purple crescent beside his mouth. Along the hat's edge his hair was gone, as closely and raggedly shorn as Caleb's had been when he'd first come home.

Luis passed a hand back over one side of his head, a caress of the bared skin, and tried to smile. "My father happened. Listen, tell Caleb I'm sorry. I'm leaving, so he can tell what story he likes. People here will be happy to blame me. And he's just a little kid. He forgets this, I think."

"Where are you going?" she asked as the bus roared up behind her.

"San José. You can tell him that too. Tell him he was wrong about that."

She didn't know what to say. She wanted to make him stay somehow, but how could she begin that argument, knowing so little about his options? Could she take him home with her? He hoisted the duffel, eyeing the bus grimly. Even in pants, Luis had always possessed a determined feminine composure, but the loss of the hair turned him graceless, naked, his Adam's apple jutting out, and she wanted to lend him a jacket or something to hide behind.

"Where's your car?" she asked.

He pointed up the street. "I sold it to Manny. My half. The other is Ranito's."

"*Luis,* you —" Others began to board, but he waited for her to think of an end to her sentence. "Where will you sleep? Do you even know people there?"

"I will know them. Don't worry about me." He set a hand on her head, exactly as Caleb had in the garage back at home, before he got on his old BMX bike and rode away.

Then the hand was gone, and Luis and the bus were gone in a cloud of dust, and Tomasina and Sofia were spooning up ice beside her saying, "Was that really the boy who wears a dress? I would not even know it was him!"

At home she found Caleb in his room, sitting against the headboard of his bed reading *Human Impact on the Global Environment*. The news, she thought, would upset him even more than it had upset her in its indistinct way, but he seemed only mildly interested. "Good for him. And I guess he's got some money, if he sold the car."

"But he's all alone," Lark said, feeling mainly that she would miss him being around. Caleb would miss him.

"He was always planning to go, you know. And if that's what he gets from his father for one stupid kiss — I mean, for real. What else is he going to do?"

"What did he mean, 'tell Caleb he was wrong about that'?"

He gave her a pensive half smile. "I told him he wouldn't actually go. So I guess I was wrong."

"What is it, Marlene?" said Mitch Abernathy, crisp after three messages on his voice mail, and then, "I'm sorry, no, I don't mean to be short with you, I just don't have time. I'm working a case." No, not kidnapping, he said, just a missing person with complications, but he couldn't go into the details. Almost instantly she felt jealous of this person he was protecting, and more jealous of the inevitable woman — wife, mother, daughter, girlfriend — whose frantic calls would supersede her own, past as much as present.

"How's Caleb?" he said next, because he had a minute. One.

"Well," she said, "he's having girlfriend problems. There was this phase, when he was very upbeat and talkative, when I thought he might be ready to give us more. But now I'm just not sure he can handle it. It's a lot of pressure for him. He understands there's a clock and all. But I'm feeling sort of like he has to be left alone to make the decision. To speak or . . . not."

She'd been pussyfooting around this topic for a while, and so far she'd been unable to rest on a resolution without veering into the opposite argument ("But sometimes I think he's waiting for a serious push. He's not used to doing things without adult direction, and it makes him a lot more secure —

happy, even — if he's not given so much of a choice"), especially when it was Mitch on the phone. In a battle, she wanted to be on his side, pushing if he needed a push. But this time she took a breath and made herself stop.

"Maybe that's all you can do," he said. She could hear it in his voice — he was distracted. "You know," he said, very gently, "it's not my case anymore, right? It hasn't been for a long time, but now it's officially closed on my end. So it's really Julianna and those guys in Spokane you should have this conversation with."

"I know. Um, sorry, I —"

"Don't be. Really. Look, I'll call you later, okay? When I have some time." Despite the emotion in his voice, she felt how this was the first step of his not calling.

At the school-bus stop, she sat in the Land Rover, her sketchpad with its damp-curled pages balanced between the steering wheel and the open window. As usual, the blue-crowned motmot posed in its tree. She was compelled by the unlikely shape of its hanging tail, a bar ending in a pair of rackets on the finest of stalks, mere threads, so that from any distance the tail appeared to stop and then conclude some inches later, past an intervening section of invisibility. It claimed specialness for those two lollipop feathers at the tip, so distinctive to the silhouette. In size they were close to the leaves of the motmot's tree, and she began to sketch in some of the surrounding leaves as if each were as rare and as worthy. She drew the shapes of light between leaves as if each demanded the same permanence. She flipped the page and, unhinging her focus, tried first to see and then to draw everything but the bird, each shape around it. Then the bird dove to the earth, into the green, leaving a hole in the light where it had been.

The bus arrived and emitted two children, Caleb and Isabel. They stood in the road speaking together, while Marlene tucked her sketchpad behind the seat. Isabel walked over to Marlene's window. "Hi," she said, morose.

"Hi, sweetie. Haven't seen you in a while. How about a ride home?"

Isabel shook her head. "I'll walk." She said good-bye to Caleb — they didn't seem to be kissing much anymore, but Caleb looped his arms around her head and spoke into her ear for half a minute. Then he climbed into the Land Rover and they sat watching Isabel walk away.

For over a week now, he'd been coming home alone from the bus stop while Lark went to town with her friend from school. "Where do we move now?" he asked, plainly feeling sorry for himself.

She smiled. "Look, kid. You're not going to believe me, but you're right at normal. No teenage romance out there is any less weird and confusing."

He laughed, an involuntary snort. "You think? Even if I just want her for, like, a shield? Or a security blanket? That's what my therapist says."

This struck Marlene as a little direct for a therapist. She pondered it. "Do you think you might really like boys?"

He shook his head, slowly, brow pinched. "I don't know. It doesn't feel like that. Maybe I'm just drawn to what's familiar. I have this giant hole in my life, in myself, and I try to fill it up with whatever's in front of me. So I'm told."

She nodded, the assessment sounding uncomfortably applicable to herself, though she didn't pause to sort through it. "Your therapist?"

He frowned in concentration. "I'm saying it wrong. It's more like I'm looking for the missing piece of myself, like trying to patch a wound. But it's not Isabel, right? She's just protecting me while I try to find the thing."

"You think *she* knows this?"

He nodded. "I don't know if she minds too much. She sort of gets that I'm fucked up." He gave her a look that wavered between shy and smirky. "You know, some girls are kind of into that."

"Is that so?" Marlene stroked his arm, cranked up the engine.

As she started down the hill, he said with some alarm, "Are we going to town?"

"No. But you don't need to be afraid of town, you know."

"I know. I'm not."

"I have a possibly interesting appointment. I thought you might like to come along."

He asked no questions then, resigned in his peculiar way to whatever it was. Farther down the road, when she glanced over at him, he was staring fixedly into the dashboard, and she recalled the expression she'd caught in his face a few times when he played the piano back home. "Is there a word," he said, maybe to himself. "I think there's a word, for the feeling that your life is going on somewhere else without you."

She smiled softly. "You know, when you go off to college, especially if you decide to go to art school or something like that, you are going to be so interesting. In a good way.

And you'll fit right in."

They drove down toward town, turned off before the soccer pitches and began to climb again, the road rocky and edged in precipitous channels. She'd driven only a handful of times in this country and still wasn't used to it. "Right at the fork," she said aloud, and told Caleb to look for a wooden sign with a quetzal painted on it. At the sign, she pulled into a driveway so washed out, dipping as if into a creek bed and then steeply climbing, that she wondered whether she ought to stop where she was. But she went on, and they bumped and crawled up a hill toward a tall brown house, beyond which sky peeked through a framing density of broad, waxy leaves. "Petra's house," she said.

He looked at her without expression. "Are you getting some drugs?"

"Oh, ha-ha, funny," she said, faking a lack of surprise that he'd gleaned this item of Petra's résumé. "I just want to see where she lives."

Petra greeted them at a screened door that led into a mudroom, then the kitchen. A typical tico house tended to be cinder-blocked, low-ceilinged and basic, but this one was American owned and designed, so the ceiling was high and the kitchen opened into a living room with a wall of windows on one side, the hardwoods everywhere pale and new. It was airy and spacious, yet compared to the chilly vastness of the Finca Aguilar it felt cozy. Doors standing open onto a balcony admitted a breeze. Along a back hall were three bedrooms, occupied by roommates who were traveling, and a bathroom. Upstairs was Petra's large bedroom and en-suite bath. Petra took them up and out through open French doors onto her private balcony, where there was a hammock and hanging canvas chairs and a view out to the Gulf of Nicoya. "Told you it was great," Petra said.

"Gorgeous. What do you think, Caleb?" He nodded from the bedroom, busy peering around at Petra's photos, ashtrays, and art objects, a satiny bra strap that peeked from a drawer.

Marlene drew Petra aside. There had been some drama happening of late at the wildlife center. Marlene's involvement had started when a gossipy volunteer, having confirmed for her that Stancia and Petra were a couple, had gone on to suggest that Petra was not exactly a willing participant, that Stancia was always doing this with young girls. The news worried Marlene enough that she confronted Petra, who said no, actually, she was in love, while Stancia was much more hesitant. The real problem was that Stancia had been presuming upon the relationship to get involved in Petra's drug business, pressuring her to sell more than she wanted to and funneling the proceeds back to the wildlife. Petra felt used, unable to trust that Stancia had any real feelings at all. But shortly after she revealed this to Marlene, the mood had turned sunny again: Stancia wanted Petra to move into a spare room of her house. Perhaps it was only a placating gesture, but Petra was taking it.

Talk to her, though, Marlene had urged. Let her know how you feel, and find out what she expects; tell her where the line is. "You two talk?" she asked Petra on the balcony now.

Petra nodded, shrugged. "I think it's okay. She's still not ready to be open, about us, but we'll see. She says we'll stop with the heavier sales." Petra — who was twenty-two but always seemed to Marlene such a baby with her anime eyes — lifted her pierced brow. "I managed to get her a little worried about getting caught. Then who takes care of the animals?"

So Petra was preparing to move over to Stancia's place, where she could live more cheaply and be closer to the animals, and her roommates were on their way out as well. "It gets fantastic light, doesn't it?" Marlene said, back in the bedroom, examining the windows, which took up half the wall.

"I think you could get it for nine hundred or even less," Petra said. "The owner would like to get a family in here, rather than these random college students."

"Are we moving here?" Caleb asked. The question was bizarrely without emotion, considering Marlene had never once mentioned leaving the Finca and had not fully formed the thought of such an option within her own head. He'd expressed more concern over spending an hour in town.

"We're just looking," she said. "I'm wondering, a little, how this country might seem to us from a different angle." This was not quite the cloud forest, Petra had told her. It was misty at times, breezy, rainbow-laced, with a resident sloth and plenty of toucans, but comparatively dry and clear. And within walking distance of town. She could almost picture a future in such a place, her own, the rooms more commodiously arranged for family life. They could get a dog, maybe. A cat. Two cats. And here in this rangy upstairs bedroom was a space etched in light and leaves where the father to her children would be.

Tico, she told herself. If she were smart about it, she'd go snare a hot little gringuero like Randáll, young enough to keep wrapped around her finger, who could set them all up with resident visas. This kind of permanence, perhaps, in this clear, bright air, would be some answer to what Caleb felt the lack of.

Or was it her? The Finca made her so restless, with its whiteout days, its tendency to trap her without a vehicle. The kids seemed content enough with their routine and managed more mobility than she did, being free to hop the bus to town after school, and they had no reason to mind living with their grandmother. Truly, Hilda made all their lives quite easy and had been more than generous with the hospitality. Though she was often negligent of them, off in her own world, doing her own laundry and sometimes fixing her own meals as if they were not there, she had not yet given a single indication that she was tired of them. But it was precisely Hilda's mild and untroublesome presence that was beginning to chafe on Marlene. She felt parented. She missed those nights at the Finca when she and Lowell had been the adults, and Lowell had been more present then, more reliable, less likely to revert to the skulking, evasive boy he became in his mother's presence.

She instructed Caleb not to mention Petra's house to Lark or anyone else, since she had no real intention of moving. It was only listening to Petra extol the house's charms that had made her curious, and about Petra's life perhaps more than about some possibility for her own. But once she'd seen the place, her brain began to fill its rooms with half-formed scenes of her own life. She began, a little, to miss the Finca — its gardens and gothic landscapes, the volcano, even the sodden air. The way her tiny honeymoon bedroom with its private porch could make her feel entirely alone in the world. And then she would dispel the notion, remind herself she had a home and no business going anywhere. She had no income, aside from what continued to flow her way without argument from Jeff.

They spoke less often now, and even Lark had trimmed back her calls to a few per week. After the Nicaragua trip, Caleb had gone through a spell of mentioning "Dad" with casual sangfroid, as if they had their own separate relationship, and taking long turns on the phone, but that had been during the slightly manic time of his pairing with Isabel. For a minute or two Marlene had even considered again whether to reconcile with Jeff. Caleb's demeanor seemed to urge it, and his talkativeness gave her and Jeff in turn something light and hopeful to talk about. But Caleb's mood lived on slender precipices. He seemed convinced that people in general did nothing but watch him and think about him, and that his father had the clairvoyance to have seen him kiss or be kissed by a boy in a dress like the rest of Santa Elena and beyond — though Jeff knew nothing of the incident. Lately when Lark was finished talking, Caleb sometimes could not be found, and Lark handed off the phone glumly to Marlene. Her son's strange logic, she discovered, worked on her as well: if Caleb happy made her kindly disposed toward Jeff, then Caleb in distress made her bitter and blameful.

"Maybe we should start thinking about a divorce," Jeff said one night, plainly fed up with her sniping.

"We should do that," Marlene said. "I'm sure she's very cute. You'll be eager to make some new babies together." Sometimes, alone in her room, she felt she was being unfair to Jeff, but when his voice came through the phone, it was as if all along he'd been the one in her ear accusing her of unjust treatment despite his crimes. She sighed, weary. "Maybe she's already pregnant with your brand-new un-fucked-up baby. It's fine, Jeff. Go on and get that new life started. Just remember you have children here, too. School isn't cheap, and we may need a new house."

"A new . . . what?"

"I don't know, sometime? Our own place to live?" She was shouting, furious with him that she had formed the words aloud, and to him first. Standing by the Finca's check-in desk, she scanned the empty dining room, all but a few of its lamps turned off — the denizens, perhaps, scattered to their rooms for the night. "I'm just reminding you of your . . . financial obligations."

"You don't need to remind me of that," he said, cold with sarcasm.

She tried to get a grip, to unscrew her voice. "Okay. I know. Sorry. This will all be fine. I imagine you'll want to do it soon. We're not getting any younger here. And your new wife is going to have plans, I'm sure." Silence on his end. Marlene went on in a light and wandering tone. "I shouldn't judge. Maybe she's a sweet girl. Maybe she didn't even plan to settle down in the suburbs until you just one day knocked her up, conveniently."

"Right, Marlene." His tone was strange, dazed and bright. "You guessed it. You know everything." He hung up.

In the canvas satchel she used most days as a purse was a tiny baggie of Petra's valium, just a few for nights she couldn't sleep. She took only one, washed it down with beer while she played over the conversation and tried to decide whether her husband had just confessed to an actual pregnant girlfriend. In the dark kitchen she waited for a crack of light at the swinging door that would frame Lark's head — it was not unlikely that Lark would have been in the dining room long enough to overhear the yelling. But it was Lowell who found her, sobbing by then and no longer aware of the door or fully in touch with her rational mind, which knew Jeff was only being sarcastic, trying to hurt her with a strained scenario she'd created herself. Then again, she knew too well that Jeff preferred his decisions made for him, irrevocably and by grand accident.

Lowell picked her up from the floor where she'd crumpled and held her, saying nothing. His shirt smelled of reefer and dryer sheets and Lowell. After a few minutes he stood her against the counter and used the cuff of his sleeve, hooked over a thumb, to dab her tears. He worked hunched over and peering into her face, as if performing some delicate operation like removing fine shards of glass from her skin.

"Your brother is an asshole," she said.

"Totally. God, the biggest. Big, giant asshole."

She burst into a giggle, returned to her senses enough to feel embarrassed. Her beer bottle came up empty. He held up a finger between their faces, again slow and precise, like a doctor assessing a head injury. "Allow me," he said, and broke open the fridge, hooked out a pair of fresh bottles.

"You know" — Lowell opened the bottles and handed her one; he drank from his own and set it on the counter — "you should probably cut my brother a break. Whatever wiggy shit he's feeding you, it's mostly insecurity. That's my guess. He's far away. He knows I'm here. He has a pretty good idea of what I'm about to do."

"What are you about to do?" Her voice, almost defiant, rattled with chill.

"It can't be helped," he whispered, very close to her now.

She was still thinking he was wrong about this, that it could and should be stopped quite easily. But no one was around anymore to take that initiative.

Here she was, head fogged from the valium and beer in the dark of his room, where she'd become a pale gleam of full-on naked-ness in the ambient window light and chillier for it, propped up half-seated on the lip of the pool table, and he was . . . she wasn't sure how clothed or not, with only the top of his head in reach, his face between her legs. She was trying to remember if he'd ever gone down on her before, in that long-ago time when they both were younger and suppler of flesh and more high. Maybe once, uncommittedly, but tonight he had navigated with avid assurance over the bet-ter part of her somewhat less lovely body, wandering the more interesting byroads, before settling in at his present station. That he'd acquired some grown-up skills and was bringing them to bear with patience was a surprise, both pleasing and unsettling. She'd pictured surrender as a rush, blind and animalistic and, above all, quick, a climax more her own responsibility than his. The last thing she'd expected from Lowell was any sort of leisure time in which to notice what they were doing.

From somewhere came a long, muted banshee screech in a minor key, and a shudder rose up through the table under her, too hard for ecstasy or a shift of the drug in her head. "Um, what," she said, "the fuck."

Her hip bones in his hands, he set his speculative chin on the mound of her pubis. "Just the earth moving. A little." He was tense, though, waiting to feel it again.

"God, here goes the rest of the north wing. We're going into the valley." She looked at him with fond resignation as if merely sad that they couldn't finish. But better this than the consequences facing them tomorrow.

"No, we're not." He stood and efficiently flipped her over, his mouth at her spine, and she found that he'd gotten himself naked after all.

In his bed, a couple of hours later — the building stayed quiet — it was turning into one of those nights in which they would not sleep, only talk and goof around and work themselves up to the next slightly more raw and laborious fuck. It was like a dare as it went, more and more dangerous if safe meant impersonal and uninvolved. Or maybe they were only going to wring the last of it out of their systems and be done. She kept looking for the point at which she could call a halt, give them a chance to retreat.

Kissing her neck, he said, "Are you going to hate me if I go to San José on Friday?"

"What?"

"It's business stuff. It can't be helped." He didn't seem to notice that he used the same sentence that had somehow gotten her down here and naked. "Wanna come with?"

Mystified, she hoisted herself onto an elbow and studied him, drowsy and supine, doodling on her right breast with a fingertip. Was she being wooed or blown off? A trip to the city appealed to her, but it was too much, too quick. "Gosh, you know," she drawled, "I probably should have mentioned this earlier, back at the after party, but I have kids. Two of them, actually. And also birds to feed every damn hour."

"Bring the kids," he said. And then, "No, you're right. It will be . . . boring, and I'll be tied up. I'll be back Sunday."

The soft promise of the last stopped her again. Did it mean something different than it would have a day earlier, when she'd have been complaining only of missing his company? For a moment she couldn't get her breath. "What is this? This is — no, wait, don't answer that. Don't say anything."

He zippered his mouth, at her command. She folded herself onto his chest and he dangled fingers in her hair, arranging strands of it over the hairless part of his torso like clothing. She asked, "Does your business in the city involve angry people?"

"Only very dull people, I'm afraid. Contract lawyers. I'm settling a deed for someone. I swear. If you wanted to come, I'd let you watch the whole gripping drama unfold."

"You know," she said, "Caleb needs contact lenses." A flash of awareness made her grimace — was she really having this routine, domestic, all-but-married conversation in the midst of one of the more illicit acts she'd ever committed? But this was how they talked, and her idea was too compelling to hold back. "And apparently San José is where to go for an optometrist. Wanna take him along? A day off from school won't hurt him. I really think he could use the break from this place. And maybe y'all can talk, you know? He needs that."

"Okay," he said, thoughtful, tentative. She knew it bothered him that Caleb's adoration had shifted loose somehow, in what they had decided together was at least half attributable to the unfathomable moods of teenagers. Still friendly with his uncle, he was cooler than he'd been, and Marlene felt only now, in the back of her mind, how much her presence in this bed must have been tied up in a hope for Caleb, for Caleb and Lowell.

"But, um, let's talk later," she said, seizing hold of him so abruptly he grunted. "About that. And the grocery lists and the oil changes and etcetera." One more and done, she told herself, and should have told him, but she knew already how false it would sound. This was a surprise too. The value of surrender should have been in revealing, reminding her, how inadequate the prize.

Well before dawn, before they had slept at all, she disrobed him of her hair, returned to her own bed on the off chance of secrecy in their household, that the ruddy glow of him might not have tattooed itself on her skin for all to see.

CHAPTER FIFTEEN

In the FBI file of photographs from the house of Charles Lundy was a shot of Nicky that had hung framed in the bathroom until his friends began to visit. Taken before his thirteenth birthday, from an angle slightly above, it showed only his head and a suggestion of bare upper body, his shoulders and chest blurred like the background by the sharp focus on his strangely glowing eyes. He didn't look at the camera but glowered off to one side, soaked in the orange and golden light of sunset through an unseen window.

It was Jolly's favorite. "I love how powerful you look there, so entitled and casually cruel, like a lion. Like a boy king."

Nicky looked at the picture and didn't believe that boy was him. Within the house, love gave him confidence, but he shrank from an open door or the thought of what lay beyond. He obeyed any mild suggestion of Jolly's like a command. The few requests he had only just started to make were pathetic, like that Jolly stay home with him instead of go out for an hour, once a week, for their groceries.

Against all evidence, Jolly began to insist that the photograph was the film-caught image of Nicky's secret soul, his true self. The first time Nicky prepared to leave the house alone, Jolly stood him before the photograph and said, "That's you, the young lion, the boy king. Carpe diem, right? *Fortes fortuna juvat.* Which means you'll be what?"

"Brave."

"All right. Go show them who you are."

What an unlikely gift, that to have a boy who moved with confidence through the world, yet belonged to him, happened to be Jolly's most treasured fantasy. How many other boys might he have become, reshaped to order by the hands of other men?

On the Calle Central, near Avenida Ocho, in the Barrio Dolorosa of San José, was the office of an optometrist who spoke English, recommended by the young American fund-raising coordinator of the Cloud Forest School. Caleb had the address and the doctor's name, in his mother's handwriting, tucked into his back pocket. He and Lowell caught the Chicken Bus before dawn, and Caleb settled into the window seat while beside him, Lowell, groggy and unshaven, went almost immediately back to sleep, his duffel hugged along his body like a lover.

At first light, the bus idling and motionless for no apparent reason in some tiny mountain town, Caleb leaned his face against the grimy window and searched for Melia among the people who passed. A little girl dragged the toes of pink Mary Janes through the dust, following her mother — too young. Another, scooting past on the back of a motorcycle, clutching a man's waist, gave the bus a pensive glance — too old, and just a plain girl, only unlit people to be seen from his window. Jolly didn't believe in ghosts, though he treated Nicky's gently. He considered them a symptom, an indication of the extremes of his deprivation when he'd lived in the basement. "It's not so strange," he'd said. "You needed someone to talk to." Nicky had been willing to buy into this idea, at least partly. The ghosts had stayed behind in their basement, after all, and didn't turn up for visits at Jolly's house, where they weren't needed.

But what did Caleb need with a ghost? "I don't know if I see her or not," he told Jolly. "She's different from the others. And she doesn't really speak. But — I feel like she's there. Does it mean I'm still crazy?"

"You're not crazy," Jolly said, a refrain from the past. "You never were. You're sensitive. A little altered, perhaps, so you think differently. It's a kind of gift, if a harsh one. It's who you are, the Nicky I know."

And what had Melia's ghost ever said? *You have left someone behind* — if that. And why in English? Jolly argued that Caleb had heard what he needed to hear, from his own mind, and that the someone he'd left behind was Jolly, obviously. Since they'd been restored to each other, had the ghost returned? She had not.

It made sense. With the real Melia, a terrified little girl, it had taken a long time before she'd been willing to part with a single word. But once Nicky had convinced her that he was a kid like her, that he and Jolly were there only to fix her broken arm, she began to attend to him as if he might be a person, and her first question — was it her only one? — had been a cracked blur of Spanish ending in "su papa?" "Sí," he told her, pointing to Jolly. "Mi papa." Though she didn't smile, he could tell the news reassured her: if the man was a papa, he might be okay.

"I remember," he'd told Jolly on the

phone. "She liked that. She'd be upset if we were separated."

The bus lurched, rumbled ahead on its downward trajectory alongside the abyss that sometimes opened with hardly a visible edge below Caleb's window. The bus was a skyscraper, so out of proportion with the terrain that he felt he could heave his weight against the window and send the whole vehicle toppling from the road into the valley. How many buses on this route ended their journeys thus abruptly? *Human Impact on the Environment,* he thought, the barrel-roll plummet taking out old-growth trees and monkeys and sloths and boa constrictors as it went, each creature rolled up with them and added to their weight. *My love, let's roll all our strength and all our sweetness up in one ball and bowl it through the gates of life . . .* Or was it *hurl? Tear?*

Lowell snored beside him, his face turned inward and pillowed on the duffel. Caleb watched a lock of hair drop boyishly over Lowell's forehead as the bus downshifted, and he reached to lift and set it back in place. Lowell did remind him of Jolly sometimes, especially asleep, though Jolly was younger and trimmer and would have been offended by the comparison.

They were pulling in at a rest stop, where

people rose and filed out toward a soda shop with painted signs that said "Ceviche" and "Pollo Frito" and "Welcome." "Wakey, darling," Caleb sang in a soft lilt. "Wake up, my love. There's breakfast." He tipped his face an inch from Lowell's, the hand still lightly in his hair as Lowell sighed, eyes blinking open. "Did you think I was my mother that time?" Lowell made a face and set a hand on Caleb's chest to move him back.

He wasn't sure when his mother and Lowell had given up all pretense and started doing it in earnest, but they were no longer hiding it very well. In the past week, and especially over the last few days, they'd become furtive and generally weird enough with each other that the night before last, when they'd abruptly left the dinner table together on specious business, Lark had cried, "Sheesh, what's *with* them anyway?" Caleb answered — in the same instant that it occurred to him — "They're fucking," and Hilda rose up like a cobra in her chair and said, "*Hush* your mouth!" with some volatile tremor in her expression that could have passed for delight. Lark's face crumpled in genuine horror. Caleb slapped two hands over his mouth to stop a laugh and said to Lark, "I'm kidding. That was just a joke. A bad joke."

"Was it?" Lark whined. "Really?" He swore it was. Hilda frowned in the direction of Lowell's room and took Lark into the kitchen to help with dessert.

Dropping them at the bus station, his mother had tried to avoid Lowell altogether with the good-byes but finally succumbed petulantly to a goofy, over-the-top squish hug, a kiss he planted on her ear with a loud "Mwah" as if it were all just the Lowell-and-Marlene show as usual. Whatever. Caleb supposed he was entitled to feel snide about it, or if not — he wasn't sure in what way he cared — to at least give Lowell all the shit that occurred to him.

Before noon, they pulled into the bus terminal of San José and joined a crowd flowing past street vendors selling gallo pinto, sunglasses, pineapples, pastry horns filled with dulce de leche. "Watch your pockets," Lowell told him, and they carried their bags with the straps crossed over their bodies. In no hurry, they wandered through the dim warehouse of a street market, packed with rows of brightly lit stalls: spices, fish, flowers, small electronics, pet food, handbags, dried staples, lottery tickets, cheap toys, gleaming fruit piled in bins and hanging densely overhead.

"Look," Caleb said at a stand where a fat, toothless tica perched on a stool, her counter displaying rows of tiny glass vials and medicinal-brown bottles; baggies of dried mushrooms, leaves, flakes, powders, and bright pastel bath salts; feathers; amulets; candles; and jars of incense marked in symbols. "¿Usted es una bruja?" he asked her. She nodded once, with a squinty smile, a slow bow of her head. Lowell, who didn't like to pause anywhere long enough to engage a seller's attention, said, "Interesting!" and tugged him along. Caleb had formed half a thought to bring something unusual home for Luis before he remembered that Luis was here in the city, somewhere, free to acquire all the rare ingredients he might like.

Out on the street crowded with pedestrians and honking traffic, Caleb was surprised by all the signs for Pizza Hut, KFC, Payless shoes. Lowell, having gone back to sleep at the breakfast stop, was ready for lunch. "You feeling homesick for any of this American shit yet? We can get some Big Macs."

"Not really. Jolly didn't let me eat junk," he said, though this wasn't strictly true — there was always the potential bargain to be made, within reason. "When I was ten, I used to sneak out with my dad for this stuff.

But I sort of lost my taste for it, I think." The crumpled fast-food bag, translucent with grease, a finger-squashed burger bleeding ketchup onto its open blossom of foil, fries limp and glittering with salt — he was never visited with a craving for these items Chet had liked to set out of reach for him to see and smell, getting cold, waiting for good behavior.

They'd stopped on the sidewalk beside a McDonald's and Lowell pointed in at the Spanish menu. "Look, they serve McPinto."

They ate lunch at Pollo Rey — better roast chicken, Lowell insisted, than any to be found in the States, though Caleb wasn't hungry, his stomach acidy and light. Farther up the street, they checked in at the Gran Hotel, where Lowell always stayed in the city and which happened to be right on the main plaza that fronted the National Theater — the Teatro Nacional. From the window of their fourth-floor room, Caleb looked down on the theater's great butter-and-copper-green neoclassical façade. He could see its ground-level vestibuled statuary, the central portico topped by three upright Greek figures — gods, angels, statesmen, fates, he couldn't have guessed from his vantage, though he knew them in fact to be muses. He examined the figures through his field binoculars. The central one, raised above the others by the peaked roof, was a winged boy teasingly draped in what could only have been a bedsheet, holding a laurel crown aloft in one hand. "You'll recognize him," Jolly had said. Caleb felt a little sick with recognition. He scanned the people in the plaza, but much of it was blocked by trees. Palms sweating badly, he put the binoculars back in his bag.

Jolly had a passport again. It didn't mean he was out of danger, or unmonitored from a dozen angles, only that the proceedings against him had reached an impasse, allowing his lawyer to exert certain pressures. If he were smart, he'd use such hard-won and improbable freedom to stay locked inside his house like a law-abiding citizen and maybe, at most, peruse the Internet for pictures of these places Caleb might be. But how smart was Jolly, after all? A smile warming his voice, he said, "When it comes to you, have I ever done anything that wasn't pretty damn stupid?"

The Teatro Nacional. No way to choose a time, even a day. But the fates had always been on their side, and maybe they still were, one last beneficent move in store to correct the course. "I don't know if it's possible, kid," Jolly said. "But just in case, look for me there."

His mother had made him an appointment with the optometrist for Friday at four o'clock. She'd given him her credit card — *Get at least a three-month supply of lenses,* she said — and a travel wallet to keep it in under his shirt, and at the last minute she'd given him his passport in case the doctor or the hotel needed to see it. Only as he sat in the hotel room, checking the whereabouts of these items while Lowell used the john, did it occur to him that he'd been given the means to go anywhere he pleased. He could walk out now, hail a cab to the airport, be on a plane before Lowell had the first idea of which direction to look. When the bathroom door opened, Caleb shoved the flat wallet back under his shirt as if it were something he'd stolen.

On their map, the optometrist's address was only a few blocks west and south. As they set off, Caleb led Lowell on a detour past the front of the theater. "San José's greatest architectural treasure," he narrated, mocking a little to cover his nerves as he glanced around at the benches, fountains, and plantings that faced it. If Jolly were anywhere, he'd be here, under the winged boy, rather than in the larger plaza off to the side. But he would not be here. Certainly not yet.

"You see okay in these?" the optometrist asked him doubtfully, meaning his glasses. After dialing each eye through a few dozen lenses, asking "One? Or two? Better? Worse?," he opened both of Caleb's eyes to the machine's sharpened view — a new prescription markedly stronger than the glasses. The contact lenses were disposable ones, and the doctor placed them on his eyes, then removed them and showed him how to do it himself. He practiced a few times, suppressing the reflex to blink at a fingertip headed straight for his eye, then reaching into his eyeball and peeling out the transparent skin. In the mirror, his face looking back at him appeared broader, cleaner of line, its bones more prominent; his brown hair was long enough to fall if it pleased into his newly uncovered eyes: a face more Caleb than it had been minutes before.

"Do you want colored?" the optometrist asked, and Caleb learned he could choose blue eyes, amber eyes, eyes of hummingbird hues, emerald or violet. No, he said, clear was fine, but then wished he'd asked to try on one or more of these, just to see what they might make of him.

He needed a new prescription for his glasses as well. Lowell and the doctor both urged him to choose new frames from the vast office wall, but there were too many options, too much choice, enough change already, and he said only that it would be too expensive, more than his mother had expected. He would just keep the old frames. This, however, meant leaving them behind to have new lenses put in. He could to pick them up the next day. When the doctor asked for the glasses, Caleb's hand locked around them, wouldn't move, and he considered changing his mind just to keep them close. Lowell put an arm around him. "It's okay, bud," he said, and Caleb gave them over.

Outside, the world had crept inches closer, all of it right in his face. Examining San José under a lowering sun, he could feel the lenses shifting, his eyes under their new skins watering just enough to blur the view faintly at its far edges and then blink it clear.

"Give it a day," Lowell said. "You won't even know they're there."

At night, the Teatro Nacional was lit in spots of gold like candleflame, the crowning boy muse gazing skyward, wings spread for takeoff. A few dozen people milled beneath

— tourists snapping photos, coupled teen-agers, children playing chase around the fountain. A street band played marimba music near the curve of the long stone bench where Caleb and Lowell sat, the band's guitar case propped open for change.

Lowell had drunk five beers with dinner, or three and some allowing for what had gone down Caleb's throat. Caleb could have ordered his own for all anyone in this country cared, Lowell claimed, but he deemed it more respectable if they shared. Under that influence Caleb could almost begin to think of the weekend's tryst as their own, dinners alone together, sharing a room. In any case, there was automatic comfort in being at heel, on any man's leash. Lowell was more attentive than normal, nudging him to talk, observing his moods. And solicitous, so that when Caleb suggested they sit out in front of the theater after dinner, Lowell said that sounded like a great idea.

Besides retrieving his glasses the next day, they would be conducting Lowell's business in the afternoon, though Caleb wondered if his present life might be ended before then. He said, "So this contract thing tomorrow. It's land, right? Like that property we drove out to that day?"

"It is, actually. That very piece. I sort of hook sellers up with the buyers. And then I handle some of the particulars, because they're all in the States. So that's basically what we're here for."

Caleb nodded. "You know, I heard about this thing some people do. You want to hear about it?"

"By all means, bruh."

"Okay, lemme see if I can get this right. What you do is you start with an investor, say in America, who wants to get a little piece of Costa Rica for cheap. Maybe he wants to retire there later. You sell the guy some land. Then you get some ticos, say some relatives of Stancia's, to move onto the property since the new owner, he's definitely not looking, right? He's off in America playing golf. So the squatters get rights. Then the investor guy, he finds out he's got worthless property and has to pay a bunch of money to get the squatters off. Or maybe he just decides to sell at a loss. Probably he sells. Then you pay off the squatters, move them somewhere else, start the whole thing all over again. I heard people can make some money like that."

"Well." Lowell nodded, thoughtful. "That would be damn interesting, if you were a guy who could afford to buy a bunch of land to be selling in the first place."

Arms spread over the back of the bench, Caleb made one full scan of the plaza, its passing people, the pairs and solitary figures seated on other benches. "Or you could just be the middle man." He chuckled, thinking of it. "Kind of like a land pimp, maybe. Plus you could get paid on the side to keep squatters off."

Lowell chuckled also, nodding. Hard to tell, in the shadows, if he looked displeased. "And where did you hear this little story?"

"I don't know. Someone was telling me."

"Caleb," he said, leaning on a hand that scritched his stubbled jaw, "let me ask you something." A canny pause made Caleb brace for some pointed interrogation on his source, an I-know-all-your-secrets tit-for-tat. He almost hoped for it. Vaguely, he suspected that everyone knew everything he assumed hidden, that they were all waiting for the right moment to snatch him up and hold him to account. But Lowell sounded uncertain, self-conscious, saying, "You like having me around, right?"

"Sure."

"You, um, may have gathered that I'm a bit of a fuckup. Sometimes. And I can have trouble with boundaries, especially around kids. I used to teach high school, you know?

But I had this problem with . . . maybe with being a grown-up, a role model. I don't know. I don't always know, like, where the line is." He was getting flustered, intense. "Like with you. I'm always sneaking you beer, and what are you, fourteen? I want us to hang out and be buddies." He trailed off as if lost.

"Fine by me," Caleb said, puzzled.

"I'm not saying this right." He took a big breath, started again. "You've been gone. And now you're back. And you have people trying to be a family for you."

Caleb flinched and nodded into his lap, ready to plead guilty. "I know."

But this speech wasn't about him, it seemed, or about how hard it was to be his family. It was still about Lowell, who shook his head in a kind of despair. "I'll tell you. Your grandmother . . . is not too happy with me. She thinks I ought to leave. She thinks I'm tearing your already torn-up family apart. But I don't know. I think I might be putting it together. And I'm really sort of wondering what you think."

"Me?" They had landed somewhere unexpected, and he relaxed his grip, a little, on the privacy of his own turmoil. "You're asking the wrong person. I'm the destroyer. Agent of destruction."

"Not now you're not."

Caleb looked up to check the boy muse for some other, better idea of himself. "It doesn't even feel like my family. I feel like I'm the one who should leave, sometimes. But I know it would just make things worse. Way worse." He pulled his feet up onto the bench, knees to his chest. "Hilda really wants you to leave?"

"She's mad about other things too. I don't think trafficking in cloud forest has helped my general standing. But if you can believe it, she's more worried about you folks. And she has suggested my leaving as the proper course of action, yes."

"Maybe we should leave together."

Lowell took an audible breath in the dark. "I'm going to assume you're kidding."

It came to him then that Lowell was on assignment. And probably there were a number of elements to the assignment, relative to Caleb, including winning his approval and earning back his affection, but the crucial one would have to be bringing him back home to his mother. This meant Lowell was probably never going to let him out of his sight. But Caleb wasn't worried. He'd already stopped looking around so much. He wouldn't need to see Jolly, only to be there, to be seen. They had time. Jolly could be watching him now, in no hurry to approach. He'd know Lowell on sight, possibly as easy to recognize as Caleb was with all his changes. He'd watch to make sure they were staying at the Gran. He'd figure something out.

Or: he wasn't coming and would never be there. This alternative was at least as likely. Caleb could accept that. In fact, maybe it didn't matter to him one way or the other, though the sine-wave segments of time in which he believed Jolly's arrival in the plaza to be impossible were the same in which he wanted to slide closer to Lowell on the bench.

The impulse, to move closer, made him confess, "You know, I figured something out, just recently. I could never run away. It's like a handicap, I think. *Lark* could run away easier than I could. It's because I'm afraid, or because I don't know how to choose that way — to pick a life, pick a direction. Jolly used to feed me all this shit about being brave, like he'd tell me I was. Brave. But he was just trying to create something in me that wasn't there." Lowell watched him closely, troubled, and Caleb smiled reassurance. "So, I'm saying, you don't have to worry. There's zero chance I'm going anywhere, on my own. But if you take me, I'll go."

"How about if we both just stay?"

Caleb blinked at him, a little sleepy. "Are you the type who stays, Lowell? You can give it a try. I don't mind. Lark might, but she'll live."

Lowell was quiet, pondering, as Caleb's gaze followed a tall woman in a very short red dress, lots of dark hair piled high on her head, striding in glossy white high-heeled boots along the theater fence. She was out of place, all of her just a little too extravagant, too much, and he thought *hooker.* Then *transvestite.* She was gone and he wanted to run after her.

"What?" Lowell asked. "Who are you looking for, anyway?"

Caleb shook his head, set his forehead to his knees, eyes squeezed shut. Lowell asked if he was tired, and he lifted his face. "You know Luis? I called him a coward. He had this stupid idea he was going to run off and work in a whorehouse, like that's glamorous, right? That's where you meet some prince. I told him he'd never go, I guess because *I* wouldn't, and then he went. Now he's here somewhere and he's . . . He's really innocent. He shouldn't be here."

"Well. We have time. Want to see if we can find him?"

■ ■ ■ ■

The next morning, while Caleb slept, Lowell was up and hunting information. The obliging concierge had sent him to a bellhop, who sent him to a busboy who marked his map. Caleb woke at his return. He'd slept through the night, it seemed, without waking to devise an accidental path to Lowell's bed, or to creep out to the plaza and wait for fate to arrive. The blanket of sleep remained tucked around his brain as Lowell pulled open the curtains, then took a seat beside him on the sunlit mattress with the morning's discoveries.

But he needed his glasses. "I can't see."

"Oh, right. You have to put your contacts in."

Caleb groaned, using Lowell's shoulder for a pillow. "Just bring it closer."

Lowell lifted the map into a shaft of sunlight, pointing to different marks. "Here," he said, "are some gay bars. And somewhere over here is a brothel. And here" — Lowell's finger traced several streets north and south of the hotel, marked in rows of red X's — "are travesties."

"Travesties?"

"According to my friend Jesús, they are

sad cases indeed and to be avoided if possible. But yeah, that's the word here." Lowell imitated the doleful accent of Jesús as he pointed to the streets. "Travesties here, travesties here, travesties here. No no no."

"Did you tell him you were looking for a travesty?"

"More or less." He knuckle-rubbed Caleb's head. "You sleep okay?"

He had dreamed of Melia, the girl removing a green sucker from her mouth and passing it to him with a serious expression like this was her job, the way babies at a certain stage will diligently hand over every object. The stuffed dog, the sling made from a man's shirt, the tangled hair — all those features she shared with her ghost, but the ghost never had the sucker that he could remember. The real girl had one, her cracked lips stained green with it, but she'd kept it to herself.

Lowell roused him in time for the tail end of the breakfast buffet, where Caleb made the argument for staying behind at the hotel while Lowell arranged his land transfer, a dull affair likely to last all afternoon. "Yeah, but see, what matters," Lowell said, "is that your mother will take a pair of scissors to my balls if I let you so much as hit the head by yourself."

"I'm fourteen. You can't watch me every minute. Besides, you've already given me like twelve chances to escape." He bugged his eyes like Isabel's in their still-strange bareness. "Here I am."

Lowell forked up eggs and gallo pinto, looking philosophical. "You know, dude, when you keep talking about escape, it makes me wonder why. There are other things that could happen to you, you know. It's a scary foreign city. Travesties everywhere, running amok."

But Caleb guessed how it would go. All he had to do was back off just a little, play like it didn't matter that much to him, and Lowell relented. He almost had to. There wasn't really a "responsible dad" option here, only mommy or cool uncle, and Lowell picked the latter. It was the only one that held out hope of winning him back. Before he left, Lowell exacted twenty promises, starting with no bar tab, no friends in the room, no making friends in the first place, and ending with the varied and unlikely circumstances under which Caleb nevertheless would not budge from one of three places: the hotel room, the lobby, or the bench in front of the Teatro Nacional, where he thought he might sit and read his book for school. "What's your promise worth?"

Lowell asked, a serious and reasonable question, so that Caleb thought about it before he answered.

"So what if something happens to you?" he asked then. "What if I'm sitting here all day and you never come back?"

This stymied Lowell for a moment. "If I don't come back, then I'm dead. Or arrested. Or in a hospital, maybe. None of which is going to happen. But there won't be anything for you to do about any of those things except go up to the room and call your mother. That's all you do. Then you sit up there ordering all the room service and Spanish porn you please until she gets here."

Somehow Caleb had gotten himself nervous, and sitting in the plaza no longer seemed as simple. How untethered might he become? "You'll do fine," Lowell was telling him by the time he left, clean-shaven but dressed in a variation on yesterday's clothes — a man who needed a tie for nothing in his life. "I trust you. I'll grab your glasses and be back by five at the latest, or I'll leave you a message at the desk."

The book was *Great Expectations.* He'd read it already, with Jolly. In a patch of breezy shade he sat with one green Converse All-Star pulled up on the bench — Caleb's shoe, Caleb's waffle-knit shirt, Nicky's expensively faded and ripped jeans, worn to school on his last day in Providence. Caleb's hair, Caleb's face. People passed continually, and any near movement or voice lifted his gaze from the page he wasn't reading. Three boys near his age rode skateboards around the plaza, two of them shirtless, and he watched their show-off moves whenever they were near.

Being where he needed to be — he'd hardly thought farther than this. Distant men turned to him with Jolly's face. Staring into Dickens, he felt someone take a seat nearby, not too close, and speak his name. He's not coming, he reminded himself. He won't be here. He calmed himself this way and hoped it was true, because he didn't want to get Lowell in trouble. He didn't want to crush his mother, Lark, everyone, though what else could he do? He'd never have broken any of those promises to Lowell, unless Jolly came, or any stranger who knew how to pick up his leash, and then it wouldn't count. It would be out of his control.

Then what? Then they would go. But not home. Wherever they went, it would not be to their anonymous lichen-colored house in Providence, six months before.

He looked up. As there and not-there as any ghost conjured out of Nicky's need, Jolly stood at the bench five yards away. Until it happened, Caleb had worried that he'd cause a scene in the plaza, running straight for the man like he was home plate. But he was there, and Caleb sat unbelieving, uncertain which way to run.

Marlene, wiping dog-kibble mush onto her sweatshirt, jogged to the desk to catch the ringing phone.

"Marlene. Good. It's Mitch." His clipped voice gave her no time to be surprised or consider what feelings it might stir. "Listen, where's Caleb right now? Is he with you?"

"No, he's . . . gone to San José."

"Fuck," Mitch said flatly. "San José. Fucking goddamn. Who is he with?"

"His uncle." Her heart fluttered — too much urgency in Mitch's voice for this to be about information needed for the case. "They left yesterday morning, on the bus. I . . . talked to them last night. They're at the Gran Hotel." She heard him breathe, added despairingly, "He went to get contact lenses."

"I am so sorry. Listen, don't panic. Charles Lundy got on a plane. He landed in San José about an hour ago. I'm going to see if we can get the police there to help out, but that may take a while. I . . . oh, fuck."

"Mitch —"

"Has the uncle got a cell?"

"No."

"Call the room then," he said, "and see if you can get the uncle on the phone. Let him know Lundy is in the city. *Discreetly.* Do *not* let Caleb guess why you're calling. You got that? Do it right now and call me back."

"Okay, but they won't be there. Lowell, my . . . brother-in-law, he had business this afternoon." An odd flash crossed her mind: that Lowell's business could have some connection to Lundy, to Caleb, to — god forbid — *pedophile rings,* that he'd purposefully gotten Caleb away from her in order to . . . No, that was crazy. But she was too flustered for certainty.

Mitch said, "Can you reach him where he is?"

"No. I don't know where . . . Mitch, what does this mean? How could Lundy even know Caleb's in San Jose?"

"Well, have you had *any* hints that he and Caleb could be in some kind of communication?"

"No." It was unfathomable, a danger she

had never thought to look for. Lark materialized close by, round-eyed, listening.

In a daze, Marlene hung up and dialed the hotel. "What is it?" Lark asked, and Marlene shushed her with an emphatic pointed finger. She left a message on the room's voice mail, straining to sound calm: Lowell, call me, emergency. She dialed back and left the same message for him at the hotel desk. "What emergency?" Lark whined in a whisper as Marlene dialed Mitch back.

"You know what," Mitch said, in a weary tone of resignation. "Darlin', I'm getting on a plane. I'm not going to trust this one. I'll be there, with Caleb, as soon as I can be. I got Julianna Brewer on the other line — those Spokane folks might race me, see who's got the faster plane." He was speaking lightly, trying to reassure her. "You just sit by the phone and try to get to the uncle. He's got the best chance of keeping Caleb safe. He's closest. You know it's possible this is just some weird coincidence. And if not, it's possible Caleb knows nothing about it."

When they hung up, she took Lark by the arm, roughly enough that Lark's mouth fell open. "Sorry, honey, but listen. Your brother's phone calls. Do you know if he's talking to anyone he shouldn't be? Or e-mailing?

Do you ever overhear his calls, anything that sounds odd to you?"

Lark shook her head slowly, at the edge of tears. "I don't know. Sometimes he says it's Isabel but it's not."

Marlene pressed her lips together against the crumpling of her face. "Could it be Charles Lundy?"

"I don't know," Lark wailed.

An hour later, no calls, not even Mitch checking in with no news. She could no longer wait by the phone. She called the hotel, left another message for Lowell: she was coming, he should wait in the room with Caleb, she'd explain when she arrived. She would have run for the Land Rover with nothing but the keys if Hilda hadn't been there to remind her that she didn't know where she was going, that she'd get lost and lose time. Hilda would drive. Lark insisted she was going too, might have clamped herself into the backseat and refused to budge if Marlene hadn't remembered that someone needed to feed the birds. Three baby blue-crowned motmots — they'd die without Lark. On the way down the mountain, Marlene and Hilda dropped Lark, with her toothbrush and a box full of birds, at Isabel's house.

CHAPTER SIXTEEN

Caleb didn't remember deciding to go with Jolly to his hotel room at the Gran. He was aware only of the looped gold-on-red pattern of the hallway's carpet passing beneath his feet and then the door of 320 opening and closing, shutting them in. At the click, some bound-up, caterwauling kernel of pure Nicky broke free to cling shaking in Jolly's arms, his face in Jolly's neck, immovable. He let Jolly lift him to the bed, a storm of blood in his ears, and they sat locked together, Jolly's breath congested, his hand finding skin under the back of Caleb's shirt. "Oh, god," Jolly was saying, both hands now hopping from one spot to another of Caleb's back as if surprised by each new part of him. "I can't believe this. I can't believe I have you."

"I can't believe you came." Had Caleb grown so much in five months, or was Jolly smaller, like the house on Waverly Way that had shrunk so much in his absence? That this was Jolly, present in the flesh, was beginning to feel not just unlikely but, as the roaring quieted, unworkable, wrong. "They're going to know," he said.

"I don't care." Jolly eased him loose, grinning. "Let me look at you."

Jolly still had the puffy look, especially around the eyes, which were nevertheless wild and bright, and his hair was cut short. "No more glasses," he was saying, "and your hair. God, you look good, though." Two hands inspected Caleb's hair, measured his cheekbones and jaw and the spread of his shoulders, Jolly's eyes blinking and troubled, then lost as his hands moved lower.

"We can't stay here," Caleb said, worried, annoyed for a reason unclear to him. "Be here. I have to —" As Jolly's face dove into his neck, he squirmed out of the embrace and stood, went to the window to check the plaza. "He'll freak if I'm not waiting when he gets back. We need a plan."

"Take off your clothes," Jolly said.

Caleb stared at him, feeling something sharpen in his head, begin to declare itself. "What are you thinking? Why did you come?"

"To be with you."

"How? Where? We can't" — he gasped,

almost a sob — "go back *home*. We can't cross a border. They'll know if we do."

Jolly gazed up at him from the bed, rapturous and stunned. "So we'll . . . maybe we'll stay in this country. Hide out in some little town. We can go to the coast and get a boat. There are ways. We'll find a way."

Something was missing, and it took Caleb a minute to locate it. Where was the hyperactive caution? Whenever they had ventured forth to take a chance against the world — to the dentist or the eye doctor, to go sledding or to school — Jolly had driven him crazy with lists of every misfortune that might befall them, the what-ifs and thenwhats. Nicky, as he gained confidence in the world, could generally find a snidely simple answer to most objections. But he'd never had to wonder whether some new gamble had been thought through.

Caleb swallowed, took a breath. "This is a bad idea. For you to be here, at all. You shouldn't have come." The pain of saying this blindsided him, sparked tears, and he went back to the bed. He folded into Jolly's arms and laid them down.

"You're all I want in the world," Jolly said, holding him tightly. Did he sound uncertain? Or only worried, lost? Their bodies wouldn't line up right, with that perfect jigsaw interlock Nicky could always find when he needed it. "We're supposed to be together," Jolly said. "We'll make it happen. It has to. Or why should I bother living?"

Jolly's hands began to move purposefully — of course he wanted sex. Even if his head had been on straight, it would have been his first order of business in this room.

"Quit, Jolly." He said it almost gently, extricating himself. "I have to go. Now."

"What?" Jolly's startled face showed plainly that even a minute of separation was unimaginable, that the small debates aside — sex or no sex, and where they should run to — all their real problems had been solved by the fact of their being in the same room.

"I'm serious. I can't be gone when he comes back. You'd better figure something out." Looking down at Jolly, who still gaped from the bed, he wondered for the first time if the man was capable of taking care of himself, let alone both of them. "I'll call your room when I can."

It was a relief to close the door behind him, give his brain some space to work. He might have suspected he was being tested if the familiar foxy glint had been there, but Jolly looked like a man with a concussion, a man who hadn't slept.

Caleb's watch said ten after four, early

still for Lowell to be back. He went up one flight, let himself into 426. No Lowell, no sign he'd returned. The message light on the phone flashed.

Two messages, in the four hours since Lowell had left. Caleb played them. The first was his mother, her voice cool and measured to a slightly unnatural degree. "Lowell, call me when you get this. Immediately. We have an emergency. Caleb, if you hear this just . . . tell Lowell to call me, okay? Love you."

The second was again his mother, from half an hour before, in the same torqued-up, chilly tone. "Lowell, this is very important. If you get this, please just stay in the hotel room, you and Caleb. Don't leave the room. Please. I'm getting in the car right now. I'm coming there." Muffled voices behind the phone. "Hilda and I, we'll be there by eight o'clock, eight thirty, I hope. Just wait for us. I'll explain when I get there."

He listened again — the whole story was in her voice: *danger* — then erased both messages, his brain speeding along on oiled rails. He dialed room 320. "Jolly, when did you buy your plane ticket?"

"At the airport this morning. Very last minute."

"Well, the FBI knows. They know you're here and they know *I'm* here. They called my mother. She's driving down here, right now, to get me. And I'll bet you anything the FBI is right behind you."

"They don't have jurisdiction."

"You sure about that?"

Jolly sounded tense. "I have a right to be here. Wherever I want to be."

"That doesn't mean you get to run off with an underage boy!" he cried, sarcastic, outraged. He took a breath, pressed a hand over his eyes. "Look, we can fix this. Maybe. But you have to go. Get back on a plane and go home. Or Spain, whatever. Anywhere. Just get out of here."

"No. I'm not leaving without you."

"You are. Because I'm not going with you." It felt right as soon as he said it, right because the alternative was impossible and right because he didn't want to go. Had he only just now felt it as his choice? He didn't want to go. All he wanted was to fix the mess before his family found out more than they already knew.

"Nicky, you don't mean that."

Caleb, he wanted to say, but he was being sucked into the vortex, regretting already the pain in Jolly's voice. He owed Jolly all he had. "Please," he said, "at least get out of the hotel." He pictured Mitch Abernathy, Julianna Brewer, downstairs at the desk. "Don't even check out. Just go. Maybe I can stall them."

"Baby, you're worried over nothing. The feds can't touch me."

"Maybe not legally. But you know what? I've gotten to know a few of these agents. Pretty well. And there's one or two of them might be willing to take you on a little car ride, with a bullet."

Jolly laughed at that. "Oh, really?"

"Yeah, and Luis, he told me about a river near here, the Rio Tárcoles, where these huge crocodiles just wait right under the bridge, dozens of them, for people to throw stuff off — it's like the perfect place to dispose of a body. Who's to know how people go missing in Costa Rica?"

"Crocodiles! I love it."

Caleb laughed too, relieved that Jolly was finally sounding grounded, more like himself. Maybe he'd wake up to reason. "You know who it'll be, taking you on that ride?" he said. "I got the perfect combination. Mitch Abernathy and my mother. God, you're so dead. Leave now, Jolly." He hung up the phone.

He lay on his bed and stared at the ceiling, wishing he'd kept his mother's messages to play back. She'd wanted to speak to Lowell — to alert Lowell, not Caleb. Because she didn't trust him. But maybe it was possible for her to believe Jolly had come on his own, stalking Caleb through some unknown source of information. And if Jolly had known, for instance, no more than that the Vincents were living in the country, then San José was the main airport, the logical place to start, and maybe with no greater scheme in mind than to thumb his nose at the feds.

When the door clicked with Lowell's key, Caleb closed his eyes, feigned waking. Lowell had his glasses, asked about Caleb's day, began speaking of his own. "I'm ready for a beer," Lowell said. "Hungry for dinner yet?"

"Starving," Caleb said, afraid that if they lingered at all, the phone would ring. "Let's go out. Not the hotel restaurant, somewhere else."

At five thirty, they walked out past the front desk. No Julianna, no Mitch, though Caleb pictured every uniformed bellhop calling *Señor! Sir!*, dashing up to Lowell, handing him a message. "You all right?" Lowell asked with a chuckle, grabbing him by the back of the neck, and Caleb smiled, released a breath. Nothing for him to do now but erase it all from his mind and keep

Lowell out for as long as he could. No one would begin to chase down Jolly as long as they were still trying to find Caleb.

But did he expect Jolly to listen, to run? As they turned to walk toward Avenida Central, Caleb saw him watching from the plaza, sentinel in the shadow of a tree, beneath the boy whose wings burned in the lowering sun.

At a restaurant called Picasso's, they ordered sea bass casados and beer. "I can't stop thinking about Luis," Caleb said, to explain, to push aside, his preoccupation. Jolly had followed from three storefronts back at least as far as the restaurant door. "That he could be in trouble . . ." As he spoke, the importance of finding Luis grew little claws to hook him — he *could* be in danger, though the trapped and desperate boy he pictured was less Luis than Nicky, waiting in his basement for any savior.

Lowell had done some scouting that afternoon, the optometrist's office being adjacent to a zone of bars marked on Jesús's map. Not much happening there during the day, but he'd come away with the location of one of the seedier clubs known for drag shows, rent boys, and private sex rooms. "Might be worth checking out," he said. "I can drop you back at the hotel and grab a cab over there."

"No, I need to go with you," Caleb insisted. "Would you even recognize Luis, however he looks now? And it's a bar, right? So like you said, no one will care."

Lowell was not keen on the idea. "You think you can handle a gay bar?"

"Me? For real? Can *you* handle it, that's the question."

"This doesn't sound like just any old gay bar," Lowell warned. But he gave in, said, "You just stick close."

Stick close was Caleb's primary impulse, Lowell his protection against — what? No shadow of Jolly in the streetlights and headlights and fluorescent-lit doorways as they left the restaurant. No cabs seemed to follow theirs. But even if he was pursuing still, he wasn't going to grab Caleb and throw him into a van. Caleb would have to decide to go. Wouldn't he? Like that cream-colored horse in the paddock: pick a direction. *Taffy! Bo!* He felt that his only real chance of making a choice might require Lowell in sight at the same time, calling.

It was going on eight o'clock — his mother and grandmother soon to arrive at the hotel — when the cab dropped Caleb and Lowell at a cinder-block structure painted red with yellow shutters. El Rojo, it was called, though a name appeared nowhere. From the street, through a low portal of a doorway, the club pounded with electronica and glowed redder than its façade. Deep toward the back a strobe flashed, and above the dark heads of men he could see a blond boy in silver shorts and nothing else writhing on a dais.

"I can't go in there," he said, barely able to speak. The glimpse through the door might have sent him running but for Lowell at his shoulder, who didn't flinch, assessing the view.

He checked Caleb's eyes, then the street behind them. "You can't wait out here," he said, his voice flat and quiet. "You can come in, or we'll get the fuck out. Forget the whole thing. Your call."

A man inside the door said something impatient in Spanish that amounted to "In or out?" — a choice still being offered. Caleb drew a breath and stepped in. Lowell handed over a cover charge. The doorman did not ask for ID, though he glared down at Caleb with stone-dead eyes.

The place was larger than it looked from outside, with an island bar and more go-go boys scattered through the room on separate stages. Other rooms opened at the back. The early crowd was not really dancing, just milling about, sipping drinks, idly watching the boys. The blond had the showcase spot, and Caleb's eyes kept going back to him. His body was slim, hairless, shimmering with oil and glitter, and in the smoke and the swim of his lenses the boy could have been fourteen or past twenty. It was possible that Caleb himself was the only person in the place under eighteen, since age of consent was supposed to be strict here, especially when it got anywhere near the legalized prostitution. But who could say? In seconds, he'd performed a kind of radar sweep of the room and knew the dancers were boys, the patrons were men, and that except for a cluster of possibly college-aged gringos who looked a little lost, he was the only one in the place under twenty-five not for sale.

Jolly, he couldn't help knowing, would have liked most of the boys — the blond for sure, also two wire-thin ticos with neat tufts of chin hair. He even have to break the law. "Barely legal" was within his range. Nicky, of all boys, had been merely the one in need of rescue. In some ways, between the two of them, Jolly had been the victim — still was, if Caleb without quite realizing it had enticed him to Costa Rica, made him risk his freedom, his life, only because the one he loved had asked it.

But Caleb couldn't think about that, couldn't let himself remember that Jolly was here at all. Already some small part of him was sounding a faint, high-pitched alarm, a call to ditch Lowell and be where he could be found.

None of the boys he could see was Luis. Lowell kept a possessive hand on his neck, moving him through toward the back rooms. Out of the dark, the glances of men were strangely rare, vacant, passing. He'd become unappealing, or was only disguised, amid boys all stripped and elevated under lights like the theater's winged muse. The relative invisibility let him relax by degrees, until he began to feel something like the jadedness he'd claimed at dinner. Even this early, the air was thickening with sex, but it wasn't a prison; it was just a bar. Anyone could choose to leave.

Lowell made contact with a trim-bearded man who gave him a friendly look. Maybe it was flirty, but Lowell didn't hesitate to lean up and shout in the man's ear. As they spoke, his hand fell from Caleb's neck, and Caleb took slow steps down a hallway, past men camped along the wall, toward a back room where he could see a stage show in progress. In a voluminous curly black wig and eyelashes of cartoon proportions, a performer strutted — hard to tell over the main room's thudding whether she was singing or speaking into her microphone.

When Caleb reached the doorway, a new performer was taking the stage, in a great headdress made of fruit, two go-go boys dancing behind her as she lip-synched salsa. But they all seemed a bit bored, and the crowd paid little attention. A few curious or bemused glances passed Caleb's way, but only one man in the room, from the shadows of the opposite wall, spotted him with the intensity of a hunting cat. To this man, he glowed a different color, fluorescent green, under powers of vision either distorting or keener, truer, than that of the others.

Lowell caught up with him as the performers exited. "So, this is not the real show yet, I guess," Lowell said. "Kind of a warm-up. But that guy said the drag queens are these older dudes who've been doing it for a while. All those ones up on the pedestals are rentable, for 'private dances' of different sorts in little rooms in the back. The drag queens too, maybe? He didn't know."

Caleb lifted an eyebrow at the bottle of Imperial Lowell drank from. "Did he buy you that?"

"No." Lowell grinned, leaned against the wall. In a playful swipe, he caught Caleb's elbow and drew him closer, flashing a malevolent glance straight at the hunter across the room. Caleb hadn't thought it would be visible: his own looking, the man looking back. At Caleb's ear, Lowell said, "So I guess there's a guy back at the rooms who handles the transactions. Wanna go, uh, find out what's available?"

Caleb pictured Luis, rentable, waiting in some booth for a customer. Luis in the gold lamé mini, a tall wig, and white patent-leather boots. Luis in boy's clothing, his head shaved, bruises still discernible. Either way, he'd appear younger than any of the others, awkward, with a displeasing tense reluctance in his demeanor, like Nicky at parties. How long would it take to achieve the sleek boredom of the others?

"He won't be here."

"Yeah, I'm thinking not." Lowell finished the beer. "I got a better idea. Let's va-manos."

Outside, they stood against the wall waiting for a cab. Lowell's friend inside had advised him on where to find a likely brothel of a more standard sort, not far, but Jesús had warned him not to walk anywhere. They'd be mugged as soon by travesties as by gay bashers. At the nearest corner, travesties stalked under streetlamps in precipitous heels. On the drive over they had passed several, one so lovely and delicate she might have been a girl, one rocky case in a cock-eyed wig who hadn't bothered to shave, the others somewhere in between, females of a polished but tall and burly sort with eyes like street brawlers' under heavy makeup. None looked remotely like Luis. None looked as tentative or out of place as Luis would look on these streets. A brothel was starting to sound hopeful, like comparative safety.

"Have we given any thought," Lowell asked, "to what we'd actually do with this kid if we found him?"

Good question. And maybe there would be nothing *to* do, if Luis had cast the right spell, conjured himself a pretty life. Or even a marginally livable one. But trying to picture the uglier places he might have landed made Caleb almost tearful. "I just want to know where he is. See if he's okay."

"Okay," said Lowell, in a steadying tone.

In the cab, Lowell asked the driver to take them along the travesty walks. He rode with an arm hooked out the rolled-down window, making inquiries whenever he found a friendly face: a new girl, he said, seventeen

586

or so, maybe going by the name Valencia? He found a few who knew English, one impatient that they weren't interested in a trick, one swearing she herself was Valencia, and one saying with a hand to her heart, "Pobrecito! I hope you find your friend. I will watch for her."

The brothel was a flat-fronted row house without a marker of any sort, but the driver pointed out the door as if he knew it. *Wait for us,* Lowell tried to say, but in his Spanish it came out more, Caleb thought, like *Hope for us.* The door was gated, the windows barred and covered, nothing to see from outside but dimly, through the door, a set of narrow stairs leading steeply up. Lowell pushed a buzzer. Upstairs they could hear voices, maybe a TV. It took a second buzz before a voice that could have been male or female hollered down, "Qué quiere?"

Lowell, with a queasy grimace, hollered back, "A boy. Mirando un chico. Tengo dinero."

At the top of the stairs, someone in a knee-length skirt peered down at Lowell, who had stepped to the fore. A buzzer sounded. As Lowell opened the gate, Caleb said, "You know, if you were wondering, taking me to a brothel is probably one of those lines you were talking about." He'd passed beyond the numb dread that had gripped him at the club's door, as if the perimeter to the underworld had been guarded by an electric fence. Now that he was in, he was calm enough that it was all seeming a little funny, strange and familiar at once.

Lowell said, "Later we'll go over the things we're not telling your mother."

The steps were sticky with grime and served as storage for boxes and buckets and dead plants so that Lowell and Caleb had to sidle up single file, past peeling wallpaper. At the top was a kind of lobby, floored in mismatched linoleum, low-ceilinged, lit by two small lamps. Sheets were tacked over the windows; the walls were unpainted plaster, undecorated but for a pair of fist-sized holes. The TV noise came from farther back in the house, beyond what looked to be a kitchen, emitting strong smells of cooking.

Two tough-looking boys in jeans and tanks lounged on a sofa; a third, shirtless and wearing the shy pout of a child though he was not one, sauntered up to the kitchen doorway for a look at them. An angel was tattooed on his shoulder; a trail of black hair ran from his navel into his jeans. *You,*

Caleb thought, selecting with Jolly's eyes. Counting nothing but physical attraction, Jolly might have chosen this boy over Nicky. The boy held a long feather that he toyed with against the door frame in a way that called to mind Luis, but the feather was not brown-mottled and delicate like the ones in Luis's collection; it was stiff and grimy white, like all that was left of the boy's own wings.

Behind a podium stood the one who had buzzed them in, an elaborately pretty young woman who was surely not a woman. And not Luis, though she looked enough like him beneath waves of dark hair that Caleb had to blink and look again.

Their hostess spit out something in Spanish that Caleb took as "What is *that*?" and she meant him. Her voice, too, was reminiscent of Luis's.

"Habla inglés?" Lowell asked, while Caleb tried to hide a little behind him. "We're looking for someone, a boy named Luis. A travesty? New here?"

"No travesties here," sneered this person, offended, as if denying they had rats, roaches.

"No?" Lowell couldn't help but snicker. "You," he said gently, "for instance, are not one?"

"I am Miss Gravy," she said, or this is what Caleb heard through her heavy accent. "I am not for sale. And no children here."

"Oh, he's . . . young-looking. He gets that a lot. Look, we don't want any kind of sexual, you know, services. We just want to find our friend."

"Maybe named Valencia," Caleb interjected, his voice louder than he'd intended. Keeping behind Lowell, he stood nearest to the boy in the kitchen doorway, who was giving him a full-body scan, his expression somewhere between skeptical and intrigued. "Or he might be a boy," Caleb said, half to this boy. "With his head shaved, kind of ragged."

"Your friend," said Miss Gravy, "maybe does not want to be found."

Kitchen Boy gave Miss Gravy a look. Either he had a permanent pout or he wasn't liking Miss Gravy too much, Caleb thought. "¿Cómo se llama?" Caleb asked him, sotto voce, before he'd thought to do it.

"He has no name for you," Miss Gravy snapped, while the boy said, "Ramón." Miss Gravy pointed an imperious finger into the house, hollering the boy off like a dog, and he slunk back out of sight. The two on the sofa, having decided Lowell had no money to spend in their direction, looked half asleep with boredom, though one idly rubbed his crotch now and then in case something might change. The buzzer sounded below, and Miss Gravy hissed at the crotch-rubber to attend to it. To Lowell, she said, "This is a business."

"I gotcha," Lowell said, hands up. "If you know where he is, I can pay for your time."

She sighed. "This boy is not here." Then there was hollering below, a man yelling *Gravy* and a lot more in Spanish. She marched between Caleb and Lowell to the head of the stairs and hollered back. Caleb had to step back out of her way, and there just at the edge of his vision was Ramón back in the kitchen, beckoning with a head tip for him to follow. Caleb didn't hesitate. The place was cruddy and run-down, but otherwise there was nothing unfamiliar in it. Nothing hiding behind any door here could surprise or hurt him.

Beyond the kitchen, he followed Ramón between a TV blaring a game show and six or seven boys who crowded before it in an effluvium of beer bottles and snack bags. Caleb gave them a smile and a wave, and they stared back astonished, turned to follow him with their eyes. Smiling, Ramón said something to him ending in "viejo" that

591

he took for "You are not an old man."

Had Jolly really asked why, without Nicky, he should go on living? He should give this place a try, Caleb thought. Before that afternoon, the idea of Jolly with one of these boys would have been unendurable, from any distance, but now it didn't bother him much. A chance to make the suggestion to Jolly would have amused him.

Thwacking the feather in a steady tempo against his denim-covered leg, Ramón led Caleb down a branching hallway with mildewed carpet and many rooms, some with sheets for doors. Here the fry oil and stale beer stench was infiltrated by a faint but unmistakable acrid mix of new and old piss, new and old semen — the smell gave him pause. But it was benign in its way, lacking in one or two volatile elements that would have tripped the alarm in his brain, made him step back and out. Open any door and he would not find Nicky. Or Melia, seated on a bed, arm wrapped in a man's shirt, though the place called to mind the house where she'd been more than any other: rank carpeting along a hallway of doors where one or two girls looked out to see who was passing by, all that rattling equipment.

At the last doorway, Ramón pushed aside

a curtain, held it with a coy grin for Caleb behind him. They were in a small, dark room smelling of patchouli and sweat, with a bed on one side and a cracked mirror on the other, mounted over a dresser where several candles burned. Ramón pulled the chain of an overhead bulb. On the bed was not Luis but an enormous, naked white man. His belly rose in a gray-furred hump above the sagging mattress. Hanging off the end toward the door, his broad feet were pink and innocently clean, splayed by the heft of his thighs. His head was bald and outsized, with fleshy jowls and no apparent neck, and his wrists were bound with hand-cuffs to the headboard. He blinked at Caleb with watery eyes and made no sound other than the wheeziness of his breathing.

Ramón, mouth pursed, arms crossed, gave Caleb a laughing glance. "Americano," he said, as if this explained the man. With the feather's tip, he slashed at the nearest foot, making it flinch and wiggle. In a tone of command, he addressed the man in rapid Spanish, emphasized with a slap to the mound of belly that made Caleb jump. The man answered in Spanish as if begging, softly and slowed by the effort to breathe. Ramón spoke again, and the man said to Caleb, with a gentle, professorial precision,

"You are also American, he says. Are you lost, son?"

"No," Caleb said. "I'm looking for someone."

The man nodded sagely. "He wants me to translate." The two exchanged more words. The man said, "Your friend was here but he was sent away. He was too young. Also, not the right look, too feminine. A transvestite? They do not work in the brothels. They work on the streets."

Ramón, the white feather parked in his back pocket, rooted in a closet and came out with a Braves cap. "He left this," the man on the bed translated. "Dropped it. You can buy it back for him."

"How much?"

"Five thousand."

Caleb looked askance at the hat, something Luis must have picked up at the secondhand shop in Santa Elena, which was packed to the walls with these American castoffs. "Ask him why the hostess out there said maybe my friend doesn't want to be found."

The man put the question to Ramón, who did not seem to have an answer other than some disparagement of Miss Gravy. "You will know that better than he," the man said.

Caleb considered the fat man, whose face

was flushed and wet and who seemed unable to move in any direction. "Do you, um, need help?"

He smiled dreamily. "No, darling. I'm just fine."

A commotion came from the hall, Lowell calling for him, then yanking back the curtain. "Fucking christ on a cracker." He took up Caleb by the scruff, frozen at the same instant by the vision of the man on the bed. "Well. Uh, hello, there? Sir."

"Wait." Caleb leaned toward the manacled man. "Ask where my friend would go. Is there another brothel? Miss Gravy, where would she send him?"

His pout back, Ramón spun the hat on a finger. Caleb added, "Tell him a thousand for the hat. Five for the hat and an answer." The boy rolled his eyes and relented.

"She sent your friend to the youth shelter," the man said, then added, "There is a good one here, I believe."

"Thanks," Caleb said, then "Gracias," to Ramón, plucking the hat from his finger. He asked Lowell to give the boy the five thousand colones. Lowell, bemused and impressed, extracted the bill, while Caleb turned the hat over doubtfully. "¿Lo quiere?" he murmured to Ramón. "To keep, uh, quedarse?" Ramón looked ambivalent over this proposal; they both shrugged and smiled. They were having a little conversation. Caleb pulled the hat onto his own head. "Que lo pases bien," he said to Ramón, with a nod to the Americano as Lowell led him out.

It was ten o'clock — still early, perhaps, for most of the action on the streets, though it was Saturday night, and the travesties were out in gleaming hordes. The cab conveyed Lowell and Caleb slowly along the designated streets, just to look from a distance into the painted faces. Lowell seemed energized, ready to be further amused. "So, youth shelter next?"

Caleb shrugged. "If he's there, I guess he's okay, right?"

For a few seconds, following Ramón down the brothel hall, he'd believed that Ramón would throw open a door and there would be Luis — chained to a bed, perhaps — and Caleb could save him. Simple. Simple, that is, if Luis wanted saving. And then what? Carry him back home? Put him in the room next to his in the south wing, feed him like one of his mother's wild birds?

He'd wondered before if he was in love with Luis, if somehow Luis got him around the question of liking girls, liking boys. And wasn't that love, when people affected you this way? He had no chance with Luis, had he even wanted one. Yet for much of the night, he'd forgotten to wonder where Jolly was or if he could be waiting, even now, in front of the theater.

"He is seventeen," Lowell reminded him. As he leaned to watch out the window, the black scorpion tattoo on his neck was lit with streetlight. Caleb felt tender toward the thing, wanted to pet it.

"Eighteen in like a month," Caleb said. "Still, I feel like it's my fault."

Lowell slumped back, turned to smile. "What is?"

By the time they pulled up to the hotel, Caleb wanted his mother. And there she was, behind the lobby glass, pushing out the door, running for him. It was all he could do to be mildly surprised and interested to see her, not to grab onto her for dear life as she did him.

Chapter Seventeen

"Where is he?" Caleb asked Julianna, a mild experimental probe. "If he's really here, I want to see him."

Almost immediately, as his mother had turned from embracing him in front of the Gran Hotel to harangue Lowell, Caleb was whisked apart, into the care of Julianna. They sat on the beds in her second-floor room. Like Jolly, she seemed subtly altered from herself, older and more tired, though still beautiful in her way. From time to time, Mitch Abernathy traded places with her, and once his mother came in for a longer talk, and he could tell that outside the room there was a lot of conferring going on. He was asked if he'd seen Jolly, received any word from him, but no one called into doubt his blinking, baffled show of ignorance or turned on him with the accusation: we know you communicate, we know you lured him here, obviously we know. Everyone was soft with him, their voices muted. They were relieved to find he'd never been in danger.

They didn't know where Jolly was. "You know him pretty well," Julianna said. "Why do you think he'd come here?"

Caleb shrugged. "I'm sure he found out we moved to Costa Rica. Isn't that in the news?"

"Do you think he's here to try to get to you? Maybe take you back?"

"He's not a kidnapper."

"No." She tipped her head, curls falling from her shoulder down one cheek. "What would you do, if he contacted you somehow? Or if, say, you saw him in the street?"

"What do you think?" They had made up, somewhat, over the phone. Though their recent calls were shorter and less frequent, she'd stopped pushing him for a statement against Jolly. Being with her in the Gran brought him back to their hotel room in Spokane, and he kept his voice as soft as hers, his anger in check. He was still angry with her. But he couldn't help wanting her back, even if she was a lie, a trick.

Somber, she watched him, waiting for a real answer, so he said, "I'd talk to him. I really *want* to talk to him, you know. You all act like it'd be so dangerous, but I'm not scared of him. We're . . . close. He means a lot to me. But it's not like I'd run off with him. I wouldn't want to."

She nodded, smiling a little, and didn't question his use of the present tense. "I believe you. And it's a testament to how strong you are, that you wouldn't go. I think it might have been different a few months ago, when you were more susceptible to him. But now I can see the difference in you, Caleb. I think you're just about strong enough that you don't need him anymore."

When his mother came in, she wanted to hear about the eye doctor, about his night out looking for Luis. She seemed only relieved, after tearing down the mountain to find him, that his evening had in fact been so safe and innocent, sex clubs and brothels with his uncle! "You really think Luis would go to a place like that?" she asked, sympathetic, as if she knew Luis and cared for him too. "Surely he's got other options."

He spent the night as guarded as he had ever been, between the beds of Mitch Abernathy and Julianna Brewer. It embarrassed him, to be treated like a child or some jewel of some extraordinary value and not a teenager who could take care of himself, but in the eyes of a certain invested segment of two bureaus of the FBI, he would be forever eleven years old, forever the victim. At least it was only these two who had arrived on the mission, not their partners and supervisors and all the shrinks and half the agents of each office. Playing bathroom tag with his guardians, always one agent in the room, Caleb ranted a little. "Do you all not know how many kidnapped kids there are who are in real trouble right now? Help *them,* why don't you? Save *them.*"

"If we knew where they were," Julianna said, "we would do that."

The next morning he was released for breakfast downstairs, at a tiny two-seater beside the window with Julianna — not his mother, his grandmother, Lowell. They'd gone somewhere with Mitch Abernathy, were not even in view. "Is this some kind of trap?" he asked, glancing around the sunny dining room, marking each corner that led to a hall. "You think Jolly's here?"

"No," she said, and sipped her juice. As if to prove it, she let him go to the men's room alone, and he found it empty. He looked into the stalls. Ridiculous to think that Jolly would be here, crouched on a toilet, waiting for Caleb to happen in. He pictured his family off with Mitch at the Rio Tárcoles, helping him feed the crocodiles.

And what did Caleb want to talk to Jolly

about? Julianna kept asking, unsatisfied with his general answers, as if he were hiding something from himself.

As they were finishing crepes full of mushrooms and cheese, Mitch appeared in the doorway and flashed a signal that made Julianna grin. She wiped her mouth with her napkin. "Looks like it's time for you folks to get home."

Caleb felt sick. "Did you kill him?"

She frowned. "No, honey. He's fine."

But he would not see Jolly again. Was it any easier to take the second time, knowing they had him, somewhere, and would not show him? It should have been. The itchy need to see him, speak to him (about what?) remained. Maybe it was only that, once again, they had missed the good-bye.

Jolly was "in custody" — here or back in the States, Caleb couldn't tell. "Did he break a law?" Caleb asked. All that mattered for now, Julianna told him, was that a judge had revoked his passport, so he would be grounded again. And probably this escapade would affect the original case, but they'd have to wait to see. So far, the American news crews hadn't caught wind, and the bureau would do all it could to keep the story quiet — the story being that Charles

Lundy had flown to Costa Rica to hunt down his former victim but was thwarted before he could find the boy.

The Land Rover was already loaded. Caleb hugged both agents good-bye. He was fond of them and irritated by them and loyal under pressure, in fluctuating but roughly equal portions, the way most kids he knew felt about their parents. He got into the backseat with his mother.

He couldn't get a clear read on why the agents and his family were all treating him as if he were a mental patient, but he was beginning to relax a little. At first he'd thought they were psyching him out, pretending to believe him, but now it seemed they might go on believing. From the start, they'd all spoken as if Jolly had acted alone. So maybe Caleb could be innocent after all.

His mother squeezed his hand across the backseat as Lowell drove out. "You probably didn't sleep much. How are you feeling?"

Guilty. "Fine."

She shook her head. "I guess this has all been a little upsetting."

He shrugged. "I guess. It's just dumb they even care where he goes. I mean, there are actual kidnappers they could be chasing. Or terrorists or something."

"And you never found Luis. Lowell" — she leaned up to the driver's seat — "is there anywhere else we could look for Luis?"

They drove around San José asking directions until they arrived at the youth shelter. No Luis there — most of the kids were out for the day — and no one would say whether he'd been there or not. Marlene suggested they check the travesty walks, which on a Sunday morning were empty but for a pair of stragglers sharing a cigarette on wobbly heels, one in a stole of spotted fur. "It's okay," Caleb said, feeling depressed, useless. He leaned at the window and watched idly for Luis, for Melia, missing her strangely. Where had she gone? How stupid would it be if Luis's half-assed spell had really banished her? He knew, in fact, that it could not have, that she would not be dealt with that way. They passed storefronts, mostly gated or closed behind rolled-down metal doors.

"We should stop by the Mercado Central while we're here," Hilda said. "It's something to see, all the vendor stalls."

"Closed on Sundays, isn't it?" Lowell said. Then, "There's that other one, down by the bus station. It seems to always be open."

Marlene said they should get home before Lark went "berserk," though she'd called

604

Isabel's house that morning from the hotel. Still, the market was on the way, and they came upon a spot to park. They'd go in just for a quick look.

It was the same street market Caleb and Lowell had stopped in on Friday, the dark warehouse with aisle after aisle of merchandise sorted at random into lighted booths. "I have an idea," Caleb said to his mother, who had paused at a produce stall to puzzle over a row of bins containing twelve kinds of mystifying fruit labeled in Spanish. "Someone to ask about Luis."

She followed, but Caleb was turned around, couldn't remember on which aisle he'd found the old bruja with her stall of remedies. He tried random lanes, aiming for the soft angle of light he recalled coming from the street. Then he was there, before the fat old tica on her stool, and standing in the aisle beside the counter was a thin young woman in a fringed scarf who said, in that startlingly low, smoky voice, "My stalker is here. Where are your glasses?"

Luis's face was brightly feminine, with coral lips and makeup that covered what bruises remained. He wore a black dress dotted in purple flowers, a purple scarf wrapped about his head and throat. The silky tassels of fringe along his forehead and cheeks were as pretty as jewelry. Caleb might have thrown his arms around this girl, but he stopped short, held himself back. He laughed out a breath, grinning. "I was looking for you."

"Funny you are here," said Luis, puzzled and blinking. "I have something to tell you."

Luis was staying at the youth shelter, working as an apprentice to the old bruja. "She doesn't admit it yet," Luis said, eyeing the woman, "but she likes me a little. She calls me Luisa. For this" — he made a dismissive gesture at his face, the scarf, the dress — "which is, just for now, easier. When I have my hair again, maybe I will be Luis."

Marlene hung back, waiting for one of them to look her way. "This is your mother," Luis said. "So you did not run away."

"No. Are you kidding?" Caleb turned to her and she came forward, took Luis's hand.

"Luis," she said, a little giddy. "We've met once, I think? So nice to see you again. I like your . . . scarf. I'll just be over here." She crossed the aisle to browse another stall, then walked to meet Lowell and Hilda, who had turned the corner after them.

"So already I am learning many things," Luis said. "Like a new trick for you."

The word *trick* tripped him, but Luis went

behind the counter, rummaged in a sack. "What happened to the whole prostitution plan?" Caleb murmured when he returned.

Luis gave a coy, one-shouldered shrug, his expression pleased and knowing and somehow less virginal, enough that Caleb raised an eyebrow at it. "What? Boyfriend? Man friend? Ale-Za?" Luis wouldn't say.

"Here," he said, and placed a very small plastic zip-lock bag in Caleb's hand. Inside was a fine grayish dust. "Put that under your pillow when you sleep. The ghost will come to your dream and tell you what to do."

In Marlene's former three A.M. Internet groups, a certain vocal faction was big on "mother sense." Talk to enough mothers of missing children and you could expect at any minute to hear as a doctrine of faith that "a mother knows": "Do you feel him? If you feel he's alive, then he is. You'll know." Some claimed they could feel pain or fear in their child; they could intuit a direction, a temperature, a smell; one woman felt when her daughter was splashing in water, or had the hiccups. Some used the same power to accept that a child was dead; they sensed graves of water, leaves, shallow earth.

Wing nuts, Marlene had decided, though

at different times she'd subscribed to every special power she was alleged to possess, tried on for fit a few of those confident claims. They had never done much to make her feel better, and feeling better was the only benefit she could see: the believers were a calmer, lighter bunch. Some were damn near ethereal.

As she rode shotgun down the mountain, the best article of faith she could summon was that surely by now she must be disaster-proof. The idea kept her reined at the rational side of panic, even when she and Hilda lost half an hour misnavigating the outer barrios of San José, even when, from the artery of Avenida Dos, trying to locate the Gran Hotel, they made what must have been nine wrong turns. When Lowell and Caleb did not answer at their room, she experienced no more than twenty seconds of blankness, of shutting down. Then she proceeded to the next steps — to ask at the desk for anyone who'd seen Caleb leave, seen who he'd been with, to find a phone to call Mitch — enough steps to fill the time, less than an hour, before Mitch arrived.

Greeting each other, they each wore a strange, grim smile, as if to say, *Here we are again.* Mitch, she could tell, was right at the edge of being amused by her unprecedented lack of hysteria. *Did I do this?* she thought then, slightly horrified. *Did I lose him on purpose?*

When it got motivated, the FBI could be stunningly fast with the information. Twenty minutes after walking into the hotel and planting Marlene in a lobby chair, Hilda beside her, Mitch reported back to them. "I'm afraid there's not much doubt that they've been in contact, by phone and e-mail, apparently a good bit. Lundy took a room here earlier today, but it's empty now. Caleb's things and the uncle's are still in their room — including their passports, so that's good. No sign of a struggle any-where."

"So that means?"

Mitch flipped a paperback distractedly against his thigh, lifted the cover to face her. *Great Expectations.* "Recognize that?"

"Caleb's," she said flatly.

"I figured — it's got a stamp from his school in the cover. And it was on the floor in Lundy's room. That doesn't mean any-thing for certain. But I think we'll proceed on the assumption that Caleb is with Lundy, and your brother-in-law is maybe out look-ing for him. There are a few other possibili-ties, so . . . The book doesn't necessarily even put them together. Remember that."

"So, what, he dropped it, and Lundy picked it up?" Her voice was airless, pitched high with stress. "Caleb doesn't drop things. He doesn't lose . . . *books.*"

Julianna Brewer, arriving half an hour later, offered a brighter take. "Look," she said, "it would be pretty hard for Lundy to get Caleb out of here against his will. And if Caleb went willingly, he'd take his passport, right? If they're planning an escape, maybe it hasn't happened yet. So there's a good chance he's still with the uncle. Or maybe he met with Lundy and already sent him away."

Marlene had been stuck at "they've been in contact," but now she tried to cling to this idea that Caleb was simply out somewhere with Lowell. Could she feel which man her child was with? Some slimmer antenna of hers ought to have been sensitive to Lowell as well, primed to stretch out through the cosmos and tap him on the shoulder, but the cosmos gave her nothing.

When Lowell and Caleb arrived in a cab, looking bewildered at their reception, she flipped back to disaster-proof, weak with relief that it had all been some kind of mistake. It took time for her to slide back to "they've been in contact." By then Caleb had been temporarily reclaimed by the FBI;

610

as recompense, she was allowed to attend Lowell's questioning.

They discovered then that Lowell had left Caleb alone all afternoon. So surely he and Lundy had been together, and in some way that Caleb had arranged for. Lowell at first was firm in his disbelief — he'd gotten no hints. Caleb had been napping in the room when he returned. All evening he'd been concerned about finding his friend Luis — even at moments very concerned, to a degree that seemed unwarranted. And that afternoon, he'd seemed a little hesitant about staying alone.

"I don't understand," Marlene said, "how you could leave him alone at *all.*"

Lowell, with a searching sincerity, said, "I'm sorry, Marlene. But at the time I felt like he needed it, in some larger way. Like what he needed was to be trusted."

As Mitch and Marlene jumped in to snap his head off, Julianna, having put Caleb in her room, held out a halting hand with an air of discovery: "No, wait. He's right. And that's our way in. Probably, I have to say, our only way."

After another hour shut away with Caleb, she emerged looking grim, with a provisional game plan. "He needs us all to trust him, even when he's lying. Because he's not really doing it deliberately. He's right on the edge, between two loyalties, two versions of himself, and if he feels doubted, or feels like he's in trouble for doing something bad — well, for him that's the same as not being liked. He'll go where he feels safe. He'll stay if he thinks that you're in his corner, that you believe in him."

So let him lie? Believe his lies, call him on nothing? Mitch said, "Problem is, he's a teenager. At a certain point, he's going to do what he wants, and there won't be a whole lot of recourse. Then it's no longer kidnapping. He's a runaway. So we have to be pretty careful."

Marlene and Hilda moved into Lowell's room for the night, shared Caleb's bed. "You should call Jeff," Hilda said, but Marlene said it was late there, no point in worrying him now. Once they were home she could call with the full report. Thus far, Hilda had made no mention to Marlene about Lowell, though Lowell had relayed Hilda's disapproval before he'd left town. "I'm getting the blame," he said. "Looks like you're getting a pass." All evening he'd waited until they were away from the FBI, with Hilda in the bathroom, to really take Marlene into his arms and hold her. Her initial rage hadn't lasted long. In every break, he'd been telling her about his time with Caleb, and even in his more reckless decisions she could hear how attentive he'd been to Caleb and what he might need. If Julianna was right, maybe the trust he'd given Caleb that afternoon had kept him from leaving.

In the morning, as on the previous night, she found herself positioned for strategizing between Mitch on one side and Lowell on the other — her two men. Lowell now and then draped an awkwardly brotherly arm over her shoulders. Whether or not Mitch read something from the two of them or even tried to, he held himself apart. He was on the phone, marching away, making things happen.

A night with Caleb had convinced Julianna that he'd actually refused a chance to leave with Lundy. "That's all you need to remember," she said to Marlene. "Give him the credit for that decision. He didn't go."

And they gave her son back to her. Keep hold of him this time. Hold by letting go. In a way she would have to seduce him into staying, flatter him with a lie of her own about who she believed he was. But if she wanted more than lies between them, he'd need extra room — for who he was now and had been and would be — within what she allowed and called good.

Again she found that Lowell had been right, insisting that not everything was a sham: Caleb was sincere in wanting to find Luis. And what a relief, a gift, on their way out of town, to actually find him. Caleb had not gone with Lundy. He had decided to stay. He was invested in this life, just enough, and it answered him with miracles. Turning away from the reunion to catch Lowell and Hilda, she burst into ridiculous tears. "That's him," she said, explaining. "That's Luis."

If either boy had asked it with even a hint, she would have loaded Luis into the Land Rover without a second thought. But Caleb said good-bye and returned to them. He had Luis's e-mail address written on his hand.

They drove north on the Pan-American Highway, windows down. She sat in the middle of the backseat so she and Caleb could talk over the road noise, quietly, about Luis. She'd noticed that Caleb took care with the soft Spanish *s* when he said Isabel's name, but for Luis he let it turn to the American *z,* more like *Louise.* He said, "I think he might have a boyfriend." So much less guarded, even his eyes, the glasses like one more piece of Charles Lundy left behind them — if she forgot for the moment that the glasses were in the car with them, in Caleb's bag. He was pensive, melancholy.

"Does that bother you?"

"I don't know. A little." He smiled briefly, shrugged. "I guess it's good. He's too old for me, right?"

She rubbed his knuckle with a thumb. So many unmentionable referents lurked beneath those words, and she surprised herself by saying, "Like your babysitter when you were ten."

"Haylie."

At the time it had seemed to her only cute, utterly normal, just a little boy's crush, but the girl was twenty-five. Had he not been abducted, that dream might still have shaped his whole life, in lesser ways, with its unreasonable power: to be old enough to interest her. To leave behind his childhood and join her where she waited, in adult freedom.

"Luis won't always be too old for you," she said.

He shrugged again. "I just wanted to know he was safe. That's all." From his hoodie pocket he drew a little bag of gray powder, toyed with it in his fingertips.

"What's that? Did he give you a potion?"

He nodded, tilting the bag in the light. The dust inside sifted slowly from one corner, back to the other.

"What does it do?"

"It's for . . . memories, I guess. If you want to get rid of them."

What to say to that? She didn't even touch him. "Does it know which ones?" she asked.

"Supposedly."

"You don't have to swallow it, I hope."

He shook his head — a relief, since she wouldn't want him ingesting this stuff. But he'd chosen to show her. Everything he did could not be hers to control. *Trust,* she told herself. *Let go.* He peeled open the bag, held it tipped at a careful, shallow angle just outside the open car window. The ashy powder — maybe it was ashes in there — blew away into the air behind them, so fine a cloud she couldn't see it go.

March 4, 2006

The man who brought her into the room was white, skinny, brow-beaten. "It's been broke a couple days," he said. "I told them it needed a doctor. Ain't gonna heal with a sling."

He was not one of the ones in charge, just some underling or customer with a crush on the girl who had designated himself her protector. He kept his hands lightly on her shoulders, while her glare, burning with anticipatory rage, shifted from Jolly to Nicky. Her first glance identified Nicky as one of Them. So impossible did this seem that it took him a minute to feel it.

"Her name's Melia," the man said. "She don't talk."

Nudged forward, she set her heels, began to whimper. "Whoa, whoa, hold on," Jolly said, hands out to stop the man. "Don't touch her, okay?" He brought a low stool forward and sat, looking up at the girl from chin level as he spoke softly, haltingly, in Spanish. He asked her about the dog. He asked her the dog's name, if he could hold it. She clutched it tighter and didn't speak, but she softened a little with listening. A few more sentences from Jolly got her to glance down at the top of the dog's head.

He asked Nicky to bring the black medical bag, in which he rummaged and withdrew a translucent sucker, green. He unwrapped it and held it out. Watching his face steadily, she took it and put it in her mouth, the dog still pinned under the same arm. Jolly smiled, murmured something encouraging, and Nicky felt a twinge of jealousy, Jolly's close attention drawn so fully to this other child.

"You want her on the bed?" the man asked.

Leaving the girl to her sucker, Jolly stood and tried to talk the man into stepping out of the room. Lollipop stick protruding from her mouth, the girl looked at Nicky and he looked back, not knowing how to convince her he was just a kid like her. He took off his Mariners cap and ruffled his bleached hair. An instant later he caught the skinny man's gaze on him, remembered where he was.

The man wouldn't leave, but he moved back against the far wall and stayed quiet. The girl backed into a little alcove with a shade-covered window, far enough removed from them for her to extract and examine her sucker. Jolly began unpacking bags, setting out equipment, directing Nicky to help with different items while ignoring the girl.

Nicky, his cap back on, kept an eye on both girl and man, making sure they both stayed where they were supposed to. "She seems less scared," he said quietly.

"The sucker's drugged," Jolly said. "Works best on the little ones. And she's just terrified. Doesn't know *what's* happening to her, poor thing."

Jolly set up the portable X-ray machine and digital developer beside the bed, explaining each to Nicky. He'd seen these machines many times without feeling much curiosity — they'd last been use on his own chest, when he'd been dozy and Jolly's explanations were no more to him than a pleasing vocal rhythm. But now he was Jolly's assistant. ("My son," Jolly had said to the men in charge. "He's going to assist.")

Once they had her sitting on the edge of the tall bed, Jolly eased loose the wrapped shirt. Her arm was swollen into ugly colors from elbow to wrist. "Yeah, I'd say that's broken," he said to the girl with a soft smile.

Nicky stood alongside. The heavy curve of her eyelashes came to just below his chin. Tangled hair hung in her face, which was smudged with dirt and snail-tracked from snot and old tears, her lips swollen, chapped, stained green with the sucker. She smelled of sweat and semen — not just semen, but that familiar nasty mix of old and new semen, with a dash of urine, a dash of blood. She was unbelievably pretty. From behind, he reached with both hands to draw the hair back from her face, lightly enough that she didn't flinch. "Give her a roofie," he said. However faulty his memory of parties and substances had become, he knew that if something extreme was going to happen to you anyway, a roofie was the way to go. And he knew Jolly had them; every now and then Nicky snuck into the bag and borrowed himself one.

Jolly lifted his eyes to Nicky's, considering. "Takes too long, lasts too long. Let's try another sucker."

Her eyes drooped a little with the second one but flashed open again as they attempted to lay her onto her back. She went rigid, began to cry. The skinny man loomed close. "You're making her nervous," Jolly said to him. "Step back to the wall. We're fine over here."

Nicky liked the *We're fine,* Jolly's easy trust of him as an assistant no matter how foreign the situation. "Está bien, dulcita," Jolly said in his dreamland voice, with the lightest fingertip stroke of the girl's hair, his other hand below her throat. "I hate to use a needle on her," he said in the same voice to Nicky. "But I have to numb up that arm eventually. Best do it now. I want you to lay your arm across her collarbones where I have my hand, just kind of casual like you're resting it there. Get down as low as you can and get her to look at you. Be ready for her to struggle; keep her down with that arm."

Nicky crouched by the bed, his arm across her light but braced, his face down on the bedsheet beside hers. "Hey, chica, over here," he called in a sweet murmur like Jolly's, while across the bed Jolly drew up a syringe. Nicky made himself look at her face only. The Spanish eluded him, and he began singing, *The wheels on the bus go round and round, all through the town.* The impulse made him laugh, and his laughing, at least, caught her attention. He tried to think of a song in Spanish — *La cucaracha, la cucaracha* — and this made him laugh a little more. The unsmiling girl seemed at least fascinated with him for a moment, then she let out a brief wail as Jolly said, "Hold her." And then sweetly, the same to each of them, "Terminado; hace mejor. Nice work, Nicky. And that was the worst of it, so the rest won't be so bad. I'm going to position her arm, so you just try to keep her still. Talk to her."

Nicky kept his face close, stroked her hair with light fingertips. "All over," he said. "Está bien." Her eyes, still pooled with tears, looked over at Jolly and her arm then back at him, becoming expressive, questioning, because it didn't hurt anymore, and he answered in the same words, nodding. "Está bien. Sí?" He tried to think of what else to say and found the Spanish close by, and also what she needed to know. "Él es un bueno médico. Un bueno hombre."

"Nikito," Jolly murmured. "Bueno español!"

"How do you say 'hold still'?"

Jolly shook his head. "Can't remember. That would have been a good one to look up, huh?"

Nicky returned to his refrain, *está bien*. So much of the CD instruction from the ride there had been about ordering food, finding a bathroom. He tried, "¿Cómo te llamas? ¿Melia?" She shook her head no, and he felt a rush of pleasure that she'd responded to him. Of course it wasn't her name. Of course some man had named her whatever he pleased. "No," he said with a soft smile. "No es tu nombre. ¿Cómo te llamas?" She said nothing. "¿No es Melia?" She shook her head again, but she wasn't going to speak. He asked Jolly the word for dog, said, "¿Es tu perro? Es un bonito perro." She hugged it closer. The semen smell of her, the fire not gone out of her eyes, was painful this close. He'd seen younger boys in such places, but never so afraid, so far from what they knew of home. And this was a girl — a brown-skinned little girl surrounded by white aliens with freaky anatomy who didn't even speak her language. Still she looked fiercer, stronger, than he had ever felt in something like her place.

. "¿De dónde, tu?" he asked her. "¿Dónde está tu madre? Tu padre?"

"Nicky."

He blinked up, and Jolly gave him a tiny shake of the head. *No.*

He barely knew what he'd asked. Jolly, positioning the X-ray, reached across the prostrate girl and laid a hand to his cheek. At the touch Nicky wanted to leave, realized he had already begged it with his eyes, but something — the touch, or Jolly's expression — pulled him back to the big picture.

Jolly had been hesitant to bring him to this place at all. It was either bring him along or leave him home alone for a night. And the girl was nothing to Jolly, a blip of concern in the universe of Nicky. He'd help her if he could, but he'd abandon her here with her mangled arm the instant he thought Nicky was in trouble.

So he had to be okay. He turned back to the girl, said, "Está bien." He stroked her hair and made himself smile. "Él es bueno hombre. Simpático hombre."

He was still fumbling with the grip on himself when suddenly the girl was whispering to him, several words ending in "su papa?" The touch, he figured, made her ask. "Sí," he said, and pointed. "Mi papa."

Jolly showed him the girl's shattered bone on the computer screen. "A simple one to fix," he said, reading as easily the welter of resistance from Nicky's mind. "I know. I don't like it either. But where she's from, it could easily be worse. The world is a wretched place. We help a little. We make her life bearable, and she has a chance. Yeah?"

Later, once Jolly had reduced the break and wrapped the arm in a sock sleeve and cotton batting, he began building the plaster cast. The skinny man had finally gone away.

The girl was sitting up, slightly drowsy and numbed from the shoulder down, willing even to smile a little. She seemed to understand the cast and its purpose, and held her arm out obligingly and made some comments about it they could only shake their heads to. "No comprendo," they said. "No comprendemos." Giggling, Nicky said, "Somos Americanos estúpidos," and she nodded grimly, which cracked Jolly up. Nicky finger combed her hair, dipped a sleeve of the shirt-sling into the leftover water brought for the plaster and used it to clean her face, while Jolly talked him through each step of the casting process as if Nicky might be entrusted with the next one.

When they were done, one of the overseers came in, and Jolly explained that he needed to see the girl in a month, preferably at a closer location, to check the bone set and remove the cast. The man handed Jolly a thick envelope full of bills and said also he could take a turn with the girl for his trouble. With an upturned palm, he offered the girl on the bed.

Jolly counted the bills. "This girl? Are you joking? She needs rest. A *month* of rest, understand?" Nicky smiled, knowing the lie well — Jolly used it liberally for any small injury at parties: *Leave this one alone;*

doctor's orders. "Take her, let her sleep. You have an older girl, maybe, fifteen, sixteen? A calm, quiet one, very experienced?"

To care for the little one, Nicky assumed. "We have many girls," the man said.

He went out, leading the little girl by her good hand, the dog riding in the blue sling Jolly had supplied her with. Nicky didn't think fast enough to look away before her querulous gaze turned back to him from the door, stayed on him until she was gone. He wanted to follow her, almost, but for what? Watching as Jolly packed equipment, he tried to word the question he didn't quite have yet.

CHAPTER EIGHTEEN

From: drj128@hotmail.com
To: spidermonkey99@yahoo.com
Subject: world enough and time

Todo está bien, sí? Sometimes the bold move is merely foolhardy, as the wiser of us knows (that's you). You'll be the teacher before we're done. Endless admiration, endless adoration, world without end. If it's safe on your side: 509-833-7823.

Caleb was surprised to find the message waiting when he checked, a few days after returning home, and especially surprised by its unwritten news: Jolly was back in Washington, but not in jail.

During their month of calls, it had been simple to set up these secondary e-mail accounts, which they'd hardly had cause to use until now. With the Internet café looking over his shoulder, Caleb started replies, erased them. Words, stupid words. Put together, they wouldn't say what he meant. Or they contradicted themselves and said nothing. He wrote down the phone number and signed off the account.

The next day, getting off the school bus in town, negotiating the sidewalk alone, he was still the boy who kissed the boy in the dress. "That's your *chisme*," Isabel said: people in this town were going to talk, always, and the favorite joke at present seemed to be that he was easily tricked, too stupid to know a boy from a girl. Whistles, muttered comments, soft laughter — he could expect it in certain pockets, like in front of the ferretería, where young men with nothing better to do hung out. Luis, who had gotten it worse just for being himself, had kept mostly indoors, at the Trogan Lodge or Soda La Perla, appearing on the street stealthily when necessary. But the bullies were afraid of him, too. They believed in his magic. Caleb had seen Luis turn and back one off with no more than a piercing look and an enigmatic gesture of his thumb and forefinger, measuring an inch of the air between them.

At the Trogan Lodge, Caleb climbed the porch, past a cluster of scruffy white guys playing guitars, two singing harmony. Inside, another group shared a pizza from a Kako's box. There was no one near the phone station, which sat in a corner close to the front desk. Caleb hovered, waiting while Dante finished settling a bill with a guest, then asked if he could use the phone.

Aggressively unhurried, Dante wrote several lines on a Post-it, affixed it to the ledger, then turned a page back and forth, too occupied with things that mattered to respond. "It's for guests," he said coldly, just as Caleb was about to speak again. "Are you a guest?"

Caleb breathed. "No one's using it. I —" He swallowed and tried again, steadily. "I have a calling card."

"The fuck you say?" Dante blinked at him in mock fascination, and the look turned to a leer, mouth tilting toward a nasty smile. "How about you blow me for it?"

Caleb sighed, as if bored with a request Dante was forever bothering him with. "All right. Where? Let's go."

Dante stood, slowly. Over the ledge that made a narrow counter around the desk, he squinted, assessing the offer and its tone and Caleb's bland, unflinching gaze. Suddenly he laughed, a big cracking open-mouthed laugh, and delivered a snakebite-swift punch to Caleb's shoulder that stung like hell. "Go on," he said. "Use the damn phone. What do I care?"

Caleb went to the phone, began pushing in the numbers. "Little shit," Dante was saying with a chuckle to another guest who'd happened by, sounding almost fond. He ignored Caleb for the length of his call, which was about ten minutes, ignored him still when Caleb hung up and went back out the door, where the porch musicians sang, "I know you, rider, gonna miss me when I'm gone." A little rust-colored dog sat listening, and Caleb sat on a sunlit step by the dog, stroking its head until the song was done.

Since being back home, he'd been thinking of the other girl, Yolanda. To him she'd seemed like most of the boys at parties, unbothered by sex if not into it. She had smiled, yawned once or twice, teased him — she might as well have been taking a bath, painting her nails. Besides, she'd been two years older than him. But how far back had she been Melia, or Nicky? Did it matter? He was sure he could never have made the decision to become one of Them, but he saw how putting his dick into that girl had done it for him.

He didn't want to talk about Yolanda, though, or about what Jolly had done to him with her. If he'd had all the time in the world, and more privacy, he'd have told Jolly about Dante, whom he watched through most of the call from behind the shallow barrier of the phone box. *You cannot be bullied. You are not afraid.* Jolly's breathing told him immediately that the phone had been the right choice: the intimate contact gave Jolly less of an opportunity to defend himself.

"Jolly," he said, "I need you to do something for me. It won't hurt you. It will help you." He sounded like Julianna. "You can use it for bargaining, maybe, for your case. Promise me you'll do it."

He heard Jolly's complicated breathing, his resistance to *no,* his resistance even to *Tell me what first.* "If it's something you need, yes. You know I will."

"The girl, with the broken arm, Melia. All those girls. You need to tell the FBI where they are. How to find them." He paused, forced out the name. "Chet, too. You know where he is. I know you do."

"Nicky. I . . . First of all, I don't know that I do, actually —"

"My mom says I won't be able to live my life unless I tell the truth first, all of it. I

631

think she's wrong. I don't think I have to tell it all, and I won't, about you. But I need this told, Jolly. This much. And you're the one who can tell them. Whatever you know."

Jolly's soft groan was like pleasure, almost sexual. "I didn't know I'd raised a black-mailer."

"You didn't. I'm only saying this is what I need from you, if you love me, if you ever really loved me. You taught me this, Jolly, to decide for myself, to choose. This is the justice I want. But I need your help. So it's your turn. Choose me, or choose them."

To gamble it all on love — he was aware of the risk. *It's not love,* people like his therapist and Julianna were always saying, in direct and indirect ways. It's manipulation. It's sociopathic behavior. It's self-interest. If there's a bet to make, bank on self-interest. That pathetic skinny man who'd convinced someone to call the doctor — did he love Melia? Nicky, even at the time, had wanted to slit his throat, less for what he'd done to the girl than for being a coward, so helpless against his cravings. He knew it might be naïve to think Jolly was different. To believe Jolly could give him what he asked, purely from love, nothing in return. But he did believe it. And he wasn't entirely wrong.

■ ■ ■ ■

On the night that Lowell's bedroom at the Finca Aguilar snapped loose of the foundation, Lowell was not in it. He was in Marlene's, upstairs in Petra's old house, killing scorpions. Hilda's home at the cloudy summit had never had the hordes of the dreaded arachnid that Lowell claimed it did, but this house — which they'd dubbed the Finca Marlene though it had never been a farm — yielded one or two each day, skittery little brown ones, fat black beasts like on Lowell's tattoo. They especially liked to hide in the bedsheets, which made for edgy sleep. With Lowell beside her, Marlene felt somewhat more protected, at least in the way herd animals felt safer in numbers: one more set of eyes, one more target.

"And they seem to all be in *your* bedroom," Lark said to her. "Wonder why."

"Ouch," Marlene said, with some sincerity. Her daughter had acquired a tight clique of girlfriends and was turning into a teenager before her eyes: taller, thinner, suddenly a smartass.

And the next night, on top of this daughter's judgment, she had Hilda to contend with, established in the spare bedroom until someone could certify that the rest of the old hotel was not preparing to fall off the mountain. Alone at the Finca, Hilda had been awakened by what she thought were gunshots, maybe the Rosales boys setting off fireworks, though she'd had a moment's worry for Rafa — Ranito — who was rumored to have drawn the ire of a local gang of Nicaraguan marijuana growers. Hilda didn't like to think such dangers had come to Monteverde. She wondered, too, what sky-splitting sounds might issue from the volcano, if the time had come for that once-a-millennium, town-burying apocalypse she forgot to dread. Not until the next day did she discover Lowell's room canted lakeward at near thirty perilous degrees, with the pool table, the Ping-Pong table, his bed, and everything else pressed to the outer wall, having apparently crawled there with insufficient momentum to break through, yet. The stairs had fractured in the lower flight, but from the outside, where the family gathered cautiously to peer in through cracked windows, they could make out the heap of furnishings in suspension against the wall, too much weight in a flimsy net.

"See," Hilda said to Lowell, "I told you. You've broken the house."

"Mom, I really don't think that was me,"

Lowell said, pretending not to know what she meant.

What exactly Lowell and Marlene were doing with each other remained undecided, despite its growing number of detractors, and Marlene could see it was never going to be ideal. But what did she expect? He was her brother-in-law. As a houseguest, Hilda was pleasant to them both and refrained from further comment, but Lowell would not even climb the stairs until Hilda was safely out of view, as if she might believe he'd been sleeping somewhere else. With Lark, he went on gamely playing uncle, but if he received sarcasm in return he had to be grateful she'd spoken at all, and he seemed about to give up. What was he going to do when they had to tell Jeff?

"Let's just not tell him," Lowell said, reclined on his elbows in bed. "I mean, what is this anyway, right?"

She got up to open the balcony doors to the valley breeze, the night's calls. In the dark, she could stand naked at this open precipice and feel unseen, but with the lower balcony so near, she always closed the doors during sex. "Just a thing?" she said lightly. "A fling? No, I'm sure a name could do it damage."

But with his other bedroom poised to

drop into the valley, they'd lost the pretense that he was actually living in it. And she had no real questions about his commitment. She felt it, more than anywhere else, in his small, daily interactions with Caleb, and in Caleb himself, his shields lowered almost to nothing.

When she sat down with Lark, the words she could not have sorted with Lowell came readily enough. "It's just another kind of family, for now. I had to try it, for Caleb's sake. It's what Caleb needs. You can see that, right? I know you want him to want to be with us."

Lark nodded, grudgingly. Her hair had grown long enough to fall below her shoulders, and she tossed it back with a jerk of her chin, a new gesture. "Everything's for Caleb, I guess. Everything will always be for Caleb." Even her neck appeared longer these days, her expression coolly composed.

"Not always, though it probably seems that way. When you want to talk about some other reasons why your dad and I can't be together, we can do that."

"Whatever. Can I *go* now?"

Wow, the sarcasm. Sometimes Lark delivered her bons mots in Spanish, giving the translation only on request. Marlene believed she could see Lark through this mask she'd fashioned for herself, a temporary protective construction. Since turning twelve at the end of April, she'd grown closer than ever with Caleb, the two of them murmuring in code or walking off down the hill into town or lounging in one bedroom or another with the music going. No matter the anger Lark felt on her own account, on her father's, she adored her brother, and she saw Marlene's point. She'd push, but she was not going to risk dislodging any block from the foundation of Caleb's contentment.

Jeff, Marlene sensed, did not yet wish to know the details, as she had abruptly dropped all references to his personal life. *When will everything be normal again?* remained the undercurrent of his every call, but Marlene in all her impulse and error had resolved for herself that *normal* was a false god. Getting to know her son required, in so many ways, moving closer to the strange, the uncertain, accepting it into her life, enlarging the context for him. And it wasn't unnatural to her. There were days in which sketching or painting on her balcony over the Gulf of Nicoya felt more true to her own self than anything she'd found during those years in the suburbs of Atlanta. The house suited her, and she thought she could stay in it, stay in the country, another two years. After that, the gods of normal might prevail on her to return to the States so that Caleb could finish high school. Maybe they would take Isabel along to wherever they went, a ready ally for necessary traumas of a new school, senior year.

If Caleb was still talking to Charles Lundy, he gave no hints, and she didn't ask. They had a restraining order against Lundy, for what good it could do. Caleb remained as secretive as ever about his calls — his bedroom in the new house had its own extension — but they were far less frequent, and she knew the numbers that appeared on the bill: his therapist, Julianna, Isabel, no mysteries. For his birthday he'd asked for a guitar and was taking lessons, practicing diligently, his slow chord changes already beginning to sound like songs.

When the rains came in June, sheets of daily drenching, she got a call from Mitch: Lundy would be serving nine months, for custodial interference. "This is better than we'd hoped," he insisted. The real news was that Lundy had been cooperating to help find the other perpetrators. "Some of them, at least. We may be able to help some other kids out of it. And it looks like Caleb had an influence there. Neither of them is saying so, but Caleb's been asking Julianna some pretty pointed questions about exactly the information Lundy's giving us. We think it might mean he's turning a corner on that loyalty. All on his own, like we hoped."

From the mudroom window, she watched the watery flash of the bus's stoplights at the bottom of the drive. Then two kids in ponchos and boots tried to outrun the deluge up the steep drive, leaping the river that rushed through the diagonal chasm at its center — ridiculous, to call this a driveway. Lark, trailing, went in up to one knee. Then they were in the house, panting and grinning, peeling out of wet things, calling each other names.

"The river got you, huh?" she said to Lark, anticipating the outrage.

"Whatever," Lark said, almost happily. She pointed an emphatic finger out the window. "It's *all* one river."

Caleb ruffled water from his hair. He was fifteen, two inches taller than she was, alive and present, saying "Whaat?" with the low note of dread that meant he could see her examining him.

She patted his cheek twice. "Nothing."

"Did you hear the news?" he said. "The jaguars are free."

■ ■ ■ ■

Setting loose the jaguars had not been intentional. For many months, Stancia had worried over the structural integrity of the enclosure, and a volunteer work crew had spent a day shoring up the lowest corner with dirt and rocks along the buried fence. With a release location still years away, for cats that were unlikely to prove good candidates for release, Stancia had given in and begun arranging placement for them at a zoo in California — no small feat since most reputable zoos had all the jaguars they could hold. Then the rains came. The college boy volunteer who drove the truck out that day hurled twenty pounds of trash fish through the feed slot before he noticed that nothing was arriving for the meal.

Within a week, the larger cat was hit by a pickup truck halfway down the mountain toward Tilarán. Its stomach was full of chicken and housecat, and it had a load of buckshot in one haunch. The other headed east, or north, or southeast, depending on which rumored sightings one chose to believe. It vanished into half-distinguishable tracks and anecdotes, one more reason parents in the outlying rural areas gave their children to keep their curfews and stay close to home.

Hilda contended that the jaguar was living in the valley below the Finca Aguilar. One day it even ventured onto the lawn, down by the mango tree where the howler monkeys that had set up camp in its branches let loose an unprecedented ruckus of shrieking barks, an alarm call different in pitch than what she'd heard before for eagle or snake. In her poncho and boots, she had tromped straight out to investigate, and through a density of fog she glimpsed the golden spotted coat, slipping back into the trees. Rain washed away scat and tracks alike, and no one was ever quite sure whether to believe her.

Hilda had stayed only a few days at Marlene's new house before moving back to the Finca. No one thought she should be living there anymore, though, and by August she'd reluctantly begun plans to raze the hotel and rebuild, starting with a small cabin that could be expanded in the future. "And why should I care, really," Hilda said, "what sort of building is on it? The land is what I love." The next hotel might take the form of multiple small cabins ranged along the hillside, and one of these might house Marlene's family, in whatever future form it had assumed.

"I told them," Jolly said, on Caleb's last call for a long time. "I told them where I thought it was. I just got it wrong." His directions to where the girls were kept had been good. But for Chet he'd sent the FBI up a steep, unpaved mountain road in Idaho that ended where no house had ever been. "I just don't remember it, I guess. I was only there once or twice. It's all I have, I swear to you."

Julianna said they would keep looking in the area. "He could be telling the truth. Or he could have a good reason for protecting this man. Men in these circles keep evidence on each other."

De dónde? Where are you from?
Soy de los Estados Unidos.
Lark was not asked the question as often as her Spanish workbooks suggested she might be, but still, she'd spoken the answer many times in conversation, usually with older ticos who thought she was cute, trying to talk. Lark and Caleb, side by side, could answer with exactly the same sentence, or in the plural, *somos.* But were they really from the same place? If Lark could never know the Gone, then Caleb could never know the country she was from, the

country of lost brothers. The country of left behind, while everyone you know to love in the world is out looking for your lost brother.

Most of the rainy days after school she spent in town with her friends, at Tomasina's café or Soda La Perla or Kako's or the panadería, where they ordered snacks and fruit sodas and talked. She wasn't sure how it had happened — spontaneous combustion, maybe — but one day she and Tomasina became a foursome with two other girls, plump Jaclyn and a new girl from Australia, Margo, each of them having simultaneously discovered that the others were funny: amusing as individuals, but especially hilarious in this group. Always there was something to laugh at, and they were all a little stunned at how quick-witted and well-matched they were. They weren't the girly-girls — they were the other ones, the smarter ones, no real chatterers or high-pitched gigglers among them, but they did generally have to speak very fast, in order to express in full each moment's available hilarity, and sometimes also a little loudly, in order to share the comedy with those who had none. They spoke in English peppered lightly with Spanish, from which Lark built a collection of stock Spanish phrases used mainly in this group, each one so laden with inside jokes that no one else ever got the extent of it.

It was hard to be so funny at home. Her family didn't provide her with the right sort of sounding board on which to bang her wit. What she brought home to them was quieter, drier: ice-pick jabs delivered like punctuation now and then to anyone else's conversation in progress. Of course her mother assumed she'd "gotten it" — like a case of mono — from her friends. Lark thought it would be more accurate to say she'd "gotten it," in a strange way, from Caleb. Not that she could entice him much to join her in open digs at Mom and Dad, but she could tell he enjoyed her offerings.

And she'd launched a new way of speaking when she and Caleb were alone, by grumbling to him the first night Lowell had come by to "visit" at their new house: what were they *doing* up there? Not that she didn't know, in an elementary way — she and her friends had a million jokes about sex and who was doing what to whom. But Caleb answered in some eye-opening detail. He was amusing himself, spinning tales to gross her out, but eventually she could play along — because it was hilarious in a whole different way — and after that it was easier for him, now and then, to tell her some of the things that had happened to him. Already she knew how to draw him out, Dian Fossey style, by staying unreactive, indirect; by being as much as she could one of him.

He told her about the girl, Melia. On a fogged-in Sunday in May, when they were in town — from their new house they could walk down into Cerro Plano or Santa Elena when they pleased — Caleb halted and spoke the girl's name. They were approaching the church where he'd kissed Luis. Through the fog they could just make out a dozen little girls in white dresses, lined up before the church gates, veils floating to their shoulders from flowered crowns in their hair. They shuffled on white patent-leather shoes, exchanging grins and wild-eyed looks, pressing lace-gloved hands to their mouths in a struggle for decorum. First Communion. Lark remembered that Tomasina's brother Antony would be in the boys' line. But it was the girls, strangely silent for all the fidgeting, almost vanishing in the white air, who made her breath catch, who made Caleb put an arm around her to stop her from taking a step closer until the line had processed unevenly forward into the church. "Which one?" she asked.

"All of them," he said.

The FBI had found some girls from that house, but no one could tell Caleb whether one of them was this particular girl of his memory, with no real name that he knew. That means no, he said; they didn't find her.

"But how would they know?" Lark asked. By her arm, he said. If she was alive, she'd have a callus on the bone to show for knowing him — knowing Nicky. Dead, she'd have it, too, and Caleb thought she was: all bones by now, like Zander, in some other basement that would never be found.

But Lark could believe in the unlikely. It was the kind of thing that happened in her country. Every day, like Caleb, she saw girls who could have been Melia, in this life or another. Sometimes, quietly, she'd point one out to him, say, "That could be her. Maybe she's home."

ACKNOWLEDGMENTS

For significant assistance with the research needed to tell the kidnapping story and its aftermath, many thanks go to Robbie Burroughs and Kera O'Reilly of the Seattle FBI, who surely had better things to do. I'm also grateful to Erin Boris, who granted my first access to the Cloud Forest School (Centro de Educación Creativa), and to the fabulous Bethany Romano, who spent a few years tirelessly fielding my questions about it. Additionally, thanks go to Melissa Arguedas, Jennifer Cordeau, and Alden Jones, who assisted with different elements of the research in Costa Rica; to Mike Hopkins for miscellaneous matters from soccer to gaming; and to Man Martin for palm reading lessons. Many pieces of this book would not have been possible without my travel sidekick and intrepid field researcher, Brad Fairchild: *muchos besos,* for everything.

Deepest gratitude to my extraordinary readers who helped shape the book in so many ways: Jennifer Haigh, Lauren Cobb, Susan Rebecca White, Peter McDade, Beth Gylys, and Jessica Handler. Special thanks also to my fabulous agent, Mitchell Waters, for all kinds of ridiculous faith in me, and to my editor, Margaret Sutherland Brown, for taking on this book and adjusting it so deftly.

Much of this novel was written at artists' colonies and owes a tremendous debt to these special places. Yaddo, MacDowell, the Hambidge Center, the Anderson Center, and the Hawthornden International Retreat for Writers all hosted me, fed me, and nurtured me through different stages of the process.

Lastly, I'm eternally grateful to the National Endowment for the Arts for awarding this book a fellowship and to Georgia State University for its generous support.

ABOUT THE AUTHOR

Sheri Joseph is the author of *Stray,* winner of the Grub Street National Book Prize, and *Bear Me Safely Over.* Her short fiction has appeared in numerous literary journals, including *The Georgia Review, The Kenyan Review,* and *The Virginia Quarterly Review.* She has been awarded fellowships from the Sewanee Writers' Conference and the Bread Loaf Writers' Conference and residencies from the MacDowell Colony, Yaddo, and elsewhere. In 2010 she received a National Endowment for the Arts fellowship for the first chapter of *Where You Can Find Me.* A resident of Atlanta, she teaches in the creative writing program at Georgia State University and serves as fiction editor of *Five Points.*

The employees of Thorndike Press hope you have enjoyed this Large Print book. All our Thorndike, Wheeler, and Kennebec Large Print titles are designed for easy reading, and all our books are made to last. Other Thorndike Press Large Print books are available at your library, through selected bookstores, or directly from us.

For information about titles, please call:
  (800) 223-1244

or visit our Web site at:
  http://gale.cengage.com/thorndike

To share your comments, please write:
  Publisher
  Thorndike Press
  10 Water St., Suite 310
  Waterville, ME 04901